MID CONTINENT PUBLIC LIBRARY
15616 E. 24 HWY
INDEPENDENCE, MO 64050

3 0 0 0 4 0 0 3 5 4 7 6 2 3

ANGELBOUND

ACCA

CHRISTINA BAUER

D1431400

WITHDRAWN
FROM THE RECORDS OF THE
MID-CONTINENT PUBLIC LIBRARY

First Published by Monster House Books, LLC in 2016
Monster House Books, LLC
34 Chandler Place
Newton, MA 02464
www.monsterhousebooks.com

ISBN 9781945723025

Copyright © 2016 by Monster House Books LLC

All rights reserved. This book or any portion thereof may not
be reproduced or used in any manner whatsoever without the
express written permission of the publisher except for the use of
brief quotations in a book review.

WITHDRAWN
FROM THE RECORDS OF THE
MID-CONTINENT PUBLIC LIBRARY

For Matthew Bauer

CHAPTER ONE

.A.

I haul ass across a tenement rooftop. The sky threatens rain, but what else is new? This is Purgatory, after all. *Land of blech.* On the next building over, Desmond the klepto demon scrambles his lizard-like butt off as he attempts to escape. *"Attempts"* being the key word in that sentence.

At every step, my fiancé Prince Lincoln keeps a steady pace by my side. A warm sense of happiness seeps through my chest.

We're demon hunting together again. At last.

Ahead of us, Desmond leaps onto another rooftop. This part of town is cramped and deserted, so he can easily scramble around without freaking out the general populace. Desmond's a lanky dude with green skin, a flat nose, and an enchanted book in his possession that he just snatched from me when I exited my limo.

What a douche.

Anger pulses through my bloodstream. Desmond stole the *Rixa Codex*—a small book of evidence that's hugely important.

I want it back *like now.*

I force my breathing to slow. Even though the book is crucial, I need to be patient. Plus, the chase is all part of the fun, right? And hell knows I haven't had any demon-fighting fun in ages.

Speaking of which, what's the rush to grab Desmond anyway? It's not like he stands a chance against both Lincoln and me.

From the corner of my eye, I give my guy a quick once-over. *Hmm.* Someone looks mighty spicy in his new black body armor.

Maybe if I let Lincoln run ahead a little, I can get a quick peek at his butt.

I take care to pant excessively while slowing my pace across the uneven shingles. Sure, it's unlikely that I'd actually be tired at this point. Like every native of Purgatory, I'm a quasi-demon. That means I'm mostly human with a little bit of demon DNA. It's what gives me a kick-ass tail as well as powers across two of the seven deadly sins, namely lust and wrath. My lust side grants me a pretty face, curves that stop traffic, and auburn hair that looks amazing without any product. Thanks to my inner wrath demon, I can fight like hell and run full out for days.

Even so, sometimes a girl just needs to slow down and check out her fiancé's butt, so that's what I do right now. *Carpe assem.*

Lincoln runs ahead of me. "For the record, I know what you're up to."

"Sure, it's called conserving energy. Why should we kill ourselves to catch Desmond?"

"Ah, then this is *only* about the klepto demon?" Lincoln leaps super-high over some kind of ancient television aerial. From this angle, it's a mighty lovely sight. "Not my glutes?"

I'm so shnagged.

"Fine. I like the view."

"We're hunting a demon, Myla." There's no missing the smile in his voice. Lincoln loves it when I'm sassy.

"Hey, I can multitask."

More smiling-voice-ness. "I've noticed."

Here's the deal. Six months ago, I was the baddest-ass warrior in Purgatory's Arena. Then, I got transformed into a supernatural called the great scala, which means that I'm the only being who can permanently move souls to Heaven or Hell. Trouble is, if I'm hurt, it's a showstopper for the spirit world. Long story short, until a Scala Heir is named, I have to be a responsible demigoddess. That means working behind a desk instead of killing things. It sucks. Hard.

"I concede your multitasking skills." Lincoln makes another mouthwatering leap. "You've got two minutes to dawdle."

Whoa.

"Did you just say dawdle?" I put on a tone of mock-outrage. "What are you, eighty?"

"I'll pass along your critique to my royal tutors."

"Like they'll listen." I snap my fingers. "Hey, I've got an idea. How about you watch some television?" *Or any, really.* "That'll help you sound like you're from this century."

"Last time I checked, resembling a young human wasn't one of my life goals, and you're not changing the subject. One minute of *dawdle* time remains." He places extra-emphasis on the word *dawdle*, the cheeky monkey.

"Eh, bite me."

"No comment." He looks back over his shoulder and winks. When the situation calls for it, Lincoln does love to use his teeth, and not in a bad way. At all.

After that, my guy goes quiet, so I return to ogling mode. Lincoln is tall and broad-shouldered with strong bone structure and messy brown hair. He's twenty—a year older than me—which some say is too young for us to get hitched. *Whatever.* I can't wait for our wedding. Plus, Lincoln's a kind of demon hunter called a thrax. His people are part angel, obsessed with tradition, and live deep under the Earth's surface. Lincoln's their high prince. More importantly, he's whip-smart, honest, noble almost to a fault, and a great kisser. Now that we're engaged, we've been working up to bigger things than kissing. It involves a lot less body armor and tons more skin.

Mmmmm, a partially naked Lincoln is a beautiful sight.

"Time's up," says Lincoln.

"Boo."

3

"Honestly, we have to hustle. We need that codex."

Okay, Lincoln has a point. The *Rixa Codex* is where we've been storing up evidence for a trial against Acca, a House of thrax asswipes who need to be brought down. Once we get that book back from Desmond—and use it to record our last interview for the thrax court—then we'll finally have enough proof to officially tear Acca apart. And after what those freaks put me through last month, I really want to destroy them. I mean, who enters into a secret pact with none other than Armageddon, the King of Hell? *Acca, that's who.*

Lincoln and I almost died cleaning up that particular mess. In fact, Lady Adair of Acca *did* end up dead. She might have been a bit of a bitch, but still. The whole situation isn't something we can let slide.

I pick up the pace so I'm running shoulder-to-shoulder with Lincoln once more. "For the record, you spoil all my fun."

"Huh." Lincoln glances in my direction while arching his brows ever so slightly. "I know for a fact that I'm your main source of fun."

I stick my tongue out at him. *He's totally right.*

Lincoln laughs, which is a rich and rolling sound that makes everything in Purgatory seem a little less crappy. Together we leap toward another rooftop and land in perfect sync. A few pigeons flap off. When Desmond sees us closing in, he pulls a vial from his pocket, downs the contents, and picks up his pace. For a demon who has to waddle-walk everywhere, that guy sure starts hustling. The vial probably contained a velocity potion.

That said, even if Desmond can go extra fast, I'm not worried that he'll actually escape. While most full-blooded demons fall into the not-too-bright category, Desmond brings *dumbass* to an entirely new level. He can't stop stealing junk, dresses like a homeless clown, and has stalker issues with my family. Yet the biggest giveaway of Desmond's stupidity is the fact that he's running away from us right now.

Come on, showing your back to a pair of hunters? Seriously? That's like predator crack. The dude must have a death wish.

Desmond jumps off the roof to land on the pavement in a roll. That's no easy feat when your spine's extra long. *Interesting.* I've never seen Desmond so motivated before. Lincoln and I share a puzzled look before leaping off as well. We sprint a few blocks in silence.

"Does any of this seem odd to you?" Lincoln finally asks.

"I was thinking the same thing. This isn't Desmond's MO."

"Precisely."

For months, Desmond's been trailing my family in the hopes of stealing random bits of our junk. No real shocker there. Mom's the President of Purgatory and I'm the Great Scala. As a result, we both have our share of stalkers. Some are cute, even if they do rummage through our trash, looking for keepsakes. Others are creepy.

Like Desmond.

I shake my head. "Normally, Desmond never runs. He just hands over whatever he stole. Which is what should have happened back at the limo."

"It's what he did last time, and without any complaint."

"Yeah, that was at the Toys for Quasi-Demonic Tots thing."

Last week, Desmond lifted some stuff from Mom's purse while she was speaking at a fundraiser. Not a great idea. While Mom's the President of Purgatory, my father's a badass archangel. All Dad had to do was glare at Desmond, and the klepto handed over what he took. That time, it was Mom's brush and an old Tic Tac from the bottom of her purse. Like I said, Desmond's not the brightest star in the demonic sky. Sure, it's in his nature to steal, but most klepto demons are a little more strategic about it.

Okay, a lot more strategic.

A sinking feeling runs through my belly. Maybe Desmond isn't too smart, but someone else is. "He could be a pawn here, you know. Who would expect Desmond to get mixed up in something seriously evil?"

Lincoln's voice gets crazy calm. "Go on."

"Let's look at the facts. Desmond is running from us. You know we can't resist that."

"True."

"Next, how does a klepto demon go so fast on those stubby little legs? That vial must have contained a velocity potion. Enchantments like those are pricey. You don't pay for them with stolen Tic Tacs. And then there's what he took. To grab the *Rixa Codex*, Desmond had to know when and where we'd be…And whether we'd have the book."

"All of which requires some serious scheming."

"Exactly. The whole thing is totally out of character. Desmond's a demon who spontaneously grabs junk. He doesn't plan complex heists."

Lincoln's full mouth thins to an angry line. "And now, he's lifted our codex, the very evidence that we need to put Acca behind bars." Thrax are all about tradition. Since we've challenged the House of Acca to court, thrax rules state that one side must go to jail. If it isn't Acca, then it's Lincoln and me.

Prison. What a sucky way to spend your honeymoon.

The more I think about it, the more I'm convinced. "Desmond is doing someone else's dirty work. Guess who."

A muscle ticks by Lincoln's jawline. That means he's pissed. Only one group gets him this angry. "Acca."

"Yup." *Boy, do I ever hate those fuckers.*

The House of Acca wants to rule the thrax homeland of Antrum. Since Lincoln's next in line to the throne, my guy stands in their way. Which is why Acca tried to marry Lincoln off to their Lady Adair. Too bad for them, Lincoln fell in love with me first, mostly because an oracle angel named Verus stuck her nose in our business. *Long story.* Anyway, not only does Acca still want the crown, but they also really, really, really want me dead. Meh.

More silence follows as we run along and ponder. Lincoln's the first to speak again. "There's a flaw in your logic. Acca must know that we'll get the codex back from Desmond."

He's got me there. Even if Desmond has a dozen spells on him, we'll still take that klepto down. I mean, I haven't even called on my little supernatural buddies for help yet. To move souls to

6

Heaven or Hell, I have power over tiny lightning bolts of energy called igni. If worse comes to worst, I can summon my igni to send Desmond back to Hell, and keep the codex right here. Sure, that would be a total pain in the ass—once igni start moving souls, it's hard to get them to stop—but I have that option as a last resort.

So what's Acca really up to?

My tail arches over my shoulder. It's a beauty, what with being all long, black, and covered in dragon scales. The arrowhead-shaped end jabs in Desmond's direction. That's its way of saying we need to grab the klepto, fast.

"Don't worry, boy." I give my tail a comforting pat. "We'll get him."

Desmond rounds a corner, and the street turns from bad to worse. The downgrade in neighborhood quality is awesome, in my humble opinion. Here's why. Most of the after-realms have issues with demons sneaking in and causing trouble. On Earth, it's the thrax who clean things up. In Purgatory, that work falls to our police. However, our government's still reeling from Armageddon's recent invasion (I kicked his ass back to Hell, by the way). As a result, our police haven't been cracking down on demonic squatters.

Long story short, crappy areas like this one? They're classic hangouts for the truly evil. My heart thuds faster in my chest. Deserted ruins filled with über-nasty demons?

The day's looking up.

I grin from ear to ear. "I think I know what plan Desmond was given."

"Do tell."

"We're not supposed to fight a klepto demon."

"Could've fooled me."

"Desmond's leading us somewhere else."

Lincoln nods slowly. "Such as straight into a Class A battle." Thrax categorize demons by letter. Class A are the hardest to kill.

"Fighting a Class A would be soooooo awesome." I shoot Lincoln a sly look. "Maybe we'll get to take down another tinea." I let out a wistful sigh. "Together."

Lincoln chuckles. "I love your idea of date night." I know that laugh. Lincoln is as excited as I am.

"How about we make this even more interesting?" I ask.

"What are you thinking?" The husky tone in Lincoln's voice says that he knows exactly what's on my mind.

"We bet on who makes the killing blow to the Class A."

"And the prize?"

"Same as always. The winner names the next kiss."

This is my favorite game in the history of ever. Whoever wins the bet gets to demand when and where our next kiss will take place. And no matter what the time or location, the so-called loser must comply. Typically, these interludes don't end with kissing, either. Our last bet was who could first cross the Plains of Rixa on horseback. Lincoln won and demanded a kiss in the royal stables. We ended up naked, and I was picking hay out of my hair for days. The whole thing was beyond great.

I wag my eyebrows. "So, what do you say?"

"You're on."

Sweet.

Desmond turns down another deserted road. Actually, *road* is a generous word. It's more of a pathway through piles of rubble. Lincoln and I speed along behind our prey. I would skip-run if it didn't slow me down.

I am so winning this bet.

Bring it on, Desmond.

CHAPTER TWO

$\mathcal{A}$

To stay hidden from view, Lincoln and I crouch behind a pile of rubble. Twenty yards away from us, Desmond approaches a deserted hospital building. The place is six stories of ruined concrete that lurches at an odd angle. In other words, it's pretty typical for this part of town.

As Desmond nears the main door, his head swivels from side to side on his long lizardy neck. The reason? Our klepto demon friend has been trying to find us for a while. He thinks Lincoln and I have given up the chase. *Oops.* As a result, Desmond's adopted both a fake limp and a hacking cough. Both are an attempt to alert us to where he is and give us time to catch up. It's not a great strategy, but the dude plays it up with gusto.

Desmond limps a few paces forward. "Here I go." *Cough, cough.* "Into the hospital." *Cough, cough.* "I wonder what the west wing is like? Maybe I'll go there now." He pauses by the front door and scans the area. All the blood drains from his scaly green face, giving him a decidedly pale appearance. He's really taking this hard, which confirms my suspicions.

No question about it. Desmond was trying to lure us into the lair of a badass demon.

"Boy," says Desmond in a full voice. "I sure hope the prince and great scala don't come looking for me here." He inspects a small sign by the door. "In Purgatory Hospital DH-27B. At the west wing."

Desmond scans the area once more. Eventually, his thin shoulders slump in defeat as he limps into the hospital.

Once Desmond's gone, I shake my head. "Poor guy. He did everything except shoot off a flare gun."

"Probably would have if he'd brought one." Lincoln rubs his square chin. "Purgatory Hospital DH-27B. Does that mean anything to you?"

"Nothing in particular. It's a standard-issue building. Total cookie cutter."

Purgatory used to be run by ghouls, a supernatural race obsessed with order and sameness. They're also cheap bunch of bastards, so our hospitals not only look alike, but they also have all the same crap equipment.

"Anything dangerous?" asks Lincoln.

"This place wouldn't have any special devices that could hurt us, if that's what you're wondering. Under the ghouls, hospitals only held the basics for patching up a broken arm, maybe stitching a wound or two. That's about it."

"Have you ever been inside one before?"

"Quasis mostly went to ghoul hospitals to get a form 87-J. It proves you're sick so you can legitimately skip school."

Lincoln gives me a sly look. "In other words, you've never been inside a place like this."

"Yeah, you know me. Not a big fan of the rules. All I cared about was fighting in the Arena." Hard to believe that just six months ago, my biggest worry was how to get out of high school and into more Arena battles.

Anticipation hangs heavily in the air. Lincoln pulls his baculum from his belt. These are two silver sticks that he can ignite with angelfire and transform into almost any kind of weapon. The fact that my guy is getting them ready now? It means he thinks the same thing that I do.

This is about to get ugly.

Sweet.

I tap my chin. "So, what do you think? Should we slip in through the roof?" Lincoln goes on demon patrols all the time, so he knows how to engage the enemy in the field. Approach isn't as important when you're fighting in the Arena. You walk out your respective entrance archways, and then—BOOM—the fighting starts.

"There's good ground cover to reach the west wing," answers Lincoln. "Let's go that route. Desmond was kind enough to state it as his final destination."

"And once we're there?"

Lincoln pats his pocket. "I have a charm that should help."

"Cool." For the record, I'm not much of a magic girl, but I do admire the charms that thrax use on demon patrol. The House of Striga makes them. Each spell is camouflaged to look like some kind of junk you'd already have in your pocket.

"This way." While staying low, Lincoln slips along a zigzag path of half-smashed walls and piles of rubble. I keep close behind. Soon, we reach the hospital's western wall, which is a tall panel of cracked concrete lined with high windows. Lincoln kneels beneath the closest window frame. Our gazes meet. Energy zings through my limbs. *Battle, here I come.*

"Ready?" he asks.

"Hells yes."

Lincoln reaches into his pocket and pulls out what looks like an old gum wrapper. *That's a revealment charm. Nice.* I've seen those before—revealments enable you to see and hear through walls. Lincoln holds the small sheet of paper before his lips and whispers one word. "Ostendo."

The wrapper disappears in puff of purple smoke, and the wall before us transforms. Cracks deepen until the concrete seems to crumble in on itself, revealing the room beyond the wall. I stifle the urge to applaud. *That's some cool stuff, right there.*

The magic shows us an interior waiting room, and man, is it ever a mess. Overturned chairs and shredded magazines line the floor. The reception desk is a smashed-up wreck. Dust covers everything.

Desmond paces the floor, leaving a trail of three-toed footprints behind him. "They could still be following me, you know."

At this point, I must say a word on the awesomeness of revealment charms. Right now, I can see and hear Desmond, but he can't detect me. I mean, I could set off a firecracker, and he wouldn't know. Cool, right?

A man and woman answer Desmond in unison. "Perhaps."

Their low, sexy voices set my inner wrath demon on alert. *These are enemies.* At the same time, my other demonic side recognizes their particular brand of power. *Lust demons.*

I crane my neck, trying for a better view. *Can't see them at all.* Whoever these demons are, they're standing just outside the range of Lincoln's charm.

I shift my weight. *Still nothing.*

Beside me, Lincoln checks the charms in his pockets.

"Do you have another revealment?" I ask.

"That was my last one. I have other magic, but none of it would address this particular problem." Lincoln rubs his neck, his eyes lost in thought. "What do you think is in there?"

"Lust demons, pure and simple."

Lincoln shakes his head. "I'm not so sure. Lust demons rarely fight in pairs, let alone speak in unison." He focuses on the hospital interior so intensely, I think laser beams might shoot out of his eyes. "With one exception."

A shiver twists up my neck. When it comes to demons, I'm a self-taught expert. I know the *"exception"* that Lincoln's talking about, and it's extremely rare. "Dyad demons."

"Let's hope I'm wrong."

"Yeah. Let's."

Dyad demons are super-hard to kill. They always move as a mated pair, male and female. Both have lust powers, which can be tough in a fight. I don't dabble in this kind of thing, but many lust demons give off an aura of compulsion that turns regular folks into compliant servants. I don't fall for compulsions myself. Even so, all those waves of power coming at me? It can be mega distracting. So, lust demons are already tricky in a fight.

But dyad demons? They have even darker abilities.

Dyad men can summon a black mist that freezes everyone nearby, trapping you inside your own body so you're awake yet unable to move. Fun times. Meanwhile, dyad women are shape shifters. I'm not talking about the kind that only turns into a wolf or whatever. Dyad women can become anything with a pulse, from bugs to dragons. Totally badass.

To make matters worse, dyads are linked by a power field called a tether. It's a sort of black cloud that hovers about an inch above their skin. A dark cord of the same material then connects the demons to each other. To kill either demon, you first have to break the tether. The good news is that once the tether is cut, they'll eventually die. But in the meantime? You have a couple of majorly pissed-off baddies on your hands. Some dyads fight for hours, even after their tether's been cut.

A weight of foreboding settles into my bones. *Dyad demons. Ugh.*

From inside the ruined hospital, the man and woman speak in unison again. "You lost the prince and great scala. We must move on with our plans."

"No," says Desmond. "Give them a few more minutes. I know those two. They will come for the *Rixa Codex.*"

"We have a better idea," they say. "Hand over the book. Aldred wishes it to be safe."

My breath hitches. It's one thing to suspect that the Earl of Acca is trying to ruin your life. *Again.* It's another to hear some random demons confirm it.

But they did.

The facts swirl around in my head. Aldred, the Earl of Acca, definitely hired Desmond to steal our codex. Simultaneously, he contracted two mystery demons to murder us in cold blood. For the millionth time, I wish I could deep-six that dude. Even so, Aldred has too many supporters among the thrax. We must dismantle the House of Acca, and to do that, we need the courts. We need the *Rixa Codex*.

Desmond sniffs. "You want to avoid a battle. Aldred's orders were clear. You're supposed to kill them before I do anything else. After they're dead, I must take the codex to the Lady."

My brows lift. *The Lady?* I look to Lincoln. "Any idea who that is?"

"Not a one."

The paired voices speak again. "The Lady doesn't want to travel to the Wheeler Institute again. Earth is such a long journey this time of year. Give us the codex. We'll take care of everything."

Desmond pulls the book from his pocket. It's a small white volume that's no larger than my palm. "I don't know if I should." He hides the codex away once more. "It's not wise to trust demons."

"We're more than just demons," they say. "We're friends."

"Call me Dusk," adds the woman.

"And I'm Mourn," says the man.

At last, the two demons step into view. Both are on the short side with pasty-white skin, black hair, and dark eyes. Their features are so smooth and perfect, they remind me of mannequins. Dusk wears a long evening gown made of crimson silk, while Mourn wears a matching red suit. Although they stand side by side, there's no mistaking the field of dark energy that rests right above their skin. A cord of the same black stuff curls across the floor, connecting them both.

That's definitely a tether.

My heart sinks. *Dyad demons for sure.*

And they stand between us and the *Rixa Codex*.

Crap.

My mind races through everything I know about this demon class. If A is the toughest, then dyads are A+++. The best way to kill dyads is with an ambush. Straight-on assaults rarely succeed. But how could I approach them without it being an obvious attack? I'm the most famous lust demon in all the after-realms. Unlike Dusk, I can't easily change my appearance, either. I glance over to Lincoln. "You got any ideas?"

"Not yet."

Inside the hospital, Dusk and Mourn step closer to Desmond. "Tell us how you began working for Aldred." Waves of demonic power wash over me. Dusk and Mourn have started working their lust demon mojo.

Desmond puffs out his chest. "Oh, Aldred noticed how I follow around the President of Purgatory and the great scala."

Dusk and Mourn speak in sync again. "So you made a deal with Aldred?"

"Yup. A good one too."

"Then you know how the man works. We also have an agreement with the Earl of Acca. We can't hurt you."

By the way, this is how Aldred controls people: crappy magical agreements. He also specializes in blackmail. For example, Lincoln has never stopped trying to put together an alliance of all the thrax Houses against Acca. Even so, the second someone is close to signing? They back out under sketchy circumstances citing their *"good name"* or the *"safety of their family."* In other words, blackmail.

All of which is why Aldred and Acca need to go buh-bye.

"You can't hurt me?" Desmond's yellow eyes widen. I can clearly make out the vertical slits in them. "Truly?"

"Of course not. So why don't you hand over the codex and go home?" Another pulse of power moves through the air. The lust demons are now pushing their mojo to eleven. "You want to do this, don't you?"

Desmond's features go slack. "If I gave you the codex, would Dusk give me a kiss?"

She blinks her heavy-lidded eyes. "Perhaps."

"Then, sure. I'll hand over the book."

"Good." Mourn raises his right hand, and a small cloud of black dust curls around his palm. "Because our deal with Aldred was very particular. We agreed not to harm you, with one exception. If you betray his orders, then you're fair game."

Desmond keeps up his goggle-eyed stare at Dusk. "So I get a kiss?"

"No, you just betrayed Aldred's orders," Dusk explains. "He instructed you—and only you—to deliver the codex to the Lady, didn't he?"

"Sure." Desmond keeps up his stare-fest with Dusk's mouth. He has no idea what they're saying at this point. I'm starting to feel a little sorry for him.

That said, they haven't frozen him solid, which is what will happen to Lincoln and me the second we make our presences known.

Unless we can come up with a way to protect ourselves from the freezing magic of a dyad demon.

Which no one's ever done before.

Yipes.

"You've disobeyed the terms of your deal with Aldred," says Mourn. "Now, we can end your sad little life." The black dust flies away from Mourn's palm. Instantly the dark power envelops Desmond, freezing him in place.

My hand moves to my throat. I knew dyads could turn their opponents into statues. That said, I had no idea it would work so quickly.

Next it's Dusk who raises her hand. A flurry of red particles whirl around her body, obscuring her from view. A moment later, the lovely woman is gone, replaced by a massive praying mantis with a red exoskeleton and long razor-sharp forearms. She tilts her tiny head, and a gleam of red demonic power flits through her overlarge eyes.

That's one nasty sight, right there.

Swiping her arm, mantis-Dusk slices right through Desmond's neck. I choke back a gasp. Desmond's body is still frozen in place, but with a line of blood across his throat. Not good.

Dusk turns to Mourn. "That wasn't so hard."

"It never is."

"What do you think Aldred will give us for the codex?"

Mourn sets his hands in his pockets. "You won't offer it to the Lady first?"

"She won't want it." Dusk shrugs her thin insect shoulders. "She only volunteered our help to find it because Aldred begged her."

My forehead creases with thought. Whoever this Lady is, she and Aldred are in deep cahoots. Too bad that doesn't narrow down her identity any.

"We did the right thing." Mourn shoots a disgusted look at Desmond's frozen body. It's beyond weird that the klepto still stands upright, even though there remains a bloody line across his throat.

"Of course," says Dusk. "We had to get rid of him. Desmond was certain to bungle things up. The Lady relies on us to ensure her missions succeed. That codex will go to the Wheeler Institute."

Mourn snaps his fingers. The black dust that had surrounded the klepto demon vanishes. Desmond tumbles to the floor, his body and head rolling in different directions. Now I've seen my share of gore, but... *Yuck.*

My disgust quickly morphs into a rougher emotion. Bands of anger tighten up my torso. Sure, Desmond wasn't a Boy Scout. He didn't deserve to die that way, though.

I turn to Lincoln. "Killing Desmond pisses me off. Seriously."

"Personally, I'm holding my rage for when they go after the book."

My attention snaps back to the *Rixa Codex.* Desmond's death aside, losing that thing will cause us a world of trouble. Like honeymoon-in-prison trouble.

"Can you get us in there?" I ask.

Lincoln sets his hand in his pocket. "I have a charm for that, but once we're inside" —he frowns— "we'll need some kind of force field, or we'll end up as dead as Desmond."

We share a long look, and I know we're both thinking the same thing. When we next speak, it's the same word: "Igni."

"It's perfect," I add. "Igni create a power field to move souls to Heaven and Hell. It should protect us."

"But they don't normally do this kind of thing, am I right?"

"Technically, no. But they're pretty adventuresome. I'm sure they'll give it a try." In fact, my igni attempt all sorts of things. Most don't work. For example, last month I said the Beelzebub Bus Terminal was going to Hell. They took that as an order and tried moving it there, pronto. It took three days to put the fire out. At least, the old terminal was another deserted ruin, so no one got hurt.

"What if it doesn't work?" asks Lincoln.

"You mean, what if we get frozen like statues?"

"Precisely."

I bob my head, thinking. "In that case, the igni could zap us to Heaven."

"You won't be able to speak to them."

"I mostly chat with them in my mind."

"Right." Lincoln lets out a slow breath. "Even so, we shouldn't do this. A better time will come. At this point, it's way too risky."

My internal wrath demon roars to life. *Risky? What about the codex, Aldred the asshole, and the headless Desmond?*

"No way. My igni can definitely do this." *Maybe.*

"They've never attempted anything like this before, have they?"

"True." I raise my pointer finger. "But when have we ever let certain death stop us before?"

Lincoln shakes his head and smiles. "Plus, there is that bet between us."

"Now, you're thinking." I love that I am such a bad influence on Lincoln. Two months ago, he never would have agreed to this. "I *will* win that bet."

"I'm convinced," says Lincoln. "Let's give it a try."

"On it." Closing my eyes, I call out to my igni with my mind. *Come to me, my little ones.*

First, laughter echoes inside my head. The voices are childlike, reminding me of little bells. These are the light igni—the power that moves souls to Heaven. A moment later, deep rasping tones fill my brain. These are the dark igni, the power that shifts spirits to Hell.

And they're coming to help.

Suddenly, tiny white bolts of power appear around my palms, each one no more than in inch in length. They swirl and dive around my hands like a school of fish.

Only, you know, ones that are made of white lightning.

Did I mention that my life is weird?

Normally, I would address the igni in my mind, but for Lincoln's benefit, I decide to talk out loud. "Welcome, my little ones. I need your help. Lincoln and I are about to fight a pair of dyad demons. We need you to form a shield of power around our bodies. Keep that male dyad from freezing us."

The voices grow louder as more igni appear. Hundreds materialize and start flowing around Lincoln and me. The sight is lovely—it's like being surrounded by fireflies. Still, something about the whole thing feels off. I frown. "This isn't right."

Lincoln scans the power shields that surround us both. "We need more. Our energies should be linked together, just like the dyads. Can your igni to form a cord between us?"

"Good thinking."

"That's why I wear the crown."

I roll my eyes. Maybe Lincoln's been hanging out with me too much. The man is getting downright snarky. "Did you hear that, my little ones? We need you to make a rope that connects Lincoln and me."

In response, the igni giggle while winding themselves into a cord of power that winds between me and Lincoln. I search through my soul, wondering if our energies are joined. A fresh pulse thrums through the center of my being. My eyes widen with a realization.

It's Lincoln's heartbeat.

"They did it." I can't help but smile. "I do feel you."

"And I you."

Our gazes lock. We're linked, body and soul. I want to live forever in this moment. However, that's not to be. Lincoln and I have to kick some ass. "You said you had a charm to could get us inside?"

19

Lincoln pulls another item out of his pocket. This one looks like a paperclip. He jams it into a crack in the concrete wall. "That ought to do it." He turns to me. "Shall we?"

"One sec." Today, I'm wearing my dragonscale fighting suit, which comes with certain necessary accessories for situations such as this one. For starters, there's a facemask under my collar, which I now pull out to cover up. After that, I quickly slip on my matching dragonscale gloves. Normally, I double and triple-check that the seals on my wrist and neck are in place, but we've spent too much time out here already. "I'm all set."

"Assault Plan Delta?" asks Lincoln. Thrax have different pre-set scenarios for battle. Assault Plan Delta is a two-person attack where Lincoln turns his baculum into a net made of angelfire.

"Check." Battle energy whizzes through my system, making it hard for me to stand still.

"Let's begin." Lincoln speaks the word to activate the charm. "Displodo."

The paperclip sizzles like a sparkler, only one made with purple fire. For a few seconds, nothing happens.

After that, the entire wall implodes.

With an earsplitting crack, the concrete before us shatters. Bits of stone fly off into the reception area. A gaping hole opens in the gray wall. Mourn and Dusk stare at us, openmouthed. They have returned to their regular human forms, and damn, do they ever look pissed.

I crack my neck from side to side.

Bring it on, guys. We're ready for you.

CHAPTER THREE

A.

Dusk and Mourn waste no time getting into battle mode. Mourn raises his left hand; black particles of power appear around his palm. At the same time, Dusk transforms into another humanoid insect. This time, she becomes a massive red scorpion. At least, the back end of her is a scorpion, anyway. That part comes complete with a tail and a poisoned stinger. From the waist up, Dusk is still her human self. Only now, she's covered in a thick exoskeleton. I hate to admit this, but she looks pretty tough.

On reflex, my hands go to where my hood connects to my fighting suit. The seam isn't secure because I rushed getting ready. It will just have to do.

Lincoln raises his arms high, a baculum gripped in each hand. A line of angelfire winds between the two silver rods. The flaming cord quickly weaves back and forth until it becomes a full net made of white fire. Lincoln tosses the fiery web toward Mourn, who uses that moment to release his dark spell.

Black particles fly away from Mourn's hand. The black cloud heads straight toward Lincoln and me. I steel myself, waiting for the magic to strike. Will the igni be able to protect us? The dark mist presses in close around our shield of igni. The tiny black particles vibrate as they try to break past the power that surrounds Lincoln and me.

They don't get through, however. The igni hold.

I grin. That means it's time to fight.

Since his baculum is netting up Mourn, Lincoln pulls out a regular short sword from the sheath on his hip. Raising the weapon high, Lincoln leaps through the newly made break in the wall and races straight for the tether cord that links Dusk and Mourn. With any luck, Lincoln's regular blade will slice right through their connection.

For my part, I have a dual-action scorpion-human bitch to deal with.

I leap through the hole in the wall and rush straight for Dusk. She skitters forward on all her buggy legs, and damn, that woman can go fast. As she closes in, I sock her with a series of body kicks that send her flying. All of which bring up some interesting points.

Number one. Kicking an exoskeleton hurts like fuck.

Number two. Dusk can't get booted very far before her tether stops her. It looks like she and Mourn have about ten yards of room to play with. Good to know.

Number three. Dusk has some excellent fine motor skills, despite the fact that her hands are covered with insect shells. I know this because the bitch ripped my hood off as I sent her flying over my head.

Damn. I really should have taken an extra minute to get my gear on properly. Something to remember for next time. I actively ignore the little voice in my head that says there may not be a next time. *Screw you, voice.*

Dusk regains her footing and glares at me, her irises flaring red with demonic power. "Your skin is exposed now, Scala. One scratch from my stinger. That's all it will take." Her scorpion tail sways menacingly behind her. "And you'll be dead."

My wrath power streams through every nerve ending I've got. My mind clears as I go into battle mode. My thoughts turn eerily calm as I calculate the vectors and approaches between Dusk and me. There are a few that seem super promising.

Think you're taking me down? Think again.

Meanwhile, Lincoln hacks away at the tether between Dusk and Mourn. He's not making any progress. In fact, his blade is half melted from the effort.

Mourn lets out a howl of pain. The angelfire net has burned through the dark shield of power that surrounds him. Now, a criss-cross pattern is burned into his face. Mourn whips off his coat. That can't be good. Using the fabric to cover his hands, Mourn tosses the fiery net aside. The baculum extinguish. Lincoln scoops up the metal rods from the floor.

Dusk and I circle each other. "Did you see that?" I ask Lincoln. No question what *"that"* is. It's how Mourn's face currently looks like he got hit with a waffle iron, thanks to the baculum's fire.

"I did."

"Assault Plan Gamma Xi."

"Perfect."

Mourn reaches behind his back and pulls out a pair of daggers. The edges of the blades gleam with green goop. More poison. He holds his weapons in a loose grip for tossing. The demon's not going to fight hand-to-hand with Lincoln. Good pick, actually.

While Mourn stands still, Dusk gets moving. She races for me, her tail going berserk behind her. The stinger end slams into the linoleum floor as she races along. Damn, she has some force behind that thing. It smashes straight through the floorboards, sending plumes of dust into the air.

My tail arches over my shoulder. The arrowhead end curls forward in a move that says, *Come at me.*

"That's right, boy." I make the same motion with my hand. "Come on. If you didn't bust up the floor so much, you'd be here already."

Dusk leaps into the air, all her eight legs moving to pin me down. As she lands, I punch her right in the larynx while my tail gives her a solid torso hit. She tumbles down beside me but quickly rights herself. After that, Dusk lunges for me, her armored fingers reaching for my throat. I drop and slide across the floor, making a path right under her torso. As I move beneath her, my tail cuts a line through the exoskeleton on her belly.

Nothing like a dragon-tail to slice through what bugs you.

A few yards away, Lincoln reignites his baculum as a pair of short swords. Mourn whips his first dagger at Lincoln and misses. Barely. Lincoln rushes toward the tether line.

Mourn releases the second dagger. It lands harmlessly on the floor, embedding itself up to the hilt. That Mourn's got a good arm. He's also got more throwing daggers. The guy already has two fresh ones prepped to go.

Lincoln doesn't wait for another volley of weapons. He brings his arms down, aiming the flaming short swords straight for the tether. The fiery blades easily slice through the cord of dark energy.

Their tether is toast. The battle's looking up.

At this point, Mourn and Dusk lose their freaking minds. Both shriek in rage. Dusk is pretty distracted, so I take the opportunity to do an aerial somersault over her scaly back. While I'm midair, my tail cuts through the tip of hers, severing the poisoned stinger. It falls to the ground with a satisfying *whump*.

I make sure to land so I stand nose-to-nose with Dusk. My plan? Use my favorite weapon—that would be my tail—and make the killing blow. I'm deep in battle mode and laser-focused on my enemy.

But, yeah. I also want to win the bet with Lincoln.

My tail arches over my shoulder, ready to strike, when Dusk pauses from her roars of rage. She jerks once, her body going stiff. After that, her eyes roll back in her head as she falls over, dead. I lean over her corpse. A short sword sticks out of her back.

Crap, now that's Lincoln's kill.

My guy stands over Mourn's dead body. Clearly, Lincoln tossed his short swords simultaneously. He took them both out at once, which is not easy to do with short swords, as a rule.

That's super impressive.

My battle rage wanes, giving rise to another emotion. I really want to kiss him, but I can't. I lost the bet. Ugh. He's going to be impossible.

A smug smile rounds Lincoln's full mouth. "Are you all right?"

"I'm fine."

He steps over to Mourn, picks up his baculum, and extinguishes it. "Are you sure?" There's a shit-ton of swagger in his step as he walks over to Dusk and does the same thing.

"Positive."

Lincoln stands right in front of me. Barely a wisp of air separates our bodies. His warm breath cascades over my lips. He tilts his head. "Want to kiss me?"

"Maybe." I slowly lick my lips. "You know how I love to watch you kill stuff."

Lincoln raises his hand, showing off the *Rixa Codex*. How exactly did he find the time to retrieve that book while taking out two Class A demons?

Crap, now I really, really, really want to kiss him.

Lincoln leans in even closer. "I'm not calling the kiss yet."

"I figured that out." *Jerk.*

"Maybe after we get our final interview for this." He raises the codex higher. "I might change my mind."

I groan. Dang, I almost forgot the entire reason we were running around with the book in the first place. We were off to Purgatory to interview someone for evidence to place in the *Rixa Codex*. "Who are we supposed to interview again?"

Laughter dances in Lincoln's eyes. "That would be Mrs. Pomplemousse."

"That's right." She's an ancient broad who was mistreated by Aldred. Her big claim to fame? Aldred confessed to her that he was in league with Armageddon, making her our best potential interview of all. There's no way we can skip it.

"Mrs. Pomplemousse." I step back, shaking my head. "Why is her name more of a mood killer than three dead demons?"

"Because it's us." Lincoln tucks the codex into his pocket.

I scan the room. *What a mess.* "I'll tell Mom to send a cleanup crew later. For the time being, we should probably haul ass to Mrs. Pomplemousse. We're super late as it is."

"Agreed."

I silently vow that no matter what happens, I am not letting Lincoln torture me about this kiss. I'll be Miss Cool. Miss No-Lust Demon. Miss Awesomesauce Who Can Lose A Bet And Not Give A Crap.

Maybe.

CHAPTER FOUR

A.

Lincoln and I rush down an empty street that's lined with identical row houses. Mrs. Pomplemousse lives at number 13. In this area, all the façades are two stories high, made of brick, and fronted by tiny lawns with mostly green grass. For Purgatory, that's fancy stuff. Tall windows look out from the second floor of each dwelling. As we walk by, I get the sneaking sensation that those windows are actually eyes, and they all watch us with evil intentions.

Great. I'm seeing nasty faces in buildings. Might be time for a nap.

In short order, we reach Mrs. Pomplemousse's door. Lincoln knocks. While we wait for her to respond, I lean on my guy's shoulder. Before coming here, Lincoln and I made a quick stop at the limo where we changed into our *"average person"* outfits. I'm now sporting skinny jeans, Bolshie boots, and a red sweater. Lincoln's got on camo pants and a long-sleeve T-shirt. The cotton waffle weave is very comfy to lean against, actually.

Naptime sounds better by the minute.

From the other side of the door, there comes a chorus of rattles and clinks as the occupant undoes what must be a half-dozen locks. The portal slowly swings open, showing a grandmotherly lady with a plump body and a dragonscale tail like mine. *Yes!* She's a fellow wrath and lust demon. Furor class. How did I not know this about her?

I frown. *Oh yeah, I didn't have time to read the briefing too closely.* I really need to nail *"preparing before you start something big"* issue. First, there was the sloppiness with my fighting hood. Now, I didn't even know Mrs. Pomplemousse was one of my demonic kind. It's not like there are a ton of quasi-Furor out there.

Oh, well. I'll definitely start being more diligent. Tomorrow.

"Hello, I'm Mrs. Pomplemousse. You must be Lincoln and Myla." She's wearing a too-tight suit for this occasion, complete with a matching pillbox hat and veil. It's sweet.

Lincoln bows slightly at the waist. Old ladies love that shit. "Apologies for our late arrival and casual appearance."

She purses her wrinkled lips. "Did you have to kill some demons?"

"Oh yeah," I answer. "Two of them."

"That's wonderful, dear. I used to fight in the Arena myself when I was younger. Why don't you come inside and have some cookies?"

You don't have to say *"cookies"* to me twice. "Why, I don't mind if I do." I walk past the threshold to find your basic grandmotherly setup. There's faded green wallpaper printed with tiny flowers. The scent of old people and mothballs fills the air. Some overly poufy furniture surrounds a small table that's been set for tea. And best of all? An impressive pile of cookies sits at the center of the tabletop.

Time to make myself at home.

I plunk onto a huge chair and scan the yumminess. Mrs. Pomplemousse has a nice assortment of munchies here, I must say, including ginger snaps, chocolate chip, and some kind of fudge thingies. All homemade. I might ask if she'll adopt me.

Mrs. Pomplemousse plunks onto the couch across from me and beams. "Don't stand on ceremony, my dear. Eat up."

So I do. "These are really yummy."

Oops. I might have said that through a mouthful of ginger snap.

Lincoln settles onto the chair beside mine. "Mrs. Pomple-mousse, I must imagine this is all rather surprising, us asking you to provide a recorded interview and all. Plus, Myla and I are not anyone's idea of typical company."

Mrs. Pomplemousse starts pouring herself tea. "You aren't, but I'm a tough old bird. And Myla and I are both from the Arena. It takes a lot to shock us."

I raise my arm. "Testify." This time, I have the sense to cover my mouth with my free hand while I chew and speak. Who says I won't make a great Queen of the Thrax? I'm already getting this regal manner stuff down.

"In that case, we'll begin." Lincoln sets the codex on his lap. "This is a magical book that will record your testimony."

"Oh, you don't need to record me. I'll go right into court and help you take that bastard down." Her tail flicks behind her.

"Thank you so much for the offer," I say. "But that's not possible."

"You see, we thrax have our traditions," says Lincoln. "And only thrax and other parties who are directly involved in the lawsuit can come into one of our courts."

Mrs. Pomplemousse purses her lips. "That seems odd."

It's no shocker that Mrs. Pomplemousse knows dick about the thrax. Purgatory used to be run by ghouls, and ghouls turned everything into a learning opportunity on sucking up to—wait for it the ghouls! Television, libraries, magazine, schools...It all centered on the ways to make our overlords happy. There was never any information shared about other realms. As a result, most quasis know very little about the thrax, other than the fact that they're demon hunters. And since quasis are part demon, they're convinced all thrax want to kill them. Long story short, my people don't have a lot of thrax love.

Plus, ever since our engagement was announced, my people seem to really hate Lincoln. In fact, I spend an inordinate amount of time explaining to the Purgatory media how Lincoln doesn't actually kill quasis on sight. That said, the quasi worries aren't totally unfounded. To tell the truth, if Lincoln and I had first met in a dark alley—instead of at a formal ball—then, yes he might have taken out his baculum and challenged me to a fight. So there's that.

Still, the Lincoln-loathing does seem to be getting a little better. I had an interview last week where they didn't only focus on the fact that Lincoln might murder me any minute.

Baby steps.

Mrs. Pomplemousse fidgets with her pillbox at and veil. Based on the suspicious gleam in her eyes, she still isn't buying the whole story about thrax and their odd traditions.

"Let me explain—" begins Lincoln.

"I'll take this one," I say. "I *am* a quasi, after all."

"As my lady commands."

For the record, I'm making a huge sacrifice here to explain things to Mrs. Pomplemousse. Why? More talking means I cannot stuff another fudge thingy in my mouth. What I do for love. "You see, Lincoln's people are demon fighters who live deep underground on Earth. Demonic forces would like nothing better than to break into Lincoln's homeland and kill everyone. As a result, the thrax must be very careful about who goes in and out, especially in court."

"I suppose that makes sense." Mrs. Pomplemousse gestures to the book in Lincoln's hands. "In that case, how do we proceed?"

"This device will magically record your words," says Lincoln. "It's the only evidence that's admissible in thrax court. Once I officially start the interview, you'll answer the questions, and everything that we say and do will be captured in the codex. The Arbiter in Antrum will review all the evidence and decide the case. Does that make sense?"

"Yes, young man. I'm ready. Begin your questions."

"Thank you." My guy looks regal and smooth a lot of the time, but never more when he's sitting in some random grandma's living room and conducting magical interviews. He makes the place seem as important as a palace.

Did I mention that he's also a good kisser? That, too. Although, Hell knows when I'll get to enjoy that again.

Stupid bets. Stupid demons.

Lincoln grips the codex in his palms. "I, Lincoln Vidar Osric Aquilus from the House of Rixa, High Prince of the Thrax and consort to the Great Scala Myla Lewis, do hereby begin this interview of evidence."

The codex rises from Lincoln's hands and then hovers in the center of the room. A flare of white light pulses across its cover.

Mrs. Pomplemousse eyes the book warily. "So it will just hover up there?"

"Yeah, that's pretty much it," I say.

"No more surprises," adds Lincoln.

I lean forward and rest my elbows on my knees. "Let's begin with the easy stuff. Please tell us your name and where you used to work."

"I'm Dolly Pomplemousse. I used to work at Ghost Tower Six."

Here's why that's an important job. Souls come to Purgatory to get judged for either Heaven or Hell. As the great scala, I'm the only one that can send them to their final destination. While the spirits are awaiting trial, they are housed in Purgatory, using what we call Ghost Towers.

"And what were your duties there?" asks Lincoln.

"At the end of every day, I would fill out form 793-BDG for our ghoul overlords." She lowers her voice. "It was a very long form that recorded all the day's activities."

I let out a low whistle. "I'm sure it was." Ghouls adore paperwork. "And did anyone interesting ever visit your tower?"

"Yes. One day, a thrax named Lady Adair came by for an inspection. She *said* she was a diplomat." Mrs. Pomplemousse folds her arms over her plump chest. She totally suspects that Lady Adair was lying. But the truth is, Lady Adair did get a job as a diplomatic envoy to Purgatory. Not that she did any actual work. Mostly, Adair used the role to try and cause trouble.

"And what happened on that inspection?" asks Lincoln.

"She came into the tower with her father, the Earl of Acca. All of us workers were supposed to act like nothing was happening. You know, so it would seem like a real inspection of how the tower worked. I was in my office and needed a pen, so I went into supply closet 37-X to get one."

I lean forward because now we're getting to the good stuff. I can feel it. "What happened next?"

"The Earl and Lady Adair came into my office and closed the door. After that, they pulled down the blinds as well. I was hidden inside the closet and something told me, *"Dolly, you should stay put."* So I did. Although…" She fidgets with her pillbox hat and veil.

I roll my hand, encouraging her to continue. "You can tell us anything. No one's going to judge you." *The Earl, on the other hand, is another story.*

My words seem to help. Mrs. Pomplemousse clears her throat and continues. "My closet was open a crack, so I snooped. Those two seemed mighty suspicious to me."

Good instincts there, lady. "What did they look like?"

"The Earl was a portly fellow who dressed like an actor from a Shakespeare play. His daughter was wearing a long gown. What a pretty little thing she was."

"Did they talk to each other?" asks Lincoln.

"Oh, no."

Lincoln frowns. "The Earl and his daughter didn't speak?"

"Not that I heard."

My shoulders slump. *Did we come all this way for nothing?* "I thought you said you'd overheard the Earl say something incriminating to his daughter?"

"I'm sorry to disappoint, but that wasn't the case."

Lincoln and I share a long look. *Busted.* Sure, we've gathered some good evidence so far. However, none of it directly links the Earl and Armageddon. Obviously, when Lady Adair's body transformed into the King of Hell, it was clear that both of them were in cahoots. And hells bells, I know that Aldred orchestrated that whole thing—Adair certainly wasn't the type to set up a master plan with the King of Hell on her own. That said, no one would go on record saying they knew Aldred was in league with Armageddon. Insert comment here about Aldred and his blackmailing skills. Long story short, we'd had high hopes for Mrs. Pomplemousse.

I reset my empty cookie plate onto the table. "I'm sorry, Mrs. Pomplemousse. I'm afraid we wasted your time."

"Now, now. I said I didn't see him speaking with his daughter, that's all."

Great. Whatever. I half rise from my seat. "Got it."

Lincoln sets his hand on my wrist, stopping me. "Then who did the Earl converse with?"

"Why Armageddon, of course."

The breath leaves my body. *Yes!* I sit right back down. "How did that happen?"

"The girl transformed into the King of Hell, right before my eyes." Mrs. Pomplemousse sets her hand over her heart. "I swear on my life, that's the truth."

"We believe you," says Lincoln. Both he and I saw the same show back in Antrum, when Armageddon tried to use Adair's body to break back into our world. He didn't make it out of Hell, though. Adair paid the price. "What did they talk about?"

"The Earl asked Armageddon about their plans to steal the throne from the House of Rixa."

I could almost dance for joy. This is the best testimony we've gotten so far. It directly implicates that the Earl of Acca was plotting with the King of Hell to overthrow Lincoln's family. Color me pumped.

Lincoln leans back in his chair. "Let's go through what happened, step by step."

It takes about an hour. Still, we get everything we can think of from Mrs. Pomplemousse, from the color of Lady Adair's dress to the exact words from Aldred's mouth. In the end, Mrs. Pomplemousse looks pretty tuckered out. Lincoln and I aren't exactly feeling fresh, either, but the evidence is airtight.

I lean back on the poufy couch and turn to Lincoln. "What do you say? Are we all set here?"

"I think so." Lincoln stands up and cracks his neck from side to side. "I'll just finish the recording, and we'll be through. Thank you so much for your time, Mrs. Pomplemousse."

The elderly woman sets her teacup down with a *clink*. A crafty look appears in her eyes. "Now, now. Don't you want to know the rest?"

My brows lift. "What else is there?"

"The Earl and Armageddon talked about another plan." She snaps her fingers, trying to remember. "It was an academy of some kind."

My heart pounds at double speed. "What kind of academy? Do you remember the name?"

Mrs. Pomplemousse taps her chin, her forehead creased with thought. "Ah, I have it. The Wheeler Institute. If things didn't work out with Adair being possessed, then they always had that."

All the oxygen seems to get sucked out of the room. *The Wheeler Institute.* That's the same place Desmond had talked about. It's where he was supposed to take the codex.

I focus every ounce of my attention on Mrs. Pomplemousse. "What do you know about the school?"

"Nothing beyond the name. I'm sorry." She sips her tea. "However, I'm guessing this Earl of Acca fellow wishes you harm. If so, then I should think the last place you should go is the Wheeler Institute."

Says her. "Did Aldred and Armageddon say anything else?"

"Not a word. That Armageddon fellow laughed himself silly and then left Adair's body."

I fold my arms over my chest. "And what did Adair have to say about what happened?"

Mrs. Pomplemousse's gaze flickers to Lincoln. A blush crawls up her cheeks. "Well, it's not easy to explain."

Now, I have a pretty good idea why Mrs. Pomplemousse is feeling awkward right now. Adair had some wackadoo concepts about Lincoln. Calling her crazy-ass possessive of him is an understatement. I wave my hand dismissively. "Trust me, Mrs. P. Whatever Adair said, you can bet that Lincoln and I have heard it already."

"All right, if you insist. Lady Adair wanted to know if Armageddon had appeared. Her father confirmed the demon's recent visit. After that, Adair asked if Armageddon had promised to help secure her birthright." Mrs. Pomplemousse looks away. "She seemed to think that birthright was primarily Prince Lincoln."

Mrs. Pomplemousse looks so jittery, I feel like I have to say something. "This is not a shocker, believe us. What happened next?"

"The Earl dragged Lady Adair out of my office. That was all I ever saw of them."

"You said you filed daily reports," says Lincoln.

"That's right."

"Did you file one about that incident?" I ask.

"Of course. My report covered the Earl, Adair, and Armageddon. I even mentioned the Wheeler Institute. No one ever followed up. Later, I tried to find the document. Unfortunately, it had disappeared."

The wheels of my mind spin super-fast. The ghouls ran Purgatory until Armageddon invaded. I kicked both of them out of this realm. When Mrs. Pomplemousse started her job, the ghouls were running things, sure. But by the time Adair was a diplomat, Armageddon and the ghouls were long gone. In fact, that's why Armageddon's been itching to find a way out of Hell. It was my igni that put him there.

"Let me get this straight," I say. "When this all went down, my mother was Purgatory's President."

Mrs. Pomplemousse sucks in a shaky breath. "I meant no disrespect."

"No, it's fine. For a while, Mom kept up a lot of the ghoul's old practices, even the silly reports that no one ever read."

"Exactly. That's what would have happened at the Ghost Towers."

I frown. "Not likely. The Ghost Towers were run by Walker."

Now, Walker's a ghoul and my honorary older sibling. He's also a genius at operations, architecture, and all sorts of random stuff. I can't imagine him missing something like a report saying that Armageddon appeared in our Ghost Towers.

"I don't know about that. There was a lot of worry in those towers when Armageddon attacked. We kept thinking the walls would burst and release angry spirits everywhere. It was just a form. With so much hullaballoo going on, it could easily have been misplaced."

"I suppose so." I open my mouth, ready to push further, but Mrs. Pomplemousse rises first.

"If you don't mind, I do think it's time to call our discussion to a close. It's been a rather busy day for me."

"Of course," says Lincoln. "Thank you again, Mrs. Pomplemousse."

"My pleasure. It's nice to speak with two sweet young people like yourselves." She gestures to my tail. "May I?"

I shrug. "Sure." Mrs. Pomplemousse is ex-Arena. If she wants to pet my tail, I'm cool with that.

My tail slips out from behind me. The arrowhead end points toward Mrs. Pomplemousse at an angle, like offering a hand. Mrs. Pomplemousse smiles and shakes my tail. "I followed your career in the Arena, you know. Myla Lewis. You were the best."

"Thank you." Sadness creeps into my bones, weighing me down. I really miss being able to hunt demons whenever I want to. I clear my throat. No point worrying about the past. My Arena fighting days are over. "We'll leave you to your evening."

"Much appreciated."

Lincoln snaps his fingers at the hovering codex. "I hereby close out this recording of evidence." The book flares with white flame once more. After that, it returns to its regular white color and lowers onto Lincoln's palms.

The interview is over. That said, our fight with Acca now has a real start.

As we walk out of Mrs. Pomplemousse's house, I want to feel the excitement of our interview victory. After all, this is our best piece of evidence yet. Still, the words about Armageddon's backup plan set me on edge.

The more I think about it, the more I don't like the sound of the Wheeler Institute. Not one bit.

CHAPTER FIVE

A.

I'm the great scala, the future queen of the thrax, and a badass quasi-demon warrior. With merely a thought, I can send a soul to Heaven or Hell. My people call me a goddess.

But, yes, I still live with my parents.

Don't get me wrong. It's on my list to find a cooler HQ while I'm in Purgatory. And I'll get around to it one of these days. Pinky promise. However, at this point? My limo is dropping Lincoln and me off at the front door of my parents' mansion. True, we should rush off to Antrum and get the codex back in the court's official vault, but I'm hungry, and I smell like dead demon and old lady.

I need to take a break. And since my dad is nothing less than the General of the archangels, there aren't many places in the after-realms that are safer than Mom and Dad's house.

Let the snacking commence.

I step out of the limo and pause. My parents' house never fails to stun me. The place is a leftover from when the ghouls ruled Purgatory, so it's a cross between a Gothic nightmare and high-tech superstore. Did I mention that ghouls love gadgets? They do.

Getting into the house is quite the process. We're forced to enter in about a million codes and undergo a few magical scans. At last, Lincoln and I walk through the front door. "Mom? Dad?"

No response.

That's not a big surprise. My parents are busy running Purgatory most of the time. Mom is the visionary, trying to create new programs. Dad is a genius at organizing troops to do, well, anything. Lately, Dad's been all about cleaning up straggler demons and removing rubble that's leftover from Armageddon's invasion. He'll be thrilled when I tell him we found and killed a pair of dyads. I'll leave out the part about Aldred and Armageddon being in league with each other. That's nothing new to my parents in general, and my father in particular. Plus, any news about the King of Hell upsets Dad. He was imprisoned there for twenty years. That's not something any of us like to chat about.

I make a beeline for the kitchen. It's a modern space with lots of gizmos and stainless steel. I scan the counters. Nothing yummy there.

Time to start rummaging through everything.

I tear through every drawer and cabinet I can find. All of them are empty of anything delicious. Bummer. My favorite snack is demon bars. They're basically chocolate-caramel goodness with a little granola thrown in. That way, it seems like health food. I live on these things, and since I'm part demon, my so-called bad eating habits don't affect my figure. Go me.

I search through a few more cabinets, finding nothing but *real* granola, which is a total waste of my time. I check the back corner of some of the larger drawers, which are my favorite hiding places for extra bars. Still nothing.

Lincoln stands in the doorway. "I thought your mother threw out all your demon bars." Mom's on a kick to try to make me eat healthier.

I crouch down and look under the sink. "She thinks she did." My fingers brush across the familiar smooth wrapper. "Bingo." I pull out a mashed-up demon bar. The wrapper isn't too torn up.

I deem thee totally edible.

A smile quirks the corner of Lincoln's mouth. "You're actually going to eat that?"

"Sure." I pull off the wrapper. "Watch me. Yum, yum."

Lincoln shakes his head slightly. "You'd have more energy if you ate actual food, you know."

And with that comment, it's official. Lincoln's judginess is ruining my snack break. I glare at him. "Why don't you go find a carrot, babe?" I stuff another bite of bar in my mouth. "I'm busy."

"Not hungry. I ate a healthy and balanced breakfast."

I'd stick out my tongue, but it's covered in food right now. Even I have standards. Instead, I wave my hand over the general vicinity of my mouth. "Still eating here."

Lincoln leans against the doorjamb and hitches his right foot over his left. "Once you're done with your gourmet dining experience, we need to get ready for Antrum." He raises the *Rixa Codex* in his hands. "This thing must go into the vault." That codex is filled with hundreds of hours of interviews, including our Mrs. Pomplemousse coup.

Those bastards at Acca are so going down.

"Sure thing." To travel to Lincoln's land, we have to use an enchanted platform called a Pulpitum. For the record, traveling this way is super fun. Seeing Lincoln's people? Not so much. They're totally twitchy around me.

To be fair, Lincoln's people have reason to fear me. Lady Adair had a goodly amount of the thrax nobility following her, and she hated my fucking guts. Later on, when she turned into Armageddon, I summoned my igni in front of all the thrax nobility... Aaaaaaaand I might have gone a little overboard. And when I say *"gone a little overboard,"* I mean that I separated the souls of all the thrax nobles from their respective bodies. It only lasted for a short while, and it made sense at the time, I swear. But after that, they're terrified of me. Oops.

Still, I did the right thing. Me and my igni posse got rid of Armageddon in the long run. That said, it doesn't change my favorability ratings with the thrax. Considering the fact that I'll rule these folks for the rest of my unnaturally long life?

Being looked at in abject horror gets really old, really fast.

But I am not deterred. No, I have a coping plan for dealing with my future thrax subjects. In my opinion, that plan involves avoiding unpleasant realities and stalling anytime I have to visit Antrum. Right now, it also means looking for another demon bar. Opening the fridge, I root around in the sketchy bottom pull-out drawers. There's one hidden under a bag of mushy apples. "Score."

"Myla, we should leave soon."

I tear open the second wrapper. "Absolutely."

"Which means we need to change our clothes."

"Fine."

"And considering we were both fighting a pair of rather nasty demons, we should also shower."

I bite off another chunk. "Yup. Any minute."

Lincoln grips the waistline of his shirt and pulls it over his head, inch by yummy inch. I toss my half-eaten demon bar on the countertop and stare my eyes out.

Damn, my guy is gorgeous.

Lincoln is all muscle-y without being obnoxious. And he has all these battle scars from fighting demons, too. Delish.

Lincoln undoes the top buttons of his camo pants. They're almost low enough where I can see something interesting, but not quite. My inner lust demon roars to life inside me, draining all coherent thought from my head. My mouth falls open as I manage to squeak out one word. "Hey."

A smug grin rounds Lincoln's mouth. "Let's get ready." He steps closer, stopping only when our bodies are inches apart. My heart is pounding so hard, I can hear my pulse *whoosh-whoosh* in my ears. He leans in until his mouth is right above mine. "I'm taking a shower. If you come with me, perhaps we could discuss our bet."

With that, he saunters out of the room.

Damn.

Bastard.

He's totally going to get me to stop stalling, follow him, and smooch. Lincoln killed the dyad demons. That means I should really make him use up his *"next kiss"* request at the very first opportunity, or he'll torture me for ages.

I stare at my half-eaten demon bar. He also wants me to stop eating crap. I'm no dummy. This is all part of a huge plot against my Myla-ness. *Well, I won't put up with it.* Folding my arms over my chest, I rest my hip against the counter. "I'm not following you, you know."

The distinct rip of a zipper sounds from the next room.

Stay strong, Myla. I'm a competitor. A winner. Lincoln does this all the time. Manipulating me with my lust demon. I won't stand for it anymore.

I will not give in.

The rush of water sounds as Lincoln turns on the shower. My lust demon roars in my head. All my resolve crumbles into nothingness as I rush from the kitchen and speed over to my parents' bathroom.

Now, let the record show that my parents have a truly epic shower. It has about a million nozzles that shoot the perfect temperature of warmness from all directions. I've been wanting to try it out with Lincoln for ages. Sure, I may be a virgin and have limited experience with men, but I have a vivid imagination and a hot fiancé. Total lust demon bonus.

I step inside the steamy bathroom. The place is all white tile and stainless steel fixtures. The shower is a clear glass number, so I can easily see Lincoln's naked backside. This moment is basically lust demon nirvana.

At last. I can truly ogle his glutes with abandon. And his back and arms, too. Let's not forget about those.

Lincoln glances at me over his shoulder and smiles. That's what you call a boudoir grin. A come-hither look.

I am so coming hither.

I grip the handle to the shower door. Lincoln rakes his hand through his brown hair, which is all wet and streaky, just like his skin. Wow, that's a great look on him.

"Myla?"

"Hmm?"

"Your clothes."

I look down. Damn, I forgot about my jeans and zip-front sweater. I give Lincoln a sly smile. "You know exactly what you do to me, don't you?"

He winks. *That's a yes.*

Reaching to my throat, I start unzipping my sweater at the neckline. That's when the worst words in the English language echo into the bathroom.

"Hi, honey! We're home!"

Ugh. I really need to get my own place.

Lincoln chuckles and nods toward the door. "You better get out of here."

My lust demon isn't having any of this. "But we're getting married on Sunday anyway. It's now Wednesday. That's less than a week. We're pretty much hitched." I'm actually mighty proud of myself. Despite being mindless with lust, I got out a somewhat logical argument.

Lincoln shakes his head. "Even after we're married, we won't have love showers with your parents around." He turns away from me again and douses his hair under the spray. The guy looks like a shampoo commercial. It's hypnotic.

"Myla baby?" *Ack.* Mom's voice snaps me out of my trance. I rush out of the bathroom and close the door behind me. My parents stand out in the hallway, looking really smug. That's when I realize my sweater is zipped down past the point of decency. I pull that sucker up and fast.

"Hey, Mom. Dad." *Fuck my life.*

"Lincoln's in there." The way Mom says it, that's definitely not a question. It doesn't help that she's all Madam President today, what with her purple suit, platform heels, and judgy expression. Sometimes, I feel like I'm just a younger-looking version of her. Not today, though. I don't think my face could ever make that particular frown. Clearly, Mom's not happy about the whole love shower thing. Well, this isn't my favorite life moment, either.

Shoot me now.

I realize my parents are staring at me. Maybe they have been for a while. At last, Dad looks contemplative in his gray suit. No judginess there. Then again, he's an archangel who's been alive since the dawn of time. This can't be his first love shower type situation.

I worry my lower lip with my teeth. What was Mom saying again? Oh, yeah. The not-a-question about who's in the shower.

"Yup, Lincoln's in there, all right." My face burns about six shades of red.

"I warned you about this," says Mom. "You mustn't place yourself in situations where you'll be tempted to have sex until you're ready. Verus cautioned you, too."

"I'm well aware of what Verus said." *That meddlesome oracle angel is always ruining things.* I mean, not including the part where she manipulated Lincoln and me to get together. That rocked.

"The igni want you to have the Scala heir," continues Mom. The fact that she's given me this speech a hundred times won't stop her, though. "You can't even sit on the same toilet seat as Lincoln and not get pregnant. The same thing happened to me, you know."

"Oh, I know."

"Your father and I used a condom and about twelve spells against fertility but—"

I raise my hand with my palm forward, the universal signal for "*whoa there, partner.*" "Too much information, Mom."

"Cam," says Dad. "Maybe we should—"

It doesn't help. Mom's on a roll. "Not that we don't want a grandchild. We do."

"That's crystal clear." I raise my pointer finger high. "Hey, I've got an idea. Let's change the subject." I shoot my father a pleading look. "How's everything with you, Dad?"

"Fine." Dad gives me a conspiratorial wink, which I totally appreciate. "Hey, I have another idea. Why don't we visit the living room and give Lincoln some privacy? Besides, I want to hear all about your latest evidence-gathering mission about Acca." Like always, Dad wears his gray suit with a blue tie. He's the definition of dashing with his cocoa-colored skin, bright blue eyes, and gleaming white-toothed smile. I love him to pieces.

"You'll adore this one," I say. "There were demons involved."

Mom frowns. "What kind of evidence were you gathering, exactly?"

I am so happy with this change of topic, I can't even tell you. Before Mom and Dad got back together, my relationship with my mother was one long conversation about me wanting to fight in the Arena...And her worrying herself sick about that fact. Long story short, this is now-familiar territory: Mom kvetching about me taking risks while doing something. So much better than the whole love shower situation.

"I can't wait to tell you." I hightail it to the living room like my ass is on fire. One I get there, I find the familiar outlay of high-back chairs, dark tables, and velvet curtains. All it needs is Dracula and a few bats, and the look would be complete. Stupid ghouls. Who told them they could decorate?

Dad plunks down onto a high-back chair. "So, what did you kill?" As General of the angels, my father knows his demons and battles. More stuff to love about him.

"Lincoln took down a pair of dyads. I helped, but he got in the final blow." *Jerk.*

"Dyad demons." Dad's brows rise. "Those are rare."

All the color drains from Mom's face. "What? Were they dangerous?"

I rub my neck. I don't want to alarm my mother. She still gets crazy-fidgety about the idea of my fighting baddies. "Maybe."

Mom sets her hand on her throat. "Oh, no. The Earl of Acca must have sent them against you."

For the record, Mom may worry about me, but that doesn't mean she isn't right most of the time. I have lots of experience with fear and Mom-management, though. It's best to tell the truth early and while using short, one-word sentences.

"Yes."

"That damnable Earl of Acca." Dad lands his fist on a nearby table with a *thunk*. "The man wants to rule the thrax again. He will stop at nothing."

Another item for the record: Dad's totally right, too. The House of Acca had the throne before Lincoln's House took power. That was hundreds of years ago. Even so, Acca has never adjusted to the new reality.

Lincoln strides into the room. Wow, that guy can sure shower fast. He's changed into his official prince kit, which involves a long black tunic over fitted leather pants. "Acca also sent a klepto demon to steal our evidence book."

Mom gasps. "Not Desmond? He's a little odd, sure. But I thought he was harmless."

I roll my eyes. "Well, now he's a little dead."

Mom puts on her presidential voice. "Myla, you should have more respect for life."

"Hey, Desmond tried to trap Lincoln and me. We chased him to get the codex back, and he led us straight into a pair of dyads. Technically, the demons killed Desmond, not Lincoln and me." I make a wincey-face. "The three of them are over in sector 27. Hospital DH-27B. Sorry about the mess."

Dad shrugs. "All in a day's work. I'll get a team on it."

"Thank you," says Lincoln. "Desmond also said something about sending the codex to the Wheeler Institute. Does that name ring any bells?"

Mom shrugs. "I've never heard of it."

"I'll look around. The place sounds vaguely familiar." Dad leans forward to rest his elbows on his knees. The lines of his face turn rigid with rage. Not a good sign. "This has Armageddon's name written all over it."

Here's where things get tricky. Dad and Armageddon have a long and nasty history. About five hundred years ago, Dad led the angelic forces when Hell invaded Heaven. The net result was the infamous Battle of the Gates. A then-common demon named Armageddon rallied a whole legion of baddies to attack my father. Dad led the opposing forces and got them all to retreat. Long story short, Dad kicked Armageddon's butt and banished all the demons from Heaven. That was ages ago. Armageddon still holds a grudge, though. Years later, when Armageddon became the King of Hell, he traded Mom's safety for Dad's incarceration in the underworld. My father spent twenty years as a prisoner of Armageddon, a demon who thinks that torture is fun.

Needless to say, I avoid any mention of Armageddon if I can help it. Even so, in the way that Mom sees risks to my safety in everything? That's how Dad is with Armageddon. And just like Mom, he's also usually right.

I try to put on my most unreadable face. It's a long shot, but it's still worth a try. "I don't think we need to bring Armageddon into this." Notice the double-speak here? I said we don't need to bring Armageddon into things, not that he wasn't there already. It's a verbal trick I learned from Lincoln.

Dad's eyes glow blue with angelic rage. "So, Armageddon is involved."

Clearly, I need to work more on that particular verbal trick.

"Yes." I take care to keep my voice level and calm. "It's all part of some backup plan between the Earl and Armageddon." Once again, ever since the Battle of the Gates, the King of Hell has had it in for my father and my family.

"I'll get to the bottom of this; don't worry." Dad fixes me with his I'm-an-archangel-and-I'll-kick-ass face. That's a good sign. It means he's handling the Armageddon angle pretty well so far.

I force on a smile. "Thanks, Dad."

"In the meantime," says Lincoln. "We need to get that codex back to Antrum."

"Right." I slowly rise. "I'll change into my Scala robes."

Mom's face brightens. "Don't forget. Tomorrow is your big day in court."

"I won't forget." *Not that I could if I wanted to.*

We make our goodbyes, and I head off to get ready. I try to force myself into a happy mood. After all, I'm getting married in less than a week. The codex is back in our possession. Even better, the book is filled with the perfect evidence to bring down Acca and protect Lincoln's throne.

So why do I feel a buzz in my body, the same one that happens right before a big battle?

I can't escape the sneaking suspicion that everything is about to go to Hell. Literally.

CHAPTER SIX

A.

After the infamous "love shower incident" with my parents, I get ready in record time. Now our limo is taking Lincoln and me to a Pulpitum, which is a magical transfer station for Antrum. I'm wearing my white Scala robes. Lincoln's still in his princely getup. Normally, I'd be excited to spend some time with my honey. But we're going to Antrum to put the *Rixa Codex* back into the storage vault. That means we may face the Earl of Acca.

Not exactly a barrel of laughs. The thought of seeing that creepy Aldred makes me sick.

I glance out the window. We're driving through another random back alley. Huh. I knock on the black divider panel to the front seat. Our regular limo driver is out sick, and one of the gardeners, Gunnar, is filling in. The dude looks like a Viking and acts like a pussy. I'll be glad when our regular driver is back.

I knock on the divider again. "Hello?"

Gunnar's voice crackles over the intercom. "Yes, Great Scala?"

I push down the red intercom button. "We should have been at the Pulpitum ten minutes ago. Are you lost?"

"Um, no." Gunnar's voice shivers with fear. "I'm not lost. Not at all. Why would you ever think that?"

Oh, yeah. He's so lost.

I hit the button again. "Make a right on Beelzebub Avenue and follow it until you hit the round building. You can't miss it. The thing looks like a cupcake."

Which reminds me I never finished that second demon bar. The great scala is hungry.

More crackling sounds as Gunnar drops the handheld microphone thingy in the front seat. He does that twice before he gets the thing firmly in his grip again. "But your followers might be there." Gunnar's voice starts wobbling so much, he might have been yodeling. He's totally scared of my groupies. Not that I blame him, mind you. Some of them *are* pretty scary.

Lincoln shakes his head. "Your fans always camp out at the Pulpitums. There's no way to avoid it. Besides, my parents were expecting us hours ago."

I pat my messenger bag with the magic codex inside. "Plus, we still need to get this into the vault." I hit the microphone button again. "Just keep going, Gunnar. We'll be fine."

"Yes." His voice comes out as a peep.

As if on cue, a crowd of my quasi-demon fans spills over onto the roadway. There are about fifty of them in total. They quickly surround the limo and block the street. That's quite an achievement, considering how there are clearly some quasi-sloth-demons in the mix. Gunnar slows down to a crawl. The crowd huddles closer, trying to peep past the tinted windows. Random shouts echo around us.

"Great Scala, come out where we can see you."

"Promise me I'll go to Heaven. I'll do anything."

"Bless me, Great Scala."

A middle-aged woman steps up to my window. Her rat tail lashes behind her as she yells at the top of her lungs. "Marry a quasi!"

A demon growl rumbles through my chest. That kind of comment really ticks me off. I get that they need time to stop hating thrax, but my choices are just that. Mine.

The woman leans in closer. "Don't turn your back on your own people!" It's a good thing these windows are tinted, or this random chick would see a very unladylike hand gesture from yours truly.

Lincoln sets his hand over mine and guides my arm down. When he speaks, his voice is super-gentle. "Try not to let them bother you."

He has a point. I inhale and exhale a few calming breaths. My inner wrath demon calms a little.

Lincoln gives my hand a gentle squeeze. "Better?"

"Yes, thanks." Lincoln really is a sweetie.

I straighten my shoulders and get ready for the nasty shouts that are sure to happen once we step out the limo door. So what if my people don't want me to marry Lincoln? I can handle it.

As we close in on the Pulpitum, I'm starting to feel pretty good about my bad self. That's when the crowd launches into *"Save our Scala,"* an awful song that goes with the tune of *"Kumbaya."*

> *"Save our Scala now*
> *Save her now*
> *Save our Scala now*
> *Save her now*
> *Save our Scala now*
> *Save her now*
> *Oh, save our Scala*
> *From marrying that evil, lying bastard."*

My tail lashes behind me in an angry rhythm. *How dare they?* I mean, I know my people don't like Lincoln. But songs? Really?

I turn to my guy. "What the fuck? That doesn't even rhyme. Or fit into the tune. They have to speed-sing the whole last part. It's beyond stupid." My tail punches a hole in the leather seat. That's the fourth time it's done that this week. I could not care less. Freaking quasis.

Lincoln seems positively serene for a man who was just called an evil, lying bastard. "Your people are very clear in their attitudes. I like that about them."

I can't believe what I'm hearing. "How can you be so calm?"

Lincoln shrugs. "Years of practice."

I fold my arms over my chest. "If you have any pointers, I'd appreciate them. What do you do? Meditate or something?"

"I remind myself of something Mother told me."

Lincoln's mom is Octavia, and she's a cool piece of business. Calculating. Ruthless. Awesome. Whatever she has to say, it must be helpful. "Can you share those words of wisdom? Because as of this moment, I'm about a second away from calling my igni on these creeps."

"Okay." Lincoln's leans closer to me. His body is all warm and comforting. "Who knows you, Myla?"

"Everyone."

"I mean, who *really* knows you?"

Oh, that.

I tap my chin for a bit. "There are my parents. Cissy." She's my best friend. "Walker." He's a ghoul who's my honorary brother. "And you." That last thought makes me smile.

Lincoln gestures to the window. "So those people outside don't know you, yet they are reacting because of how you live your life. Does that really have anything to do with you?"

I ponder that one for a full minute. "I guess not."

"You're a symbol for something inside those people, nothing more. You represent some corner of their own souls that they love or hate. You can't take either their praise or their hated too seriously."

I frown. "But I do like the praise part."

"If you accept their praise and light, then you must take in their hatred and darkness, too. And that's a horrible road to walk down. Because, ultimately, you have nothing to do with how they see you or treat you. It's all inside them." He cups my face in his hands. "Allowing someone into your heart...That's a privilege you must only grant to those who truly love and know you."

A weightless feeling seeps into my bones. "Wow. That makes total sense." I give him the barest of kisses. True, it's breaking the rules of the bet, but at this point, I don't care. "How'd you get so smart?"

He smiles. "I told you. Octavia."

"Somehow, I think this is more than your mother. You're an amazing man."

Our gazes lock, and the temperature in the limo seems to spike about fifty degrees. My lust demon instantly awakens inside me. Nothing like super-smart words of wisdom from your honey to put you in the mood. Suddenly, I'm rather shocked that Lincoln and I have never fooled around in a limo before. Lincoln meets my gaze, and the way he's looking at me? I might as well be naked.

Fooling around in a limo. We should definitely give that a try.

I am so convincing him to call the kiss. Right now.

Gunnar's voice crackles over the speaker again. "We're here."

Or not.

With that, my lust demon gets pissed. This is the umpteenth time she's been thwarted today. "Gah!" It's not my most eloquent complaint, but it captures my mood perfectly.

Lincoln's face turns unreadable, which is nothing less than amazing. My guy can go from molten-hot to Mister Cool in two seconds flat. I shake my head. Lincoln chuckles.

"What?" I ask.

"Did you have some unseemly plans for my person, Myla Lewis?"

"As a matter of fact, I did."

"Good. Remember them for later."

Still Mister Cool. I really have to learn how he does that.

Gunnar opens the limo door beside me. A row of guards in purple body armor line either side of the walkway to the Pulpitum. The crowd stays behind them. This is Purgatory's new army that was started after I drove Armageddon out of town. These troops are led by Cissy's boyfriend, Zeke. His guards don't fool around when it comes to keeping us safe.

It almost makes me want to take back all that nasty stuff I said about Zeke being a tool for ignoring Cissy all those years while she pined away for him.

Almost.

As I slide out of the limo, I tightly grip the satchel that carries the codex. Desmond ripped that thing away from me once. In retrospect, he probably was using a ton of stealth potions while he did it, but still. No way will I allow anything like that to happen again.

We exit the limo and step toward the Pulpitum.

The annoying shouts continue as we hustle past the mob and rush toward the round building. Like Lincoln said, there's always a crowd here, waiting for someone famous to transfer somewhere cool. I should get used to it. They call out more irritating crap, but my tail waves to the throng. It really doesn't care what they say as long as attention is involved. What a ham.

The guards stay outside as Lincoln and I enter the Pulpitum. It's strangely quiet in here compared to the chaos outside. The Pulpitum is a circular chamber made of stone. Like always, the place is lit with fires that burn in these copper bowl thingies. A large metal disc takes up most of the floor. Lincoln and I step to the center of the round platform.

"This is Lincoln Vidar Osric Aquilus. Activating standard station."

White laser beams pulse across the Pulpitum. This body scan confirms who we are. When it comes to security, the thrax are all high tech. Other than that, they're pretty much stuck in the Middle Ages. Not that I blame them for the high-tech security part. There's no place the demons would rather break into than Antrum. After all, it's home to all the demon killers in the after-realms. Where better to attack if you're demonic? Long story short, thrax spare no expense on the Pulpitums, and that's a good thing.

A man's disembodied voice echoes through the chamber. "Identity confirmed. Good afternoon, Your Highness. And greetings, Great Scala."

"Thanks, Marty." Like all Pulpitum operators, Marty is actually back in Antrum at Transfer Central. More high-tech fanciness.

A rustling of papers sounds through the intercom. "It seems that you're late. Queen Octavia and King Connor were waiting for you at the Courthouse Pulpitum, but they got called off to another emergency."

Lincoln's brows quirk slightly. "What happened?"

"A demon patrol went missing."

The thrax divide up the Earth's surface into regions. Each House has a territory that's theirs to guard against demonic activity. When thrax warriors talk about demon patrols, they're referring to a group of five fighters from a particular House that visit Earth on an eight-hour stretch. The patrols plan demonic protections, watch out for bad activity, and—if they're super-lucky—they get to kill stuff, too.

I love joining demon patrols.

I frown. This is totes weird. Demon patrols never go missing. "Where did that happen?"

"Some place on Earth, Great Scala. It's called Nova Scotia."

The name means nothing to me. Then again, my high school was run by ghouls. If it didn't involve learning how to suck up to our undead overlords, they weren't big on teaching it. It's a goal of mine to grab Lincoln's royal tutors and catch up on things. You know, after I find a way to get more demon kills into my schedule. A girl must have priorities.

"Where would you like to go today?" asks Marty.

"Courthouse Pulpitum," answers Lincoln.

"Confirmed and ready at your signal."

Lincoln wraps his arms around me, and I lean into his chest. Hands down, the best part about Pulpitum travel is that it requires snuggling. The worst part? The Pulpitums are enchanted to actually fly through the ground, yanking us between areas in the after-realms. In this case, we're about to fly from Purgatory to Antrum (aka underground Earth.) For all their worries about security, the thrax don't give two fucks about safety. There are no guardrails on this thing. If you get too close to the edge, your face could get burned off by magma.

"Launch transfer on my mark," says Lincoln. "Three...two... one...mark!"

The round platform beneath our feet shudders for a moment.

The platform hurtles into the ground. The Pulpitum disappears, replaced by streaks of brown earth, red lava, and multicolored minerals. Every so often, the disc whips from side to side, which is why the snuggle is so key to staying upright. I may take a few opportunities to pretend to lose my footing so I can slip my thigh between Lincoln's legs. What can I say? I'm part lust demon.

The platform lurches one final time, and our journey is over. We've come to a halt at the end of a long black corridor. This is the Courthouse Pulpitum. Lincoln pulls out his baculum and lights them up as a torch. The angelfire casts a beam of shifting brightness down the passageway.

That's when I notice him. The Earl of Acca. The hallway lights are out, and Aldred stands just inside the shadows. Waiting.

My tail makes a lewd gesture over my shoulder, and I don't even smack the arrowhead end. This is a huge bummer. I'd expected Lincoln's parents to meet us here, not this freak in thrax clothing.

Speaking of outfits, the Earl wears his traditional thrax tunic, which is a long velvet shirt. In Aldred's case, that tunic bears the symbol of a gloved fist, aka the sign of the House of Acca. The Earl has receding red hair, a barrel chest, and small black eyes. Plus, his face is all lit up with a too-bright smile. *Prick.*

"Greetings, My Prince!" The Earl bows slightly at the waist before turning to me. "And you, Great Scala."

Lincoln glares at the Earl. "What do you want, Aldred?"

I nod. *Good question.*

"Why, the other Earls and I merely had a few queries for you."

I stare off into the shadows. "Earls? I don't see anyone. Who's here, exactly?"

Aldred waves his plump hand. "Some of the other Houses happen to be close by. Nothing to fret your pretty head about."

I lower my voice an octave. "This pretty head can send you to Hell right now."

"How very amusing of you, Myla." Aldred chortles like I just made a charming joke. That really sets my blood boiling.

"The great scala asked you a question," says Lincoln. "Who else is here? Step forward."

Three other Earls shuffle into the light. I instantly recognize their faces and insignias: the Earls of Kamal, Striga, and Horus. Together with Acca, these are what the thrax call the four Great Houses. They're the most powerful groups in Antrum outside of Lincoln's House of Rixa.

Unfortunately, over the years, it seems like most folks have fallen to Aldred's careful information gathering, deal-making, and blackmail schemes. It's rumored he has dirt on everyone in Antrum, even Lincoln. My guy says he battles that rumor by never doing or saying anything he wouldn't want to be discovered. If our places were reversed, I think my head would explode.

Lucas, the Earl of Striga, steps forward. Like all thrax from the House of Striga, Lucas looks pale, tall, and lanky in his purple robes. His waist-length dreads are gray and strung with beads of spell achievement. "We were ordered here to witness the conversation between Aldred and Prince Lincoln."

"Quiet, Lucas," snarls Aldred. "You'll speak when tradition dictates."

Lucas toys with one of his many beads of spell achievement. "Or I'll simply cast a vomitus spell on you, and we can all go home."

I smile like it's my job. The Earl of Striga is the bomb, pure and simple. It doesn't hurt that his House is the main source of magic in Antrum. That seems to give him some leeway with Acca.

"I asked you a question, Aldred." Lincoln's voice gets deeper with anger. "What do you want?"

"Why, to see the magic codex that holds all the evidence against my House, of course. Our court date is tomorrow morning. However, the vault keepers tell me the *Rixa Codex* isn't there."

What a dick. He totally tried to set us up with Desmond.

Therefore, it feels super-sweet to raise my messenger bag high in my hands. "The codex in is here."

A flicker of unease moves across the Earl's piggish face. "Then show us the item in question."

"With pleasure." Lincoln pulls out the codex and raises it high. Aldred's neck burns red. The other Earls sigh with relief. Lincoln slips the codex back into my messenger bag.

"We never doubted you had it," says the Earl of Kamal.

Sure, you didn't. Creep.

"What a waste of my time," says Lucas. "I would never have come here, except Aldred asked the other major Houses to be present for an official review of the evidence." He shoots a nasty look at Aldred. "That's your right under thrax law. Even so, you shouldn't abuse it."

Aldred puffs out his chest. "Tradition can never be abused, only upheld."

"That's untrue and you know it." Lincoln's voice is deadly low, and every inch of him oozes badass. It makes me want to kiss him again. What can I say? I'm part lust demon.

A flurry of footsteps sounds in the long corridor. Torchlight flashes in every direction, blinding me.

"Stand aside!" I'd know that voice anywhere. It's Octavia, Lincoln's mother.

My tail does a happy dance over my shoulder. Octavia is a nasty woman, and I mean that in the best sense. *This is getting good.*

The Earl of Striga gasps and steps back into the shadows. *You better hide, buddy.* Lincoln is an only child. Saying his mother is overprotective is pretty much the biggest understatement of all time.

Both of Lincoln's parents come into view. They're both in full regal mode today. Octavia wears a black velvet dress with her long hair in a tight bun. Connor has on his silver battle armor. Today he reminds me of an eagle, what with his imposing presence, broad shoulders, and longish white hair.

These two aren't playing around.

Connor marches right up to the Earl of Acca. For the first time, I notice the legion of Rixa guards that fill the corridor behind them. "What are you up to, Aldred?"

The Earl of Acca raises his chin. "Merely protecting my own House. We do know how to take care of things, you know. At one time, Acca ruled all of Antrum."

"Right," Connor sniffs. "And the place almost went down in flames as a result."

The change of leadership from Acca to Rixa happened hundreds of years ago, so you'd think everyone would be cool with things by now. Didn't happen.

Connor taps Aldred in the center of his chest. "Leave my son alone. He should be spending this time preparing for his nuptials, not dealing with your tricks."

"And what of my House? My family?"

"They'll be fine," says Connor dismissively. "You won't, though."

I can't begin to tell you how much I love seeing Connor stand up to Aldred. For ages, Lincoln's father was a huge pussy when it came to the Earl of Acca. It's beyond awesome to see him come into his own.

Octavia steps up and kisses me lightly on the cheek. "You look lovely, my dear. We're so excited for your wedding on Sunday." She glares at the other Earls. "Aren't we?"

A chorus of "Yes, your Majesty" sounds through the air. I'm half surprised they don't make kissy noises too.

Lincoln steps forward until he's standing nose to nose with Aldred. "Desmond is dead, and so are the dyad demons. Your plans have failed. Try anything like that again, and I'll tear you apart piece by piece, tradition be damned. Do I make myself clear?"

Aldred bows. "I don't know of what you speak, but I shall endeavor to please."

What a lying liar.

Lincoln sets his hand on the base of my back and guides me through the packed corridor. Everyone steps away to make room for us as we go. We're halfway to the vault when I speak in a whisper that only Lincoln can hear.

"I don't believe him, Lincoln."

Lincoln's face is stony. "The Earl?"

"Yes. He's not done being a douchebag. He still has plans within his plans."

"He won't win."

I hip-check him as we walk along. "I know. Just promise me one thing."

"What's that?"

"I get to be there when you kill him."

He gives me an easy smile. "Anything for you, my sweet fiancée."

As we head into the vault, I keep thinking one thing over and over.

I am so going to love being married.

CHAPTER SEVEN

A.

Lincoln and I walk down a stone access passageway deep in Antrum. We're heading toward the entrance to the Vault, the place where precious thrax information is kept, including evidence for trials. With every step, I'm careful to keep the messenger bag with the enchanted codex pressed tightly against my chest. No way am I losing that thing again.

Lincoln's parents keep pace behind us as we head deeper underground. The four of us have been walking through the maze of passages for a while now. We haven't seen anyone else around, which isn't surprising. The Vault isn't exactly a thrax hot spot.

At last, the passageway opens into a small reception room. This is a boxy space that's lit by torches. It holds the circular portal-door to the vault itself, as well as a line of guards. Like the Pulpitum, all thrax Houses take turns supplying warriors to guard the Vault.

Today's group is from Acca. *Ick.*

Lincoln and I step into the reception room first. As we march into the torchlight, the Captain of the Guard eyes me from head to toe. He's typical Acca—average height, light skinned, and his hair is the color of spun gold. Not sure what kind of conditioner they use in Acca, but it really makes some of their tresses looks like metal. If they ever got around to bottling that goop, they could charge a fortune in Purgatory.

"What is this? You're not supposed to be here." Unlike the other guards, the Captain wears a tunic and chainmail that appear to be made of gold. He glares at us while setting his hand on the pommel of his sword.

Connor steps forward out of the shadows. "It is the royal family, my man."

"Ethan," corrects Lincoln. "The Captain's name is Ethan."

Everyone stares in surprise at Lincoln. I know he memorizes the guard rotation for his personal chambers, but Lincoln tracks the Vault as well? I can only smile. My guy is so stealthy.

"Ah, Ethan," huffs Connor. "We're here to see Cryptan, the Protector of the Vault."

Protectors are regular folks who get offered an eternal job. Personally, I got drafted into my supernatural gig as the great scala. Cryptan volunteered, though. Unless he meets an untimely death, he'll spend eternity doing the same thing over and over, which in his case means sitting alone in a vault. Not my bag.

"Cryptan is well, my King. My team checks on him every hour. He responded to my hail some twenty-seven minutes ago."

"Thank you," says Connor. "You may return to your duty."

If you didn't know Connor, you wouldn't think he was super-pissed right now. That said, I've been hanging with Lincoln's father long enough to know when he's angry. The way his fingers drum on his thigh? The man is pissed. Ethan will get his ass handed to him later, I can guarantee it. In Connor's mind, you don't go around pointing swords at his son's fiancée. However, Connor sees himself as too royal to reprimand anyone directly. For my part, I can't wait to have a crown and the authority to kick verbal ass down here. Right now, I have to keep my mouth shut. That said, once I'm Queen? Closing down stupidity will be a total job perk.

"As you command, my King." Ethan goes back to stand against the wall once more, but keeps glaring in my direction.

"You have a problem, Ethan?" I ask.

"I'm simply doing my duty, Great Scala." The way he says "*Great Scala*," you'd think I'm something he scraped off his shoe. "Keeping Antrum safe."

Meaning I'm a demon in his homeland.

What a dick.

I take a step toward Ethan, ready to give the guy a piece of my mind. I am so tired of this demonist bullshit. Lincoln grabs my elbow, stopping me. "Connor will handle him. Not to worry."

"Fine." Still, I make my eyes flash with demonic red light, just because I can. Ethan visibly trembles, which is a most satisfying sight.

Lincoln steps up to the Vault door. It's a small metal portal with a heavy iron handle and one of those spinny-dials you find on old-fashioned safes. It's not much as doors go. However, this place doesn't need tons high-tech in order to be secure. It's got Cryptan, the protector who guards this Vault. For the record, I know Cryptan asked to guard this place alone for all eternity, but I still think we should give him two weeks' vacation every year. This is yet another area where I plan some reforms once I become Queen. Bottom line? Using enchanted workers gives me the creeps.

Lincoln pauses before the door. "I am Lincoln Vidar Osric Aquilus, High Prince of the Thrax, and I request access to the Vault. Here with me are my parents and bride-to-be."

"What's the pass phrase?" Cryptan's voice sounds deep and crackly from disuse. It's yet another reminder of how rarely he sees or talks to anyone. Poor guy. At the very least, we should enchant a dog to keep him company. Sheesh.

"Aquila immortal," says Lincoln.

"That's right."

The iron door slowly swings open. Cryptan stands in the shadows of the inner Vault. He's a handsome middle-aged guy with short brown hair and a somewhat dazed look on his face. That said, Cryptan is also mega-huge, a fact that is highlighted by the oversized armor that he wears. Today, his helm is tucked under his left arm. "Greetings, royal family." His mismatched eyes catch mine and twinkle. Cryptan is kind of a flirt. "And to you as well, Great Scala. I could sense someone coming and hoped it was you."

"Hey, Cryptan." I start to offer him a high five and think better of it. I'm pretty sure his gauntlets have spikes on them. "Did you get a chance to look at any of the books I left you?"

"Books?" Cryptan frowns. "Are they in Latin?"

"Of course." It was a real pain to find them, too. "They were on battle tactics. Written by Julius Caesar."

Cryptan takes a few steps backward. "I forgot, Great Scala. I shall endeavor to read them before you return again."

I mock-glare at him, careful to make my eyes glow blue with angelic power. "You better."

Lincoln and I share quick glance. He feels the same way I do about Cryptan. The guy needs some hobbies outside of standing around.

We all step deeper into the Vault. The place is a large chamber made of shiny black stone. I'm not sure how big it is, actually. The room just stretches off into the darkness. Beams of white light pour down from the vaulted ceiling. Inside each pool of brightness, there hovers a single codex. Supposedly, there's a book here for every thrax House that has ever been in existence, even if it was only five people and a cave. It's a little mind-blowing.

It's also rather lovely. I'm used to seeing an enchanted codex that's all white. Here, all the magic books take on a different appearance. Once they enter a beam of light in the Vault, the volumes turn larger and translucent. The recordings inside them flicker to life, like highlights from a television show.

Ah, television. I miss it already. Did I mention that's one reason I don't like hanging out in Antrum too long? I need me some Human Channel.

Anyway, hundreds of columns of light stretch off into the darkness, each one holding a single codex that hovers about six feet above the floor. Images of long-gone thrax appear inside the transparent interiors. Most of them look like someone I could see walking around Antrum today.

As much as I complain about how the thrax are stuck in the past, there are moments like these where I totally get it. Lincoln and his family are part of a long line of people dedicated to keeping humans safe from the forces of Hell. They follow sacred traditions of the past so others can face the future without fear. All their open and honest faces flicker at me through the semidarkness. It's beautiful.

Cryptan marches toward one of the empty columns of light. "You have the codex for me?"

I reach into my messenger bag and pull it out. "Here you go." A question pops to mind. "When you said you could tell we were coming, was it us or the codex?"

"Both. All protectors can sense the object they are protecting, as well as human souls. I know the soul-signature of some of the guards outside." His upper lip curls with disgust. "It isn't pleasant." He grins. "Not like you."

"Thank you." I blush a little and hand him the codex. Lincoln shakes his head. There's a small smile on his face. Lincoln's more the protective than jealous type. It's one of the many things about him that I like.

Cryptan takes the book and sets the magic item into a nearby beam of light. Instantly, the images inside come to life. For whatever reason, the ones that show up first are the thrax children we interviewed early on. Their mismatched eyes stare at us from within the clear depths of the codex. Lincoln wraps his arm around me, and I lean into his shoulder. We've been thinking about starting a family. I want to, but I know everyone says we're too young to get married, let alone have a kid. Add in the whole *"don't even share the same toilet seat"* speech from Mom, and I know I'll get pregnant right away. Add it all together, and it's got me hesitating to start a family.

Then again, when have I given a crap about what everyone else thinks anyway?

Lincoln's father stomps over, stands beside us, and clears his throat. Dang, I'd almost forgotten he and Octavia had come along, they'd gotten so quiet. Connor rakes his hand through his white shoulder-length hair. His voice is gentle. "You shouldn't let it bother you, you know."

I angle my head for a better look at him. His mismatched eyes are wide with sympathy. "What do you mean?" I ask.

Octavia rushes to stand at her husband's side. "The children."

"What about them?" Now, I'm really getting confused.

Connor sighs. "We know how things work with the great scala."

"You do." My voice comes out flat. What most people know about the great scala is nothing. What few records there were got destroyed by the ghouls. People are forever making up rules about my situation.

This ought to be interesting.

"What do you know, exactly?" I ask.

Connor's face goes from Mister Sympathy to Captain Happy. It's a little weird, as a matter of fact. "The igni were created to move souls to Heaven and Hell. Their magic has certain limitations based on blood. Having the blood of a human, demon, and angel empowers you to move souls to Heaven and Hell, am I right?"

"You're spot on." Connor really researched this. I must say, I'm impressed.

"The igni are very selective about who can have this responsibility. At any point in time, they only allow two people in all the after-realms to be born with the blood of a human, demon, and angel. That's the Scala and the Scala Heir, am I right?"

"Correct." I can't shake the feeling that another shoe is going to drop, though. No one understands how my powers work. Even I don't understand everything. All the records have been erased, and when the igni try to explain, it's all a bunch of gibberish.

A gleam of satisfaction shines in Connor's mismatched eyes. "This is where things turn unfortunate. I'm sure you both know that the Scala Heir is almost always the child of a thrax maiden and a Greater Demon."

Octavia steps forward. "We checked through all the records with Cryptan. That's been the genesis of the Scala Heir for more than five thousand years."

Connor's voice turns gentle. "That isn't to say that mixed-blood parents don't try for children. It simply doesn't happen."

My brows lift. Now, I know where they are going with this. Ugh.

Lincoln's body stiffens beside me. "You don't think we'll be able to have a family, do you?"

"We know you won't." Connor still seems way too pleased with that fact for my taste. I know he likes me as a person, or at least as a force of nature. Lincoln's dad almost threw a party when he found his son was in love with the great scala. In fact, he thought it would be a superb way to get the upper hand with Aldred and the House of Acca.

A chill prickles down my limbs. *Acca.* Connor is happy we can't have kids, and I'd bet a million bucks that has something to do with Aldred. If we don't have children, then the throne goes to the highest ranking Earl left alive. One guess who that is.

I want to punch myself in the face for being so stupid. Why did I think Connor would actually change and be anything but Aldred's toady?

Connor pats Lincoln's shoulder. "That's all right, son. Your mother and I love you both anyway."

Hells bells. This isn't happening.

Lincoln focuses his attention on me. His right brow is raised in a look that says, *"I'll go with your lead here"*. Which I totally appreciate. I don't want to share my fertility status with just anyone, but I can make an exception for Lincoln's parents. It will be their grandkid, after all. "You have your information all wrong."

Connor and Octavia speak at once. "We do?" Octavia looks excited. Connor? Not so much. All of which supports my *"Acca getting the crown"* theory. Well, screw them. Aldred can learn to live with disappointment.

"It's like this," I say. "The igni have made it absolutely clear that they want my child to be the Scala Heir." I don't get into the details. Even so, it all has something to do with Verus and one of her visions for the future. Bottom line? Verus and the igni are in cahoots. And since neither of them will ever tell me anything useful about their alliance, I actively ignore it.

Connor frowns. "Even so, it can take a long time to get pregnant."

"You might want to talk to my mom about that." Which is all I'm saying on that particular subject. Let them put two and two together and see what they get. Which is the igni facilitating a pregnancy the second it's possible.

A long moment passes. Cryptan, who's been characteristically silent this whole time, finally pipes up. "You're with child, Myla?"

"Not now, no. But, you know." I shoot Lincoln a flirty look. "Soon."

Octavia wraps me in a huge hug. "Oh, I'm so excited for you both! A grandchild. What a warrior that boy or girl will be. I can't wait." She turns to Connor. "Isn't this wonderful news?"

Connor pulls at the neckline of his armor. "We better go." He gestures to the codex. "The evidence is safe in the Vault." He chin-nods toward Lincoln, which is a move Connor usually does when Lincoln's completed something amazing. Nine times out of ten, it's something that Connor should have done anyway. "Great work gathering the interviews, my son."

"Myla and I teamed on this. She deserves credit, too."

"Of course, of course." Connor doesn't give me any additional credit, though. He just starts mumbling to himself and marches out of the Vault.

Octavia gives me another hug. "Don't mind him. Many men have a hard time adjusting to the idea of grandchildren."

"Octavia!" Connor's voice echoes in from the outer hallway.

"I'm coming." She rolls her eyes. "He'll be in one of his moods. I can tell."

"You don't have to follow him," says Lincoln. He's protective of his mother when it comes to Connor. Full disclosure: I've joined that club, too.

"Prevention is simpler than cleanup, my boy. When Connor gets in a foul mindset, he can cause all sorts of trouble that I must then fix. Plus, these rough moods are rare. Your father's a dear most days."

To you, maybe. But to Lincoln? Not so much. Connor basically handed over all major kingly responsibilities to Lincoln while my guy was thirteen. In other words, Connor keeps the crown while Lincoln gets all the work. That was a huge amount of pressure to place on the shoulders of someone whose biggest concern should have been acne, not ruling millions of thrax and keeping billions of humans safe. Octavia's too in love with her husband to see the truth.

"It's best if I go now." Octavia kisses Lincoln lightly on the cheek. "I'm so proud of you." She rushes from the Vault at a pretty nimble pace for an elderly lady. Then again, Octavia was once a warrior.

Cryptan gestures toward the door. "You had best depart as well. Too many secrets are held in this Vault. No one should loiter about." That's Cryptan's standard statement after we hang for a few minutes. That said, I'm not letting him off the hook so easily this time.

I wag my finger at him. "You promise to read the books I left you?"

"That I do, Great Scala."

"Okay, cool." I turn to Lincoln and pat my stomach. "I'm hungry."

He chuckles. "You're always hungry."

I shrug. "Welcome to your future."

"How about we head to my study? I can have meals sent up." I don't like the flinty look in Lincoln's eyes, at all. My guy is scheming about something.

"What's going on?" I ask.

"Now that the codex is safe, I'd like to find out some more about the Wheeler Institute."

"You've been obsessing about that ever since Desmond said the name, haven't you?"

He winks. "What else would you expect?"

From the guy who memorizes guard rotation schedules? Nothing less. "Where do you think we can we find some maps?" I ask the question, but I bet a million dollars Lincoln's already thought this part through.

"I keep the best ones in my study."

"Of course, you do." Arx Hall only has about a dozen libraries. Leave it to my guy to sneak out all the good stuff for his private collection. I wrap my hand around Lincoln's forearm. "Lead the way, babe."

Demons? The Wheeler Institute? Snack time?

Count me in.

CHAPTER EIGHT

A.

Lincoln and I step down yet another gilded passageway in Arx Hall, his family's castle in Antrum. After leaving the courthouse Vault, we took a transfer platform directly here. It's one the many benefits of Lincoln being High Prince. The House of Rixa has his own set of Pulpitums. Sure, before it was faster to use the public Pulpitum to get straight to the courthouse station, but now? We'll take the private Pulpitum back, thank you very much.

It's a short walk to Lincoln's study. A Rixa knight stands guard before the golden doors. "Good evening, Your Highness. Great Scala."

I nod and smile, which hopefully hides the fact that I have zero idea who this dude is. "Hey."

"Hello, Felix," says Lincoln.

"Will you be staying long?" asks Felix.

"A few hours at least," answers Lincoln. "Please ask the kitchens to send up something for dinner."

My tail knocks on Felix's breastplate, and the guy almost jumps out of his armor.

"Sorry about that," I say. "That was just my tail. He doesn't like being ignored." I pat the arrowhead-shaped end and talk in a baby voice. "Do you, boy?"

Felix's chainmail jingles as he leans forward. "And greetings to the great scala's tail."

My tail straightens. That thing is such a ham.

Felix pats his breastplate with a *clink*. "I almost forgot. There was a message for you, Great Scala." He pulls out a small envelope from behind his armor. "I should have said something right away."

I pull the envelope from Felix. "That's fine. Thank you for getting it to me."

Felix goes back to his station while Lincoln pulls open the door. We step inside, and I think what I always do when we hang here.

I love this room.

Lincoln's study is a huge stainless-steel box. It's easily one of the most modern places in Arx Hall. The thrax keep records on almost everything by using rolled sheets of parchment, and Lincoln stores his copies here in movable glass walls. Yeah, he's that badass. Each wall is about three feet deep and is set on a track that's built into the floor. Inside the storage walls, there are shelves to hold all of Lincoln's rolled treasures. A whole troop of servants do nothing but sort through new sheets and put them carefully away.

There's a small seating area by the main doorway. It's not much: some leather chairs and a table. Right now, that tabletop is stacked high with the latest documents waiting to be filed. I plunk down into a chair and examine the envelope from Felix. It's addressed to Myla-la, which means it could only come from my parents. I tear the message open.

Lincoln slips into the chair beside mine. "What does it say?"

I read aloud.

Dear Myla-la,
I'm working my contacts and researching the Wheeler
Institute. Come to the clubhouse tomorrow night after

your court appearance. By then, I may have some information for you.
Dad

Lincoln arches his brows. "The clubhouse?"

"It's where Dad hangs in Heaven with his archangel buddies."

"And it's a little clubhouse." Lincoln seems unconvinced.

"In the way that Hell is a little nasty. The formal name for the place is the Dominion Line. It makes the humans' Hoover Dam look like a shithole." I toss the message onto the pile. Tomorrow night feels like ages away. I'm curious about the Wheeler Institute now.

"Where's do you store the stuff on Earth again?" I ask.

"By the right wall."

"Cool. I'll look for the Wheeler Institute and that area where the demon patrol disappeared in, uh…" I snap my fingers.

"Nova Scotia."

"That's it."

"Sounds perfect." Lincoln scans the pile of documents. "I'll find the latest patrol reports."

I speed over to the right wall while Lincoln sifts through the pile of parchment. He quickly drags off a document from near the top of the stack. "Ah, here it is." He scans the sheet. "The patrol disappeared in Boulders Beach, Nova Scotia. Ring any bells?"

"No, but I'll check for it." I step over to the correct section and drag out the glass wall. All the rolled parchments are marked with hanging tags. I find the area where the tags list all the human cities and institutions in Nova Scotia. "There's nothing here on the Wheeler Institute or Boulders Beach."

"Maybe they were misfiled." Lincoln pulls out wall after wall and scans the tags. Minutes tick by before he's through. "Nothing. Not a single scroll on the Wheeler Institute or Boulders Beach."

"Could you have missed those places?"

"No, the Earl of Striga comes in once a month. He casts spells to find any missing cities or reports. Unless Boulders Beach and the Wheeler Institute were founded in the last four weeks, then they should have been in here."

"Oh. That sucks." Not much else to say other than that. Someone must have gotten in here. But how? I know for a fact that Lincoln asked the Earl of Striga to cast about a dozen protection spells on this chamber. My guy doesn't trust Acca not to snoop around. As extra security, Lincoln has a twenty-four-hour guard outside. I rub my neck, trying to think of any other reason why the documents would be gone. "You have servants who file stuff for you. Could one of them have taken things?"

"Unlikely. There are a number of serious spells here to ward against that." Lincoln marches over to the main door and pulls it open. "Felix, how long have you been on patrol?"

I can't see Felix. Even so, I can hear his voice echo in from the outer hallway. "All day, Your Highness."

"And has anyone come or gone from my study?"

"Only the messengers. They came twice to deliver new parchment. I watched them each time, just as you ordered. They set the sheets on your table and left. Is there something wrong?"

"Perhaps. Send word that I want the Earl of Striga here immediately." Lincoln starts to close the door, thinks better of it, and reopens it wide. "And Felix?"

"Yes."

"Have the kitchens rush up something for the great scala to eat."

Yes! I cup my hand by my mouth. "I want demon bars. Cook has promised to stock them."

"She means pizza," says Lincoln.

"What's a pizza?" asks Felix.

"It's bread, cheese, and tomato pie. And remember. Get the Earl of Striga here within two minutes." With that, my guy closes the door, turns to me, and gives me his most winning smile. "Now, what were we discussing?"

Right.

I know what Lincoln's trying to do here. Mister Smoothie wants to avoid the fallout from derailing my demon bar order. I level him with what I hope is a serious look. "For the record, demon bars and pizza are *not* equal on the snack food value pyramid."

Lincoln tries to keep a straight face. "And who made this pyramid?"

"Me. It's my personal pyramid of value. And by the way, who doesn't know what a pizza is?"

"Almost everyone here. Most thrax don't leave Antrum. They aren't trained to be warriors, so they've no business going to the surface where demons are. Besides, it's a lot of work keeping a million people cleaned, housed, and fed down here. They have other things on their minds than human food."

"Okay, I get that. That said, we should still bring some decent snack foods and DVD players down here. Enchant them or something. Believe me, the average thrax wants television, phones, and videogames. They just don't know it yet."

"The average thrax...Or you?"

He has me there. "Um, yeah. It's totally me." Lincoln and I have agreed to split our time between realms. Right now, I'm looking at six months every year with nothing to do but read books and act royal. That sucks.

A knock sounds on the door. "Your Highness? It's Lucas."

"Come on in," says Lincoln.

The Earl of Striga enters the room. His long purple robes have the Striga pentagram embroidered on the front. As he walks forward, his long gray deadlocks sway behind him. His spell achievement beads click and clack, showing off all his magical knowledge. In other words, the Earl of Striga is a badass warlock. "How can I be of service, Your Highness?" He turns to me, and the movement makes the beads in his hair jingle. "Great Scala."

Lincoln folds his arms over his chest. "I fear that someone's been in here and taken parchments without permission."

The Earl's mouth falls open. "I'll investigate immediately, Your Highness." He closes his eyes and murmurs a spell. Circles of purple flame appear around his body. They have a special magic name—spell circles—but I think of them as supernatural Hula-Hoops. They slowly shift up and down his torso.

My brows rise. There must be a half-dozen Hula-Hoop thingies here. This is a pretty serious casting.

At last, the Earl opens his eyes again. Beads of sweat line his forehead. "The wards here are broken. Someone came into your study, perhaps a month ago. They took some documents." He shakes his head. "I can't believe they broke through all my protective spells."

"Do you know who it was?" I ask.

"That I can't determine," says the Earl. "I'll need to bring in some help. Perhaps Elder Faustina could be summoned."

"I don't think you need to bother," I say. "There aren't a lot of folks that can break through your spells. And one month ago, Lady Adair was running around Antrum with Armageddon under her skin. Using his power, she could easily have broken in here."

The Earl steps back. "That couldn't have happened. You need to learn about our ways, Great Scala."

Puh-lease. I can't believe he's saying this to me. Especially after what happened with Lady Adair.

"Excuse me, but weren't you at the temple *in Antrum* when Lady Adair turned into freaking Armageddon before our eyes? We've got solid intelligence that Armageddon has a plan that involves the Wheeler Institute. Now, we don't know the specifics of that scheme. Even so, I'll bet it's about one thing: getting the King of Hell back into Antrum. He's not a complex demon. All he wants is to kill me and my family, and he'll never stop trying." It's getting a little annoying, actually.

The Earl sighs. "I suppose you're right."

Damn right, I'm right. "There's something else we'd like you to do."

"Anything." The Earl looks happy to move on from the whole Armageddon-in-Antrum convo.

"Can you tell us where the Wheeler Institute is located on Earth?"

A small smile rounds the Earl's mouth. "Yes, easily." He closes his eyes, speaks a few words, and opens them again. "There are more than one hundred Wheeler Institutes on Earth."

"Are there any located in Nova Scotia?" asks Lincoln.

"Yes, in Boulders Beach."

I fist-pump the air. "Hells, yeah!" *Finally, we're getting somewhere.*

"Are you pleased for your father, Great Scala?" asks the Earl.

Lincoln frowns. "What do you mean?"

"That particular Wheeler Institute has a Heavenly patron, the archangel Xavier. He's the father of the great scala, isn't he?"

My eyes almost bug out of my head. "Oh, yeah. Xavier is totally my dad. But he's never mentioned being the patron of any school." That said, a ton of places have him as a patron-whatever. Not many of them register on his archangel radar, though. Dad's picky.

Lincoln steps to my side and wraps his arm around my waist. His face positively beams with excitement. "This is excellent news, Lucas."

"It is?" The Earl looks downright flummoxed.

"Yes, we need to get to the Wheeler Institute in Boulders Beach."

"I could help you search for more documents here," offers the Earl.

"Documents won't cut it," I say.

"Someone's gone through a lot of trouble to make those parchments disappear," adds Lincoln. "They won't be easy to recover, and we don't have a lot of time to gather evidence from the school."

"And we want it," I add.

Here's the deal. Sure, we have the testimony from Mrs. Pomplemousse. However, that's only one direct implication of Aldred's alliance with Armageddon. We'd hoped to have more testimony, but when push came to shove, everyone seemed to forget everything, mostly because Aldred was blackmailing them. And evidence from friends and family isn't admissible. Stupid thrax rules. Long story short, if there's evidence on Earth, we're getting it.

The Earl's eyes widen. "Evidence? You mean against the Earl of Acca?"

"Yes," I answer. "We think this school could be related to Aldred's alliance with Armageddon."

"Myla and I simply must visit the Wheeler Institute. Hard evidence is critical at this stage."

"Can you really afford a jaunt to Earth?" asks Lucas. "Tomorrow is Thursday. Your case closes Friday. Per thrax law, you have only two days to present your evidence and related arguments to the Arbiter." By the way, the Arbiter is the protector of the thrax court system. She's like Cryptan, only a chick and a lot more frightening (or so I've been told.) Most people spend months planning their two precious days of speeches and arguments. Right now, it looks like Lincoln and I will wing it.

"We are going," says Lincoln solemnly.

Lucas sighs. "Have you even written an outline of what you'll say?"

"We said. We're on it." Don't get me wrong. Lucas is a good guy, in general. But he does have a tendency toward mansplaining.

Lucas keeps on going like I haven't said a thing. "Starting 9 a.m. tomorrow morning—and continuing through Friday at 5 p.m.—the Arbiter listen to your arguments as you highlight evidence from your codex. You have two precious days to make your case. Right now? It's far too late to be out gathering new findings. At the end of the day on Friday, the Arbiter decides your case. Then on Sunday, your wedding takes place. There's no room in that schedule for a covert mission to the Earth's surface."

"Myla and I have it covered." Lincoln steps closer to the Earl. "What you need to ask yourself is this: how much do you want to end Acca?"

The Earl shivers so violently with rage, it sets his beads jingling. "That bastard Aldred has blackmailed my people for years. I want him gone. I'll do anything, My Prince."

"And I believe you." Lincoln sets his hand on the elder man's shoulder. "But I need your help."

"Tell me. What can I do?"

"We'll need spells, potions, and charms. All of them must be fine-tuned for only Myla and me. That way, we can investigate more quickly."

"Agreed."

"And one more thing…"

"Yes?" asks the Earl.

I worry my lower lip with my teeth. I know Lincoln well enough to guess what he'll ask next. The Earl is not going to like it.

"Lucas, you must cast a compulsion spell to keep all of this a secret."

The Earl takes a half step backward. "I would never betray you, Your Highness."

"I know you wouldn't wish to, my brother. But we've already seen your magic has been breached. Someone got into my study in the first place. Unless you cast an unbreakable compulsion on yourself, they may be able to pull information out of you against your will. Too much is riding on this mission. Myla and I can't take any chances."

I step over to Lincoln's side. We do this double-team-intimidating thing on people sometimes. Our process is simple. Lincoln scowls. My tail swipes threateningly behind me. It works every time. When I speak, I take care to lower my voice. "We need your compliance on this. It's important."

"Fine, I'll do it," says the Earl as he speeds toward the door. "I'll need to get some supplies first."

Lincoln and I exchange a dry look. Compulsion spells can hurt like fuck. No doubt the Earl wants to avoid the pain for as long as possible. We can't take that risk though. Even if Lucas does hate the Aldred, the Earl of Acca has a way of getting people to do what he wants. "Hey, buddy?" I ask.

The Earl stops and turns around. "Yes, Great Scala?"

Lincoln waves the Earl closer. "How about casting that compulsion spell first?"

The Earl's face falls. He catches himself quickly though. "Of course." He starts mumbling more incantations. A bunch of purple light-hoops start swirling around him.

I lean my head on Lincoln's shoulder. "How long does it take him to cast spells?"

Lincoln bobs his head from side to side. "These will be personalized spells, and Lucas casts with power from Lucifer's crown, so..." He purses his lips. "About an hour."

"Huh." We didn't have any of this magic stuff in Purgatory. Most of it is new to me. "And he'll be casting us a bunch of stuff. It's going to be a long night."

Lincoln kisses my temple. "At least we'll spend the evening with questionable pizza and excellent company."

I wrap my arm around his waist and give him a squeeze. "That we will."

CHAPTER NINE

A

I'm so sleepy I could punch someone. Why? It's now Thursday morning—very early Thursday morning, I might add—and the Earl of Striga, Lincoln, and I have been hanging in Lincoln's study all night, preparing for what I'm calling Secret Mission: Wheeler Institute. It's not the best code name. Then again, it's also 3 a.m. I'm creative during daylight hours and then, only when I'm killing something. At least, I'm wearing my Scala robes. They sure are comfy.

The Earl raises a small amber amulet in his fist and mumbles another incantation. He's casting a spell of hiding on the amulet. Once it's done, I can wear that necklace, walk around the Wheeler Institute, and no one will ever recognize me. Sure, humans can't see my demonic side anyway, but if the school is in cahoots with the Earl of Acca, that's another story. Who knows who might be running around there? If they're from the after-realms, they would know who I am in a heartbeat. Not worth the risk.

The Earl slumps onto a leather chair. "It is complete." He hands the finished amulet to Lincoln, who slips it into his man-bag of supplies for our mission. The Earl has been a real trooper in terms of helping out. We have a ton of charms and amulets in there now.

I offer the Earl my fist to bump. "Great work, you!" The guy stares at me like I'm insane, so I drop my hand. I keep forgetting how most thrax have lived their lives under a rock. Literally.

"Thank you, Great Scala." The Earl nods, making the beads on his long dreads jingle again. "Is that all you require?"

Lincoln scans his man-bag. "Yes, we're well prepared. Thank you."

Lucas stares guiltily at the floor. "When do you plan to leave for the school?" In truth, Lucas knows the answer; he's only asked this question a dozen times tonight.

Lincoln looks to his funky wooden wall clock. "We have to be in court in less than six hours."

"And then after court—" I almost volunteer that we're meeting with Dad before going to the Wheeler Institute, but I stop myself in time. As much as Lucas is being helpful, it's not great strategy to tell him more than he absolutely needs to know. That's another trick I picked up from Lincoln, by the way. I clear my throat. "Tonight we'll head over to the Wheeler Institute."

Lucas frowns. "It will be late by the time you arrive."

"They're in summer camp," says Lincoln. "It's not as formal."

"Plus, Lincoln and I need to plot out some cover stories and strategies. We'll put together something that they'll buy; don't you worry."

"I try not to." Lucas worries a bead of spell achievement with his fingers. "But I wish I could do more. I should go with you…Or send some agents along."

Lincoln leans forward, resting his elbows on his knees. His mismatched eyes turn super-serious. "So why don't you?"

Lucas sighs. "That's not easy to say."

Sure, it isn't. Now, I have a pretty good idea why that's the case. This is the perfect opportunity to find out if I'm right. "The Earl of Acca has something on you, am I right?"

Lucas sighs again. Shakes his head. Stares at his shoes. He doesn't reply, though.

That's totally a yes.

For the record, it used to stun me how Aldred got such a tight grip on all the other Houses. I mean, the guy has crap skills as a warrior, which is all the thrax care about. So why does everyone bend over backwards for him? The man is great at digging up dirt and blackmailing. And after what I overheard from the dyad demons? He also loves putting together deals, some of them sealed with magic.

Not that this makes the situation with Acca less awful. Still, it's good to understand your enemy.

"I take it back," I say. "You don't have to answer that." *Because basically, you already did.*

Lincoln leans back in his leather club chair. His eyes are still narrowed, which means he's scheming up a storm. "Thank you for what you've done, Lucas. If you'll excuse us, Myla and I have additional planning to do."

"Yes, Your Highness." Lucas slogs from the room. I'd feel sorry for him, but then where would the pity stop? I'm sure that Aldred is blackmailing pretty much everyone except Lincoln and me. Us, he wants to kill. We're lucky like that.

Once Lucas is gone, I turn to Lincoln. "And that, my dear sir, is the only thrax who's got any spine against Aldred…And it's not much of a spine at all."

Lincoln chuckles. "Which is why we need to run through some game plans. We know it's the Wheeler Institute. We know it's in summer session. And we know I have a more authoritarian air while you give off a youthful vibe."

I blink prettily at him. "You're saying you want to play teacher and student?"

"I think it's our best bet. We could run some scenarios based upon that ruse. Maybe even map out a few ways to approach the school and its students, that kind of thing."

"Sounds like a plan."

Suddenly, the door to the study swings open. Only one person can enter any room in Arx Hall without announcing herself first. Octavia. Sure enough, Lincoln's mom speeds into the chamber.

"What are you doing awake?" She tightens the belt of the long black dressing robe that she's wearing. "Aren't you due in court in six hours? You're supposed to be presenting your case to the Arbiter today."

Lincoln rises and kisses her lightly on the cheek. "We're discussing wedding plans, Mother. What else?"

"Are you?" asks Octavia in a sly voice. "Because I've been planning this event with Myla's mother, Camilla, and I know for a fact that neither one of you has shown any interest in the details."

We go through this all the time. Lincoln tries to stall Octavia, but she always gets the information in the end. I decide to cut to the chase. "We were scheming with Lucas."

Octavia purses her lips. "And I suppose you won't tell me what those schemes are about?"

"No, Mother." When Lincoln says this, it's in his no-nonsense tone. Unlike the stalling maneuver, this one always works.

Octavia glances at the closed door. "And I suppose you had Lucas cast a compulsion spell not to discuss whatever you three were *really* up to?"

"Yes, so don't bother trying to wheedle it out of him." Lincoln folds his arms over his chest. "Now, what are you doing here, Mother?"

She folds her hands neatly at her waist. "Would you believe me if I said I wanted a friendly visit?"

"Not at all," replies Lincoln. "You never visit after 9 p.m. And besides, I can see the edge of your fighting suit under your robe."

"Oh, bother." Octavia pulls the robe even more tightly around her. "I need you both to come with me. I've gotten some strange reports from my servants."

"Sure thing," I say. Octavia has about the best spy network in the after-realms. Nothing happens in Antrum without someone whispering it into the Queen's ear, often within seconds after the fact.

"Follow me." Octavia steps over to the far wall and pulls out one of the moving glass panels. She exposes a hidden passageway set behind the stainless steel.

Lincoln groans. Still, he pulls on a fresh tunic and some breeches. My guy can't go wandering around Antrum in jeans. His people get twitchy about stuff like that. "How did you find out about that doorway, Mother? The new passage was supposed to be a secret. You don't even want to know how hard I worked in order to keep it hidden."

I raise my hand. "He worked really hard." We had Striga cast about a hundred memory cleanses to keep everyone oblivious. Even one of those takes forever.

Octavia lifts her chin. "Well, try harder next time."

Lincoln clears this throat. "I had a question. How did you find out I was building it?"

"A woman never shares her secrets."

Lincoln chuckles. "On second thought, I'm not sure I want to know."

Octavia steps into the hidden passageway inside the wall. Lincoln ignites his baculum to use as a torch. "Where are we off to?"

"The Vault. I know a secret way to get there."

I pause. "Is something wrong with the codex?"

"I don't know." Octavia straightens her spine. "My spies tell me that Cryptan has been injured."

My insides twist with worry. *Cryptan's hurt?*

With that, we hustle our butts of into the semidarkness. There's a warren of hidden corridors that all look the same to me. Good thing Octavia and Lincoln seem to know their way. Still, it feels like forever ekes by before we're out of the hidden passages and into the courthouse. Soon, we're standing before the Vault door itself. The same dicky Acca Captain is still on duty—Ethan— which gives me the creeps.

Octavia marches toward Ethan. She's in full bitch-queen mode, which is really something to see. I want to cower under a large piece of furniture, and she isn't even directing her anger at me. "When was the last time you spoke with Cryptan?"

"Good evening, Your Majesty."

"It's past three o'clock in the morning."

"Good morrow, then." His words drip with acidic hate. That's not good. No one mouths off to Octavia. It's simply not done.

Something is wrong. Very wrong.

"You're supposed to check with him on the hour," says Lincoln. "When was the last time that Cryptan responded to you?"

Ethan's face stays eerily calm. "Only a few minutes ago."

One advantage of being part demon is that I have a pretty good bullshit detector. And what Ethan just said? Total crap. The guy is lying.

"I see." Octavia steps up to the door and pounds on it. "Cryptan! Open up!"

There's no reply.

"The man's fine," says Ethan. "I'm sure Your Highnesses have better things to do than double-check my work." He gestures toward the exit. "Now, if you don't mind."

"I do mind." Octavia glances at Lincoln. "Son?"

"With pleasure, Mother." Lincoln takes out his baculum. The pair of silver bars aren't lit with angelfire. That said, they're still pretty heavy items in their own right. Lincoln slams them into the side of Ethan's head. The man falls to the ground in a lump, unconscious. Lincoln scans the other guards. "Anyone else want to interfere?"

No response. *Wise choice, people.*

Octavia extends her hand. "Then give me the keys."

Another guard down the line steps forward, a gleaming set of skeleton keys in his hand. "Your Majesty."

Octavia swipes the keys from him and gestures toward Ethan. "Get him some first aid."

Part of me knows that knocking Ethan out was harsh, but more of me suspects that Cryptan is hurt and Ethan was involved somehow. Frankly, the dude's lucky to be getting first aid.

While the guards drag off Ethan, Octavia fiddles with the spinny dials and locks on the round metal door. Why does one portal take so long to open? It seems to like an hour ekes by before Octavia can even get the door to budge. My breathing quickens.

Finally, Octavia pulls open the round metal door. Lincoln, Octavia, and I rush inside the Vault. What I see makes me gasp.

Blood. Everywhere.

A huge body lays on the floor, motionless. *No, no, no.* I race over and fall on my knees beside the body. "Cryptan. Are you—" The words catch in my throat. His armor has been slashed through so much his torso has been cut in half.

He's dead.

"Cryptan!" I cry.

Lincoln kneels beside me. "I'm sorry, Myla. I know you two were friends." He looks up at Octavia. "The body's still warm. Who could have done this?"

"Who, indeed?" A voice sounds from the opened door.

It's Aldred.

My blood boils with rage. What is that asswad doing here? The Earl of Acca parades into the Vault along with the rest of the guard who'd been all-too-conveniently waiting outside. I swear, there weren't this many of them here a minute ago. Aldred must have called in reinforcements. Now, there's like fifty Acca warriors here.

"I thought there might be trouble tonight. And look what I discover." Aldred points to Cryptan's body. "Our sacred protector is dead."

Cryptan's blood drips from my fingertips and down my white Scala robes. Fury pounds through me. It's not a coincidence that Cryptan is dead and Aldred shows up two minutes later with a bunch of warriors. I rise to face Aldred. "What did you do to him?"

Aldred ignores me and makes a great show of scanning the room. "One of the books is missing." He steps over to the spot where our evidence codex used to be stored. "Oh, no. The *Rixa Codex* is gone. And since these magical books can't be destroyed, someone must have taken it!"

Heat pools behind my eyes, and I know my irises are lighting up red with demonic hatred. I'd been so concerned about Cryptan I hadn't even noticed that the codex was stolen. What a bastard that Aldred is. This entire thing was his doing, I'm sure.

Lincoln stands beside me, his jawline trembling with rage. "I knew you'd do something to upset the trial. But this?"

Aldred waves his arm dismissively. "You're too blinded with lust to see the truth. The enchanted books in here are filled with the secrets of our people. They are filled with so much magic, they're indestructible. Your fiancée stole one of the most valuable: the codex for the ruling House of Rixa." He glares at me. "Never trust a demon."

"I had nothing to do with this."

"Is that so?" Aldred steps over to the wall and pretends to notice some markings there. "Look what I found! The imprints of an arrowhead-shaped tail. Those are extremely rare, aren't they? Right now, only one person in Antrum has such a tail. You, girly. It looks like Cryptan put up quite a fight before you killed him."

Lincoln grips my hand with more force. "This is obviously a setup. No one will ever believe you, Aldred."

Octavia moves to stand beside us. If she's concerned about the fifty soldiers blocking us from the exit, then she doesn't show it. "I won't allow this."

Aldred jabs a chubby finger in my direction. "You've all been blinded by this demon. Remember your responsibilities. With Adair gone, Lincoln should be wooing my next eldest daughter, Avery. That's what our marriage contract had said."

"I never signed that document, Aldred." Lincoln's voice is deadly low. "In fact, I stepped away from forming an alliance of the lesser houses in exchange for you dropping this marriage farce altogether, don't you remember?"

"That was done under false pretenses. I had no idea you'd take up with a demon."

"She's not a demon; she's the great scala." Lincoln inhales slowly. A muscle twitches along his neck. It's taking everything he has not to ignite his baculum and go to town.

I give Lincoln's hand a reassuring squeeze. "Stop trying to distract from the main issue here. This isn't about me. It's about your dreams of ruling."

Nice work, me. My tail and I exchange a high-five. That was some pretty logical maneuvering for someone with serious rage issues.

Lincoln gives me an approving nod. I could just about jump over the moon, I feel so awesome about that. "Myla's right." Lincoln returns his attention to Aldred. "You need to give up on these dreams of my marrying into your family. It's over. I'm engaged to Myla, and we're getting married Sunday."

"The demon girl is the one who must give up," snarls the Earl. "She made you drag me into court."

I roll my eyes. "You are so full of crap. Lincoln hates you and you know it."

"What I am is innocent of all charges. Armageddon is my sworn enemy."

"Whoa, whoa, whoa." I shake my head. "I need a minute here. How can you keep spewing out lies like that?"

"Because I'm not the liar. I'm not the murderer, either. This is all on you, demon. You used your lust charms to wheedle your way into Cryptan's life. And when you knew the codex didn't have enough evidence? You killed him in cold blood so you could steal away the proof of your failure. You'll never prove my guilt by Friday, and both of you will spend your lives in jail." Aldred turns to Lincoln. "Is it really worth it? A life in prison to cover up for a demon whore?"

Demon whore? "Watch your mouth, or I'll send you to Hell early."

"Not before I slice him in two." Lincoln takes out his baculum. "Address Myla properly."

"My mistake, Great Scala," says Aldred. Still, he doesn't seem too worried about Lincoln's baculum or my threat to send him to fiery down under. That's not a good sign. Aldred points to the empty spot where the *Rixa Codex* once stood. "First things first. You have no evidence."

"We'll gather fresh testimony," says Lincoln. "There's a lot of time between now and Friday."

"No, there isn't any time at all." Aldred pulls out a scroll of parchment from the folds of his tunic. "I have a signed writ here from your father, the King. The House of Acca has just been awarded the Rights of Prisonry in Antrum."

Rights of Prisonry. That means they now run every jail. "I thought Kamal ran the prisons."

"Time was, they did." Aldred lifts his chin. "Now, it's Acca." He taps a spot on the writ. "And as we all know, in cases of murder on thrax lands, all suspects must be held indefinitely in prison." He glares at me. "I've a nice cell already picked out for you."

The world seems to stop spinning for a moment. I knew Lincoln's father was acting strangely, but to sign a writ like this with Acca? To get me carted off to prison before our day in court? I never would have expected this betrayal. Neither would Octavia, it would seem. She marches over to Aldred and takes the sheet from his hands.

"That can't be right." Octavia scans the document carefully. "This must be a forged signature. Connor would never do such a thing." The words come out as more of a question than a statement, though.

My heart sinks. Lincoln has always called it. He said Connor would never allow Acca to end up in jail. I thought maybe Connor had gotten over his Acca love-fest. Looks like I was wrong though. And knowing Aldred's love of blackmail? He must be holding something awful over Connor's head.

Aldred pulls the parchment back from Octavia. "I want no trouble with you, my Queen. Myla is coming with me."

I've never wanted to kill anyone more than I do Aldred right now. "And Lincoln?"

"Ah, yes. We're detaining him for questioning as well."

"Let me guess." I smack my lips. "The detaining process includes slapping my fiancé in a prison cell."

"It's standard operating procedure for prisonry in Acca."

I roll my eyes. "You just made that up."

"Whine all you want," says Aldred. "All that matters is one simple fact. Neither of you are going to court today, I'm afraid."

Right.

I turn to Lincoln. "What are our options? Tell me we don't have to do this."

Lincoln's mismatched eyes fill with despair. "I wish I could say that."

"You see?" asks Aldred. "Our High Prince Lincoln is an honorable man. He will always respect our laws and traditions." Aldred waves the parchment in his hand. "And he must follow the dictates of his King."

Now, there are times when I wish that I were Queen of the Thrax. Now isn't one of them. In fact, I'm pretty psyched that I'm only a supernatural being who isn't in any way a permanent thrax official. Why? Because I get to say this.

"Lincoln might have to follow your stupid rules, but I don't."

Aldred frowns. "You think you can pull that same scheme that you did with Adair? Use your little tricks to threaten my people with Heaven or Hell in order to get your way?" He pulls out a small amulet from under his tunic. "Well, that won't work again, girly. I've gotten protection from the likes of you. The only time you can touch my soul is when I'm dead."

"I can help with that," says Octavia.

"Don't fill the air with your false threats," retorts Aldred. "Everyone else may be afraid of the so-called great scala. I'm not. Both she and the prince coming with me, and there's nothing anyone can do to stop it." He glares in my direction. "Right?"

I open my mouth to tell him to stuff it, when an image appears in my mind. It's the message from my father. *Meet me in the clubhouse.*

That's exactly what I'll do.

"I have no intention of using my powers on you or your people." I shrug. "Not at this very moment, anyway."

The look that comes over the Earl's piggish face can only be described as gloating. "Glad to hear it."

I look to Lincoln and lower my voice to a whisper. "You know what I'm thinking?" I shoot a quick glance upward, aka the Heavenly direction.

Lincoln catches on right away. "I do. The clubhouse."

Boy, do I ever love this guy. He can guess my thoughts like nobody's business. But he does need to understand the risks here.

"I've never pulled physical bodies up to Heaven before, Lincoln. Only souls." Since I'm part demon, getting me in Heaven will be especially tricky.

"You can do anything, Myla." Even though he's whispering, there's no mistaking the excitement in my guy's voice.

My heart warms with his confidence. "Be ready to move on my signal."

"I will."

Aldred sets his hands on his hips. "Are you two done with your little discussion? Ready to accept reality?"

"Yes." I make a great show of sniffling. "Lincoln and I will follow your rules. First, you must let Octavia go."

Aldred waves to his soldiers. "Allow the Queen to exit."

Octavia scans Lincoln and me carefully for a few seconds. Her mouth slowly winds into a small smile. She's two steps ahead of us, I'm sure. "I'm glad you'll do your duty, my son."

"Always, Mother."

Octavia leaves the chamber. Once the sound of her footfalls disappears, Aldred refocuses on Lincoln and me. "Now, let's return to business, shall we?"

Let's not.

"Hang on, Lincoln."

Lincoln pulls my back against his chest. "Like this?"

"Perfect."

"I said enough of your yammering to each other." The Earl waves to his troops. "Move in. Take them by force if necessary." The soldiers charge across the darkened floor.

That means it's time to go.

I raise my arms over my head. From my soul, I call out to my igni.

Help me, little ones. Take me and Lincoln into Heaven.

Music instantly fills my mind. It's sweet singing that only I can hear. These are the voices of the light igni, the forces that pull souls to the Pearly Gates. Hearing their lovely music instantly calms me.

Suddenly the room fills with the brightness of a dozen suns. Thousands of igni materialize around Lincoln and me. They are small lightning bolts of power, each one no longer than my thumb. The igni whirl and dive around us in a column of light that spans from the floor to the ceiling. Aldred's troops try to break through, but it's no use. My igni hold them back with ease. The guards' shadowy forms are barely visible beyond the wall of tiny, shifting lightning bolts.

"That's it, Myla," Lincoln whispers in my ear. "You're doing it."

I pull in more igni until the column grows taller than ever before. It starts to bore through the ceiling of the cave, up toward the Earth's surface. The music of the igni turns deafening. Supernatural energy thrums through my soul. I pump in even more power.

Move us, body and soul, my little ones.

Their childlike voices become even louder. I don't understand much of what they say, however there are words about Lincoln, love, and the future of the after-realms.

Our feet start to rise from the floor. The shifting lights of the igni column swirl around us. Beyond that, I can see crossbow bolts slam into the rounded wall of light. The projectiles fall harmlessly to the floor. *Go igni.* Lincoln and I lift higher, then pause. There isn't enough energy. Panic zooms through me.

It's as I'd feared. The igni can't move both body and soul.

I look over my shoulder to my angelbound love. Lincoln's face contorts with worry. We've stopped moving toward the ceiling, but at this rate. In fact, we've drifted a few inches lower.

My igni can't do this. They might very well drop us soon. And based on how the guards are closing in, I don't think we'll get another chance at escape.

I inhale a deep breath and scream with all the power in me. "I said, move!"

The igni song grows louder than ever before. Lincoln and I fly upward on a bolt of light. We're moving. Now it hurts like hell, though. A part-demon chick isn't meant to go whipping physically into Heaven. At least, not without an escort like my father to cast a million protection spells on me. Pain radiates through every cell in my body. I won't give up, though. Lincoln's arms stay tight around my torso. He won't let go, either. Although the agony is terrible, I know one thing for certain.

We can do this. We can reach Heaven.

CHAPTER TEN

I hold on to Lincoln as we hurtle upward. A column of igni swirls around us, blocking out any view of the outside world. Although I can't see a thing, the sense of movement is unmistakable. There's no doubt about it. My little lightning-bolt buddies are drawing us onto a supernatural plane.

Here comes Heaven.

With every passing second, the air currents turn more intense. My limbs feel like they're being torn off. Pain radiates through my bones. Getting into Heaven is never pleasant when you're part demon, but this is especially painful. I grip more tightly onto Lincoln, pressing my cheek against his firm chest. Even through the wind roars in my ears, I can still hear my guy's steady heartbeat. He's part angel, so this stuff doesn't hurt him. Touching him helps.

A minute later, it's all over. Blissfully-still air encompasses us. The igni disappear. Lincoln and I now stand before the Pearly Gates. I inhale a shaky breath. I've never seen the gates up close before. They're a huge pair of doors made from intricate loops of shifting igni. This is one of the places where my little ones hang out when they aren't helping me zap stuff around. On either side of this entrance, a barrier wall stretches off into the distance. It's enough to make you feel ant-like in comparison.

No one else is around outside of Lincoln and me, although that's no shocker. Human souls get zapped into Heaven's interior by yours truly. Angels fly their way in and out of Heaven. The Pearly Gates are rarely used.

I scan the clouds for angels. There are none in sight. That's strange. Dad told me that angels flew past the gates all the time.

Lincoln gives my hand a gentle squeeze. "Are you all right?"

"Getting into Heaven hurts like a bitch. Once I'm here, it's cool." From what Dad told me, it's that way for full-blooded demons, too. It was one of the reasons why they never expected an invasion from Hell. *Oops.* "How are you doing?"

"I've been better." There's a sad look in his eyes that I've never seen before.

I cup Lincoln's face in my hands. The bristle on his cheeks tickles my palms. "Don't worry about the codex. Mourn and Dusk said it was supposed to go to the Wheeler Institute. I'm sure that's where it is right now, and we're already prepped and ready to visit. We will find the codex again."

"I hope so, Myla." He leans into my touch. "The thought of being parted from you…"

My mouth falls open. Lincoln is not an *"I hope so"* kind of guy. He's Mister Confidence. Something is off. "Hey, I know it sucked to have Aldred ambush us, but we're warriors, right? We bounce back."

"We'll try."

I'm about to give him a quick pep talk (okay, lecture) on being positive, when the sound of flapping wings fills the air. A shadow falls over us. Considering how bright everything is, the darkness feels heavy as a blanket. Looking up, I see a dozen angels flying toward us. The sun is behind them, so their faces stay hidden in shadow. Even so, I can tell that one angel has golden wings. *Bet that's Dad.* Golden feathers are an archangel thing.

A deep voice booms down from the skies. "Myla-la?" *Oh, that's my father, all right.* I'm so happy to see him I decide not to give my standard speech about calling me baby names in public.

I wave up to Dad. "Yup. It's me. Lincoln's here, too."

Lincoln steps away from my touch. He's usually an affectionate kind of guy, so he must be in a mood. I'll work on him later.

Dad swoops around at top speed before slowly landing before us. He wears his knightly armor and holds a baculum sword of white flame.

I grin. My archangel father is so cool.

"What's wrong?" asks Dad. "Why didn't you get official passage to Heaven?" Typically, the process involves getting an angelic posse to carry you across the border, including all those anti-pain enchantments for those of us with a demonic side.

Overhead, the other dozen or so angels hover in battle formation. All of them carry regular broadswords and wear lighter armor. My father acts as the General of the angelic army, so whenever something unexpected happens, he always calls in his troops.

"No one's attacking, Dad. We came here to follow up on your note." My father still looks distracted, so I feel it's necessary to clarify things. "The Wheeler Institute, remember?"

My father scans the cloudy ground like Armageddon himself will pop up out of the mist. Then, I realize that's exactly what had happened here, only hundreds of years ago. My father fought in the infamous Battle of the Gates, which took place right at this spot. It was the first time someone from my family defeated Armageddon. Needless to say, the King of Hell has been trying to kill us all ever since.

Dad's eyes narrow. "Are you certain there's no trouble?"

"No one is attacking, I mean it." Good thing I'm telling the truth. My father can totally tell if I'm lying. It's some kind of archangel-magic thingy.

Dad doesn't move. He doesn't extinguish his fire-sword, either. "Then what are you doing at the Pearly Gates? I planned to lead the team that would carry you into Heaven." Which would have been awesome. Getting carried around by my archangel Dad is pretty much the ultimate.

"Myla's igni brought us here," explains Lincoln.

A collective gasp comes out of the angels flitting overhead. A few voices echo down from above.

"Igni don't move physical bodies."

"It's never been done before."

My tail gives them a little salute. It loves the attention, but I'm not too comfortable with the situation here. These are professional warriors and all. Even so, Heaven isn't exactly Vegas when it comes to entertainment. Obviously, they're paying super-close attention to everything we're saying. Awkward.

"It's a complex story." Lincoln glances at the angels. "Perhaps we should go somewhere private and discuss it."

"Of course." Dad waves his arm, and the angels take off like bullets from a gun.

My brows lift. "You train them to fly like that?"

"Who else?"

"That's a pretty neat trick."

"Thank you." At last, Dad extinguishes his baculum sword. Instead of a blade of white flame, he now holds two simple silver bars in his hand. My father's mouth winds into a white-toothed smile. I swear, his teeth actually sparkle like a television commercial. "It's so good to see you, Myla-la. You look more like your mother every day. Simply beautiful."

My heart warms with affection. After so many years of wondering who my father was, it's beyond awesome to finally know him. "Thanks. I'll tell her you said so."

Dad winks. "I'm counting on it."

Did I mention that Dad's a bit of a schmoozer? Well, he is.

Lincoln stares suspiciously at the clouds that obscure the ground. I know how he feels. As a warrior, it's unsettling not to see the ground nearby. "Perhaps we could talk in your clubhouse." It's not really a question. Lincoln's ready to vamoose.

"Quite right." Dad focuses on me. "By the way, what I'm about to do may count as a new power."

"Nice." My father has a list of superpowers a mile long. They're amazing to me, but since my Dad's had them from the beginning of time, he doesn't even realize they're special, let alone keep track of them. So, whenever I run across a new one, I write it down in a journal. For example, *"finding my daughter right away when she shows up in Heaven"* is definitely going on the list. My journal's about a quarter full, and I've only known my father for less than six months. "What are you going to show me?"

"Remember how we flew into the clubhouse last time?"

"Yup." Dad's clubhouse is a massive wall-like structure. Hard to forget your father fly-carrying you over something bigger than the humans' Hoover Dam.

"Well, here's a shortcut." Dad steps up to the Pearly Gates and sets his palm on the opaque surface. Circles of white fire billow out from his hand. The motion reminds me of ripples in a pond.

"That's funky." It's not his best though. One time, Dad actually made it rain fire. You haven't lived until you've seen an archangel create a meteor shower over the desert.

A small smirk rounds my father's mouth. "I'm not done yet." Dad pulls open the huge gate and reveals one of the inner chambers of the Dominion Line, aka his clubhouse. I've been to this room before. The observatory. It's a long and tall space with floor-to-ceiling windows that overlook the City of Arches. Opening a door directly to this spot? Now, I'm totally impressed.

"Well done, Dad."

"I thought you'd like it. While we're in Heaven, I can use any door in one place to get anywhere else, if you get my meaning."

"I do." And it's totally going in the journal.

CHAPTER ELEVEN

A

We step into a long room made of pearly-white granite. There's no furniture around; this is more of a viewing area. I make a beeline for the window. The City of Arches stretches out before me. There are thousands of white buildings, all of them looping and twisting around each other. Some are solid stone. Others look as if they were cut from lace. Overall, it has the effect of white arches stretching off into the distance, all of them lurching at different angles. I rest my hand against the pane of observation glass. Small halos of vapor surround my fingertips. This view is phenomenal.

Lincoln moves to stand behind me. His warm hand rests on my shoulder. "It is lovely."

Hey, now. Lincoln's voice is so gloomy, it almost breaks my heart. "You're sad about Cryptan, aren't you?"

Lincoln pulls my back against his chest. "Yes."

"I get that." I lean my head against his shoulder and give him few seconds. No one can *constantly* be super-strong. Everyone has a right to get bummed out. Especially Lincoln.

Dad's voice sounds from behind us. "Do you two need some time?"

"We do, but there isn't any," says Lincoln. "We should get to business. It's been an eventful day." *Yow.* That's the closest my guy gets to saying everything is total shit. Leaving the view, I turn to face Dad and Lincoln.

My father folds his arms over his chest. "Tell me what happened."

With that, Lincoln explains about Cryptan being dead and our codex getting stolen. My father questions every little detail, especially anything having to do with Desmond, the now-dead klepto demon. I let Lincoln do the talking. Maybe some sharing will help him break out of his funk.

Soon Lincoln gets to the bit where Desmond and the dyad demons talked about the codex and the Wheeler Institute. Dad's been pretty chill throughout the explanation. The second that Lincoln says the word *"Wheeler,"* my father's entire body tenses. "I have some information for you."

Uh-oh. I don't like the vibe here. "Why do I have the feeling I won't like what you have to say?"

Dad starts unhooking his angelic armor and setting it aside. "You won't. It has to do with Lucifer."

In my experience, Lucifer *plus* Myla *equals* nightmare. Here's the deal. Lucifer was once King of the Angels. These days, that's Verus's gig (she's also the oracle who set up Lincoln and me.) Now, everyone's heard how Lucifer went cuckoo and lost his job. What most people don't know is that my father and the other archangels were the ones who had to arrest old Lucifer and lock him up. Even fewer know that Lucifer loved making super-magical bits of junk, which he then left lying around.

Like Lucifer's Orb.

That was the last time my life crisscrossed with Lucifer's. The guy left around a super-powerful orb that prevented me from doing my job, as in moving souls to Heaven and Hell. The Ghost Towers in Purgatory got so full, they almost exploded. Getting rid of that orb was a total pain in the ass. I don't look forward to more creations from the Lucifer collection.

I make a yuck-face. "Don't tell me. Lucifer left more magical crap."

Dad's never bullshits around when there's bad news. "That's exactly what he did."

Fuck-fuck-fuckity-FUCK-fuck.

"Let me guess," says Lincoln. "This little item, whatever it is, could free Armageddon from Hell."

"Right again," says Dad.

All reason flies out the window as I stomp my foot, toddler-style. "Come on!"

Lincoln works hard to hide a smile. "Myla, I thought you were trying to become more regal."

I stick out my tongue at him, just because I can. "Okay, fine. I'm not acting like the most mature chick in the after-realms right now. But please. I worked so hard to send Armageddon back to Hell with my igni. And since I did the sending, he wasn't supposed to get out. Ever. Do not pass go. Do not collect two hundred dollars. It was a total *"stay in jail permanently"* card. And now, he's scheming with Aldred to escape again." I grip my hands in my hair and growl. Loudly.

Dad stands frozen with his gauntlets half off. He slowly swings his gaze toward Lincoln. "You've known her longer than I have. Does she do this a lot?"

Lincoln shrugs. "Give her a minute."

Demonic rage pumps through me until I'm positive my irises are glowing red. *That'll show them.* "In case you forgot, *"her"* is standing right here."

Dad raises his hand. "But, Myla-la—"

Lincoln cuts him off. "Don't go there. It's best not to talk until she cracks her neck. Just pisses off her wrath demon."

Now, I'm pretty sure there was some more chatting about me like I'm not here, but I'm way too pissed off about Armageddon and Lucifer to process that stuff. I start pacing a line in front of the glass wall. "I sent him to Hell. Igni soul column!" Some small part of my mind knows I'm speaking in sentence fragments. I can't seem to stop, though. "Lucifer's orb. Ghosts everywhere. Aldred and his freaking schemes. Gah!" I exhale a long breath. Look out the window. Jog in place for a few seconds. *There, that feels better.* As a final touch, I crack my neck from side to side. "So, Dad. What does this have to do with Lucifer's Orb?"

My father and Lincoln share a weird look. I make a mental note to grill Lincoln about it later on. "Yes, Lucifer liked to create magical objects." Dad looks at me like I'm going to explode on him or something.

"I know."

"And you realize that his objects are impossible to destroy?"

"Yeeeeeeeah." The thrax codex system works the same way. I'm sure if Aldred had the option, he would have smashed the *Rixa Codex* to bits. He couldn't, though. Hence why it's hidden on Earth.

"Well, Lucifer made a coin that would allow the holder to open the Gates of Hell."

"Like a ghoul portal?" asks Lincoln.

"A ghoul portal only allows people to enter single file. In battle situations, you can really only get one warrior in with each ghoul. No, what Lucifer's coin would create is a massive gateway that would allow whole armies to troop through."

I pinch the bridge of my nose. "And why would he do that, pray tell?" It's like the guy sat around brainstorming stupid shit to create. *What's next? A magic plunger that sucks us all into outer space?*

"This was at the beginning of time. Hell was still called the Garden of Eden then. We thought that when human kind was ready, we could lead them out of the Garden in a great parade of achievement. Hence Lucifer's coin."

I smack my lips. "Oops."

Dad finishes taking off his golden armor. Now he stands in a brown leather tunic with matching pants. It's a pretty badass look, actually. "Yes, that didn't turn out as planned. The coin remained. It was still around after we..." His eyes get that sad, glassy look that always happens when Dad talks about Lucifer. The two of them used to be great friends.

I steal up to his side and speak in a soothing voice. "You were saying something, Dad?"

"Yes. The coin was still around after we placed Lucifer in prison. The archangel Aquila was put in charge of hiding it. Turns out, she placed it in what is today Nova Scotia."

"Let me guess," says Lincoln. "At the Wheeler Institute?"

"Precisely," replies Dad. "She also named a protector to watch over the coin, but she lost touch with that person. As you know, protectors are immortal, yet not immune from injury."

I picture poor Cryptan. "No, they can certainly be hurt like anyone else."

"I understand that this coin can open a gateway," says Lincoln. "But is it really more powerful than igni? Myla's abilities placed Armageddon in Hell. He shouldn't be able to escape."

I shoot Lincoln a thumbs-up. "Huzzah."

"Unfortunately, the coin was made before igni came into being. That means its magic isn't subject to igni energy. Armageddon can still be released."

Unfortunately, my father has the whole *"been alive since the dawn of time"* thing going for him. If he says that Lucifer's coin trumps my igni, then it's the truth. It's just super depressing.

I force myself to take in a few calming breaths. "Let me get this straight. Lucifer's coin can release Armageddon from Hell. For sures."

"I'm afraid so." Dad's face is all droopy and sympathetic. "The coin is incredibly powerful. In fact, that's why we had to hide it in the first place. Even we archangels couldn't destroy the thing. So yes, the coin is probably the only way Armageddon could escape from Hell."

I'm not sure I like the use of the word *"probably"* in that sentence, but I have bigger things to worry about right now. "How does Aldred fit into all this?"

"I can answer that," says Lincoln. "The place where the Wheeler Institute is located has been Acca demon patrol territory for centuries. Aldred's people have had plenty of time to learn about Lucifer's coin and its protector. They must have a good idea where the coin is hidden."

"So if they're looking for the coin, why send the codex there, too?"

"My guess?" Lincoln scratches his neck. "Having his patrols search around for an archangel artifact is one thing. It's not illegal. But hiding a thrax codex? Now that's a big deal. Aldred could go to jail. Demon patrols are switched out every eight hours or so. This patrol is probably Aldred's most trusted group of warriors. By having this one disappear, he could have his best team look for the coin while hiding the codex. It's not a bad plan, really."

I raise my pointer finger. "For the record, this whole situation sucks."

"It gets worse," says Dad.

My mouth falls open. "There's more than the Hell-opening coin?"

"According to Aquila, the coin also requires a long incantation in order to start working."

"That's good, right?" A little bubble of hope swells in my chest. "It means that even if they find the coin, they can't use it."

"Not exactly. Aquila left the incantation with the coin's protector. If what Lincoln says is true and Acca knows this territory so well—"

"It's true," says Lincoln.

"Then, Acca may have already found the incantation. If so, they know how to activate the coin, too."

Aaaaaaaand the bubble bursts.

Lincoln scrubs his hand down his face. "So the Acca demon patrol that disappeared is hiding the codex and searching for the coin. And since they didn't reappear, I'm guessing that they're probably still looking."

That little insight takes a huge load off my shoulders. "Good point, babe! Otherwise, Armageddon would be running around trying to kill us already."

"Unless he's lying in wait," says Lincoln.

Bad point, babe.

"That's unlikely," explains Dad. "If that portal had opened, we would know it. All the after-realms would quake from the release of that much primal power."

A realization hits me. "Wait a second." I snap my fingers. "We have a total ace in the hole here. Does Aquila know where the protector or the coin is?"

Dad huffs out a breath. "Not exactly."

I set my fist on my hip. "What do you mean, not exactly?"

"How much do you know about Aquila?"

"She's my great-grandmother," offers Lincoln. "She's Walker's grandmother or something too, right?"

"That she is," says Dad. And the way he says those words, it's clear that marrying both a ghoul and a thrax prince aren't the weirdest things Aquila has done. A sinking sensation moves through my stomach.

Please don't let Aquila be a flake.

"So," I try my best to sound casual. "How many times did Aquila marry mortals anyway?"

Dad shakes his head. "I've lost count. And Aquila doesn't remember clearly, either." He gives Lincoln a sympathetic look. "I'm sorry if this comes as a shock, but Aquila is a rather free spirit."

In Dad-speak, that means she's a total flake. Crap.

I straighten my spine. Maybe there's something we can salvage here. "Perhaps Aquila can help in another way. Lincoln and I were doing some planning for a mission to Earth. The Wheeler Institute has a summer camp going now, yes?"

"That they do," says Dad.

"Great. So we were thinking…Maybe Lincoln could pose as a teacher, and I could go as a student. That way, we could infiltrate the school and look around. Could Aquila help us with that?"

"No, yet I have some contacts who might." Dad taps his cheek, which is his move when he's contemplating doing something non-archangel-y. "You'll need to enter the school separately, however. I can get Lincoln in tonight."

On reflex, I curl my upper lip at the idea. "Really? We should go in together."

"Not a chance." Dad folds his arms over his chest. "Don't take this the wrong way, but the two of you are so in love it's obvious you're a couple. You don't want to risk blowing your cover before the mission has even started."

I'm all out of toddler-class responses, so I simply nod. "All right. You convinced me."

"What about the rest of the after-realms?" asks Lincoln. "Aldred has gotten approval from my father to place both Myla and me in prison. Everyone will wonder where we are."

Dad's face lights up with a million-watt smile. "I'm granting you sanctuary."

"You can do that?"

"Sure. Where do you think humans got the idea? Heaven has always offered sanctuary to those being persecuted." Dad bobs his head, thinking. "Only, you're supposed to spend the time in seclusion and quiet meditation. I'll pretend you're staying here in the clubhouse." His eyes narrow. "There's a catch, though."

Of course, there's a catch.

"What is it?" I ask.

"No contact with the outside world. If you go down to the Wheeler Institute, you can't reach out to Walker, your mother, or anyone else. Officially, you're staying here with me and meditating. End of story. Can you do that?"

I've spent most of my youth sneaking around on my mother, so this is no biggie to me. "Sure, that won't be a problem."

Lincoln does that chin-nod thing that guys do. "Same here."

My brain tries to process all this news so fast, my head starts to hurt. "Before we go any further, let me get this straight. Acca has stolen the *Rixa Codex*. It's probably hidden away at the Wheeler Institute, where there's a handy-dandy Acca patrol to guard it while they're also looking for Lucifer's coin. And, oh by the way, if they find said coin, Armageddon will be freed from Hell so he can kill me, Lincoln, and our families."

"That's close," says Lincoln. "But you forgot the part about how Armageddon probably won't stop with just murdering us. Once he's free, he'll go on a rampage and wage war across the after-realms."

There's almost an audible ping as Lincoln's words flip the *"Armageddon freak out"* switch in my father's brain.

"Never!" Dad raises his fist. "I'll build an army before that happens. In fact, I'll muster my troops today." My father's eyes glow blue. This is not an act, either. Dad will really herd his troops around. Plus, after what I saw at the gates? Those angelic warriors will do whatever Dad wants and fast.

"Whoa, whoa, whoa." I raise my hands palms forward in a very clear *"calm the hell down"* gesture. "Armageddon's not free yet. And if he is getting out of Hell, it's only because Aldred made a deal with him: the coin in exchange for the throne of Antrum. Armageddon gets revenge by killing me, Lincoln, and our families...While Aldred gets the throne. After that, the King of Hell goes back to where he came from. That's really the worst-case scenario here." *Which is a total lie. It's not the worst-case scenario by far. Even so, I don't need Dad freaking out.* Normally, my father's lie-detector ability would catch my falsehood fiesta, but I'm banking that he's off his game right now.

Lincoln arches his brows. He's not at all sure about the direction I'm going. "Myla..."

I shoot Lincoln a look that says *"give me a chance"* and speak super-slowly. "Don't you think it's best if we focus on the Wheeler Institute, rather than starting a major war?"

Lincoln pauses for a moment before giving me the barest of nods. "Absolutely." And with that, my guy and I are working the same angle. Awesome.

Dad and I still aren't aligned, though. A manic gleam dances in his eyes, which is honestly creeping me out a little.

"So," says my father. "You're both certain that the throne is the only thing that Aldred wants? What if the Earl of Acca has other plans as well, like taking over all the after-realms with Armageddon at his side?"

I fix Dad with my best and most serious look. "Dad, I'm absolutely, positively, and one hundred percent certain that the only thing Aldred gives a single crap about is the throne of Antrum." *Which is true. Sort-of.*

Here's what I don't say. Yes, Aldred would be happy with the throne of Antrum. But Armageddon? No, no, a thousand times, no. The King of Hell wants more than the chance to kill Lincoln, me, and our families. In fact, Armageddon's been pretty consistent that he'd like to take over all the after-realms, starting with Purgatory. Yet after being imprisoned by the King of Hell for twenty years, Dad has a tendency to go off the deep-end when it comes to this topic. It's best if I help my father focus on the little disasters here. You know, like us getting murdered in our sleep by the King of Hell.

Dad's chest keeps heaving in breaths. "Well, if you're certain that's the main threat."

"We're positive." Lincoln is all Mr. Regal again, and my father visibly calms. Once more, my guy works the prince vibe like a pro.

"Forget war," I say. "What we need is your help with getting into the Wheeler Institute."

My father shakes out his shoulders. I can almost see his thinking-brain start to work again. "You shall have my full support, children."

"Thanks, Dad."

Lincoln rubs his palms in a gesture that says *"let's get back to it."* "So, did you find out anything else about the Wheeler Institute?"

"I did. It seems to be a secluded, cult-like operation. A high school for girls only. The locals also say the place is haunted."

Haunted? That's new. "So, what's really going on in there?" I ask. "Are they having class, preparing the students for virgin sacrifice or what?"

"I'm afraid I don't know that yet. That was all the intelligence I could gather on short notice."

"Really?" I ask. "You're an archangel."

Dad sets his hands on his hips. "About that. We need to talk."

Now, I haven't known my father for very long, but I know a lecture when I hear one coming. "What did I do?"

"It's not what you did," says my father. "It's what you know. Going to school in Purgatory under the ghouls. They didn't exactly explain how things work with angels and humans."

"You can say that again." Unless it involved bowing, scraping, or preparing worm soufflé, the ghoul teachers in my high school had a very limited lesson span.

"On Earth, the Almighty severely limits what I can see or do when it relates to humans. I can't witness much of what goes on, and I definitely cannot interfere with anything that would limit a human's free will. Even showing up in my archangel form would change things immensely. Imagine if mortals all knew we existed for certain?"

I nod slowly. Although I spend my days moving human souls around, I haven't really thought about life on Earth beyond the Human Channel on Purgatory TV. For mortals, seeing my archangel father even once would change everything. "That makes sense."

"You and Lincoln are part human. The moment you step foot on Earth, I can do very little to help you." His mouth thins to a worried line. "In fact, I've already broken a number of rules just by giving you sanctuary."

My eyes almost bug out of my head. "What do you mean?"

"By thrax law, you and Lincoln should be in prison right now. Antrum is on Earth. You two are part human. I should not interfere with your laws. Technically, protecting you here oversteps my bounds."

The thought of getting my father in trouble makes me ill. "We can leave."

"And when you do, you'll be tracked by everyone in the afterrealms, including the Earl of Acca. If you're going to investigate the Wheeler Institute, then everyone must think you're somewhere else. Officially, you're staying here and meditating."

"But we can contact you, right?" Even if I can't reach out to Mom or Walker, I'd assumed that Dad would be part of this whole thing.

"I'll help you infiltrate the school. That's as far as I can go, though. Please, Myla. I can't emphasize this too severely. Offering you both sanctuary is pushing things far enough in terms meddling with human affairs. Once you go to the Wheeler Institute, no one can know where you really are. That means no messages, no contact with anyone until you leave Earth. Even me." He shakes his head. "Especially me. Understand?"

"You have my word," says Lincoln.

And I want to give my word, too, but the whole thing seems a little unfair. It's all more arbitrary-sounding rules, and after growing up under the ghouls, I hate that crap. "What about the threat of Armageddon? Isn't that enough to allow you to break some dumb rules?"

"My relationship with the Almighty is…" Dad exhales a long breath. "Complex. Trust me when I say that officially, you must be here in sanctuary. And once you're on Earth, you're to contact no one." A flicker of unease shows through in my father's blue eyes. He's taking a huge risk to help us.

"Okay, you have my word."

"Thank you," says Dad. "Now that's agreed, how will the pair of you stay hidden on Earth? If that thrax demon patrol is still around, then they'll be able to identify you."

Lincoln holds up his man-bag again. "We asked the Earl of Striga to make us amulets and other supplies. Once we're kitted up, no one will recognize us. Even if my own mother walked into the Wheeler Institute, she wouldn't see me for who I am."

"Excellent." Dad starts pacing a line before the window, which means he's going into General mode. "As I said, I don't know precisely what's happening at the Wheeler Institute. Even so, I like your ideas of masquerading as teacher and student. I can get you aliases in that vein. For example, Lincoln could use a role on the faculty that allows him to roam the grounds."

"Gym teacher?" I offer.

"Perfect." Dad looks to Lincoln. "Let's see about getting you there tonight." My father gestures to me. "Meanwhile, you'll act as a new student. We'll get you to school tomorrow morning."

"So, as a student, I just show up by myself at school?" Yes, this is a totally leading question, and yes, I know I'm pushing it here, but what can I say? I want more time with my daddy.

My father grins. "I'll be able to drop you off."

"That's awesome, Dad. You're the best." And I really mean it.

My father glances out the window. "It's getting dark." He looks to Lincoln. "One of my angels will transport you to Earth. That said, you must leave soon."

I edge closer to Lincoln. I haven't been apart from him since we got betrothed. I don't like the idea of separation, at all. "Can you give us a minute, Dad?"

"Surely." My father gestures to a door set into the far wall. "Knock when you're ready." With that, he marches away.

I stand there for a minute, dumbfounded. Lincoln's really leaving, and he's doing it right now. We'll be apart. And even if we're able to stop Armageddon from leaving Hell, I still might be separated from Lincoln if we end up in jail. Of course, we'd appeal any prison sentence and all that. Even so, who knows how long that will take?

Before I know it, Lincoln has me wrapped in a warm embrace. "I worry about the same thing, Myla."

I nuzzle into his neck. Nothing smells better than Lincoln. Forest pine and leather. "And what's that?"

"Being parted from you. This isn't a very princely of me to say, but I worry more about our separation than another invasion from the King of Hell."

I can only smile. "It isn't princely. I totally appreciate it, though." I fold my arms around his waist. "Can't we let the after-realms go to Hell for once? I mean, this room isn't so bad. We could claim sanctuary, maybe get some furniture. A few throw rugs. A mini-fridge. We could be happy here."

Lincoln chuckles, and I love that sound. "But then we'd miss out on an opportunity to kill demons on Earth."

My inner mope-fest ends instantly. I forgot about the opportunity to go after demons. The Earth's surface is crawling with them. And unlike the Arena and Purgatory, there will be no one to stop me.

"You have a point." And he totally does. I glance out the window and watch the sun dip toward the horizon line. "Let's go kick some ass."

"That's my Myla."

I kiss the tip of his nose. "No, that's just us."

And even though all Hell is about to break loose—literally—I still feel like everything is all right with the world because right now? Lincoln and I are together.

CHAPTER TWELVE

A.

Dad speeds his Bugatti Veyron convertible around another curve in the road. He and I are following the coastline of Nova Scotia on our way to the drop-off point for the Wheeler Institute. We should arrive in the next five minutes or so, which is when I'll meet Headmaster Prescott. The last headmaster I had was a ghoul, so whoever this dude is, he's bound to be a step up.

I lean back in the convertible, close my eyes, and let the sunlight warm my face. It's late September here in Nova Scotia, and the air has some of the sizzle of summer with the crisp undertones of fall. The ocean surf pounds onto the rocks along the shoreline. It's beautiful, but in a lonely kind of way.

I miss Lincoln.

Dad takes another turn at high speed. As an angel, he really doesn't see speed limits as applying to him. He's also decided to be Mister Quiet this morning. I keep asking questions without getting answers. Finally, he breaks the silence. "How did things turn out with you and Lincoln? Have you moved the wedding date?"

On second thought, maybe Dad's decided to be Mister Busybody.

"No." The way I snap off the word, it should be clear that the subject is closed. Besides, we went over this a million times after Aldred somehow maneuvered our court date to right before the wedding. Lincoln and I didn't move our big day then, and we won't move it now. Aldred would see that as a win. Besides, there's the fact that our moms and my bestie, Cissy, have been working their asses off on this ceremony. I mean, getting tens of thousands of people into one place? That's huge. Long story short? *We're not canceling dick.*

"So your mood is more than the stress of the wedding," says Dad. "You hate being apart from Lincoln."

"You got that right. It bites. Big-time."

Dad glances at me over his shoulder. He's wearing some super-fancy sunglasses, so I can't see his eyes. Still, I know him well enough now to realize that he has his *"I'm wiser than you"* face on. I know exactly how this will go. He'll say something that will make me rethink everything, and I'm not in the mood. I decide to try and stop the whole conversation before it starts.

"You are not wiser than me, Dad." There, that ought to do it.

"I've been alive since the dawn of time. I suffered in Hell for twenty years because I traded my life for your mother's. I believe I know a thing or two about situations like this."

And there, he did it. Put everything in perspective. "Okay, maybe you do know a few things."

"You and Lincoln are true partners. That's what's most important. Whatever happens, he'll be there with you at the end of eternity."

Now, I liked the first part of what Dad said, but the whole *"end of eternity"* comment makes me think that we won't meet up again until we're dead. And that a thought makes my mope-o-meter start to rise again. Still, Dad's trying to be, well, a Dad. I should encourage it. "Thanks. That means a lot to me."

"Glad to help." Dad doesn't say anything more, and that's fine with me. Besides, I need to get into the headspace that I'm a high school senior again, not the great scala. Sure, that was my life six months ago. Yet it feels like I've lived about three lifetimes since then.

I get lost in my thoughts until I realize the car has stopped. Dad has parked us near a small cluster of wooden buildings that hug the shoreline. Beyond the shore is a pretty sizable lake. And in the middle of the lake?

Hemlock Island.

Way to name it something creepy, Nova Scotia. To my mind, the lake looks dark despite the early morning light. And the island itself seems overrun with trees and shrubbery and who knows what else? We don't have a lot of nature in Purgatory. It's mostly old concrete and grubby strip malls. And honestly, I like things that way. Rundown cities I get, but the forest? That's Lincoln's world.

Just thinking about my guy has me bummed out, so I try to focus on the mission instead.

I'm in high school, I'm in high school, I'm in high school.

"This way, Myla." Dad has his sunglasses off, and his face is all sympathetic and smiley. I really wish he would lecture me again. Lecturing I can handle. The sympathetic thing makes me want to cry.

Tamp it down, Myla. Focus.

"I'm right with you, Dad."

We head toward an old wooden dock. An ancient dude in a heavy fisherman's jacket stands at the far end. With his blue pea coat and huge gray beard, the guy looks like he belongs on a box of fish sticks. Next to Fish Stick Grandpa (as I've decided to call him), there stands a middle-aged man with pale skin, a skinny-ish frame, and golden-blond hair. If the other guy looks like he fell off a fish sticks box, this guy could be an illustration in the Preppy Handbook.

Dad and I step out of the car and march along the dock, our footsteps beating a quick rhythm. I'm wearing jeans and a long-sleeve T-shirt. From what I've seen on human TV shows, this is standard stuff for a regular human high school student. But it feels really strange not being in my Scala robes or dragonscale fighting suit.

The headmaster smiles broadly at us as we approach. He's wearing khaki pants, a white shirt, and a blue jacket with some kind of insignia on the pocket. He's even got one of those cravat thingies at his throat. I decide that if humans ever made a country club edition of their Ken dolls, then that would be this man.

The headmaster extends his hand toward Dad. "Greetings, Mister Cross." Humans don't know my father's real last name, so there was no need to come up with a fake one. I had to leave the name Myla behind, though. That's a bummer. "I'm Headmaster Prescott." He then focuses on me. "And you must be Miss Mysteria Cross. How are you, Missy?"

"Mysteria." I took a long time making up that name. I wanted something close to Myla that didn't sound girly. I am so not happy with the Missy thing that Prescott's working here. "Everyone calls me Mysteria. Pronounced Miss-TEER-ee-ah." That ought to make things clear.

"You look like a Missy to me." Prescott grins, and there's something predatory in his smile. Every instinct I have is telling me to pile drive this asshole into the dock. I hold off, though. I need to get that codex to court by tomorrow.

I slap on what I hope is an innocent face. "Hey, all I want to do is fit in."

"You'll do well here, then."

"Yup." I try to keep working my innocent vibe. It's not an easy task with all the ruckus from my tail. Sure, humans like Prescott can't see it. That doesn't mean it isn't screwing around with my center of gravity, though.

Thanks for nothing, boy.

This is the situation. Sometimes, my tail takes an instant shine to a person, like it did with Lincoln. In other cases, my backside hates someone so badly it makes a big scene and acts like a total baby right off the bat.

Like now.

My tail hooks its arrowhead-shaped end into the dock and burrows in. Clearly, it doesn't want to go anywhere with Prescott.

I twist my hips and try to break free, but I only end up making myself look like I'm twerking.

"Are you quite all right, Missy?" asks Prescott.

Way to make a great first impression, Myla.

"I'm fine." I shake his hand. Since my tail has me anchored in place, I have to lean way forward to meet his grip. "I'm really excited to start school here. Thanks so much for making a place for me. I know summer camp started weeks ago."

"You're quite welcome." Prescott eyes me warily. And even if Prescott were really an angel or demon, he wouldn't see anything because I'm wearing the amulet from Lucas. Still, it must look like I'm standing at an angle that defies gravity. Not good.

Dad steps around back of me and casually pulls my tail free from the dock. I exhale a relieved breath.

Thank you, Dad.

My father strides over to Prescott and shakes the headmaster's hand. "Well, I have to run for a meeting at the clubhouse." He wraps me in a big hug. "Have fun, darling." I don't know where the *"darling"* comes from, but it sounds totally authentic. Dad really is a cool liar.

"I'll have loads of fun, Daddums." There, that sounded preppy and convincing. *I hope.* Prescott stops scowling at me, so I take that as a good sign.

Dad kisses my cheek, says his goodbyes to Prescott, and walks away. Once Dad is safely inside the Bugatti, Prescott rubs his hands together. I notice he has a manicure. Lincoln's hands are all calloused from holding a sword all day long. Manicured man-hands give me the creeps. Reason number two to dislike Prescott. "Well, Missy? Shall we go?"

Aaaaaaand thanks for reminding me that calling me Missy was reason number one to hate your preppy ass.

"Sure thing, Headmaster." I hoist my backpack onto my shoulder.

"Is that all you're bringing?" Prescott gestures to my pack.

"Yes, my parents are sending up a trunk with my other stuff in a few days." I shrug my backpack higher on my shoulder. "This is fine for now." I'm not planning to stay here past a few days, either. Not that I'll volunteer that fact.

"Don't you have more girl-things you need? Makeup? Formal dresses?"

Nunchuks?

"Ah, no. I'm more of a sporty type." He doesn't seem convinced, so I quickly add on more detail. "Also, I do my own laundry." This is totally true, by the way. For whatever reason, that seems to convince him.

"In that case, let's be off." Prescott gestures to the Fish Stick Guy. The man has been so quiet I'd forgotten he was here. "Jeeves, if you don't mind?"

My lips purse. *Jeeves? Really?* I am so sticking with Fish Stick Grandpa as his name. FSG for short because, what else should I do with my time other than make up nicknames? Pay actual attention to my new headmaster?

After Prescott asks the same thing two more times, FSG finally ambles into the boat and grabs the oars. I'm pretty sure that he heard Prescott fine and is just being an ass, which is totally cool with me. Prescott looks young and fit. It takes balls to ask some wrinkly old dude to row your fat ass around when you're totally capable of doing it yourself, even if you are wearing a cravat.

Once FSG settles into the rowboat, it's my turn to climb aboard. It isn't easy getting in, especially since I have to hold my struggling tail with one hand while keeping my balance with the other. Combine that with the water, and I'm wobbling all over the place. What fancy-ass preppy school uses an old rowboat anyway? It seems like they'd tool back and forth in one of those sporty James Bond wooden powerboat thingies. Something to ponder for later.

Prescott takes my free hand and helps me settle in, which is cool. Perhaps I misjudged him for wearing a cravat and everything. Then, my scummy headmaster somehow manages to brush my boobs a few times as I sit down, which is way uncool.

Reason number three to hate the man.

Eventually, we're all settled into the boat, and FSG rows us across the lake to Hemlock Island. My warrior sense goes on alert. This is my life now. Really? Who goes in a rowboat with a pervert to a sketchy-looking island?

Myla Lewis, that's who.

I've had some crappy ideas, but this is starting to feel like one of my worst.

CHAPTER THIRTEEN

A

FSG huffs and puffs as he hauls us across the lake. From here, Hemlock Island looks like a panel of green trees surrounded by a calm sheet of dark water. A weight of foreboding settles into my bones.

Looks like I'm in for some nature-time. Yuck.

I grew up in Purgatory, so I dig the whole rundown industrial scene. Take me to a cracked-up parking garage and—BAM—I feel right at home. To me, forests are a whole lot of irritating. In my experience, the woods are basically packed with bugs and nameless goo.

Oh, well. Anything to find that codex and get this over with. Not to mention stopping Lucifer's coin from unleashing unholy Hell.

FSG heaves on the oars once again. The dude looks wrinkly, sweaty, and ready to keel over. I tap his shoulder gently. "Would you like some help, uh…" I barely stop myself from calling him Fish Stick Grandpa. "Jeeves?"

He keeps hauling on the oars. "I've been pulling these oars…" *Pant pant.* "Every summer for forty years…" *Pant pant.* "There's no one to help."

I frown. "What do you mean no one?" I glance over at the village by the water. Now that I take a closer look, the houses have a fresh coat of paint. Even so, the windows do look mostly boarded up. "What happened to everyone?"

FSG opens his mouth, and I just know he wants to spill about why the town is deserted and he's ferrying me around by rowboat. However, before he gets a word out, Prescott gives the old dude the stink eye. FSG shuts his yap and fast.

That is so not stopping me from getting an answer.

"Why did everyone leave the town?"

"No idea." He keeps hauling and panting.

"But you stayed."

FSG stops pulling on the oars and takes in a few breaths. "My family has always been here, young lady. We're not like other people."

My tail gives him a modified thumbs-up. It's a nice gesture, even though FSG can't see a thing.

Or can he?

FSG's gaze flickers at my tail for a moment before he returns to his task.

My frown deepens. There is no way he could see my tail. Only Lincoln and my father can detect my supernatural side at this point. Lincoln can do it because he's wearing an amulet that's linked to mine. Dad can see me because his power is older than dirt. If FSG can see me, he'd have to be someone pretty extraordinary. His recent words echo through my mind.

"We're not like other people."

I lean forward. "How are you different, exactly?"

Prescott sighs. "Please leave Jeeves to do his work, Missy."

"My name's not Missy." FSG is carefully avoiding my gaze now. "Your name's not Jeeves, either. Is it?"

FSG cracks a super-wrinkly smile, and I know two things. One, the man does not visit a dentist regularly, and two, he's totally not named Jeeves.

"What's your real name, anyway?" I ask.

"Jeeves!" snaps Prescott. "Stop pestering my summer student. Missy and I have important things to discuss."

"My name's Mysteria." *Sheesh.*

Prescott keeps ignoring when I correct him. It's really getting on my nerves. "Now, Missy. I wanted to greet you personally in order to discuss any misconceptions you may have about summer camp at the Wheeler Institute."

"Sure." *Misconceptions? This is getting good.*

"What do you know about us?"

I shrug. "My father says you have the best summer camp on the planet, so here I am."

"Excellent. Indeed, we are a superb organization." Prescott gestures to me. "Why, look at the caliber of student we're now attracting. Your father is a renowned gold dealer." He lowers his voice. "In secret markets, of course."

"Something like that." I told Dad that having gold wings didn't mean he could pretend to be a human gold dealer. My father countered that he'd done something similar while riding a caravan along the Silk Road, whatever that involved. I find it's best to change the subject when he starts talking about ancient times. Otherwise, he can and will go on for hours.

Prescott's voice lowers to a hush. "My point is, I don't want you repeating anything you may have heard about the Wheeler Institute. There have been some nasty rumors that the island is haunted, but that kind of fear-mongering is completely behind us. The last headmaster did his best. Now I'm taking things the final mile."

Huh. That's interesting. "So, how long have you been running this place?"

"About six months."

I bite back a groan. *Six months? That's when I kicked Armageddon back to Hell.* No way that's a coincidence. "If you don't mind my asking, where were you before this?"

"Before?"

"Like, what school did you run or whatever?"

"Oh, I never ran any school."

"You didn't?" *That is so weird.*

"I'm an expert in Archangology." Prescott lowers his voice and starts speaking very slowly, like I'm a young child. "That's the study of archangels."

"I know." *My Dad's one.*

"In fact, the patron saint of the Wheeler Institute is an archangel."

"I know that, too." *That would be my Dad again.*

"And that's how I got this appointment." Prescott's eyes glaze over in a way that somehow reminds me of when he groped my butt. It's more than little creepy. "The Lady thought that only someone with my appreciation of the archangels would be fit to run this school."

It takes all my limited self-control not to gasp. *The Lady.* Aldred ordered Desmond to deliver the *Rixa Codex* to Earth because of the Lady. Yet when Desmond agreed to hand it over the dyad demons, they murdered him. This has to be the same Lady that Prescott is talking about.

"The Lady? Who is she?"

"A great benefactor of this school. That's all you need to know."

I try my best to appear innocent and interested. It involves a lot of blinking. "She sounds so fascinating. I'd love to learn more."

Prescott lifts his chin. "She's a very private person. All you need to know is that she hired me to clean up the school's reputation, and I have done so. Those nasty rumors are a thing of the past."

It's obvious I'm not getting any more insights into the Lady, so I decide to press for additional information about the school. Prescott assumes that I know what he's talking about when it comes to the so-called "rumors," which I don't, so I figure my best bet is to play along. "Anything in particular you don't want me to say? There are so many horrible rumors going around, after all."

"Just don't say anything negative about the school, and you'll be fine." Prescott brushes lint from the lapels of his blue blazer. "Now, there's something else you need to prepare for. You're about to meet our welcoming committee. The best students and faculty will come to the shoreline to greet you."

"Wow. That's really cool. But shouldn't everyone be in class?"

Prescott winks, like this is all between us. "This is summer semester, so we're a little more casual. Besides, your father was kind enough to make a ten-million-dollar donation that will fund a new library. I'm rebuilding most of the Wheeler Institute, you know. The library will be my greatest achievement. The daughter of the man who made it possible should feel extra-welcome in our little community."

"Huh." Note to self: add *incredibly loaded* to Dad's list of superpowers.

Prescott's icy-blue eyes bulge out of his head. "I hope that wasn't inappropriate for me to share. Would your father be upset that I told you about the money…Or that we're having a welcoming committee?"

"No, I'm sure that whatever you've said or got planned will be great. I'll make sure my father knows how kind you're being to me."

"Ah, it's nothing." Prescott leans forward and rests his elbow on his knee. "Since we have a few minutes alone, I wanted to discuss a few additional items before you meet the welcoming committee."

"Sure."

"We have rules here at Wheeler."

I fight the urge to groan. *Rules. I hate rules.* It takes some serious concentration, but I fold my hands neatly in my lap and blink innocently. "I'd love to hear them."

"First of all, no mentioning the unpleasant rumors."

"Of course not." *Besides the fact that I don't know what the rumors are yet.*

"Second, you do exactly what you're told and when."

"How specific." *Screw you.*

"Third, the whole point of our school is learning while in a natural environment. You must embrace the outdoors."

"You got it." *Especially since those outdoors may contain demons.*

"And fourth, whatever you do…" His icy-blue eyes darken. "Don't go to the north side of the island."

Bullshit. The second I have a free moment I am so hitting the north side of the island.

"Check."

Prescott grins, and that predatory look returns to his eyes. There's something leery and gross about it. In an effort to distract him, I point at the shore. There are a lot of trees, a dock, and a group of about twenty people milling about, all of them in blue blazers. "Is that the welcoming committee?"

Prescott still has a glazed look in his eyes. "What?"

"Welcoming committee. Shoreline."

Prescott clears his throat. "Yes, yes. That's them, all right."

I'm no witch. Still, the way he's acting around me, it's as if he's under a spell. "Great. I'm looking forward to meeting them." *And getting away from you.*

I edge myself a little farther away from Prescott and watch the shoreline grow larger as we close in. Hemlock Island sure has a lot of trees. I can't even see the school from here. This is nothing like Purgatory High. That place was a chipped-up block of bricks that towered over everything.

I never thought I'd say this, but I'm starting to miss Purgatory.

CHAPTER FOURTEEN

$\mathcal{A}$

FSG expertly maneuvers our boat to a sleek wooden dock. I scan the shoreline. In every direction, there's nothing but trees, trees, and more trees.

Huh. This place looks more like a forest than a fancy pants school.

About twenty teachers stand in front of the greenery, both male and female. All of them are wearing khaki pants and blue blazers. I get out of the boat, stand on the dock, and anxiously scan their faces.

My heart sinks. No Lincoln.

Along with the teachers, a half-dozen girls stand by the dock as well. They're done up in short plaid skirts, white tops, and cutoff blue jackets. Somehow, in all of this, I didn't realize there would be a dress code involved. *More rules. Yuck.*

Prescott steps off the boat and introduces me to the teachers. I make a few quick hellos and hold onto my tail for dear life. I know how its skeevy little arrowhead-shaped mind works. The second I let go of my tail, it will dive back into the planking and hold me hostage. I am not giving it that chance.

After the faculty greets me, Prescott turns to address the other students. "Now, I'd like to present the student welcoming committee. Girls, this is Missy."

"He means Mysteria."

"Hello, Missy." All six of them speak in unison, their voices sounding in a monotone. It's more than a little chilling, actually. The six of them are slim, pretty, and look well put together. Something about them is very wrong, though. It's the look in their eyes. I've seen it before many times, right before I go for a killing blow.

Fear.

These students are scared out of their minds. My battle sense goes on alert. I want to start kicking ass, now. Whatever is frightening these folks is going down, and I'm the girl to do it.

Calm down, Myla. Find the codex first.

I force my breathing to slow and my thinking-side to kick in. After a few seconds, I'm able to slap on an innocent smile. "Nice to meet you."

Prescott beams. "The Wheeler School follows an acclaimed tradition of schooling in a natural setting. That means lots of outdoors time and no electronic falderal. You girls don't mind not having cell phones or televisions, do you?"

Wait, what? No cell phones? No TV? Don't tell me I just left the only place in the after-realms that has no technology...Only to go to the only place on Earth without it, either.

While I wait for the students to reply, I work hard to hide my panic. Maybe I'm worrying over nothing. Surely, they'll all say something like *"ha ha, what a joke"* right as they pull out their phones and take a selfie.

At last, the girls reply. "We don't mind at all." And they even say THAT in unison.

So. Freaky.

"Excellent," says Prescott. "Let's go to class, shall we?"

"Like, at this very moment?" I haven't been to class in months, and honestly, the whole no-school thing was really agreeing with me. "I thought there would be a tour or something."

"I'll do that along the way." Prescott elbows me slightly. "Not that you'll remember. You girls are terrible with directions."

My face scrunches up into a look that can only be described as *what the hell?* Girls aren't good with directions? Where is he coming up with this stuff? I scan the faces of the students beside me. They look so terrified, they probably couldn't find their way out of a paper bag. I guess I'll let it slide.

For now.

Prescott claps his hands three times. "Let's go, girls! Time for the tour." He marches off into the line of trees. To be honest, I don't know what I expected from Nova Scotia. Okay, maybe some salmon, a few rocks, lots of indoor living and television, and that's about it. But this place is heavy with trees and shrubs and who knows what else. There are meandering pathways through the hefty tree trunks. Every so often, a wooden sign is propped into the ground with destinations listed on hand-carved arrows:

"Jamboree Hall."

"Angelfire Learning Bunkers."

"Exercise Grounds."

"Student Cabins."

The last one gives me pause. "We live in cabins?"

Prescott gestures through the trees. "Yes, there's one now."

I blink to make sure what I'm seeing is right. It is. "I've never been near a cabin like that one." Which is totally true. We don't do much camping in Purgatory, but the few places around are pretty rustic, to say the least. The cabins here mix the old log vibe with modern style glass and concrete. Some places even have bay windows and porches. Whoa.

"Impressive, right?" asks Prescott.

"Yeah."

"The quality living arrangements is one of the main reasons parents trust us with their children. As I've said, this is a natural learning environment. No phones, no technology. Being outdoors helps the mind to focus. And privacy is critical as well. Every single student gets her own cabin."

"That's cool." *And I mean it.* Being an only child, I'm used to my own, well, everything. Personal cabins will suit me fine.

We follow the trail to the Angelfire Learning Bunkers. Soon the meandering path opens up onto a small quad made of four long buildings. One stands along each side of a grassy square. The architecture is Davy Crockett meets the Pentagon. It's like a log cabin and a cement bunker got busy. The Learning Bunkers are cement blocks—no windows, mind you—with log roofs that slant down on an angle. Something about it makes my hair stand on end. It's like the place is supposed to be all woodsy. In reality, it's more like an armed camp.

But are they keeping someone out or in?

We walk into the first Learning Bunker. The interior takes me right back to Purgatory High. The place is all cinderblock walls, linoleum floors, and combo desk-chairs. These folks put a lot of money into the cabins where people sleep—I saw those on the way over—but when it comes to the classrooms? This is way cheap. I know since I went to a school like this, and nobody is more chiseler-like than the ghouls.

Prescott moves to the front of the classroom and pauses before the green chalkboard. "Girls, take your seats."

The other students grab chairs at the front of the class. I debate for a minute about where to park my butt. Back at Purgatory High, I always sat in the back row. This could be an opportunity for me to turn over a new leaf. Be a front-row student and listen with rapt attention to…

Country Club Ken.

I scratch my cheek. *Can't do it.* At least, not yet anyway. Maybe if I sit in on a lecture or two and he isn't a douchebag, I'll change my mind.

Prescott claps again, three times. I feel like I'm in doggie training, and it's not a nice feeling. I grab a seat in the back row.

"As the welcoming committee, you girls represent the finest of the incoming senior class of the Wheeler Institute. Therefore, you're in for a real treat today. I'm going to give you a lecture from the depths of my studies in Archangology."

The other students all lean forward, their eyes wide with anticipation. I must admit, I'm pretty interested as well. What I don't know about my father is a lot. Anything I can learn on archangels is good news to me.

"The angel we'll focus on today is the General. Now, who knows which archangel is the General?"

That would be my father.

Prescott points at a girl with red hair and a ticked-off look on her face. I instantly like her. "What about you, Harper?"

"That's the archangel Xavier," says Harper.

Prescott grins. "Quite right. The archangel Xavier is indeed a fine warrior, but he's also a virile man who's had more than thirty-seven human wives."

"What?" The word comes out of my mouth before I can stop myself.

Okay, I could totally have stopped myself, only I didn't want to.

"Missy, you'll answer questions when asked."

"It's Mysteria, and the archangel Xavier has not been married thirty-seven times."

Prescott's blue eyes narrow to angry slits. "We spoke about being obedient before, Missy. You'll answer questions when asked and not before."

I grab the bottom of my seat so I don't do something else with my hands. Like chuck the entire desk at Prescott's head.

Remember the codex.

Prescott glares in my direction. "This school is dedicated to the General, and I don't mean to take anything away from him. That said, part of what we're here for is to become independent thinkers. That's why I'll tell you what to believe about the archangel Xavier."

I dig my hands so hard into the plastic seat I'm surprised I don't snap it in two. "Fine."

"The General does have a number of families."

Not fine.

"Nope, you're thinking about Aquila."

"What?" Prescott's face turns pink.

"The archangel Aquila. She's been married to a thrax and a ghoul, at least that I know of. She's the one with multiple bloodlines. My fa—" I clear my throat. "The archangel Xavier has only been married once." *And then, very recently.* Not that I'm volunteering that part.

"Missy." Prescott's voice quavers with rage. "Interrupt me one more time, and I'll send you to your cabin for the rest of the day."

"Got it."

Note to self: get sent to your cabin ASAP because this lecture? Sucks hard.

"Another thing to note about the General is that he's a bloodthirsty warrior, not a diplomat."

Anger zings through my nervous system. Even if I hadn't just vowed to get myself sent to the equivalent of a time-out chair, there was no way I'd let that comment slide.

I hop to my feet. "My father is the greatest diplomat Purgatory has ever seen. In fact, it's how he met my mother in the first place. She was a Senator in Purgatory's legislature and—"

And I look like an idiot.

"Mysteria!"

I fist-bump my tail behind my back. *Now, he gets my name right.* Nothing like a little rage to help you focus.

"Hope, Gale...Escort Mysteria to her cabin." Prescott stomps down the main aisle to stand before me. "In light of your *real* father's donation to this school, I'm going to assume this outburst was the product of a tired mind. You'll go to your personal cabin to rest now, and when I see you for group breakfast in the morning, I expect you to be well behaved."

I put on my best mopey look. It's not as effective for Prescott since he can't see my tail go all droopy, but it will have to do. That was a big slipup back there. "Yes, Headmaster Prescott."

"That's a good Missy."

My mopey look disappears. Did he just use the words *"a good"* before my name, like I'm a pet? Unbelievable. And I thought the ghouls were bad teachers.

Prescott gestures to two students near him. "Gail, Hope. Get her going. This lecture is over." The headmaster stomps from the room, and the other students follow along. The ginger-haired girl gives me a quick thumbs-up. I make a mental note to find some time to chat with her later. *Harper.*

For now, I'm stuck with Gail and Hope, both of whom look wide-eyed and frightened. As we walk outside, I make sure to give them my most winning smiles. "So, how do you two like summer camp?" They keep staring at the grass, and I'm no ace at small talk. "This school has a lot of...Trees. And stuff."

There's a saying that you speak and get crickets. At this point, I've got actual crickets chirping away at me. These chicks aren't making eye contact, let alone using their verbal skills.

Without saying a word, Gail and Hope trudge off into the woods. I shoulder my backpack and follow close behind. Guess the perky approach isn't the way to go.

I'll simply have to improvise. It's what I do best anyway.

We meander through the trees, and one thing becomes instantly clear. This place is loaded with guards. So far, all of them are adult humans. In other words, pretty weak as opponents go. I don't spy any demons, but that doesn't mean anything. If there are ones around, they're most likely to come out at night. Only Class A jobs can run around in the daytime.

Eventually, the path ends at a log cabin. The place is triangle-shaped and modern-looking. One wall is all logs; the other is reinforced glass. We go inside, and things get even nicer. There's a small kitchenette with a dining table along with a couch and reading nook. Finally, the back wall has a door that opens onto a bedroom-bathroom combo. Only one thing to say about this.

There's no television. Boo.

Gail and Hope stand by the doorway, their gazes still locked on the floor. They keep not saying anything, and it's making the awkward factor get way worse. "So, guys..."

Silence.

"You all want to read a book or something?"

More silence.

I'm going for broke. "I've got an idea. Why don't we play a game? I call it *let's tell each other the worst rumor I've ever heard about Hemlock Island*. What do you say?"

They all file out of the cabin like I started playing "Jingle Bells" by making fart noises with my armpit. (Yes, that's a skill I have. No, I haven't used it since I was four.)

Well, that was the wrong thing to say, obviously.

I'm alone again, and I decide to use my free time to scope things out. I open the front door, ready to explore the forest even if it is loaded with squirrels and goo. Three human guards step out from the trees and glare at me.

I wave at them. "Hey, there!"

They don't answer. Verbal communication is a real issue on this island.

"I think I dropped something by the trees. I'll have a quick look around."

I step forward.

They step closer.

I step forward again.

They close in again.

Huh.

"Let me guess," I say. "Is this your way of telling me to stay in the cabin?"

Acting in unison, the trio lift their machine guns at once. Still no talking. Even so, I guess words are overrated. It's an extreme way to handle a student. I can't say I'm totally shocked, though. This island is crazy pants.

"I'll just go back inside." With as much dignity as I can muster, I retreat into my luxury prison. My tail flips them the bird as I walk away though. Even though the humans can't see the gesture, I do appreciate the support.

I plunk down into the butter-soft leather couch and take stock of things.

First, I could knock out those guards. However, that's messy and noisy, and I'd need to put on my dragonscale fighting suit.

Plus, they've got guns. And although the bullets wouldn't go through dragonscales, they'll still hurt like a sonuvabitch.

Second, I could find another way to sneak out of here.

I decide to go with door number two.

Time to check out the bathroom and bedroom windows. I hightail it back to my bedroom suite. It's more rustic-chic with lots of polished wood and glass. The bathroom has no window. There is one above the bed, though.

Bingo.

I leap onto the bed and peep out the window. The moment I look out, I notice something. Red dots of light on my chest.

Hells bells.

Now, we have really crappy television in Purgatory. Even so, I've seen enough cop shows to know that a red dot means someone is targeting me, and not in a nice way. I wave out to my mystery stalker. "Just checking the locks!" I give a hearty thumbs-up. "We're good!" The red dots disappear.

Whew. These humans are touchy.

I climb off the bed and stalk around the cabin. Looks like there's nothing to do but get ready for breakfast tomorrow. I head over to my backpack, where all my worldly possessions are. It's going to be a long night.

CHAPTER FIFTEEN

A

I spend the rest of the afternoon organizing my backpack and getting to know my pricey prison-slash-cabin.

Pros: the place has fancy-smelling shampoo and a comfy bed.

Cons: the kitchen is stocked with kale and suffering.

There's some stuff in the fridge that might be fruit, but it's green and star-shaped. I keep waiting for it to sprout legs and ask for a fight. The mini-library has zero books about demons or battle tactics, so that's a snore. And the dresser is stocked with plaid skirts, white shirts, and little blue jackets. Just to be sure, I also opened every cabinet. There is definitely no TV.

Dinner arrives at around six. Or, I should say, at six, a guard drops off a tray at my door, rings the bell, and runs for the trees. This is yet another sign that this place is more of a prison than a camp. And growing up, Purgatory was basically a prison for us quasi-demons, who were pretty much slaves to the ghouls.

Long story short, I know when I'm being kept captive. The question still remains, though. Why? Is it for our protection, to keep us from escaping, or both?

I take the tray inside. It's been a boring afternoon, and I'm excited for a yummy meal to pass the time. Instead, I get a bowl of goop that looks like tiny ball bearings and snot. I think I saw Lincoln eat this once and call it quinoa.

What I wouldn't give for a demon bar.

It starts to get dark, and I'm running out of ways to waste time. I decide to prep again for tomorrow's search for the codex. The minute I'm able, I'm going to sneak out of class—always one of my best skills—and look around for the hidden book. I try to keep a positive attitude. It isn't easy, though. Right now, I shouldn't be locked in this damned cabin. Today should have been our first day in court. At this very moment, Lincoln and I were supposed to be putting Acca away forever. Trouble is, every time we get close to ending Aldred, he weasels away from us. The current situation is merely another example of how that creep is always one step ahead.

I'm being a total downer, and I know where my negative thoughts usually end up: with me eating my weight in ice cream and demon bars. Even so, there's no junk food to be had in the cabin, so I decide to give myself a pep talk instead.

Don't worry; it's only Thursday. You have until tomorrow at 5 p.m. to find the codex and bring it to the Arbiter. You're golden.

Aaaaaaaaaand the pep talk is a no go. I'm still freaking out. A day is really no time at all.

I try to remember what Mom would say in a situation like this. My *"Old Mom"* would freak out right alongside me. Not helpful. But my new *"Presidential Mom"* would tell me to get busy and take my mind off things.

I decide to go with Presidential Mom's advice and get my stuff ready for breakfast tomorrow. This involves rearranging the already-perfectly-arranged junk in my backpack. That doesn't take long, so I decide to try on my new—gulp—uniform. I hustle my cookies to the bedroom and close the window blinds tight. Those machine-gun-toting guards are out there, and I don't want to give them a free show.

Hey, simply because I'm part lust demon doesn't mean I'm an exhibitionist.

I scope out my closet and remove the nearest skirt. The good news is that it's actually pretty silky, so that's a plus. I get as far as my zipping up the skirt and adjusting my bra when a voice sounds from the bed.

"You're killing me here, Myla."

It's Lincoln.

I spin around, and there he is. On my bed. Wearing my favorite body armor along with a look of all-out lust in his mismatched eyes. I soak in the sight of him. Messy brown hair. Cut cheekbones. Full mouth. Broad chest. My guy. It's too awesome to be real. "How did you get in here?"

He arches his brows. "Expert hunter, remember?"

"I peeped out the window, and they had those little red dot thingies on me."

"Don't worry about that. I magically jammed all their machine guns yesterday."

When he got here early. "You've been a busy guy. Is that why you missed my welcoming committee?"

"I had lots of little projects to do while the rest of the faculty were off greeting you." He eyes me from head to toe. "And you're still killing me."

There are a million things I should worry about. Like what's the real secret of Hemlock Island and the Wheeler Institute, not to mention how we're getting our codex back. But right now? The only thing I can focus on is the energy that's filling the air. I am part lust demon, after all. Heat pools behind my eyes, and my irises flare bright red.

Helloooooo, Lincoln.

Lincoln does one of those chin-nod things that only hot guys can get away with. "Come here."

I slowly saunter over. With every step, my tail slinks from side to side in a predatory rhythm. Reaching the end of my double bed, I slowly crawl up Lincoln's prone form. Warmth positively radiates from his body, which in turn heats my torso. I catch his gaze. I know how much my guy likes it when my eyes flare red, so I make sure they're blazing.

"So, I'm killing you?" This is a bullshit question, of course. I totally know Lincoln is digging me in a little skirt.

His eyes darken. "Yes." His husky tone sends a jolt right through my core.

Okay, then.

I straddle his waist, brace my arms above his shoulders, and lean in so close we're almost kissing. "Are you calling your kiss now?"

Some small part of me says that it's overly competitive to bring up the kiss thing at this point. More of me likes to win, so I just keep going.

Lincoln laces his fingers behind his head. It's a move that shows off his broad chest and heavy arms, both of which he knows I love.

The bastard is competing, too.

"You mean, the kiss I won when we fought the dyads?"

"That's the one."

He grins. "No."

I can't believe this. "No?"

"No. You're going to kiss me, Myla. And it won't count toward our bet." He lifts his head until his lips almost-maybe-but-not-quite touch mine. His warm breath cascades over my mouth. My inner lust demon goes berserk. There is nothing in the universe but his mouth and my desire to taste it. Screw the damn bet and Lincoln calling a kiss. I want this.

I lean in ever so slowly and brush my lips against his.

"Yes." Lincoln grips my hair and draws my mouth onto his, hard. We're a tangle of tongues and desire. I can't taste him enough. The straddling position is mighty nice, too. Lincoln's firm hands can easily slide up my thighs and cup my backside. Any sense of control disappears. My lust demon is absolutely in charge, and it's awesome.

Finally, I break our kiss. "I've made a decision."

"Go on." Lincoln kisses my neck, gently nipping my skin with his teeth. *Damn, that's good.*

"I want to have kids."

More kisses, this time behind my ear. "As do I."

"Then, let's start trying." I grind myself against him. "Now."

Lincoln cups my face with his rough hands. "You can't imagine how much I want to."

"Oh, I've a pretty good idea." I wiggle against him a little.

A steely glint comes into his eyes. "We need to put this conversation on hold until we're married."

My lust demon roars inside me. Frustration heats my blood. "Why do we have to wait?"

Lincoln's features are all ironclad control over a well of desire. "Now isn't the right time."

"You don't strike me as the traditional kind of guy."

A devilish smile rounds the corners of his full mouth. "I'm not. That said, we both know how your igni are. Once we have sex, you will get pregnant."

"That's not guaranteed."

"Need I remind you of what your mother said?"

And that's a mood killer. How can I forget Mom telling me how she got pregnant despite the fact that Dad wrapped his junk and cast anti-conception spells? "No need, actually."

"I want you. You know I do. But I won't take the risk of starting a family until this whole issue of Acca is behind us, one way or another. By the end of day on Friday, the trial should be over and our family will be safe."

"Oh, right." I got so worked up, I forgot about that part. If we don't find the codex in time, then Lincoln and I might end up in prison for a while. Separately. Being a solo pregnant inmate with a supernatural love-child isn't my idea of fun. Mood killer part deux.

"This is only temporary, Myla. We'll be together." He slides his right hand across the bare skin of my shoulder. I shiver. The tips of his fingers outline the edge of my bra. For the record, I'm feeling pretty pumped that I wore some of the cute new undies that my best friend, Cissy, made me buy.

Lincoln's fingers trail between my breasts and down my stomach. "There are still ways we can enjoy each other until the time is right." He brushes a line along the waistband of my skirt.

My eyes flare so brightly I'm surprised they aren't burning a hole in Lincoln's head. I want to come up with some snarky reply. It's all I can do to nod.

Yes. Let's do that. Yes, yes, yes.

"Good." Lincoln's mouth takes mine again as his hand slides lower still. "We'll have to stay quiet, Myla."

"No problem." *Maybe.*

Lincoln gives me one of those soul-shattering kisses that sets every nerve ending I have on fire. I soak in the moment and sensation. Most of my life is one unpredictable disaster after another. Times like these are rare, and so I value them all the more. The next few hours stretch out before me, filled with intimacy, touch, and delight. As I slide down into Lincoln's embrace, I decide to enjoy these moments to their fullest.

A.

It's nearly one o'clock in the morning when Lincoln and I decide to move on from *"lust demon time"* and return to the whole *"how do we get out of this mess"* conversation. At this point, Lincoln and I are lying in my bed. Lincoln reclines on his back, his left arm arched behind his head. I snuggle into his right side. My inner lust demon is happy, especially since neither of us is wearing any clothing.

"So, you mucked up their machine guns?" I ask. "What else have you been up to while we've been apart?"

"They give faculty here a lot of leeway, so long as you stay on the south side of the island. I checked out the facilities and inspected what demon patrol systems Acca had put in place." His mouth thins. "This is supposed to be their patrol territory."

"I'm guessing they did a crap job."

"They've done nothing. There are no protections for the humans out there. There should be charms and perimeters in place to discourage demonic activity. That's what a decent demon patrol is all about. But here? It's as if this land wasn't ever covered by the thrax."

"So what have they been doing here?"

140

"That's the question. It hasn't been protecting the human populace, that's for certain."

My mind turns over this piece of news. "That must be the rumors, or at least some of them."

"What do you mean?"

"Prescott warned me not to discuss the rumors about the island. Even if humans can't see demons, they can sense danger. Some of the more sensitive ones can even catch a glimpse of something. Both Dad and Prescott said the island was rumored to be haunted. Who knows? What humans think of as ghosts could really be demonic activity."

Lincoln makes slow arcs on my bare arm with his thumb. "You might be right. Some of the other teachers have been discussing the rumors as well. They say the same thing. The place is supposed to be haunted. That's why the town is emptied out. In fact, I'm surprised they even have that old boatman to take people back and forth."

"You know Acca better than anyone. Why do you think they're slacking off on patrol?"

"Demons frighten humans, and scared mortals stay holed up inside, especially at night. Acca has probably been using the fact that no humans are around in order to make it easier to search for the coin."

All this talk about the deserted town makes me think of Fish Stick Grandpa. "on the boat ride over, I learned something else that you might find interesting."

"Hmm?"

"Prescott told me that he's an expert in Archangology, and the person who was asked him come work here? The Lady."

"The same one Desmond and the dyad demons were talking about?"

"It's a safe bet. Even worse, it all took place about six months ago."

"Right when you put Armageddon in prison."

"Which makes sense, right? That's when the King of Hell really needed a way out, so he started hunting down Lucifer's coin and Aldred. My guess? Once Armageddon and Aldred made their deal, the pressure was on to actually deliver a coin. Whatever half-assed searching that Acca had been doing needed to be kicked up a notch. I think that's why Aldred called this mysterious Lady, and she called in Prescott to become headmaster."

"What else did Prescott say about her?"

"Not much. She's some kind of benefactor for the school."

Lincoln sniffs. "She's a benefactor, but it's not for the school. Most likely, the Lady is helping Aldred and Armageddon."

"Agreed." I stretch a bit. "Much as I'd hate to say this, there's only one way we'll get past all this nastiness. Sneak around." I kiss his bare shoulder. "Tell me you have a way to get us out of here."

He winks. "I have a way to get us out of here."

"That's why I love you, Mister the Prince."

"And I you." He kisses me once, gently. "There's been a lot of strange activity on the North side of the island. My guess? The Acca patrol is hiding out there. Those paths are guarded during the daytime, but it should be fairly easy to sneak in at night."

"How very, very awesome then that it is nighttime right now."

"Precisely." Lincoln's gaze turns intense. "Before we leave, I need to tell you about the rest of my day."

"Sure."

"I spent a lot of time casting charms that will protect your cabin."

I like where this is going. As much as I'm a badass, I do love it when Lincoln gets a little bossy and protective. "What did you do?"

"I added a magical perimeter around this place. Better than bulletproof glass." He hitches his thumb toward the wall. "Those guards could lob a grenade at your window, and it wouldn't leave a dent."

"Anything else?"

"Nothing else for you." Lincoln hoists himself onto his left elbow. "I'd like to have a discussion with your tail, though."

I think back to the way my tail acted on the docks. Lincoln must have figured out that it was being surly and now? Somebody's in trouble.

Instantly, my tail dives under the covers. It's a total sucker for Lincoln, and it knows what's coming. I tap the sheet. "Get moving. You know he won't let it drop."

Little by little, my tail slinks out from under the sheet. The arrowhead end points toward Lincoln's face. This is it's *"I'm ready and listening"* pose. I don't see it often.

"Now then," says Lincoln. "I'm sure you're not happy here and therefore, you're giving Myla grief. I want that to end. Do we understand each other?"

My tail's arrowhead-end does its nodding thing. *Yes.*

Lincoln reaches his arm out. "Thank you." My tail instantly winds around Lincoln's arm, rubbing against him like a cat. I yank it away. Sometimes, my tail is such an attention hog.

"I guess we should get going."

"Yes," says Lincoln. "You'll need to change into your dragon-scale fighting suit before we go." He leans back against the pillows. "I'll watch."

"Sure, you will."

And watching isn't all that he does. All of which is why we end up not sneaking out of the cabin until 2 a.m.

Sometimes, it's good to be me.

CHAPTER SIXTEEN

A

It's almost time to trek off to the north side of the island. I make a few last-second checks of my gear, including fiddling with the facemask of my dragonscale fighting suit. Once I pull this thing over my head, no one will see me in the dark. My tail bounces in a happy rhythm behind me. It seems like everyone is pumped to be leaving the cabin.

Lincoln digs around in his man-bag of tricks, an angry look on his face. I can't help but notice how we're not going anywhere yet.

"Is everything okay?" I ask.

"I went through way too many spells in prepping for today. I never suspected that Acca had done nothing to protect the area." He shakes his head. "I should have guessed."

"How bad is it?"

"I've enough charms to cover us. Barely." Lincoln starts setting some small potion bottles and charms into different little pockets on his body armor. "There are a lot of demons out there, though."

My heart pitter-pats a little faster. "How many is a lot?"

"Tons. The place is crawling with them."

My tail arches over my shoulder, tilting the arrowhead-shaped end toward me. I give it a high five. "Now, that's what I'm talking about."

"We're not killing demons tonight." Lincoln has his no-nonsense tone on, which is a total bummer. "This mission is for recon only."

"Sure, sure." *I'm so killing something when I get a chance.*

Lincoln tilts his head and eyes me carefully. "You're just yes-ing me to death, aren't you?"

I debate about lying, but that's a bad habit to get into. "Yeah, I totally was." I raise my hand, palm forward. This is a serious mission, and Lincoln and I need to be aligned. "I promise not to kill anything unless we agree on it."

Lincoln's face warms with a genuine smile. "I love you, Myla."

I wink. "It's easy to do, really." I kiss him gently on the cheek. Sometimes, that says it all.

"Well, now." Lincoln loops his arms around my waist. "Are you ready to explore the north side of the island?"

"Hells, yeah."

"Then, let's go." Lincoln pulls a small knife out of a pocket. The pentagram insignia of Striga has been carved into the handle. More magic stuff.

"That's a new one to me." Although, considering Lincoln and I haven't been together too long, most of the stuff from Striga is new to me. "What does that thing do?"

"It will cut our way out of here without attracting attention. Even the guards won't see us." Lincoln kills the lights, steps over to the wall, and kneels down. I can barely make out his blade glowing in the darkness as he makes a mark across the baseboard.

I finish getting myself ready. In this case, that means pulling my hood over my face and dragging on my gloves. This way, every inch of me is hidden.

Fear me, for I am Ninja Scala.

Lincoln pulls on his own facemask. While mine looks more like a black fencing mask thingy, Lincoln's reminds me of a ski

145

mask with meshy eyes. It's pretty cool looking, actually. Lincoln glances up in my direction. We share a silent nod.

Go time.

Returning his attention to the wall, Lincoln curls his fingers right into the baseboards, exactly where he'd just cut a line with his magic knife. Jamming his hands into the wood, Lincoln then pulls up the wall as if it were fabric. Grass becomes visible through the new hole.

My brows lift. *That's a pretty neat trick, right there. Especially considering how the guards can't see a thing.*

We crawl under the wall and out into the night. The cool air makes me shiver. Lincoln starts to slip through the trees and shrubs. There's only a thin moon in the sky, so everything is almost completely dark. Another bonus of being part demon is I have excellent night vision, though. For Lincoln's part, his angelic side gives him similar abilities.

We slink through the woods for quite some time. I don't see any of the guards. I can sure hear them, though. They are cocking their guns and gasping at every little sound. Considering the situation, I don't blame them.

There are demons everywhere.

Acca has been slacking on this territory, and it shows. The humans can't see anything. I'd imagine that they sure can sense the evil, though. I've never seen so many Class F demons in one place. There are dark pixies flitting through the shrubs. Hell bats hanging upside from the trees. Even the grass snakes have glowing red eyes. My inner wrath demon goes berserk. Every cell in my body wants to break out and fight.

I grit my teeth and keep a steady path toward the north side of the island. Lincoln keeps pace at my side. I'd give myself a high-five for holding back, but I don't want to mess up my concentration. Not-killing is hard work.

As we move along, the woods change. The trees become taller. Older. More space separates the trunks. The grounds are raw and unkempt. There's no question about it. We've reached outskirts of the Wheeler Institute. My pulse skyrockets. We're getting closer to the north side of the island...And the Acca patrol.

Lincoln and I slip farther through the trees and then, we come to a large cabin. Unlike the one that I'm staying in, it's old and nasty. The roof looks ready to fall in. In fact, there's only one good thing about this place.

Candlelight shines through the cracks in the walls.

Someone's in there.

Every nerve ending in my body becomes charged with excitement. Could this be the hiding place of our codex and Lucifer's coin? My palms turn slick inside my dragonscale gloves. It's currently early Friday morning (very, very early). If we get the codex today, we can still show the codex to the Arbiter and make our case. This could all be over so soon. And then...Our wedding. I'd be able to talk to Mom and Octavia about the plans, maybe squeeze in another fitting on my dress.

Slow down, Myla.

I force myself to inhale a few long breaths. Now is not the time to start mentally celebrating. The codex and coin come first.

Lincoln and I steal up closer to the barn. Voices carry through the night. I tilt my head. A bunch of men are gabbing about something. None of the voices sound familiar, though.

We crouch by the barn's outer wall. Here, the breaks in the wood are large enough to peer through. It takes a moment for my eyes to adjust to the bright light inside, but when I do, I see five Acca warriors. Lincoln pulls out a charm for concealment—it resembles a nickel—and snaps it in two. A small puff of purple smoke wafts into the air.

Now, no one can hear us.

"Is this the lost patrol?" I ask.

"That's them, all right."

Inside the rundown cabin, all five warriors are seated around a shabby wooden table. Everywhere in the room—tables, chairs and floor space—the place is piled high with old books and sheets of parchment. The warriors wear black body armor like Lincoln's, only theirs has the insignia of Acca embossed on their chest. Dicks.

And of all people, Prescott paces a frenzied line before them. I blink, wondering if I'm seeing things. I'm not. Prescott is here and chatting up the Acca warriors like they're old buddies.

What does Prescott want with fighters from Acca, exactly?

"I've done everything you asked," says Prescott. The headmaster is still in his country club best, only he doesn't seem so calm and collected any more. The guy's golden hair is a mess and his shirt is untucked. A wild look now shines in his icy-blue eyes. "I want my Lady back in my life. She won't speak to me unless the coin is found."

My brows jet upward. There she is again; the same Lady that Desmond talked about. Every particle of my body strains to hear what the Acca patrol says next. A long pause follows before anyone answers. My heart hammers in my chest as I get a closer look at the warriors. As thrax go, they're pretty standard Acca guys. All of them are little on the thin side with mismatched eyes and lots of golden hair. One of them is taller with an all-gold tunic and a man-bun. That's the patrol's Captain.

Prescott falls to his knees before Mister Man-Bun. "Please, Blaze."

Blaze leans back on his chair. "The terms of our deal were very clear. Your Lady is the one who set the rules here. You won't see her again until the coin is discovered."

"But I have the codex. I'm keeping it safe for you in my library. Isn't that enough?"

On reflex, I grab Lincoln's hand. *The codex is on the island; Prescott admits it!* This fiasco is so close to being over, I can taste it. Well...Over except for the bit about Lucifer's coin and opening up a gateway that could end the world. That part still bites.

"What more do you desire?" asks Prescott. The guilty look on his face says that he knows damned well what Acca wants.

"Please. Lucifer's coin is still hidden on this island. You're some kind of expert on Lucifer."

Prescott lifts his chin. "I know about all archangels."

I roll me eyes. *Sure, you do.*

"You don't know enough to find Lucifer's coin. Perhaps the Lady overestimated your skills in archangology."

I have to admit, Blaze is right on that score. What Prescott knew about my father was zip.

"I'll find the coin," insists Prescott.

"I know you will. That's why you're here."

Prescott puffs out his chest. "That, and because my Lady loves me."

Riiiiiiight. It's too much of a coincidence for some Lady to fall for an archangologist when Lucifer's coin is missing. Not that love makes you too logical. I've seen it myself with Connor and Octavia.

"We're not having this conversation again," says Blaze. "Find it."

I glance over to Lincoln. He sits still as stone, a sliver of moonlight outlining his masked profile. I can't see his face, but there's no mistaking the waves of rage rolling off my guy. Lincoln is furious, and he's not the only one. Both my hands are curled into fists. It's one thing to suspect your own people are plotting against you. It's another thing to see it firsthand.

This betrayal really pisses me off. Right now, I should be snuggling with my guy, eating demon bars, or planning my wedding. Okay, the wedding-planning stuff isn't my favorite thing to do. That said, my point remains. These losers have me sneaking around a random island instead of living my life.

Prescott scrubs his face with his hands. "I've done everything I can think of. I've searched the island from end to end."

"Look again. If you want to see your Lady, you'll find it."

"Yes, that's right. I will find it. I'll do anything for her."

Something about the look in Prescott's face reminds me of how he acted all creepy and handsy in the boat. A realization rattles around the back of my mind, so close to coming to the forefront. I lose it before I can bring it to light, though.

Blaze gestures to a pile of books on the floor. "We got some new volumes in today. Take them back to your library. See what you can discover."

I turn to Lincoln. "Tell me you know where his library is."

Even through the mask, I can tell my guy is smiling. "That I do."

Sweet.

Prescott rushes over to a pile of leather-bound tomes and scans the bindings. "These are good. Very good. Some Greco-Roman histories." Prescott scoops up the books and sets them against his chest. "I have a good feeling here. These books will be the key to finding Lucifer's coin. I know it."

"Then, you better find it soon." Blaze's voice takes on a menacing tone. "If you want your Lady back, then this is the only way it happens."

Prescott rushes to stand before Blaze. "I do. You know I do."

Blaze stands, and it's clear that he's a half head taller than Prescott, even if you don't count the man-bun. "My brothers and I don't like hiding out here. We're not allowed home without the coin, and every day that passes, it becomes less likely that we'll be able to return."

Prescott's eyes take on a wild look. "You mean the young usurper? The man who stole away the throne from your people?"

A weight of dread tightens through my insides. *The young usurper.* He means Lincoln. How many thrax really believe this to be the case? I mean, I knew Aldred thought that Rixa stole the crown from them. But what about the rest of Lincoln's people? How deep does the betrayal go?

Blaze nods. "Before our enemy gets locked up, he could cause a lot of problems for those of us in this room."

Lincoln shakes his head. I know my guy well enough to guess what he's thinking. These five are totally screwed, no matter what Prescott finds.

"I won't fail you, Blaze." A bead of sweat rolls down Prescott's cheek. "Believe me."

"You have until tomorrow. We need the coin by the coin by Friday; it's as simple as that. Our master has something special planned for the usurper this Sunday."

Sunday. Our wedding day. And Aldred plans to ruin it. Yet another reason to hate him.

"I...I'll do my best," stammers Prescott. "What will you do with the coin once you have it?"

"That's for my Master and your Lady to decide."

Those are the words that come from Blaze's mouth, but the dark look in his eyes? That tells a different story. That warrior knows exactly what will happen when Aldred gets the coin.

He'll release Armageddon.

I shiver, thinking of the last time I saw Armageddon's army march across Purgatory, leaving a trail of smoke, blood, and destruction behind them. It's not something I ever want to witness again.

Prescott steps closer to the door. "I'll take these to my office right away. And I'll find that coin. You can trust me." He rushes off into the night.

For a time, I watch Prescott race through the trees and back to the school. What is that dude's deal, anyway? I ponder for a few moments before I realize how easy it is to pick out Prescott's silhouette through the trees. We must've been here longer than I thought. It's getting light out.

I tap Lincoln's shoulder and point in the direction of my cabin. "We should head back."

Lincoln nods and together, we slip through the forest. As we step along, the night demons disappear under the growing light. Dawn will be here soon. Once we're well away from the rickety cabin, Lincoln speaks again. "Prescott's library is in his office. It's the only one on the island. That's why he was so excited about your father's donation. He wants to build something far grander."

"Can you get in there?"

Lincoln shakes his head. "It's guarded, and faculty must make an appointment to enter."

A sly smile rounds my lips. "What about students who misbehave?" This was a specialty of mine back at Purgatory High.

"They go right in." Lincoln's eye fill with mischief. "Do you think you can get sent to the headmaster's office?"

"Oh, yeah."

"That's my Myla."

It's all I can do not to yell *"mwah-hah-hah."* After what I saw tonight, I'm totally wound up about Prescott being a tool, a murderer, or both. Long story short, I can't wait to get in trouble with him again.

CHAPTER SEVENTEEN

A.

All that snooping around on the north side of the island—combined with my extracurricular activities with Lincoln—make for one tired quasi-demon. Once I get back into my cabin, I crawl back into bed, close my eyes, and fall right to sleep.

I barely have time to hit a REM cycle when my alarm starts ringing. It takes me a few seconds to remember I have to attend breakfast this morning at Jamboree Hall.

Blech.

I sit up and scrub my hands over my face.

It's Friday. Not even a full day left to find the codex.

Excitement heats my bloodstream. After last night, we know the codex is in Prescott's office. My mouth winds into a semi-evil smile. I'm so going to enjoy worming my way in there.

I drag my butt out of bed, take a quick shower, and get dressed in my new uniform. I scope myself out in the mirror and come to the conclusion that I hate all uniforms on principle.

Still, knowing that Lincoln likes to see me in skirts takes a little of the sting out of the situation. Once I'm all set, I follow the sound of the bell to Jamboree Hall. A pair of girls makes their way through the trees. Their faces look pale and their movements are jittery.

I saunter over and slap on my best smile. "Good morning!"

The two of them say something that sounds like *"mumble-mumbling."* I think that's *good morning* if you're human and spent the night terrified of the demons outside your cabin.

No question about it. Those rumors about this place being haunted are definitely due to the freewheeling demon fiesta. I still can't believe how many I saw last night.

One mystery down, a ton to go.

I follow the wooden signs toward Jamboree Hall. With every step, I get more ticked off. That damned Acca demon patrol. If they'd been doing their jobs instead of scheming against Lincoln's family, these girls wouldn't look like extras from *Dawn of the Dead*.

As I close in on the hall, real pathways start to appear through the woods. The trails all lead up to a large building that looks like a modern-style barn. It's two stories high and made of stainless steel and concrete. The huge windows are framed in glossy wood. More log cabin meet modern art.

I walk into Jamboree Hall. It's an open space with long tables across the floor and a low stage on the far side of the room. Along the right wall, a long buffet table stands, its surface heaped with food. I scan the pickings and although there are no demon bars, there's another one of my favorite treats: bacon.

Oh, yeah.

I eagerly step into line and load up my plate with all sorts of bad-for-you breakfast stuff. One thing I'll say for this place, they do not skimp on breakfast. By the time I'm through the line, I've got an omelet, cheese sandwich thingy, and a Jenga-like tower of bacon on my plate.

I'm so excited for this pile of greasy yumminess, I almost walk right into Lincoln without noticing. Of course, his tray is piled high with healthy crap. There's a bowl of granola and a bunch of figs. I stare at the tray in disbelief. "Figs? What are you, ninety?"

"Good morning," he says smoothly. "I'm Mr. Prince, one of the new teachers. And you are?"

What *I am* is about to give him crap about his fake name—Mr. Prince, really?—when I realize people are staring. "I'm Mysteria Cross."

"What an unusual name."

Ugh. He beat me to the name jab. I hate it when Lincoln wins.

"I was about to say the same thing to you."

"Such a shame I got there first."

Does my guy know me or what?

I take care to speak so quietly only Lincoln can hear me. "Enjoy victory while you can, buddy."

"I plan to. I still have my kiss to look forward to." He looks at me like he'll call it at any moment.

"You wouldn't."

"Wouldn't I?"

He totally would.

I quickly raise both my tray and voice. "I'm really hungry, Mr. Prince. So, if you don't mind…"

Lincoln is totally not letting me go so easily. "You have gym class with me today. Not sure how well you'll perform with that kind of breakfast in you."

I'm sleepy, hungry, and grumpy at getting yet more hassle about my eating habits. The words tumble from my lips before I can stop them. "Bite me, big guy."

Aaaaaaand I said that a little too loud.

The whole hall seems to fall silent. A few moments ago, about fifty students and teachers were milling about and getting breakfast. Suddenly, all eyes are on me and Lincoln. Based on the looks of shock and horror, I'm guessing people don't mouth back to teachers very often.

I lift my tray again. "I'll go eat now. Nice to meet you, Mr. Prince."

"Until gym class, Missy."

I grip my tray so hard the silverware starts to rattle. "Mysteria."

"Right."

Oh, he is so going to get it later.

The hall fills with chatter once more as I find a vacant seat next to—surprise, surprise!—another group of terrified girls who won't say dick to me, no matter how much I try to start a conversation.

I give up on chitchat and focus on scoping out the room instead. Across the hall, Lincoln sits at the faculty table. He's one of the few male teachers here and definitely the only hot one. Although, I suppose that's a matter of taste. Some might think Prescott is yummy, if you're into older dudes who play golf and grope your ass for no reason.

I chow down on more bacon and take a closer look at Prescott. What a loser.

My last bite of bacon is history when Prescott rises and strikes his fork against his water glass. The room falls silent. *Guess it's speech time.*

"Good morning, students," says Prescott.

"Good morning, Headmaster," says everyone in unison. Their voices hold an excitement level that's one notch above finding dog crap in your shoe.

"Today, I'd like to talk about an important subject. Archangology."

I refold my napkin. *What an interesting subject.*

"The patron of our school is none other than the archangel Xavier. As you know, there are some ancient texts that say an artifact of the archangels has been hidden on this very island. It's been a hobby of mine to search for it."

Hobby? Try total obsession inspired by your Lady, whoever she is. Which come to think of it, considering that his Lady is involved with Aldred and ordering demons around, means that the Lady is possibly demonic. Definitely evil.

"I've recently been fortunate enough to receive some new information about the hiding place of this artifact. It may be buried somewhere on the east side of the island. I'll need a good number volunteers to help me dig it up." Prescott scans the room. "What do you say? Do I have any volunteers?" All the students are staring at their plates. No one seems interested in his offer.

Smart girls. Handling Lucifer's coin is not something humans should do.

"Perhaps I need to sweeten the opportunity a little," says Prescott. "Whoever volunteers may have a two-minute phone call with a loved one next week."

Everyone raises their hands. I'm so shocked I almost fall out of my chair. My inner wrath demon writhes inside me. He's tricking girls into doing something dangerous in exchange for a phone call? That's it. I've had it with sitting around and being quiet, even if I could get more bacon for round two.

I rise. "What are you talking about? We students can't contact our families?"

Prescott gives me a grin worthy of a Ken doll. "It's what their loved ones agreed to when they came to this school, including your father. We've covered this before. You're here to learn, not chat the day away and fritter on technology. We do things traditionally here, by using books, discussion, and healthy exercise. There are no computers, Internet, and only one phone. It's in my office and only for emergencies."

"Wow." I tap my chin, as if seriously considering his words. "That's a terrible idea." I gesture around the room. "I mean, look at these people. They're two neck puncture wounds short of being in a vampire movie. If they want to talk to their parents, they should be able to."

Half the student body looks at me with shock. Others seem hopeful. I take that as a super-good sign because, honestly? I was worrying that they were all under some sort of spell.

Prescott's voice lowers. "You're new to this school, so I'll only say this one more time. Students speak when spoken to, and they follow the rules."

I fake a cough, but it sounds a lot like *kiss my ass*.

Prescott's takes a half step backward. The entire room gasps and falls silent. "What did you just say?"

"I'm sorry." I twiddle my fingers across my neck. "One second. I think I ate a bug or something. Let me try that again. I said…" I clear my throat. "Kiss. My. Ass."

If Prescott were a cartoon, he'd have steam coming out of his ears. "Miss Cross! Into my office. Now!"

157

Mission accomplished.

I point in a few different directions. "Which way is your office, exactly?"

Prescott grits his teeth and makes a growly sound. For such a put-together-looking dude, when he falls apart, it's really spectacular. "Miss Cross!"

I step toward the door. "You know what? I'll find it."

"I have to finish my faculty briefing, but rest assured, we will have words."

"Got it."

The room breaks out into animated chatter. About five teachers surround Prescott. They all wave their arms around and glare in my direction, evidently discussing how much I suck. As I head to the exit, a student pulls on my sleeve. I pause. "What's up?"

"Prescott's office is the cabin to the right of Jamboree Hall." She's got big eyes, red hair, and some attitude. Leave it to a ginger to break ranks and talk to me. I remember her from yesterday. She was the only girl in Prescott's class who seemed to have any life in her.

"You're Harper," I say.

"And you're Mysteria."

Not Missy. "Damn right."

Harper lowers her voice. "Thanks for standing up to him. I get that this is supposed to be an old fashioned and immersive learning experience." She makes finger quotes when she says that last part. "But he takes it too far."

I eye the door. "Let's talk about it later, okay? I don't want to…" I stop myself before saying "*waste this opportunity to peep around his office.*" Instead, I put on my best guilty face. It might look a little like I'm constipated, but I'm not a really expert in feeling guilt, let alone showing it. "I don't want to anger the headmaster any more than I already have. I'm totally new and all."

"Sure. I understand." She raises her hand. "Don't rush. His faculty briefings take forever, even if he is angry about someone."

"Good to know." *Great, actually.*

I saunter out the front door. *This is going to be fun.* If the headmaster's angry now, wait until I get done with his office.

CHAPTER EIGHTEEN

A.

Once I leave Jamboree Hall, it isn't hard to find Prescott's HQ. It's a traditional-looking log cabin, only on a huge scale. Two human guards stand at the front door, both of them men. *What a sausage party.* That can work to my advantage, though. I do my best to seem super-mopey as I slog my way closer. I pause before the guards. "I've been sent" —*sniffle, sniffle*— "to the headmaster's office."

One of the guards pushes the door open. "You should watch your mouth, girly. Headmaster doesn't like it when the students sass off."

I purse my lips. *I have to admit, hearing about my little incident already? That's impressive.*

"You know what just happened in Jamboree Hall?" I ask.

The guard's eyes narrow. "It's a small island. We know about everything that happens on our side of it."

Our side. Interesting. Guess the humans really do stay away from the north side and the Acca patrol.

I speed into the log cabin; the guard slams the door behind me. Inside, the place is basically one large room whose walls are lined with books. A large brushed-steel desk sits on the center of the floor. There's no kitchen, reading area, or bedroom like with my place. The only windows are located on either side of the front door. Unfortunately, the blinds on both of them are open.

For what I plan to do, those windows need to get covered.

Tiptoeing forward, I carefully pull the blinds down, making sure that I whimper loudly as I do it. Hopefully I won't have to keep playing the "I'm a girl and I'm crying" card as the excuse for what I'm up to.

A guard pounds on the door. "What's going on in there?"

Then again, I might have to play it up even harder.

"I don't want you to see me cry."

"Pull up the damned blinds, girly."

Huh. My initial plan isn't working. Now I'll have to call out my super-secret weapon. "Whatever you say. I'll just…Oh, no!" I whip open the front door and pop my head out. "Hey, do either of you guys have a tampon?"

They stare at me, their mouths falling open. "Uh…"

"Because I like, really, really, really need one." I glance over my shoulder and shudder. "I've got a gusher going on in here." I've found that for this tactic to work, it's absolutely critical to look sincere when saying the word *gusher*.

Am I evil to do this? Why yes, yes I am.

Does it work every time? Why yes, yes it does.

The guards look panic-stricken. "We, uh…"

I snap my fingers. "Wait, I've got it. Maybe there's something in the bathroom." I slam the door shut and wait. Here's where I see if my favorite non-battle battle strategy works yet again. A few seconds pass, and there's not a peep from the guards.

Another mission accomplished. That will keep them out of my hair for a while.

With the guards safely outside, I return my attention to the office. Harper said Prescott's briefings take a while, but I still want to hustle here. I scan the shelves of books and massive desk. What's the best way to go about this? Last night, Prescott said the codex was hidden in the library.

Books first, then.

I run my hands across and behind the books, looking for any-thing out of place. Nothing seems odd, unless you consider it a little strange that everything is dusted to perfection. Prescott is a total neat freak. Other than that revelation, the library shelves are a total bust.

On to the desk.

The brushed-steel desktop holds a neat pile of books. I rec-ognize these as the same volumes that Prescott got from Acca last night. Now, I'm no scholar. I do know people, though. The headmaster seemed super-excited about these books. In fact, he mentioned them this morning as being crucial for his search, so I'll check them out next. The thick volumes are encased in heavy leather bindings. They look hundreds of years old. I flip open the first few books and scan the contents.

Great. They're all in Latin.

Sure, I can understand spoken Latin. It's a weird side effect of becoming the great scala. I would have preferred the ability to fly or have laser beams shoot out of my palms, but whatever. Understanding spoken Latin is fine. Reading it is another matter, though. I can't make out a word of what's on these pages.

Fortunately, Prescott has already read these books for me. In fact, he's even gone ahead and marked a few pages with Post-its. *How helpful.* I stare at the ancient sheets of parchment. Lincoln would know how to read them, easy peasy. I finger the worn edges of the pages.

One of these days, once Purgatory gets more technology and Antrum gets any, I could get a functioning cell phone of my very own. Then, I could take pictures of stuff like this. After all, these books belong in a museum. I should be super-careful here. I stare at the books and ponder before coming to a momentous decision.

Meh. The super-careful way is way too much hassle right now.

I tear out the marked sheets, slip them into my jacket pocket, and refuse to feel guilty about it. After all, a demonic army means the end of the human world, including all museums. So there.

With my inspection of the books behind me, I decide to tackle the rest of the desk. Plunking down in the headmaster's chair, I pull open the drawers.

Aaaaaaaand it's official. The man is a crazy-ass neat freak.

There are pens arranged by color. Post-its stacked by size. Quill pens arranged by manufacturer. Some kind of wax thing, probably to perfectly seal envelopes. Tissues. Mini wipes. Hand sanitizer. I shake my head. At least I know I didn't get any germs on me when he groped my ass. I eye the largest drawer hungrily. It's a big one. The codex could easily fit in there.

I yank the drawer open. Small envelopes sit inside, all of them arranged into neat little piles. There must be a thousand of them in here, all jammed in tightly and with infinite care. In fact, the rows are so neat and straight you couldn't actually shove another envelope between stacks.

It's official. Prescott just graduated from nutjob neat freak to OCD. I pull out a random envelope from the top. It reads:

To: My Dearest Prescott-kins.
From: His Lady.

My stomach sours. I get the Lady part, but Prescott-kins? This is going to be gross. Still, I need to read this nastiness, just in case there's a clue hidden somewhere. The envelope has already been opened, so I pull out the letter.

My dearest man,
I'm sitting alone, missing you, and thinking of our last time together. Remember how I twisted my fingers through your long, sweaty chest hair right after we—

Whoa.

I fold up the letter like it holds the contagion for a zombie apocalypse. *No way am I reading another word.* I only got through two sentences, and now I'll never unsee the image of my head-master's nest of sweaty chest hair after getting intimate with his so-called Lady. I jam the letter back into the envelope and slam the drawer shut.

My inspection of the desk is officially over. I pat my pocket. Although I did have to read about Prescott-kins, I still got these sheets for Lincoln. Go me.

Voices sound outside the front door. It's Prescott, and he's talking to the guards. I can't tell everything they're saying, however the word *tampon* comes up quite a bit. I haul ass so I'll be standing before the headmaster's desk when he comes in.

The door opens slowly. "Missy?"

"Yup." I don't even correct him this time.

Prescott slowly steps into the room. "The guards, uh, told me about your situation."

Mr. Neat is freaking out about the tampon-thing. Nice. I make a great point of wincing.

"Whatever they said, they didn't do it justice."

"You know what? We can have our conversation later. I know you have…Things to do. You realize your error at breakfast, correct?"

"Absolutely." *Not.*

"Excellent. Don't let it happen again." He opens the door wide. I see my chance and take it. Without so much as a goodbye, I hightail it out of Prescott's office. The door shuts behind me with another slam. Frustrated mumbles sound from behind the closed door. I can just imagine Prescott talking to himself while he pulls out his wipes and sanitizer, ready to go to town on every surface I may have come in contact with.

Cool. That'll keep him busy for a while.

For my part, I now have gym class with Lincoln. Although I did grab the sheets from Prescott's book, I can't celebrate too much. After all, my big goal was to find that codex, and I came up empty. Even worse, today is Friday. If we don't find the codex today, then Lincoln and I can go to jail.

I stomp across the grass. Hells bells. I was so sure that the codex was in his office. It's beyond maddening. Both the codex and the coin are definitely on this island, but we haven't found either one yet. And worst of all, the Earl of Acca has something special planned for our wedding, according to the Acca warriors from last night. In Aldred-speak, that means trouble.

A small wooden sign has been tacked to one of the trees. It reads *"Practice Field"* and has an arrow that points toward a path through the forest. I take off at a run.

CHAPTER NINETEEN

A

I race through the forest. The path that I follow is all gnarly roots and jutting rocks. Random tree branches loom over the trail. A few almost whack me in the face.

Important point: I've seen enough Earth-made TV shows to know that, in this situation, most human females would trip on a rock, fall on their ass, and lay there like a lump. Makes no sense. Time was, I thought it might be some phenomenon about woods on Earth. Enchanted anti-feminine rocks, maybe? But now that I'm here, I find that it's super-easy to run along without falling. Not sure what's up with that.

Something to ponder. You know, when I don't have to haul ass to find a magical codex and Lucifer's coin to keep me and my fiancé out of jail and the world from ending.

So, you know, much later.

The trees open up to a large round swath of flat grassland. About twenty girls march around the periphery in three neat rows, military style. They're all wearing these weird one-piece zip-front jumpsuits. It's surreal.

Lincoln notices me the moment I step onto the green. Unlike the students, he's still wearing his low-slung khakis and blue blazer. Somehow, he makes it look good. "Mysteria Cross. You're late."

My first reaction is to tell him to bite me. I'm able to control my sass, for once. "Yes, Mr. Prince. I'll be right there." My tail, however, flips him a modified hand gesture over my shoulder. I love that thing.

Lincoln's glance goes to my tail. None of the humans can see my demonic side. Of course, Lincoln catches it right away. His full mouth tips up into a subtle smile. He knows he still got sassed and he thinks it's awesome. One of the many reasons why I love the guy.

I pause before him. "Sorry I'm late. I ran through the forest, fell, and lay there for a while." I figure if any humans are eaves-dropping, this will seem like a very plausible scenario.

"Don't let it happen again."

"No problem." *I never let it happen the first time.* The other students march by us in formation. "Is this all we do? March around in circles?"

"Pretty much. The class hasn't been taught anything more useful yet. Walking about is supposed to be good exercise. Plus, they're all stuck on the far side of the green, so we have a few minutes to chat." He tilts his head. "Any luck with Prescott's office?"

"Not with the codex." I reach into my pocket and pull out the parchment. "I did find this, though."

Lincoln takes the sheets from me and scans them. "Prescott highlighted these passages?"

"Yes. He put little Post-its on these pages. What do they say?"

"They're about protectors." He looks over the next sheet. "This one tells the story of Cryptan. It's how he volunteered to become the protector of the thrax Vault. It happened thousands of years ago." He sighs. "At least he lived a long life."

My heart lurches, thinking about our lost friend. I shake my head. Now is not the time to focus on Cryptan's death. "So it talks about Cryptan. Anyone else?"

"It mentions the protector who volunteered to look after Lucifer's coin." He flips the sheets over. "Other than saying that the protector is a man and that he exists, it's a little thin on details."

"How old is that text?"

"At least two thousand years."

"Well, if the protector of Lucifer's coin was around when that text was written, the guy would be pretty old."

Lincoln purses his lips. "He might not look old. Cryptan didn't."

"Yeah, but Cryptan never saw the light of day. Whoever this is, they've been running around under the Earth's sun for a long time." The solution appears in a flash. "Fish Stick Grandpa."

"Excuse me?"

"The guy who brought us over to the island in his rowboat. Jeeves. I could have sworn he saw my tail. That might mean he's working some supernatural mojo like Cryptan. A protector."

Lincoln taps his chin. "That could work."

"I bet his name's not really Jeeves." I lower my voice. "And I'll make that like, an official kiss bet."

"And I won't be taking that wager."

"Why not? What are you, afraid?"

"Nice try. What I am is a kiss ahead." He leans in closer and smirks, the jerk. "And I'm keeping my lead."

Crap. The *"what, are you afraid"* routine used to work so easily on Lincoln. Now he's getting used to all my tricks. I need to up my game.

Lincoln slips the parchment into his jacket pocket. "We should head over to the dock. See what we can find out."

"I like this plan."

The class has finally marched just into listening distance again. Lincoln turns to the students and raises his arms. "Class." Even though my guy isn't wearing a crown, he still works that regal vibe like a pro. Everyone stops to stare at him. "Use the rest our time to explore the woods and exercise in an unstructured manner."

Everyone freezes in place. A chorus of gasps fills the air.

Oops.

167

The cool ginger girl, Harper, steps forward. "We don't go off the paths. Ever."

"And why is that?" asks Lincoln.

Harper's gaze locks with mine. "We have our reasons."

"Whatever they are, you can tell me." Lincoln looks totally trustworthy when he says that, mostly because he is.

Harper scans the frightened faces of the other students. "It's nothing. I shouldn't have said anything. We'll go back to our cabins and hang out."

The group starts to head toward the path. The muscles in my arms and legs clench. I get this overwhelming feeling like an opportunity is passing us by. Harper is clearly a leader of some kind. After all, she's ordering her peers back to their cabins, and they're all listening. Plus, it took guts for Harper to talk to me after I mouthed off to Prescott in Jamboree Hall. And even more guts to share that no one wants to step off the official paths.

It doesn't feel right to let her leave without saying anything. "You mean demons?" I ask. "Are you worried about them?"

The other students scurry off into the woods, but Harper pauses. With careful steps, she closes the distance between us. "What do you know about that?"

"I saw them last night. Flying through the night sky. Hiding in the bushes. Linc— I mean, Mr. Prince saw them as well."

Harper eyes us both from head to toe. "Who are you two, anyway?"

"That's not easy to explain," says Lincoln. "All I can say now is that you're in serious danger."

Harper folds her arms over her chest. "And you two came here to save us."

"We did." I try to look trustworthy, too. It never works as well for me.

"I'll need more than that," says Harper.

Lincoln and I share a long look. I know what the expression on his face means. *Should we trust her?*

"Harper looks cool." I shrug. "Besides, we're running out of time here."

"True." Lincoln goes back into prince-mode. "We believe that Prescott has made some kind of pact to release a demon army right here on Hemlock Island."

"Wow." Harper rolls her eyes. "You almost had me going there. I mean, this place is creep central. But a demon army? Right."

I raise my pointer finger. "We also came here looking for a magical book, too." If we've decided to trust her, there's no point in holding back on the major items.

"Whatever." Harper flicks her finger between Lincoln and me. "The two of you are crazy. I'm going to Headmaster Prescott and telling him everything."

Harper starts to turn away, but Lincoln raises his hand palm forward. "Don't."

"You can jus—" Harper freezes in place.

I look to Lincoln, my eyes wide with shock. "Did you just put a freezing spell on her?"

"I did. It's a standard charm we carry with us on demon patrol. You never know when you'll run across a troublemaker."

"She's not causing trouble. She simply has no idea that the after-realms even exist."

Lincoln sifts through the inner pockets of his jacket. He pulls out what looks like a small seashell. "This charm will clear her memory."

Lincoln steps toward Harper, and I block his path. "We don't want her memory cleared. Out of all the students at this school, Harper is the sharpest. She already suspected we were together."

"It wasn't that hard."

"All I'm saying is that we still need that damned codex. There must be another library on this island. Sure, I didn't find the codex in Prescott's office. That said, if anyone knows where else to look, it would be Harper."

Lincoln turns the shell over in his hand. "I could charm one of the teachers."

"You don't like to take information from the unwilling."

"When did I say that?"

"Two weeks ago. Before we interviewed those quasi kids for the codex."

Lincoln sighs. "Fine. But it's a risk. I'll need to convince her to trust us, and that will require a more serious spell. If I cast it, the Acca patrol could detect that another thrax is nearby. We could blow our cover."

"You'd blow it anyway by casting a charm to clear her memory. I know for a fact that has some serious magic in it."

Lincoln reaches into his pocket, toying with the different charms there. "I don't like revealing that thrax exist. It goes against everything we stand for."

"She doesn't need to know about all your people, Lincoln. Just give her enough supernatural mumbo jumbo to make her trust us enough to answer a few questions." I step closer and grip his arm. "It's Friday, Lincoln. We're almost out of time."

Lincoln stares at the ground for what feels like forever. Eventually, he nods. "And I'll allow her to keep her memories afterward as well. We may need her help again."

I go up on tiptoe to kiss his cheek. "Thank you for breaking with thrax tradition here."

"You can thank me if it works." Lincoln takes out a key from his pocket. It's so clever how the House of Striga makes all their charms look like regular pocket-stuff.

Lincoln steps up before Harper. "I'm going to release you now." He lifts the key. "I need you to stay here and listen. If you scream or run, I'll freeze you again and erase your memory." He grips the key in his fist and clenches his fingers. It makes a crackling sound as he grinds the item in his palm. Purple dust cascades from his hand to the grass below.

Harper moves. She doesn't scream or run, which is the good news. The bad news is that she looks terrified out of her freaking mind. "What...What did you do to me?"

Lincoln pulls out another item from his pocket. This time, it's a small feather. "It's not important what I did, but who I really am. I'm about to give you a great gift, Harper. I'll give you the ability to witness you my true nature and allow you to retain the memory. This doesn't happen very often." He places the tiny feather between his palms and presses them together. When he pulls his hands apart, the feather is gone.

I gasp. The feather may be gone, yet now? Lincoln has wings. Beautiful, white angel wings that shimmer with silvery light. I've never seen anything so lovely, and I have an archangel for a father.

"Wow," croaks Harper.

I couldn't agree more. Of course, I knew Lincoln was part angel. The archangel Aquila is his grandmother. However, he never shows his angelic side like I display my demonic nature. If you're from the after-realms, my tail is really hard to miss.

I open and close my mouth, trying to speak. Finally, I'm able to whisper a few words. "You're beautiful."

Lincoln brushes his fingers along my jawline. "As are you."

"When were we getting to the angel wing part of our relationship? Because I think I really like this."

"Sometime Sunday night, I think."

So this is a post-wedding thing, showing your girl your wings or whatever. I'm about to pry for more details when I realize that Harper is almost hyperventilating. I can ask about wings later.

Harper grasps her hands by her throat. "What do you want of me, oh angel?"

Whoa. Talk about a change of attitude. I have some angelic blood in me. I wonder if I can sprout the wings from time to time. Another item to research later.

"We're here for a magical book—a codex," says Lincoln. "It's supposed to be hidden in Headmaster Prescott's library. However, we checked all over his office and couldn't find anything."

Harper grips her elbows and sways. "This is a lot to take in."

Lincoln steps closer. "We need your help. Could there be another library on the island?"

Harper stares at the ground for a long minute before she mentally regroups. "The teachers say that Headmaster Prescott used to be obsessed with his books. He changed, though. All he cares about these days is some lady."

Well. That's not helpful in the slightest.

"So nothing else on a library?" asks Lincoln.

"I'm afraid not."

Okay. Maybe Harper doesn't know anything more about a library, but perhaps she could help in other areas. "What do you know about Jeeves?"

"The old guy?"

"That's the one," says Lincoln. "If I wanted to get in touch with him, what would I do? Are there other boats we could take to the shore?"

"No, nothing. Jeeves is the only way to reach the island."

My shoulders slump. "That sucks."

"You're telling me." A shiver rolls across Harper's shoulders. "We're trapped here. No phone calls. No letters. No way back to the mainland. One girl tried swimming her way there, but she got hypothermia. It was only luck that the old guy grabbed her into his boat."

"I see." Lincoln's eyes gleam with promise. *My man's working on a plan. I can tell.* "That's very useful information. Thank you, Harper."

"So that's all you need me for?"

"Only one more thing. Never tell anyone what you saw today. The fact that people like me exist is a great secret. And if you find out anything about the codex or the boatman, find us and let us know right away."

"I will. I promise."

Lincoln takes my hand. "Let's get to the docks. Quickly." We race off into the woods, leaving a stunned Harper standing on the practice green.

"That was nice of you to allow her to keep her memory," I say.

"I wish I could take credit for being kind, but I'm not. We might need her again before this is all over." He rubs his hand over his shoulder, and the wings disappear, which is a bummer.

It takes me a few beats to stop focusing on the missing wings and go back to what this means for Harper. I know my guy well enough to know that he doesn't break tradition easily. Lincoln has more in store for Harper. "So that means...what?"

"Once this is all over, I'll come back and wipe her memory clean." His hand tightens in mine. "As long as I live, no one except you will ever recall seeing my wings. They are the essence of my soul, and as such, they are yours alone to see."

I can't help it. My heart warms with those words. And even though we're racing off to find a crazy old man who may have a coin-shaped key to Hell, I can't help but feel mighty pleased with myself.

It's not every girl who gets to see her man's wings before her wedding day.

CHAPTER TWENTY

A

Lincoln leads us on a zigzag path through the woods. This is yet another bonus of being in a relationship with an expert hunter—you never get lost in the forest. In no time, we reach the dock. It's late morning now. A low mist hangs over the lake. The mainland lies hidden under a shroud of white. Above us, the sky hangs heavy with clouds.

There's no sign of Jeeves. Or whatever his real name is.

I turn to Lincoln. "How will we summon him?"

"Jeeves is a protector, just like Cryptan was. Once we're on his territory, he'll sense us."

"That's right. He said he could sense the items he protected as well as when people came close."

Too bad he didn't detect and block whoever killed him. A weight settles into my soul. Cryptan didn't deserve what happened to him.

Focus, Myla.

I press my palms into my eyes and get my head back into the game. A memory appears. "Harper told that story about the girl who almost drowned. That's what this is all about, isn't it?"

"Yes. Cryptan could tell when someone was approaching the Vault. Perhaps the boatman has a similar skill and used it to rescue the student."

"Makes sense."

"Only one way to know for certain." Lincoln marches onto the gravel-heavy shore, crouches down, and sets his hand in the water. When he speaks again, his voice is low and regal. "I call to the protector of Lucifer's coin. You are needed right away."

Long seconds pass. Nothing happens. Bummer.

I scan the shoreline. Lincoln's supposed to be teaching gym class right now. Will Prescott notice that my guy has taken off? Another agonizing minute passes before Lincoln leans back on his launches. "We're missing something." He looks over to me. "Any ideas?"

Rubbing my neck, I consider the possibilities. "No offense, but maybe it's you."

His brows lift. "It's never me."

"Seriously. I'm certain that the old dude noticed my tail before. Did he ever look at you strangely?"

"Not at all."

"So, maybe he can sense my supernatural side more easily. My great scala-ness. Let me give it a try." Kneeling beside Lincoln, I gently set my hand into the water. Cold liquid prickles across my skin. I'm about to repeat the words that Lincoln said when my tail decides to get into the act. With a great splash, it dive-bombs into the lake, sending a plume of spray over Lincoln and me. *Looks like someone is excited to get into the action.* I roll my eyes. "Thanks, boy."

Suddenly, a rhythmic splashing echoes across the lake. My heart kicks into overdrive. That's definitely the sound of oars hitting the water...And I didn't even say anything. A moment later, the small red rowboat breaks through the mist. It's Jeeves.

I exhale and turn to Lincoln. "We were right. He is definitely a protector, same as Cryptan."

"And he's still here, which means that the coin remains."

The boat moves smoothly across the water until it pulls up beside the dock. Jeeves tosses a heavy rope across one of the cleats, keeping his small vessel in place. Lincoln and I rush to stand nearby on the dock. This is the kind of conversation you want to whisper.

"Good morrow to you both." Jeeves looks as old and wrinkly as ever. His gray beard seems extra-fluffy today. "I can greet you properly now, Great Scala."

That's a shocker. "You know who I am?"

"I've been alive a long time. I've met a Scala before. Your energy is unique." Jeeves pulls the lapels of his blue pea coat more tightly around him. "What can I do for you both?"

"We're looking for Lucifer's coin," says Lincoln.

"Sorry to say, that's hidden on the island. Even I don't know exactly where it is."

Wait, what? "So what are you protecting, exactly?"

"Access to the island. It's enchanted so this boat's the only way on or off."

My bullshit-o-meter is going off in a big way. "And that's it."

Lincoln folds his arms over his chest. "He also guards the incantation."

Jeeves shudders. "That's right. I guard the parchment that contains the incantation. The coin is no good without it."

"And where is that incantation, exactly?" asks Lincoln.

I raise my pointer finger. "Good question."

Jeeves twists his gnarly fingers through his beard. "Let me think, now. I gave the parchment away words out once, a long time ago. Can't remember the name, actually."

"Try harder." Lincoln's talking about an octave lower than normal. He's getting pissed.

"Ah, I remember. I gave it to a thrax male many hundreds of years ago. He had a spell." His face crinkles into a hopeful look. "He didn't get the coin, though. No one's found that yet."

"And the name of the dude you gave it to?" I cross my fingers. Maybe Dad got bad intel. He could have coughed up that parchment to anyone. It didn't have to be Acca.

Jeeves stares at his hands. "King Archard the Bloody."

Oh crap.

Bloody Archard. Even I've heard of that guy. He was the last Acca king and a real bastard, too. In fact, Bloody Archard was the whole reason Aquila had to haul her archangel cookies down to Antrum in the first place. She defeated Bloody Archard, fell in love with a thrax named Ryder, had some kids, and—BOOM—the House of Rixa was born.

I try to process all this awfulness. Total fail. "Let me get this straight. You definitely gave incantation to a thrax from the House of Acca?"

"I'm afraid so." Jeeves moans. "He tricked me. Used magic."

"Does Aquila know?" I ask. "Can she give us a new incantation?"

"I never told her," says Jeeves.

"You're kind of a shitty protector, you know that?"

"Why should I upset her? There was nothing to be done, anyway. Once the incantation is set, it cannot be changed. And for hundreds of years after I handed over the parchment, nothing came of it. I figured the knowledge died with Bloody Archard."

"The House of Acca doesn't lose knowledge," says Lincoln. "They pass it down, storing it up for the right time to use it."

"I'm so sorry." Jeeves's voice cracks. "I knew I should have never have even spoken to Bloody Archard, but my work here is so lonesome. Bloody Archard said he wanted to share words, not take the coin. I had no idea I was opening myself up to a compulsion spell." He leans forward in the boat, and the motion is so dramatic, the little vessel starts wobbling. "Let me make it up to you. There must be something I can do."

"You can tell us about Prescott," says Lincoln.

I shoot Lincoln a thumbs-up. "Another good call." My guy is on a total roll today. "He's got the hots for this so-called Lady of his. Know anything about her?"

"Ah, yes, the Lady. I rowed her back and forth for a few weeks about, ah, six months ago."

"What can you tell us about her?" asks Lincoln.

"She is a vision of beauty. I can see why Prescott favored her. They still write dozens of love letters each day." He reaches into his pea coat. "I have one of them here." Jeeves pulls out a small, familiar-looking envelope.

"I've seen those before. Prescott has an entire drawer of them in his office." I shiver. "They aren't great reading."

Lincoln smirks. "Then I'll take a look, since you're so squeamish." He takes the letter, opens it, and scans the contents. My guys' face turns a little green. I'm so mature I don't even tease him about it.

"Enjoying that letter?" *Okay, maybe I tease him a little.*

"Well, that was way too much information."

"Yeah, I think all the letters from the Lady are like that." I return my attention to Jeeves. "Do you have any letters from Prescott?"

"None, Great Scala."

"How about the Lady?" I ask. "Anything else we should know?"

"She was a lust demon, or partly. Took me a while to figure it out. The Lady was always under a full body enchantment."

Lincoln folds his arms over his chest. "How can you tell? Those are impossible to see through."

"I've got a good eye, and the Lady was too perfect. I rowed her back and forth every day. Never was there a hair out of place. Never saw a drop of grime on her heels. Too perfect. That's the sign of a full body enchantment."

I let out a low whistle. That kind of magick is tricky stuff. It's also not typical for a lust demon. "How do you know she's a lust demon?"

"Well…" Jeeves starts squirming again. "You may not like this, miss."

"I can take it like a girl."

"I've been around my share of lust demons. I know how they work, and the way Prescott reacted around the Lady? It's the same way he reacted when you set foot into my boat. The man turned downright lustful."

Now, my shields go *way up.* "Hey, now. I wasn't acting seductively."

"You don't need to," says Lincoln. "You're part lust demon."

I open my mouth, ready to argue. Unfortunately, Lincoln has a point. I've always known I was supposed to have powers over lust and wrath. The wrath stuff came easily, yet lust? That ability only kicked in after I met Lincoln. "Do you think it could have affected him?"

"I can say from personal experience that it absolutely did." Lincoln chuckles. "I was drawn to you from the first moment I saw you."

"That was different." For the record, Lincoln saw me while I was chasing demons around at night. That's what I consider a highly seductive situation. Not like, say, sitting in a boat, minding my own business.

"Yes," says Lincoln slowly. "It was."

Our gazes lock for a long second, and I'm so very, very happy I found Lincoln.

Jeeves clears his throat. "Well, whatever power you have, Prescott acted the same way around you as the Lady. Word is, the man was once a scholar. But ever since he came here, everything has been about that woman."

His words echo through my mind in strange ways. *It's all about his Lady.* Harper said something like that as well.

Suddenly, some of the thoughts I'd been struggling with fall right into place. I grip Lincoln's arm. "I know where the codex is."

"Where?"

"It's in his library."

"I thought you said you checked that."

"I checked his old library." I'm so excited I bounce on the balls of my feet. "But that was the old Prescott. The new Prescott wouldn't see his library as being filled with scholarly books. It would be his collection of her letters."

"The messages from the Lady?"

"Yes, he had them all in his desk. The moment I saw the drawer, I thought the codex could have fit inside it. After I started reading the letters, I got so put off that I gave up." I pound my leg with my fist. "How did I miss that?"

"After reading one of those letters myself, I can't say I blame you." Lincoln wipes his hand off on his jacket, as if simply holding one of those letters made his skin filthy.

I turn to Jeeves. "You've been super-helpful, thanks. We have to run now."

"Whenever you need me, just touch the water again."

"I will." I start to turn away, but then remember something. "Is your real name Jeeves?"

"No, Great Scala. It's Jarl. Prescott wanted something that would be more in keeping with the school."

"I like Jarl, actually."

Lincoln clears his throat. "How about we get back to business?"

Oh yeah. That. I focus on Lincoln. "We better hightail it back to Prescott's office."

"I even know a shortcut."

"You're awesome."

We race off into the forest, hand in hand. Both of us are smiling our faces off because we're about to find this stupid codex. After that, we can get our asses back to Antrum, lock up Aldred, and have an awesome wedding. Not that I know what the moms have planned for us.

As I run along, I'm almost tempted to skip, I'm so happy. That's when a little voice inside my head reminds me that even if we do find the codex, Lucifer's coin is still out there somewhere. It won't be much of a wedding if there's no one left in the after-realms but demons.

I set that thought aside. *First things first.*

And right now, that *first thing* is sneaking back into Prescott's office.

CHAPTER TWENTY-ONE

A

Lincoln leads me on another wackadoo set of paths through the forest. Note to universe: even though I'm number one, a girl, and number two, running past trees, I have yet to trip on a fucking thing. *So nyah.* In short order we're right back by Prescott's fancy pants HQ. I pause, my eyes widening with surprise.

The clearing outside the place is mobbed.

Students, faculty, and guards are all making a mad dash past the headmaster's office and toward Jamboree Hall. It's a super-strange sight. Normally, everyone shuffles around in small groups, looking terrified. Right now, they're as excited as if someone was handing out demon bars nearby...Or whatever it is that humans value.

"What's going on?" I ask Lincoln. "Is this a faculty event thingy?"

"Not that I know of. Perhaps the other students are staging an insurrection." A blissed-out girl rushes past us. "They certainly look happy enough."

"Are you kidding? Folks here can hardly organize themselves to make eye contact, let alone revolt against Prescott." I pause and tap my chin. "Although, I haven't been super-chatty with any of the other students yet. Maybe they're secretly badass."

"Only one way to find out."

More people run past. I tap the shoulders of no less than three students, trying to get their attention. Everyone ignores me. I look over to Lincoln, who's been trying to do the same thing. No one's talking to him, either, and he's supposed to be a teacher. Frustration constricts my neck.

It's Friday morning. We have until sundown today to get that codex to Antrum's courts. There's no time to get caught up in student-body drama.

I'm calling in my secret weapon.

Angling my head over my shoulder, I talk from one side of my mouth. "Go get me one, boy."

Lincoln grins. "Hey, now. Did you just give your tail an order?" That man does so love it when I'm sneaky.

"Mmmmmmaybe."

Another student jogs right by me. Clasping my hands behind my back, I pretend to be fascinated by the clouds. It's important to look innocent at times like this. The moment the girl is level with me, my tail juts out and yanks on her kneecap. Because she's human, she doesn't see a thing. Well, other than the pavement coming toward her face.

Ah, the things I do to save the after-realms.

Before the girl can topple over, I step in to steady her, making sure to get a tight grip on her upper arm. "Are you all right?"

"Fine. Excuse me." She wiggles in my grasp, but I am not letting go until I get some answers.

Lincoln moves to stand before both of us. "Juliana. I thought I asked the class to return to their cabins."

Huh. Leave it to Lincoln to have everyone's names memorized after a day. I eye Juliana from head to toe, trying for some sense of recognition. If Lincoln asked her to return to her cabin, then Juliana must be in my gym class. She's blonde haired, brown eyed, and pretty. I vaguely remember her.

Maybe.

Okay, I have no idea who this chick is.

What can I say? I'm more of a warrior than a secret agent. In my defense, though, my classmates were only marching around in circles, so it's not like I got a quality look at them.

"We did return to our cabins," explains Juliana. "The guards just came and got us. We're going treasure hunting today. And the headmaster has upped the prize. All the students who help can make a ten-minute call...To anyone they want!"

My brows lift. A ten-minute call is a big deal here. "Define treasure hunting."

Juliana bobs a bit on the balls of her feet. "The headmaster is digging some hole on the east side of the island." She pulls harder against me. "I have to go. They're handing out shovels and work gear in Jamboree Hall as we speak. We don't have a lot of supplies, so if I don't get there soon, I won't be able to pitch in." She lowers her voice. "Please. I really want to call my parents."

Damn. She's so wide-eyed and pathetic it's like trying to hold back a puppy. "I think that's all we needed to know. What do you think, Linc—" I clear my throat. "I mean, do you need anything else, Mr. Prince?"

"One last question before you go," says Lincoln. "Do you know what you're digging for?"

"It's some kind of artifact." Juliana's eyes widen. "A coin. That's it."

Lincoln and I share a knowing look. *Great.* We're finally about to get off this freaking island, and now is when Prescott rallies to find Lucifer's coin. The *"come to Acca"* talk last night with Blaze must have really lit a fire under his butt.

Thanks for nothing, universe.

I let go of Juliana's arm. "Good luck." She takes off like a shot for Jamboree Hall. I set my palms on my eyes. "Do you ever wonder if maybe we're cursed?"

Lincoln chuckles. "In my opinion, our glass is half full."

"How do you figure that?"

Lincoln sets his hands on my shoulders and angles me toward Prescott's office. "Everyone's off at the dig. There are no guards at the office door."

"Oh, yeah." A zing of happy moves through my nervous system. "Let's do this."

"Great scalas first."

Smiling, I rush up the short flight of steps to the front door and try the handle. *Unlocked, yes!* After pushing the door open, I peep into the office. The place looks exactly like it did before—all burnished steel and disinfected perfection. "No one's in here." I step inside.

Lincoln follows close behind me. "Where did you say the codex might be hidden?"

"In the place Prescott truly considers his library." I gesture toward Prescott's desk. "His collection of Lady letters is in here." Plunking down in the chair, I yank on the largest handle. The drawer slides open with ease. All those ooey-gooey love notes still remain in their perfect little stacks. A shiver of disgust rolls over my shoulders. There's no unseeing what was written in that message. Sweaty post-sex chest hair.

Moving on.

I shake my head, forcing my mind to focus on the task at hand. I dig out the letters with gleeful abandon. Haphazard piles of envelopes build up on the floor. Sweet. If nothing else, it will give Prescott something to clean up later. And if the headmaster freaks out that someone was rifling through his office? We'll be long gone.

Lincoln steals closer. "Tell me the codex is in there."

I dig out more letters and find nada. Disappointment weighs on my shoulders. "Not yet. But the drawer is really long." Leaning forward, I jam my arm shoulder-deep into the drawer.

Still nothing.

Panic tightens up my rib cage. What if I totally miscalled this one? If we don't find the codex, then Lincoln and I could go to jail, which would really suck…And not only for personal reasons. Together, we'd have a much better chance to stop Lucifer's coin from releasing Hell on Earth. That is, assuming Prescott digs up the coin in the first place.

I sigh. The way my day is going? Prescott's totally going to dig that thing up.

At last, my fingertips brush something smooth and hard. My tail does a happy dance. "Yes!"

"You've got something?"

"I think so."

Moving quickly, I haul out more letters than ever before. Angling my head, I look into the depths of the desk drawer. A glint of white shell appears in the back corner. Bit by bit, I slowly pull the object out. It's a magical codex, all right. Lifting the item up, I scan the bottom for the runes that mark it as ours.

"This is our codex, all right." I smile so hard, my cheeks hurt.

A little bubble of happy seems to descend around me. It's getting to be late Friday morning. Lincoln and I still have enough time to get the codex into the court, submit it as evidence, and put Aldred into a nasty little dungeon for the rest of his natural-born life.

Nyah part deux.

Lincoln's grinning, too. He offers me his fist to bump. "Good work, Myla."

Before I can raise my arm, my tail swoops in, the arrowhead-end curving as it knocks into Lincoln's fist. I can only chuckle. My tail is such a ham.

Lincoln's gaze locks with mine. A warm feeling seeps through my chest as my little bubble of happiness expands. For the first time in days, I contemplate all the wonderful things in our joint future. The wedding. Starting a family. Throwing Aldred into prison. Nothing but fun times. Sure, the coin is still floating around. That said, the only reason the coin's a problem is Aldred. Once he's locked up, we should be golden.

But none of that will start until we get our asses out of here. Cradling the codex against my chest, I march toward the door, pausing beside coatrack where Prescott had a collection of jackets and stuff.

"Are you cold?" asks Lincoln.

"Nope. I need something to carry this codex." I spot a leather backpack. "This will do perfectly." *Oooh, it's Prada too.* My BFF Cissy's been teaching me about these human things. I zip open the bag. It doesn't look like anything special. Then again, what I don't know about fashion is a lot. I slip the codex inside, zip it back up, and hoist the pack onto my shoulders. "There now, all set. How close is the nearest Pulpitum?"

"Not far, once the boatman takes us across the lake."

"Makes sense. I suspected that Dad was driving in circles to get here."

"Your father is a total gear head. Xavier knows almost as much about human automobiles as he does about demons."

"Wow." That's all I can say because Dad knows a ton about demons.

We step outside. The moment fresh air hits me, my skin prickles with awareness. *Something's not right here.* First of all, finding the codex was way too easy. Second, the courtyard is deserted now. Presumably, everyone's digging holes on another part of the island. That's not what has my danger-radar going off, though. An odd tension hangs in the air. I'm no expert in hunting, but I think we're being watched. I pause just outside the door. "Someone's out there."

Lincoln stands beside me, his mouth thinning to a line. "Yes."

"Should we run for the dock?"

"No, they're thrax. They'll catch up to us in the woods. Better to face them here."

My eyes almost bug out of my head. I don't know how Lincoln knows who's watching us. Still, I have no doubt that he's spot-on about them being thrax. It's all part of the expert-hunter thing he's got going on. I clasp the straps of my backpack more tightly.

Crap on a cracker. Thrax.

Lincoln kisses my cheek. "Let's see who's lurking, eh?"

"Sounds like a plan to me."

Lincoln and I move to stand at the top of the stairs leading to Prescott's office. We both look out over the clearing. It looks like a bunch of grass and trees to me. Lincoln focuses on one particular section, though. "We can see you, you know."

Actually, I can't see dick, but I'm not volunteering that fact.

A few long seconds pass before Blaze strides out from the exact spot that Lincoln had been inspecting. Once again, I decide that Blaze could be handsome if it weren't for the oversized attitude and man-bun. He strides across the clearing and pauses at the base of the stairs. I really, really, really want to jump on his head in a pile-driver-style slam, but it's

probably better to take Lincoln's lead on this. My guy has more experience with the thrax, after all.

Although, the pile driver would feel really good. This Blaze guy is a creep.

"Greetings." Blaze only addresses Lincoln, which pisses me off.

Lincoln's stance stays still as stone. "What do you want?"

"Information. I'm told you're some kind of angelic warrior."

At those words, a wave of worry moves through me. Our amulets hide our true identity, even from thrax. In other words, there's only one way that Blaze could know about Lincoln being part angel. *Harper.* My muscles lock with a mixture of rage and fear. "How do you know that?" Blaze ignores me. I'm hating the guy more by the second. "I asked you a question."

He still ignores me. The guy is so getting extra pain because of that.

"Answer her," orders Lincoln.

Blaze doesn't bother to look my way when he replies. "I have my sources."

"Don't play coy. What did you do with Harper?"

"Concerned about your fellow student?"

"Just answer the question, knob head."

"She's right here." Blaze waves his hand. The other four Acca warriors step out from the woods. All of them still wear their black body armor with the Acca insignia on their chests. Harper limps along in the center of group. My heart cracks at the sight of her. Harper's face is tear-stained, and her jacket's been torn almost in half. One of the Acca warriors holds a knife to her throat.

"This girl says she saw an angelic warrior." Blaze points to Lincoln. "I'm guessing you're a thrax who's hiding under some kind of charm." He nods toward me. "And you're his thane."

What a dick. Thanes are little better than slaves. "I am *so* not his thane."

Blaze chuckles like that was a really cute thing for a little girl like me to say. "You two must be a wayward demon patrol, perhaps from the House of Gurith?"

Much as I hate to admit it, that's not a bad guess. Lincoln's mother Octavia is from Gurith. It's one of the few thrax houses that train women warriors. Even so, Gurith is one of the lesser houses. It's about a dozen levels below Rixa, which sets Lincoln's at the top of that particular pile. A small smile rounds my lips. Wait until we take these enchanted amulets off and show Blaze who we really are. He'll wet his battle armor.

I bite my lower lip to keep my yap shut. I'm dying to spill the beans.

If Lincoln's anxious to share, he doesn't show it. I swear, my guy could play poker professionally. When he speaks again, Lincoln's voice is super-calm. "It's true. I can lay claim to the House of Gurith."

Technically, my guy can lay claim to every thrax House in Antrum, but that's neither here nor there.

"Then, let's talk, one thrax to another." Blaze gestures to where Harper shivers between the hulking Acca warriors. "This human says you're here on some kind of quest. Now what could that be?" Blaze taps his chin dramatically before pointing to my backpack. "I'm guessing you have taken the codex from Prescott's office. You stole our Earl's property. You're rebel sympathizers."

I raise my hand. "Define *rebel*."

"The true ruling house of Antrum is not Rixa, but Acca. Aldred is our right and proper King. Anyone who declares otherwise supports a rebellion. As a lesser house, you would do well to align yourselves with us, here and now."

Meaning, he wants us to just hand over the codex. Like that'll happen.

"No," says Lincoln.

A muscle flexes along Blaze's square jawline. I decide that he has a head shaped like a marshmallow. "You would deny the true King?"

I roll my eyes. "Come on. Rixa took the throne like five hundred years ago. You really need to adapt to reality."

"Perhaps you're the one who needs to change," says Blaze slowly.

"Let me clear things up. For the record, we're totally in league with Rixa. And you're not getting your hands on this codex. Like ever."

Lincoln's voice takes on a deadly tone. "Let me share with you what happens next. You're going to let us go. After that, you're turning yourselves in to the nearest Pulpitum to admit your crimes and plead for mercy."

Now, this is why my guy is total king material. My first reaction was to squish Blaze into a bloody pulp. Lincoln wants to give him and his cronies a chance to turn themselves in. Totes noble.

Blaze slides his hands lower on his hips. My brows lift. That's a classic thrax battle move, right there. Their body armor hides about a dozen mini knives and nunchuks by their upper thighs. "I'll give you one more chance, Gurith. There are five of us and two of you. Do you really think you can win?" He pauses for dramatic effect. "Now, hand over the codex and join our side."

Lincoln and I share a long look. I know what he's thinking because it's the same thing that I am.

That's the stupidest request in the history of ever.

We're about to say just that when Prescott wanders into the clearing. I blink, not sure what I'm seeing.

Prescott's here, really?

Things are about to get interesting again. And in my life, that's bad news.

CHAPTER TWENTY-TWO

$\mathcal{A}$

Maybe I'm seeing things. And by *things*, I mean Prescott strolling into an almost battleground with Acca. Just to be sure the headmaster's really here, I pinch myself. Hard.

Aaaaaaaand… Nope.

Prescott's still standing around.

Bleugh.

I eye the headmaster carefully. His usually pristine white shirt is streaked in filth. In his arms, he lovingly cradles what looks like a clump of dirt. Pure joy lights up his Ken-doll-style features.

This is such bad news.

Why? There's only one reason Prescott would look super-happy about dirt. That clump of earth must hold Lucifer's coin. Their dig was successful.

Prescott rushes up to Blaze. "There you are! I've found a cache of the most amazing angelic artifacts. You must come and see."

"Headmaster Prescott!" Harper waves manically from her spot between the two Acca warriors. "Over here!" It's not the smartest of moves, considering one of the warriors has a knife against her throat. Harper could stab herself in the jugular by mistake.

"Whoa there, Harper. Let me get his attention for you." I make a circle with my thumb and pointer finger, jam the shape into my mouth, and whistle super-loudly.

"What?" asks Prescott.

"Harper is here."

He's still not looking at her, though. He stares between Lincoln and me. "Why aren't both of you in class?"

"Because Harper has a knife against her throat." It's also why I'm standing here versus kicking ass, but there's no point overloading Prescott with details. The man is so obsessed with his Lady there's hardly room in his brain for much else.

At last, Prescott spots Harper and gasps. "What's all this?"

Blaze speaks without breaking his eye-lock with Lincoln. "You need to leave, Headmaster."

"Absolutely not." Prescott wags his finger at Blaze. "We had a clear understanding. I would search for the coin while you stayed on your side of the island. No interfering with my students. Blast it all, I even hid your silly codex for you. I've more than kept up my side of the bargain. Now, tell your men to set Harper loose."

My eyes widen with surprise. So far, I haven't exactly been a huge fan of Prescott. That said, I'm pleased that he's trying to do the right thing here. At least so far.

"No." Blaze snaps his fingers. "Secure her."

Instantly, the Acca warriors get busy tying Harper to a tree. My muscles flinch as I look for a break where that damned knife is away from Harper's throat. When it comes to battle, Lincoln and I don't need much of an attack window. That said, we do need one.

Unfortunately, Acca warriors are really good at tying Harper to a tree while keeping a knife right at her jugular. It's almost beyond belief. All they need is a train track, long mustaches, and a cry of *mwah-hah-hah*. With that, their scene of evil would be complete.

Prescott stomps his loafer-clad foot. "I said to release her, not tie her up." He wags his finger at the warrior with the knife. "And take that dagger away from her throat."

The Acca fighter simply shakes his head no. Seems like Blaze is the chatterbox of the team.

Blaze now does a total dick move. Taking advantage of the fact that Prescott's back is turned away from him and toward Harper, he starts going in for a kill. Quick as a whip, Blaze hunches over to pull a dagger from the sheath on his leg. Prescott keeps up his foot-stomping routine, totally oblivious to the danger, his back a perfect target for Blaze.

Wow. What humans don't know about battle is a lot.

Lincoln sees the move, same as I do. My guy lunges forward. With a graceful swoop of his arm, Lincoln grabs Blaze's wrist and prevents him from unsheathing the weapon. We can't stop the knife-wielding thrax who's threatening Harper, but at least we can do this.

"I thought we were discussing a possible alliance." The lines of Lincoln's face are tight with fury. "I don't negotiate with thrax who kill humans."

Blaze features turn tense with rage. "You don't want this kind of trouble, man of Gurith. I've killed Furor dragons in hand-to-hand combat." The weapon wobbles in Blaze's grasp. It doesn't fall, though. "You know what that means. I've battled fully grown dragon demons with wings. Think I can't take you?"

When Lincoln speaks, his voice comes out deep and deadly. "I know you can't."

A lead weight of worry settles into my stomach. Furor dragons are badass. I should know—I have a small part of their DNA rolling around in me. Anyone who can kill a Furor dragon is dangerous with a capital D. My guy's a great warrior and all. Even so, I've also seen how quickly someone can end up dead in a battle. All it takes is a moment and a mistake. I simply can't lose Lincoln. He's my heart.

Jumping forward, I land right by Lincoln's side. I glare at Blaze for all I'm worth. "Fuck with him, and you're in for a world of pain, my friend."

Blaze offers us a simpering smile. "Of course. We're still negotiating." He doesn't let go of his weapon, though. Jerk.

Prescott finally turns around. "Mr. Prince. Missy."

"Mysteria," I snarl. No way am I ever letting that drop.

"What are you doing?" Prescott's eyes slowly widen. "Wait. You're from the after-realms, too. Aren't you?"

"Yeah, well…" I debate about explaining what's really going on, but decide that it's way too much trouble. "We are."

At the same time, Blaze keeps his eye-lock going with Lincoln. Now this feels like safer territory to yours truly. It's really a bad idea to get into a staring contest with my fiancé. Lincoln has a way of glaring into someone's soul. It breaks his opponents every time.

Blaze is no exception. He soon opens his hand, allowing his dagger to slip back into its sheath. "May we continue our discussion of a possible alliance?" Blaze's voice shakes a little. I consider that a small victory.

"We may." Lincoln releases his grip on Blaze. The Acca warrior stands upright and shrugs like it's no big deal Lincoln just stopped him.

You fool no one, Man-Bun Dude.

"I'll give you another sign of my good faith," says Blaze.

"Go on."

"I'll release the young girl and her headmaster. Will that help?"

"Very much so."

Blaze turns to the headmaster. "Untie the girl, and you both may leave."

"No." Prescott's holding his ground, but it's obvious how his entire body trembles. "I have the coin with me, just as you ordered." He raises the clump of dirt in his hands.

My jaw drops. *Hells bells. Now he tells us.*

Prescott lifts his chin. "Before I'll do anything, I want your assurance that I'll see the Lady again." His eyes glaze over with a hungry look. "I need her."

Since the whole "*I'm from the after-realms thing*" is out in the open, I'm going for broke. "What you're feeling, Prescott? That's called a lust demon enchantment, my friend. You need a curse breaker, not more time with this Lady of yours."

Harper writhes under her bindings. Angry red welts are appearing around her wrists, neck, and legs as she twists. The knife is still being held dangerously close to her throat. "Get me out of here. We have to run!"

I shoot Harper a hearty thumbs-up. Leave it to the ginger girl to talk sense here. "Hang tough, Harper. We'll get you in a minute."

Harper moans softly. Tears stream down her cheeks. The warrior's blade pricks her throat. A thin dribble of blood runs down the pale column of her neck. Every cell in my body wants to leap over and free her now.

Screw this. I'm doing it.

I firm up my footing, ready to lunge. Lincoln's hand gently wraps around my wrist. Our gazes lock.

"Not yet," he whispers.

I grit my teeth. *Hells bells, he's right.* Harper's safe enough for the moment, and we need information while we can still get it. *Not to mention grabbing that damned coin.* I force myself to nod.

Blaze smiles breezily. "You want this over, Prescott? You know the price. Give me the coin."

"It's right here." Prescott holds up the clod of dirt. "I won't hand it over, though. Not until you vow to give me access to my Lady. Use one of those magical promises."

Blaze tilts his head. "What you're holding doesn't look like any coin."

"Warriors." Prescott brushes away some of the caked-on dirt. "You have no imagination." Within seconds, a gleam of gold appears. The coin is about the size of a coaster and covered in Latin writing. Now that the thing is uncovered, its power starts to break free as well. Even from this distance, I can feel the energy. It reminds me of the last time I held something Lucifer made—his orb.

No question about it. That's Lucifer's coin, all right.

Suddenly, my skin feels too tight for my body. This coin could release an army from Hell, including Armageddon himself. And it's really here.

Damn.

Talk about being stuck between a rock and a hard place. On one hand, I already have the codex that will prevent my fiancé and me from ending up in prison. It needs to go to Antrum, pronto. On the other hand, I still have to get a coin that could destroy all the after-realms.

I straighten my spine. There's no question. There must be a way to reach both objectives. That's all there is to it.

Blaze starts grinning his face off. "That's the coin, all right. Hand it over. Now."

Prescott grips the golden disc against his chest. "Not until you promise me, my Lady. I won't tell you again."

Blaze chuckles. "You're in no position to negotiate. You never have been." He snaps his fingers twice. It's some kind of signal because one of the Acca soldiers instantly raises his arm. A throwing dagger gleams in the warrior's uplifted hand. My breath catches.

He's going to kill Prescott. And this time, we're too far away to stop it.

Although the motion only takes seconds, time seems to slow to a crawl as the soldier lowers his arm and sets loose the small throwing dagger. The blade spins through the air before embedding itself in Prescott's back. I shiver.

The headmaster crumples to the ground, dead. Harper's soft weeping echoes across the clearing. I'm not exactly broken up over the guy's death, but that was a crap kill. There's a reason calling someone a backstabber is an insult.

Lincoln clearly agrees with me. "Where's your honor?" he snarls. "The man wasn't a warrior."

Blaze shrugs. "He deserved to die. This is my patrol territory. Here I am judge, jury, and executioner."

"You're also a coward," says Lincoln. "If you're man enough to take someone's life, then you can look them in the eye while you do it."

"Please. I gave the man a chance, which is what you wanted. Should I coddle him all day?" Blaze strolls over to Prescott's prone body and kicks the corpse over. You'd think the guy would have a little more sense of urgency, considering who we are.

Oh, that's right. Blaze doesn't know who we are yet.

Blaze leans over Prescott's body. Lucifer's coin still sits in the dead headmaster's hand. Blaze scoops up the coin and sighs. "At last, we have succeeded in our mission." He slips the coin into a pocket on his body armor. "My Lord Aldred will be pleased."

I stare at the pocket that currently holds Lucifer's coin. His *"Lord Aldred"* is never getting his hands on that thing. I make a silent vow: Lincoln and I are not leaving this clearing without that coin.

One of the Acca soldiers gestures toward Harper. "What do you want to be done with her?"

"That depends." Blaze returns his attention to Lincoln and me. "We need to finish our negotiations first. Have you considered my offer? You must see that there is no other choice. Aldred already has the incantation to activate Lucifer's coin. Our elders secured it ages ago. Once Aldred has the actual item in his possession, Acca will take the throne of Antrum."

"That's your offer?" Lincoln's features are still as stone. My guy's pissed, all right.

"I'll sweeten the deal. You seem to know this human girl. If you swear fealty to Acca right now, I might let her live."

My brows lift. *Wow, is that ever a crap deal.* Ally with a psychopath and you maybe—just maybe—won't kill someone? This dude is delusional.

Lincoln turns to me and sets his hand at his throat. "What do you say, Mysteria?" My guy doesn't have to say another word. I know exactly what he's thinking here. He wants us to take off our amulets and reveal our true identities.

Man, I am ever down with that concept.

"Yup." I twiddle my fingers by my neck. "I'm with you."

Lincoln and I turn back to face Blaze. Moving in unison, we grip the silver chains around our necks and yank the amulets off. Both charms fall onto the wooden step beneath us with a *clunk.*

The lines of Blaze's square face soften with shock. The other Acca warriors freeze. I can't help but gloat a little.

That's one super-satisfying sight, right there.

Lincoln straightens his shoulders and goes into what I call his royal mode. "I am Lincoln Vidar Osric Aquilus, High Prince of the thrax and future consort to the great scala. You have one chance to give up the coin and the girl. If you do this now, I'll allow you all to live."

My tail waves to them over my shoulder. "And I'm the Great Scala and future Queen of Antrum. Normally, I'd have killed you already. That said, my guy here wants to chat, so..." I bob my head, considering. "You've got about two minutes, tops."

"Demon!" hisses Blaze. "I'll enjoy slicing that slimy tail from your backside, bitch."

Over my shoulder, my tail gives Blaze a modified version of an obscene hand gesture. I nod in agreement. "That's right, boy." I glare at Blaze. "Respect the tail."

Lincoln moves to stand beside me. "This is your last chance, Blaze." Even though his words are hard edged, Lincoln's demeanor stays calm and controlled. "Surrender now."

Blaze's chest heaves as he considers his reply. Still, the guy doesn't even need to open his big yap. I can already tell that he's going to shoot us down.

Nice.

My thoughts slip into battle mode as my inner wrath demon roars to life. Every tree, wall, and stone falls into an intricate web of possible attack vectors. My battle plans deepen. Different offensive moves flicker through my mind's eye. There are no less than four different strategies that I could use to take these guys down while getting that knife away from Harper's throat.

I nod once to myself, the decision made. I'm going with the assault plan that uses my tail the most. After all, my backside is still making lewd gestures at Blaze. That only happens when it's super pissed. Best to let my boy get out some ya-yas.

Lincoln and I lock gazes. We've had situations like this on demon patrol before. I hitch my thumb toward my tail and then toward the other Acca warriors. The question is there but unspoken. *Can I set him loose on those guys?*

Lincoln gives me the barest of nods. *Yes.*

I bob a little on the balls of my feet. Lincoln will go after Blaze while my tail and I take out everyone else.

This is going to be so awesome I can't stand it.

Blaze pulls out two long daggers and raises them high. "Kill the usurper!"

I roll my eyes. "Finally."

The other Acca warriors take up the cry and rush toward us. In response, I leap straight up into the air, my favorite battle cry on my lips. "Eat death!"

Meanwhile, Lincoln ignites his baculum as a long sword made of white angel fire. He rushes down the steps toward Blaze.

I'm a big fan of mixing in acrobatics with my battle plans, so I take care to do an aerial flip before I plant both my sensible schoolgirl flats right onto the chest of the Acca warrior nearest Blaze. He tumbles backward onto his ass. I'd give that fall about a six out of ten, tops.

Now, if I were wearing my battle boots, I would have crunched a few ribs with the impact, too. That would have pumped the rating up to a seven or eight. *Guess you can't have everything.* I'm just happy to be kicking ass and taking names.

Lincoln's now in a heated swordfight with Blaze. I hate to admit this, but Blaze is actually really good with a sword and hand-to-hand combat. His words about killing a Furor demon come back to me. My heart leaps into my throat.

The three remaining Acca warriors get out their throwing darts and start chucking stuff in my direction. *Bring it on.* This is like crack for my tail, which has a grand old time batting the weapons away from me. My backside moves so fast, it's basically a blur. At the same time, the first warrior—aka the one I knocked unconscious with my landing—is still lying like a lump on the ground. He won't be battle-ready again any time soon, so I run toward the trio of dagger chuckers.

One down. Three to go.

I quickly size up the three remaining Acca warriors. These guys are total projectile junkies. They're standing in a perfect formation for me to take them down—one, two, three.

It's so sweet I almost want to cry.

My power of demonic wrath rushes through my bloodstream, giving me extra strength and speed. I crouch down again, leap up even higher into the air, and land on the first Acca warrior's back with a *thud*. There's a snapping noise as some bones break. That guy isn't getting up anytime soon.

Two down. Two to go.

Standing up, I go into a Thai kick, slamming my shin into the face of another Acca fighter. His nose crunches as I break it. My tail takes a breather from deflecting projectiles to wrap around the dude's neck and smash his head into a nearby tree trunk. The warrior goes down like a sack of potatoes.

Only one left.

The final warrior stares at me, dumbfounded. He's your standard Acca blondie with whip-strong limbs and a low IQ. He raises his hands in a defensive move. "Our prince says you will give us mercy if we surrender."

I glance over to Lincoln, who's still going at it with Blaze. They've now chopped through part of Prescott's office and downed half an oak tree. My fiancé is such a stand-up guy. He really would want this Acca scumbag to stay alive.

My tail swipes slowly behind me. "Fine. I won't kill you."

"Thank you, Great Scala."

I step up closer and raise my hands in a gesture that says, "*You're safe.*" The guy sighs.

That's when my tail goes to work and punches him right in the nuts. The dude hunches over and moans before falling to the ground. After that, the end of my tail balls into a fist and knocks the guy out cold.

And with that, I have kept my word. The guy isn't dead. That said, he won't be walking upright any time soon, though.

With warrior number four out of commission, I return my attention to the battle. Blaze and Lincoln are fighting it out under another massive oak tree with heavy branches. My tail goes berserk behind me. I pat the arrowhead end. "I know what you want to do, boy. I'm down with it."

I rush across the clearing and start scaling the massive tree. We don't have a lot of forests in Purgatory, and the ones that do exist have like two leaves. Long story short, they're really only good for climbing, which is why I can scale this trunk super-fast. Holding my arms out, I balance-walk out onto a limb that juts out right above Lincoln and Blaze.

Almost there.

Once I'm right above the action, I loop my tail around the branch beneath my feet. Blaze is heaving breaths now. He won't last much longer. Lincoln still looks pretty fresh, though. A warm sense of happy radiates through my chest. *Lincoln's winning.*

Blaze pulls a charm from his pocket, crushes it in his hand, and releases a poof of purple smoke right into Lincoln's face. My guy quickly counters by pulling out a charm of his own, but I don't like this. At all.

Blaze is fighting dirty.

Well, two can play at that game.

I step forward off the tree branch. My tail holds me in place as I swing around, stopping when I'm upside down and face-to-face with Blaze. The Acca warrior freezes. Blaze was so focused on fighting with Lincoln, he didn't see me coming.

Which is just how I like it.

"I'll say it one last time." I take care to use my most badass voice. "Respect the tail." Curling forward, I smack my supernaturally-tough head onto Blaze's. He stumbles backward, stunned. I jump to the ground, and my tail grips Blaze by the ankle. Twisting about, I spin and take my enemy along with me. Our 360-degree journey ends when Blaze's head smacks into another tree. He's knocked out cold.

Huh. It's like a concussion theme day here at the Wheeler Institute.

My tail lets go of Blaze's ankle and starts to do a happy dance over my shoulder. I pat the arrowhead end. "Good job, boy."

Lincoln extinguishes his baculum. Now, he holds two silver rods in his hand, nothing more. He chuckles. "'*Respect the tail.*' That's a good one."

My tail whips up to muss Lincoln's hair. They have their own love thing going. Well, as much love as can happen between a demonic tail and a hot prince. Most days, I try not to think about it too much. A few more seconds pass with my tail fawning over my fiancé before I yank it away. "That's enough, boy."

A mischievous gleam shines in Lincoln's mismatched eyes. "Why? Are you jealous?"

"No, not at all. We simply need to, you know, clean things up?" I so suck at lying.

"Yes, we do need to set things right." Lincoln's still working his sneaky-grin thing, but at least, he's letting the whole tail conversation die out, which I totally appreciate.

Stepping over to Blaze, I search through his pockets until I find the coin. It's about the size of my palm and cool to the touch. You'd never suspect this little item could bring on the end of the after-realms, yet that's the whole point of major magic, I suppose. It wouldn't work too well if it advertised itself. I zip open my backpack—which survived the battle like a champ, by the way—and slip the coin inside. A sense of relief washes through me.

"I think we did it," I say.

"Almost."

Suddenly, Blaze hops up to standing. It's like something out of a human horror movie. His face is crazed as he grips two fresh daggers. This time, he's ignoring Lincoln and running straight at me.

I want to move and fight, but seriously? What is this guy's deal? I mean, what kind of person has a head that thick? My tail really rammed his cranium into an oak tree, after all. It doesn't seem possible.

Lincoln reignites his baculum as a long sword. I blink hard, trying to get my thoughts back into battle mode. There's no real need, though. Before two full seconds have passed, Lincoln has run his long sword straight through Blaze's chest.

Couldn't happen to a nicer guy.

Blaze tumbles over, dead. Lincoln glares at the corpse. "No one goes after my future wife." He raises his baculum again, ready to strike.

I rush to Lincoln's side, setting my hand on his forearm, trying to calm my guy before he loses it entirely. It strikes me that Lincoln did the same for me, not so long ago, back when I wanted to go into berserker mode and free Harper early. "It's okay. You killed him."

Lincoln turns to face me, his eyes wild with rage. "He woke up out of nowhere and ran straight for you."

I gently guide his arm down. "I know. But you got him." I rest my palm on his cheek. "It's over now."

Lincoln heaves in a few breaths before nodding. "Right." Finally, Lincoln seems to snap out of his berserker funk. He extinguishes his baculum and sets both rods back into their holster. "It's just…Anyone attacking you, it makes me crazy."

I can only smile. "I got that."

Harper's weeping sounds from across the clearing snap us both out of our thoughts.

"Oh, crap." I sigh. "We forgot about Harper."

Lincoln and I rush over to her side. With a flick of my tail, Harper is free from her bindings. She hobbles away from the tree to stare at me, wide-eyed and frightened. "What…What are you going to do?"

It's a good question. Part of me wants to say my goodbyes, forget this school ever existed, and haul ass back to Antrum. That way, Lincoln and I can put the codex somewhere safe—along with the coin, of course—and then get on with our lives. That impulse quickly fades, however.

Even with the fact that time is running out, there's no way we're leaving here until I'm certain that Harper and the others are safe. I glance over at Lincoln. The resigned look on his face says it all.

"We're staying, aren't we?" I ask.

"Yes." He glances up at the sky. "We still have the afternoon left."

My stomach somersaults. The afternoon. And in that time, we have to secure the school and what's left of the Acca patrol. That part wouldn't be too hard, but it all depends on who has seen what. If we have to do memory wipes, it won't be easy. Those things are a massive time-suck to do on one human, let alone fifty. Staring directly into Harper's eyes, I give her my best "I got this" face. "Mr. Prince and I will talk care of everything." I wince. "Although, I have to be honest. Come tomorrow morning, you're not going to remember any of this. We have some magic mumbo jumbo that will erase any signs of strangeness, including your memory of the last week or so."

Harper hugs her elbows. "Good. Thank you."

Lincoln taps his chin. "Let's check the Acca warriors. They may have some charms that could help."

"Or we can run to the nearest Pulpitum and summon a thrax team to help us. You know, from the House of Rixa."

"Too risky. Gives the humans a chance to record all this somehow. We need to do basic damage control first. After that, we can summon a formal thrax patrol for cleanup."

Ah, cleanup. From time to time, humans see that thrax really exist. When that happens, there's a long list of protocols, spells, and traditions to follow. And it's all for good reasons, really.

I rub my neck in a weary rhythm. The court closes in a matter of hours. We have so much left to do, and I've never felt so tired. "I guess we better get to it, then." There's no mistaking the quiver in my voice. *Exhaustion.*

Ever since I met Lincoln, it's been nonstop craziness. And today is no different. Suddenly, all I want to do is hide somewhere and sleep for about a thousand years.

Lincoln pulls me to him in a deep hug. He's never felt warmer or more comforting. His voice sounds low and soothing in my ear. "I know this is a lot, Myla. Yet we've gotten this far, haven't we? At last, we have both the codex and the coin. Now, all we have to do is make sure the Wheeler Institute is safe and return to Antrum. From there, things should be easy."

I nod and nuzzle into his touch. *Yes, things should be easy.* A weight of worry settles into my stomach. *But for us, they never are, are they?*

CHAPTER TWENTY-THREE

A

Hours pass before Lincoln and I have the Wheeler Institute under some semblance of safety. In the end, we had to do a shit-ton of memory wipes. At least, we were able to raid the pockets of the Acca soldiers and steal their caches of memory charms. Even so, it took forever to wipe everyone. A student ran across the battle with Blaze, saw Prescott get killed, and freaked everyone else the fuck out. Someone already wrote the whole experience in her journal. Good thing we found that.

Once the wipes were complete and the Institute was relatively secure—including the nasty business of hiding dead or magically asleep bodies—we got Jeeves on guard duty. Mostly, his job is to hold down the fort until a Rixa thrax patrol could finish the cleanup.

With that done, we still needed to get the codex to Antrum before 5 p.m. Yipes. Lincoln knew of a nearby Pulpitum that could take us straight to the courtroom. After changing into our fighting gear, we rowed our own asses back to the mainland. There wasn't a lot of chatter between us. The air felt heavy with tension.

By the time Lincoln and I hit the opposite dock, the sun was already touching the horizon, so we ran full out to the Pulpitum. Turns out, the place was hidden inside what looks like a deserted barn.

Which brings us to where I am now: jogging closer to a Pulpitum-holding barn while I scan my surroundings. There are trees everywhere and no humans around. *Good.* I pat the backpack, ensuring the codex still remains safely inside. The weight feels solid against my palm. Worry still twists up my neck, though. The evidence in this thing simply has to work. There's no other option.

Lincoln and I step inside the deserted barn. The interior is rundown and empty. Everything smells like moldy hay and dust. Beams of dying sunlight poke through the gaps in the walls, casting odd patterns on the dirt floor. I haven't used a ton of Earth-based Pulpitums, but they're often in places like this: abandoned garages, ruined houses, that kind of thing. Barns are a particular favorite as they're also far away from the eyes of prying neighbors.

Lincoln cups his hand by his mouth. "This is Lincoln Vidar Osric Aquilus. Activating field station."

White laser beams pulse inside the deserted barn. Once the lights crisscross over Lincoln, the floor rustles under our feet. A large metal disc rises from the dirt. *The transfer platform.* I grip the straps of my backpack more tightly.

Only minutes remain to return this codex to the courthouse in Antrum.

A man's basso voice echoes through the chamber. The tone is familiar. It's Marty, the Pulpitum operator who helped us before. "Identity confirmed," says Marty. "Good afternoon, Your Highness. And greetings, Great Scala. I must say I'm amazed. We all thought you were both in Heaven under sanctuary. No one's been able to contact you."

I scrunch up my face, debating how much to share with him. *"Not much"* is probably the best way to go here. "We're back now, Marty. We can't discuss details, though. I'm sure you understand."

"Of course, Great Scala."

"We'll need transport to the Courthouse Pulpitum," says Lincoln.

"Yes, Your Highness. Are you ready for the countdown?"

"Not yet. First, we need three cleanup crews sent to the Wheeler Institute. Red level urgency. My private patrols only. Once they arrive, they're to find a protector named Jeeves. He'll give them instructions."

"Yes, I'll relay the command immediately."

"And Marty?" asks Lincoln. "Acca is not welcome to join them."

"But your father ordered—"

"Absolutely not. No members from the House of Acca are to be on that cleanup crew. The King can approach me directly if he has any questions."

"Acca will put up a fight," warns Marty.

"My personal patrols can handle it." Lincoln takes my hand. Together, we step onto the center of the metal disc. After that, we get into position by standing face-to-face. Lincoln wraps his solid arms around my waist. Something deep inside my soul quiets.

My guy's voice sounds gently in my ear. "Are you ready?"

"As I'll ever be."

"Marty, send us to the Courthouse Pulpitum on my mark. Three, two, one."

A long pause follows. Both Lincoln and I stiffen. Normally, the Pulpitum would have taken off right away.

"Marty?" I ask. "Are you all right?"

More seconds tick by before Marty's low voice booms through the deserted barn. "My apologies. We've had some issues with demonic alarms. One just went off and shut down the Pulpitum. I'll have you ready in a moment."

Lincoln and I share a puzzled look. Recently, we had some serious issues with the Pulpitum being misused by Acca. In fact, it was a key factor in how Lady Adair was able to cause so much trouble. For obvious reasons, the thrax don't have any Pulpitums that run to Hell. Lady Adair was still able to sneak her possessed ass around on them, though, thanks to her Acca buddies who were working at Transfer Central. After the problems were dis-covered, we'd been clearing out Acca personnel from manning the Pulpitums. It hasn't been easy.

A fissure of unease winds through me. Is Acca planning some-thing with the Pulpitum again?

Stay calm, Myla. The Pulpitums are fine.

Lincoln slowly rubs his chin, his eyes lost in thought. "Why the demon alarms?"

"The guests are already arriving for your wedding, including demonic diplomats. We tried to adjust the Pulpitums to allow them to enter, but the alarms still go off."

Marty's explanation sounds fine. Even so, something about it doesn't feel right. "Who was entering just now?"

"Demonic delegation from Purgatory." A rustling of paper sounds as Marty checks records. "The Acheron?"

Lincoln looks at me questioningly. I know what he's thinking even if he doesn't voice his concerns. *You've heard of them?*

I nod. "They're a family of wrath demons who were exiled when Armageddon took over Hell. They've been big supporters of my mother's."

"One moment. I need to reset my console." Another tense minute passes before Marty lets out a long sigh of relief. "Ah, now everything's working again. Transferring you to the Courthouse station in three, two—"

"Wait a moment," says Lincoln.

"Your Highness?"

"I'd asked that all Acca personnel be removed from Pulpitum duty. I have the sneaking suspicion that hasn't happened. Is this the case?"

Marty clears his throat. "Yes, you certainly asked for their removal." The way his voice sounds is nothing less than über-guilty. "I'll resume the transfer in three—"

"Not so fast." I stare up at the ceiling where I know the vid cameras are hidden. "Lincoln asked if his orders were followed."

"About Acca?" Marty's words come out as a squeak.

"Yup. Spill it, dude."

"No, the King himself overrode those orders. We still have representatives from the House of Acca doing regular shifts for operating the Pulpitums." He lowers his voice to a whisper. "They're here right now."

Lincoln starts holding me so tight it's getting hard to breathe. I loop my arms around his neck. "We'll take care of the Pulpitums soon." I make sure to say that loud enough for Marty to hear. "We have to finish at the courthouse first, right? Once we take care of Aldred, everything else will fall into place." I make sure Marty hears that part, too. The sooner everyone stops fearing Aldred, the better.

Lincoln nods slowly. This bums him out. I can tell.

My heart goes out to Lincoln. This happens time and again. Lincoln gives an order, and Connor could give a crap about whatever Lincoln decrees...Unless it has to do with Acca.

Lincoln stares at the ceiling. A muscle ticks in his jaw. "You're right."

"Hey, I'm always right."

A smile rounds Lincoln's mouth. "We're ready to go, Marty. Initiating Pulpitum transfer in three, two, one."

With a jolt, the platform speeds into the earth. Normally, I enjoy watching the streaks of rock, water, and magma fly by as we hurtle toward our destination. This time, though? The ride is anything but pleasant. All I can think about is getting this codex to the courthouse before it's too late.

Even worse, my inner wrath demon is going berserk. It senses danger from Acca, and that sense is never wrong.

I only hope we arrive in time to stop whatever they have planned next.

CHAPTER TWENTY-FOUR

A.

The Pulpitum slams to a halt. Lincoln and I now stand at the end of a long black corridor. I pat the backpack behind me. The codex and Lucifer's coin are still safe inside. I exhale a shaky breath. At last, we've arrived in Antrum with the evidence we so desperately need. At this point, all that remains is getting to the courtroom.

Lincoln and I step off the Pulpitum and into the darkened corridor. Rustling noises echo from the shadows. We pause.

My tail arches over my shoulder, ready for battle. "Who's there?" I wouldn't put it past Acca to leave soldiers in here, just in case Lincoln and I returned in time. Warrior energy streams through my muscles, preparing me to fight.

Lincoln ignites his baculum into a torch. The flickering light reveals the outline of two familiar figures seated in the darkness. I grin.

It's Walker and Cissy.

My shoulders slump with relief. Walker is my honorary ghoul brother, and Cissy is my best friend. It's beyond awesome to see them.

Cissy stands and bobs a bit on the balls of her feet. The movement makes her blonde ringlets bounce. Today she wears the purple robes of her office as a Diplomatic Senator. "They're here!" She leans over to pull Walker to his feet. "Wake up."

My brows lift. As a ghoul, Walker needs almost no rest at all. For him to have zonked out—and be so deeply asleep that he didn't hear us arrive—something big must have gone down.

Walker slowly rises. His tall stature and death-white skin are classic to all ghouls. The sharp lines of his face soften as he focuses on Lincoln and me. "At last. I came here when I got news of your sanctuary. I knew you'd return, and when you did, that this would be your first stop."

"I've been coming and going," offers Cissy. "But Walker's been here the entire time."

My throat tightens. *No wonder Walker dozed off.* He's been waiting for us at the Pulpitum non-stop. Note to self: make Walker one of the cough syrup cocktails he loves later.

A tense moment follows. There are no tearful hellos or long explanations. We all know what's at stake. If Aldred isn't put behind bars, Lincoln and I could end up in the dungeon.

"I know the fastest way to the courtroom." Walker races off into the darkness, making his long black robes billow with the movement. Lincoln, Cissy, and I try to keep pace. For a ghoul, Walker can really haul ass.

"I'm so relieved you made it!" Cissy positively beams. "How was sanctuary in Heaven?"

"It was...Fine?"

Cissy's big blue eyes narrow. "You're a crap liar, Myla. I want details and I want them now. I've been waiting here too, you know." Like all quasi-demons, Cissy has a power aligned to one of the seven deadly sins as well as a tail to match. Her sin is envy, and her backside is of the golden retriever variety. At this point, Cissy's tail is wagging furiously, which means she's super-excited. Envy demons covet gossip of all kinds, and Cissy wants to be the first to know what happened.

Eh. She can live with waiting.

"You'll get plenty of information shortly."

"But, Myla—"

"Trust me, Cis. Not now. I need to focus on the courtroom."

"Of course. You're getting your game face on." Cissy winks in my direction, which is a surprise. The girl I knew six months ago would have had an envy-inspired hissy fit. But becoming a Senator has shown Cissy what's really important. These days, she drops the envy crap a lot more easily.

"What happened while we were gone?" asks Lincoln.

"Aldred has been grandstanding all week," answers Walker. "He insists that you're hiding out in Heaven because you've no real evidence against him. He's even started a major referendum on where to imprison you."

"Of course," says Lincoln. "And the investigation into Cryptan's death?"

Walker shakes his head. "We never put any tracking systems in the Vault. Why would we? People hardly went in there." Walker's an engineering genius. He's done a ton of work in Purgatory and some projects in Antrum, too. So if there were recording thingies in the Vault, he would know. "Unfortunately, we've no proof who came and went that day."

"Aren't there any spells you can use?" I ask.

Walker frowns. "We've tried. There are many magical blocks in place. I'm not sure we'll ever see the truth of the thing. At this point, we've only Aldred's lies."

"And what of my people?" asks Lincoln. "Do they believe this subterfuge?"

"I'm afraid everyone believes Aldred. Or, at least, they say they do."

I stifle a groan. "Aldred and his blackmailing."

"That," sighs Walker, "and I'm afraid the thrax still have some issues with the demonic side of your heritage. Long story short, everyone says they believe Myla killed Cryptan and you're both trying—unsuccessfully—to frame Aldred. I'm sorry, brother."

My heart sinks. Everyone thinks Lincoln's a liar and I'm a murderer? Nasty.

"Don't worry," offers Cissy. "I've already submitted an injunction. They can't imprison you, Myla. You're a citizen of Purgatory until you're...You know."

Married. Which isn't too comforting. Not that I'm telling Cissy that. She's just trying to help.

At last, our little group turns down a new passageway. This one's brightly lit with torches. A set of black doors towers at the far end of the corridor. My breath catches.

That's the courtroom entrance.

I've never been inside this place before, but I've heard enough about it to know what to expect. Two guards in silver armor stand at the end of the hallway, one on either side of the doors. The Acca crest is embossed onto their breastplates.

My back teeth lock with frustration. *Acca's on duty. Of course.*

Like the Vault and Cryptan, the thrax Houses take turns guarding the courtroom as well. The fact that Acca has duty today? Totes sketchy. Still, at least it's only two warriors. Could be worse.

As we approach, the Acca dickheads move to block the entrance. The guard on the right is the first one to speak. "The courtroom is closed."

Cissy sets her fists on her hips. "As Diplomatic Senator from Purgatory to Antrum, I'm supposed to be here."

The guard's helm angles toward Lincoln and me. "No one gets in with *them.*" The way the guard says the word *"them,"* it's like we're the plague.

Glancing over to Lincoln, I bob my brows and eye the door hungrily. *Can we take them down?*

Lincoln rubs his hand along his strong jawline.

Huh. He's actually considering it. Usually, Lincoln's big on giving people a chance to do the right thing, while I'm more of a *"kill first and ask questions later"* kind of girl.

"You get one chance, men." Lincoln raises his hand. "Walker, crown."

I purse my lips. If Lincoln is asking for his crown, things are about to get ugly. He only uses his signs of office when he wants to emphasize authority...And kick some butt. My tail flicks behind me in an anxious rhythm. I wish we could just battle our way inside, but this isn't my realm, and I'm trying to be mature here.

"*Trying*" being the operative word in that sentence.

Walker reaches into the folds of his robes, pulls out a small cir-clet of silver, and tosses it to Lincoln. My guy catches his crown, seemingly without looking, and sets it perfectly atop his head. "I ask you once, as your Prince and future King." Lincoln's voice lowers. "The doors. Open them."

In reply, the guards pull their long swords from their scabbards. The blades gleam in the firelight.

I catch Lincoln's gaze again. Pure, cool rage lights in his mis-matched eyes. He says seven words, and with that, we're off. "I've got the guard on the left."

I grin. "Right."

After leaping up into the air, I double-kick the right-hand guard. My boots land flush against his visor. The guy's helm top-ples to the ground with a satisfying *clang*. Next, my tail winds about the guard's throat while I bend over at the waist. With a burst of supernatural force, my tail hauls the guard over the ful-crum of my back. The Acca dickwad goes flying down the hallway while letting out a sweet chorus of "*ow*" noises.

Nice.

Meanwhile, Lincoln ignites his baculum as two short swords. The guard raises his long sword and goes in for a death blow.

Lincoln shakes his head. "We don't have time to parry, my friend."

With fluid swipes, my guy slices across the left guard in a criss-cross movement. A long moment follows while the guard stands frozen in place. After that, he tumbles to the ground in four neat pieces. For the record, I'm counting the bottom half of his legs twice.

I can't help but smile. That was easy.

Time to go in and finish this.

Reaching forward, I yank on the golden handle. "Locked." I roll my eyes.

Like this will really stop us.

Lincoln purses his lips. That's his *"I've had just about enough of this"* face. "Let's get in there."

Moving in unison, Lincoln and I stand before the door and execute a front kick, putting all our weight behind it. The entrance splinters as the doors burst open.

Inside, the courtroom is a massive space that's more cave than anything else. The walls are grey stone striped with white sediment. Iron braziers hang on chains from the ceiling. Long wooden benches line the floor. My forehead creases with surprise.

The place is almost empty. Huh.

You'd think if their high prince was about to be slapped in prison, there would be more folks around.

Oh, well. No reason to stand about.

Lincoln and I march forward down the center aisle. Across the huge cave, a small group of thrax sits on benches by the far wall, right before a raised platform. A huge stone throne-like chair sits upon that stage. In it sits a statuesque woman in flowing white robes.

The Arbiter.

My pulse quickens. I've heard about this woman. She's another protector like Cryptan. In other words, she's enchanted to sit in that chair forever and act as the one and only judge for all things thrax. However, unlike Cryptan, her courtroom gets a lot more traffic, so she's not so isolated and twitchy. The Arbiter is as white as a statue, including her hair, skin, eyes, everything. It definitely contributes to whole otherworldly air she's working.

As we approach the far side of the chamber, the room becomes silent. The front benches are filled with thrax in their medieval finery. The men wear chainmail shirts under their tunics, the emblems of their houses are emblazoned on their chests. The women wear long gowns in house colors.

I quickly scan the faces, my pulse speeding faster with every passing second. On the left-hand side of the chamber is everyone that I would consider to be on Team Lincoln and Myla: our parents along with Lucas, the Earl of Striga.

Not a lot of people on the left-hand side of the room, actually.

On the right half of the chamber, there's Aldred and just about every other Earl in Antrum. Based on the scent of ripe adult hanging in the air, they've been in attendance all day, waiting to see if we'd show. Team Aldred has the other major Houses represented as well, namely Kamal and Horus. I'd expect that. But a ton of leaders from minor houses are here too. Even the Countess of Gurith is sitting with the enemy. Ouch.

No doubt Aldred pulled in every blackmail card in the deck to get everyone here as witnesses to the final failure of Lincoln and me. Creep.

We march closer to the judge, our footsteps echoing through the huge stone space. The attendees stare at us silently. Our families look super-happy. Everyone else? Not so much.

Lincoln and I pause before the raised platform. I have to crane my neck to look up at the Arbiter. Her all-white eyes soak us in. If she's surprised that we've shown up at the last second, she doesn't show it. "Who approaches the court?"

"Lincoln Vidar Osric Aquilus, High Prince of the House of Rixa."

I give her a little wave. "Hi, there. I'm Myla Lewis, the Great Scala."

From the benches to the right, Aldred hops to his feet. His almost-bald head is beaded with sweat. "Where are my guards?"

Lincoln glares at Aldred. "One's unconscious."

I raise my hand. "That was me."

"The other?" Lincoln keeps up his stare-fest. "Came at me with his sword." He doesn't need to add the bit about the guy ending up dead.

"Did you hear him?" Aldred gasps. "These two fight and kill for no reason. My guard is only the latest casualty. Don't you all see? Our so-called prince is no more." He points right at me. "He's fallen under the spell of this lust demon, the same one who killed Cryptan."

The thrax in the right-hand seats all nod. A few even murmur out the odd "huzzah."

I set my fist on my hip. "Really, guys? Sure, I'm part demon, but I'm also the Great Scala. I could, can, and—let's face it—after this

215

I probably *will* send all your souls to Hell after you die. Doesn't it occur to you to maybe suck up to me a little?"

One of the minor Earls waves his fist in the air. "Demon! Temptress! You're not meant to be the Scala. It's always been a thrax, and will be so again."

"Quite right," adds Aldred. "Her presence is a sign of our negligence. By leaving behind our precious traditions, we have brought this scandal upon our own heads. It wasn't I who brought Armageddon into Antrum. It was them! They lured my sweet daughter to her death." Aldred pounds his chest. "Under the rule of my House, none of this would have happened."

At this point, all the folks on Aldred's side of the courtroom do the equivalent of whistling guiltily while staring at the ceiling and going *nu-ne-nu-ne-nuuu*. They all know what a mess it would be to have Acca run things; they're too wussed out to say so.

"Let's think." I tap my chin. "Why did you guys lose the throne? That's right. Everyone was starving to death."

Aldred's face flushes pink. "You demon-tailed bitch!"

"That's enough," says Lincoln. His voice comes out deadly low.

For its part, my tail touches my mouth as it blows air kisses at Aldred. His face goes from pink to bright red. Say what you want about my tail, it has a demonic sense of how best to piss someone off.

The Arbiter raises her arm. The room quiets. "This court judges on evidence alone." She turns her all-white gaze to us. "You have some?"

"Yes, we do." I slip my pack off my shoulders and pull out the codex. "We've gathered tons of testimony."

Aldred frowns. "That can't possibly be the real codex."

"What?" asks Lincoln coolly. "Because the real one was hidden on Earth at the Wheeler Institute?"

All the blood drains from Aldred's face. "What did you do?"

"We got the evidence, of course." I raise the item in my hands. "Oh, and you may be permanently short one demon patrol, if you know what I mean."

Aldred's features turn slack as he slumps onto the bench. "You're doomed. Whatever you've done, it won't help you."

Sure, it won't.

The Arbiter looks at the codex in her hands. "You had two days to make your arguments in tandem with this evidence, I'm afraid that's down to a matter of seconds now. Do you have anything to say?"

I raise my hand. "Yes."

The Arbiter's all-white eyes narrow. "Go on."

I point to Aldred. "He's guilty as fuck." Aldred's face turns so red he seems ready to burst. Meanwhile, a chorus of stunned gasps echoes around the room. I roll my eyes. "Come on, you all know he's guilty. Spare me."

The Arbiter focuses on Lincoln. "And what do you have to say?"

"Nothing to add. My lovely fiancée captured my sentiments exactly."

I take Lincoln's hand. *That's my guy.*

"Then I shall prepare the evidence." The Arbiter focuses on the codex, which rises up to hover above our heads. Seconds pass, and my chest tightens with worry. Will this evidence be enough? I know Lincoln said the Arbiter is fair and all, but who knows what happens when you're magically chained to a chair for all eternity? This bitch could be crazy.

When the Arbiter speaks again, her voices echoes in odd ways through the cavernous room. "Commence the review."

The codex becomes larger and translucent, just as it did with Cryptan in the Vault. Images flicker through its depths. I recognize the faces as they give testimony, starting with the children we first interviewed and ending with Mrs. Pomplemousse. Beams of light shoot out from the codex as the different images pass through. Meanwhile, the irises in the Arbiter's face turn from white to icy blue.

I was so busy getting the evidence I never really considered the process by which it would get reviewed. At last, the Arbiter raises her arms, and the codex flies into her grasp. The moment the magical item reaches her palms, it returns to its regular appearance. The Arbiter blinks once, slowly. When she refocuses on the courtroom, her eyes are all white again. "There is enough evidence here that we wish to reopen this trial."

"What?" Aldred hops to his feet again. His barrel chest heaves with frantic breaths. "That's against tradition. You need to decide now. And there is only one true result—send both of them to jail, starting with Lincoln."

I point at his Aldred's nose. "That's the High Prince Lincoln to you, buddy."

The Arbiter sets the codex into her lap. "This is an area of law with no precedent. Never before has evidence been brought on the last day."

"Send them to prison!"

"How dare you?" The Arbiter's all-white eyes flare with bright light. "This is my courtroom, and I have set a new precedent. No one is to be imprisoned until the evidence is reviewed fully."

"What about Cryptan?" Aldred raises his fists. I have to hand it to the guy; he's not giving up. "You can't possibly—"

"Enough!" The Arbiter stands. Her imposing seven feet of height means that she positively towers over the room. "I set the justice here. We reconvene on Monday. That is my commandment. You may all leave."

Lincoln and I share a look. Little by little, we break out into huge smiles. I'm not sure who moves first, but suddenly we've enveloped each other in the mother of all hugs.

All the work was worth it. Interviewing those who'd been hurt by Aldred. The trip to the Wheeler Institute. And now, we have a chance to can win this case and legitimately dismantle Acca. I lean into Lincoln's shoulder, inhaling his sweet scent of pine needles and leather, one thought echoing through my mind.

We're so close. We might actually do this.

CHAPTER TWENTY-FIVE

A

I soak in every aspect of this moment. The press of Lincoln's arms around me. The *drip-drop* of condensation from somewhere deep in the cave. The screeching of Aldred as he loses his cool. I want to bottle this up and save it for the hopeless times, because chances are, there'll be plenty of those in my future. And when they arrive, I'll mentally return to the here and now, remembering how Lincoln and I kicked some serious ass today.

But then, Aldred's screeching gets earsplittingly loud. The moment ends. *Oh, well.*

"They are guilty!" Aldred's mismatched eyes are wild with rage. After that, he rushes across the aisle, his face flushed red and fist cocked high.

Even worse, he's coming straight for me.

The move takes me by surprise. Aldred is a lot of things, but a warrior isn't one of them. I stare at him, mouth open. This is really happening. Aldred's charging at me with the clear intention to introduce his fist to my face.

In court.

In front of all the thrax nobility.

It's too bizarre to be real. For a time, I can only stand there and stare at him. In some small corner of my mind, I realize my tail is poking me in the shoulder, trying to get me to snap to attention.

I can't.

It's simply too much. After everything Lincoln and I have been through? Somehow, watching Aldred come at me is basically the final straw in this metaphorical cow-pie of this fiasco.

At last, my warrior sense kicks in. There's no way I'm letting Aldred of all people punch me in the kisser. I shake my head, trying to get myself into battle focus.

That's when Lincoln steps in. He inserts himself between Aldred and me and grabs the Earl's fist. Aldred stops as the high-pitched snap of bones echoes through the courtroom.

Huh. Lincoln just broke Aldred's hand. And by the sound of it? In multiple places, too.

Yet another reason to love my fiancé.

When Lincoln speaks, his voice rings with rage. "Come after Myla again, and I'll break every bone in your body."

Aldred turns to the Arbiter. "Did you see that? These two are violent criminals. This court must lock them up! How can you not do this?"

The Arbiter frowns in Aldred's direction, and I swear the temperature drops twenty degrees. I shake my head. Right now, the Arbiter truly resembles a Greek statue come to life. Only, you know, one who's seven feet tall and wielding untold superpowers.

"I believe my last order was for everyone to leave," announces the Arbiter. "Not to charge each other with raised fists."

Aldred lifts his hand. The fingers tilt at odd angles. "He broke my bones."

"I saw who attacked first," says the Arbiter coolly.

"You can't mean that."

"This court deals in truth. I know what I saw." The Arbiter's eyes flare with white light. "You're not blackmailing me, Aldred. I'll support the facts. You attacked first. Under thrax law, the high prince did what was his right."

I pump my fist in the air. Go, *Arbiter*.

Aldred's face twitches with rage. "You're in league with them!"

"Disrespect this court once more, and *you* will be the one in prison."

At last, that shuts Aldred up and fast. He storms from the room with his menagerie of losers following behind him.

Too bad that's most of the thrax nobility.

As the courtroom empties, my parents rush over, showering Lincoln and me with hugs and hellos. Dad looks mighty smug with himself, as he should. After all, my father's sanctuary scheme just put one over on the Almighty. Meanwhile, Mom's looks hollow-eyed and weary. A pang of guilt moves across my rib cage. I know how my mother thinks. Chances are, she's been worrying her head off about the whole honeymoon-in-prison thing.

Octavia approaches at a slow and regal pace. It gives me a chance to appreciate the perfectness of her black Rixa gown, silver crown, and sweeping updo. She air-kisses Lincoln and me. All the while, Connor stands a safe distance back. He's also done up in his medieval king best. Even so, the man looks totally guilty.

As he should. I've no doubt that whatever Connor's been up to this week, it hasn't been helping team My-Linc. At last, Connor finally decides to approach Lincoln.

"Good work, son."

My mouth falls open. *That's it?* "*Good work?*" How about "*wish I could have helped*" or, even better, "*sorry I've been totally fighting you every step of the way.*" A million insults fly through my brain. All I can manage to get out is one sound. "Huh."

Lincoln points to the exit. "We need to talk." I fight back a smile because Lincoln's voice is about two octaves lower than normal. That means he's about to lay down the law with Connor. *Yes.*

My parents catch on that things are about to get ugly. Mom straightens the lapels of her purple jacket. "We'll return to our chambers." She's in total Presidential mode now. "It will give you all some time to talk."

"Thanks, Mom." They both speed off at a respectable pace. I return my attention to Lincoln and his parents. My guy looks pissed. Connor still seems totes guilty. And Octavia? She stares at her husband with a gleam of adoration in her eyes. Unbelievable.

At this point, it's worth repeating that for a very sharp woman, Octavia has a massive blind spot when it comes to her husband.

Lincoln slips his hand into mine. "Let's discuss the situation in my chambers."

"Yes, of course." Connor straightens his crown. "Your mother and I will be there shortly. Troubles with the Pulpitum, you know."

"We know," I say slowly. "We were the ones who asked you to get rid of Acca so the trouble would stop."

Connor fidgets with his crown some more. "It's not Acca."

"Honestly, it's all your party guests," gushes Octavia. "I can't remember a time when we had so many visitors in Antrum. Not that I'm complaining, but with thousands of people going through the Pulpitum, there's bound to be trouble."

Connor nods. "That's right. With so much extra traffic, we need all the trained operators we can get. It's the only way we can accommodate your wedding."

The logical side of me can see their point. Antrum is locked down tight against demons. As much as we complain about the demon alarms going off, at least Antrum has them. After all, it's the whole reason the thrax moved underground in the first place: so they'd have a secure way to screen everyone who comes and goes. False alarms or not, Antrum is the safest place for our big day.

I rub my temples with my fingertips. This whole situation makes my brain hurt. I wanted a small ceremony on Earth. On the other hand, our parents wanted something huge. Considering they were the ones planning the whole thing, I figured it was only fair that they have a say in the size of the event.

Okay, that's not totally true. I gave in and turned into total mush when Mom and Octavia got all misty about planning a huge wedding like they never had. How could I say no? Well, I could, but I was mushy. So, here we are.

Once the big-wedding question was settled, the mothers insisted on holding the wedding in Antrum so it would be safe. That was a shocker. I thought Mom would want things in Purgatory. If nothing else, you'd think the photo opps would help her presidency. Still, she's a stickler for safety and privacy, especially considering the creepy crawlers that follow us around. Plus, we're doing a parade later where Lincoln and I will be dragged through Purgatory in the equivalent of a bulletproof bubble. So Mom will still get her photo opps. And the wedding is in Antrum, which makes Lincoln's family super-happy. Bottom line? It's a win-win. Or it *seemed* like one.

All of which brings me back to the situation at hand. Connor is selling some story about the Pulpitums being fine, which—huge wedding or not—I'm still not buying. My vote is with Lincoln. Those things are dangerous right now.

"I get that the Pulpitums are under huge amounts of stress," I say. "That's why we need to talk about them. Plus, we must clear the air about a bunch of other stuff, too, like the fact that no one's complaining that Lincoln and I almost got chucked in prison."

"Of course we're upset about that," says Connor. "And we'll discuss it all. Soon."

Lincoln's glare gets so strong you'd think laser beams might pop out of his eyeballs. "Soon?"

Connor's face droops with disappointment. "What? You look like I won't keep my word."

Because he doesn't. Connor is forever making us wait around.

Unfortunately, this *"don't doubt me son"* stuff is Lincoln's kryptonite. Lincoln stiffens his stance. He hates disappointing his father. I decide to step in before Connor pulls out more emotional weaponry. I turn to Octavia. "You'll make sure he comes as soon as possible?"

"Yes, Myla. I promise." Octavia's face takes on that tight no-nonsense look which means this will really happen. Unfortunately, that's the best commitment we'll get at this point.

"Okay, Octavia."

As Lincoln's parents speed away, my tail loops around Lincoln's waist. I bite my lips together, forcibly stopping myself from calling any number of nasty names at Connor's back.

That old dirt bag better show up, or I'll hunt him down myself.

A.

It's been hours since we left the courtroom. I slump into one of the comfy club chairs in Lincoln's private chambers. The grandfather clock reads past midnight and—surprise, surprise—there's still no sign of Connor or Octavia. My tail has been alleviating frustration by balling up bits of parchment and chucking them at the door.

Lincoln sits at a nearby table, reading through the messages that have come in for him since we left. Whenever he's done with a parchment, he tosses the sheet to my tail.

This has been going on for hours now. It's making me crazy. Where the hell is Connor?

One thing I'll say, though. Lincoln's rooms make for a cool spot to hang out. His chambers mix up the medieval vibe with some swanky modern art and plush leather chairs. Not to mention the fact that the servants have been delivering a steady stream of yummy meals. No demon bars have arrived yet, but these guys can roast meat like it's nobody's business.

At last, there's a knock on the door. Lincoln carefully sets aside his latest sheet to rise and answer it. My shoulders slump with relief.

Connor and Octavia are here. Finally.

Octavia sweeps into the room. Whatever she's been doing, it hasn't resulted in a single hair getting out of place. "We're so sorry we're late. We spent time chatting with all the Pulpitum operators."

I fold my arms over my chest. "All of them? Or only Acca?"

The guilty look on Octavia's face says they spent the last few hours sucking up to their son's mortal enemies. My tail balls up another sheet of parchment and chucks it at the door, only missing Octavia's head by about six inches.

Good job.

Octavia gasps. "Did your tail almost hit me?"

"Yup." I pat the arrowhead-shaped end. "You're protective of Lincoln, aren't you, boy?" I stare pointedly from Octavia to Connor. "He doesn't understand why you were talking to the same people who just tried to put your son in jail. To be honest, I'm not getting it, either."

Lincoln moves to stand beside me. "That kind of behavior is precisely why we wanted to chat."

Connor starts scoping out the leftover trays of food. "And what do you wish to discuss, my son?"

Now, I like food the same as the next person, but not at a moment like this one. Connor's acting like a creep.

"We'd like to investigate the Pulpitums again," says Lincoln. "Now."

Connor picks up an éclair and eyes it. "Sure, whatever you want."

"Although, I wish you'd let us focus on these things." Octavia wrings her hands at her waist. "You should be enjoying your wedding, not worrying about the transfer stations."

"Yeah, we should," I say. "But the situation with Acca is out of control, and that makes us wary."

"Situation?" asks Connor. His lined face is the picture of innocent confusion.

I throw my hands up. "How can you ask that? I feel like I'm taking crazy pills here. Was I the only one who watched Lady Adair of Acca turn into fucking Armageddon while rigging up all the Pulpitum in the process?"

"That was a long time ago."

"That was three months ago! Acca tried to kill me and force Lincoln into marrying that psycho bunny, and you know what's happened to them since then? Zero. Zip. Nada. Nothing. If anything, Acca is going after Lincoln even more with this codex-stealing fiasco. And still, you're doing everything you can to help them."

For a few seconds, everyone stares at me, dumbfounded. Finally, Octavia speaks. "Ruling Antrum is very complex, Myla. Connor is balancing some extremely delicate situations."

"Bullshit."

Octavia gasps. "What did you say?"

"I said bullshit, bullshit, bullshit."

A tortured look comes over Lincoln's face. "Myla..."

"No, I've tried keeping my mouth shut. That clearly isn't working." I round on Connor. "It's time someone told you the truth. Lincoln and I both thought we'd moved past this strange connection between you and Acca. Obviously, we haven't."

Everyone stares at me with varied looks of shock on their faces. I take that as an invitation to keep right on going.

"Ever since you found out that Lincoln and I can have kids, you've been acting super-weird again."

Connor stiffens his shoulders. "I don't know what you mean."

That does it. Now that I've started speaking my mind, the torrent of rage I'd been holding back comes a-rolling out. I march over to Connor and poke him in the chest. He drops his éclair to the floor, and I take that as a small victory. "What does Acca have on you? Pictures of you doing it with a goat? Your balls in some kind of plus-three vise of magical obedience? Because whatever it is, you need to move on. This thing between Lincoln and me? It's happening."

"Be reasonable, Myla." Octavia gently guides me away from Connor. "We love the idea of the two of you being married. That said, the thrax are still mourning the loss of Lady Adair. She was almost Lincoln's fiancé, too, remember?"

"How could I forget?" I mean for the words to come out with venom, but they're said in a soft conciliatory tone. Lincoln's mom is an expert at turning any conversation around. I still have the vague sense that I'm in the right here. I can't quite remember why, though.

"You must give our people time to get to know you," adds Octavia. "Once they do, I'm certain they'll adore you and your marriage."

Lincoln sets his arm around my shoulders. It's a protective move that I value very much. "Myla is the great scala. The thrax should be kneeling at her feet. The only reason they hesitate is Aldred. He's using blackmail to poison their minds."

Connor sets his fists on his hips. "That's quite enough. We need to be honest here as well."

Octavia pales. "Connor, you said you'd wait until after the wedding."

"I did. However, it seems the children want to air things now." Connor rounds on me. "Three months ago, you pulled out the souls from our entire nobility. Their spirits hovered over their heads. Yes, that action got rid of Adair and Armageddon, but it scared our people half to death. You're a demon. In Antrum. Yanking out their souls. And they are demon fighters. Now, you want to marry my son and you expect them to be thrilled about that fact? There are bound to be repercussions."

Every line of Lincoln's body firms with determination as he steps between Connor and me. "Show some respect. Myla saved Antrum that day."

Octavia shakes her head. "That may be. Sadly, all our nobles saw was one demon interacting with another."

They see Armageddon and me...as equals? Possibly even allies?

"Is that true?" My voice cracks with sorrow.

"All Connor and I are saying is that, in this moment, we must do a careful dance to keep all the thrax in line. Half of them didn't want to attend the wedding."

My shoulders slump. *Not attend the wedding?* Octavia's words hit me like so many fists. "They'll never see me as more than a demon, will they?"

Octavia steps forward and takes my hands in hers. Her fingers feel so tiny and dainty in mine. "They will see you, eventually. You're a wonderful person. However, you must be patient. Besides, the thrax aren't the only one with prejudices. Your people have issues with Lincoln, don't they?"

How I hate to admit this, but she's right. I mean, the quasis did sing that *"Kumbaya"* song with hate speech against my fiancé. "Yes, I suppose they do."

Octavia gives my hands a squeeze. "These are age-old misunderstandings between our peoples. You and Lincoln are breaking new ground. That takes courage and time."

My throat tightens with grief. I get the whole *"be patient"* thing. Still, it hurts like hell. "I guess so."

Even as the words leave my lips, some small voice in the back of my head screams that I just got derailed. There was something more important at stake here, wasn't there? I try to recapture my line of thinking, Somehow, all I can focus on is the fact that the thrax can't stand me.

I blink hard, my mind refocusing. *No.* I won't let this conversation get derailed. My train of thought comes back online. "I didn't ask you here to discuss the misunderstandings between our people. And I won't be deterred from the real threat here. Pulpitums, people."

"Myla's right," continues Lincoln. "We want Acca off Pulpitum duty. I need a copy of the duty roster to do it."

Connor shrugs. "Can't give you that."

Lincoln's eyes narrow. His body fairly radiates rage. "I suppose there's no point in asking you for a list of all Acca nobility and their thanes? Now that the codex is with the Arbiter, it's only a matter of time before Aldred is convicted. Aldred isn't the only rotten apple in the Acca barrel. We need to clean up that House. In order to accomplish that, I require a full list of everyone in Acca. We must decide who will be exiled after Aldred's in jail."

"I'm working on it, my boy. There are millions of thrax in Antrum. It takes time to find everyone from Acca."

I'd say *bullshit* again, but I feel like I've used up that card today. And, if I'm being honest, I'm still feeling blue from that whole being-hated thing.

"We'll get it to you shortly," adds Octavia. "I promise you both."

"I see." The tone of Lincoln's voice says he thinks that's a whopper of a lie. "And will Aldred be at the wedding tomorrow?"

Connor's mouth thins to a determined line. "I think you know the answer to that question. Of course, he'll attend. It's what has to be done to keep the peace." Connor throws up his hands. "There's no point continually rehashing our positions here. You have one idea about how to lead Antrum. Your mother and I have another." He shoots a glare in my direction. "And no, there were no goats involved in our decision making. We've been doing this for a long time, and we know the best way to rule."

"Precisely." Lincoln's usually so calm and collected. This time, though? His words come out as an almost snarl. "We have different ideas on how to rule. So in that light, let me make one thing absolutely clear. If Acca isn't dismantled and I don't believe with every fiber of my being that Antrum is safe for Myla and our children, then I'm stepping out of the line of succession. Acca won't have to fight to gain the throne. I'll give it to them. Aldred's the senior Earl. Without an heir, the throne is his after you're gone."

All the blood drains from Octavia's face. "What?"

My mouth falls open. "You can't be serious."

Lincoln turns to me. With the slowest and gentlest of movements, he cups my face in his softly calloused palms. The warmth of his touch moves through my soul. "You are what's most important in my life, Myla. All this work to dismantle Acca was only to ensure your safety here in Antrum. If it isn't secure, then I will step down."

His words rattle around my brain. This can't be real. "But you're a wonderful ruler. We all know you've been running things for ages. And if you leave Antrum to Acca, you'll be dooming your people. Acca can't manage demons on Earth. Look what happened at the Wheeler Institute. This will affect the humans, too."

Lincoln leans in until his forehead touches mine. "I can't do any of this without you, Myla. Not even if I wanted to."

My eyes prick with tears. *I feel the same way.* Without Lincoln, I'm not sure I could move a soul, even if the igni were freaking out.

Lincoln brushes his lips against mine. "I'd be proud to live my life in Purgatory as consort to the great scala. That is, if you'll have me."

Okay, that's a really sweet speech. I mean, I knew Lincoln wanted to get rid of the threat and fix Antrum. However, I thought it was for the general good of his people. It takes me a few minutes to realize that everyone's been staring at me, waiting for my answer.

"However we can be together, that's what I want."

"So that's a yes?"

"A big yes."

Now, the strategic side of me wants Connor and Octavia to see that Lincoln and I mean business. But the feeling side? I can't let Lincoln walk away from ruling so easily. We'll have to have a long talk about this later. If Lincoln really wants to do this, I want to be sure that it's for the right reasons.

Octavia stands frozen, staring at us. I think a few hairs actually fall out of place. "You're serious, aren't you?"

Lincoln pulls me into a deep hug. "Completely."

We've embraced before, yet this one feels special. Lincoln would give up everything for me. That's huge.

The reality of the situation finally sinks in with Octavia and she rushes over to Connor. "We'll get them that list, won't we?"

"Sure, sure."

"Right." I sigh. "Sure, sure…That's what you say when you have no intention of doing anything. Honestly, how is Aldred blackmailing you?"

Connor chuckles like I just told the funniest joke in the world. He's the only one laughing, though. And the high-pitched sound of his laughter? It says I hit the mark. Aldred really is blackmailing Connor. In the long run, I suppose it doesn't really matter what that blackmail is about. The point is that Connor's a tool.

"Glad we settled all that," says Connor. Without another word, he stomps out and slams the door behind him.

There goes a lying liar.

Octavia steps over to give us both kisses on the cheek. "I'll work on him. It will be fine."

"Thank you, Mother."

"Have a good night, Octavia."

She rushes away as well. The moment Lincoln's parents are gone, I feel like someone pulled my plug. The last week has all been way too much excitement. I slump into Lincoln's hold.

He kisses my head. "You've hit the adrenaline crash, haven't you?"

"All I want is to sleep for a year. Minimum."

"I'll take you to your room."

I close my eyes and wrap my arms around his neck. "My room is attached to yours. I can walk the whole ten yards to get there."

"Not on the weekend of our nuptials. You must stay in the future queen's suite. I'm not supposed to be near you during this time."

I groan. "More traditions?"

"More traditions." There's a smile in his voice, though.

"Maybe if I take a nap here, I'll be up for the walk."

"That sounds like a wonderful plan." Lincoln scoops me into his arms. "Nap away."

I'm about to counter that actually, I can totally walk on my own. But honestly? It's really nice to be carried around by Lincoln. And I do take a little half-snooze along the journey. When I awaken again, I'm lying in a pink bed in the frilliest room ever. Lincoln starts tucking me under the poofy covers. I'm still in my schoolgirl outfit, but what the heck? Right now, it's feeling comfortable.

"This is the future Queen's suite?" I scan the over-the-topness of it all. The place is all pink, from the fluffy curtains to the plush rug. And every free inch of space is covered in little girly knick-knacks and sculptures. "It's like a unicorn threw up in here."

"I said tradition. I didn't say attractive." Lincoln starts stripping off his khakis, and although I'm enjoying the show, I'm a little confused.

"I thought the whole point of sleeping here was that I'd be separated from you."

"There's tradition, and there's the fact that we haven't been together in days." He slips under the covers, and I'm very happy that my guy sleeps totally naked. Normally, this would signal sexy-times, but right now? It's simply all the more reason to snooze in comfort.

"This is nice," I say through a yawn.

"Very." Lincoln wraps me in his arms and I cuddle into his side.

My eyes pop open. "What about Lucifer's coin?"

"I brought it with us. It's safe inside your backpack."

"That's awesome."

Lincoln tightens his hold on me, which makes me all kinds of warm and cuddly. Soon, I fall into a very sweet sleep, thinking a single thought, over and over.

This is how I will rest for the remainder of my days. With Lincoln's arms around me.

Not bad at all.

CHAPTER TWENTY-SIX

$\mathcal{A}$

That night, I dream about sleeping. It's totally weird yet not exactly upsetting. All I do in my dreams is snooze while feeling happy, cuddly, and warm. In fact, the whole experience is so awesome I find it tough to wake up. Eventually, I have to, though.

Although I'm only half alert, thoughts of the day start rattling around my head.

It's Saturday.

Yesterday, we got that damned codex into the courtroom.

Tomorrow, I get married.

And then, there appears the most delicious thought of all.

There's a very naked man between my thighs.

I smile through my drowsiness. Today just get a hell of a lot better. My eyes flutter open. I lay on my back with Lincoln atop of me, his arms braced on either side of my head. I can't help but admire his broad shoulders, ripped chest, and lean waist. Being part angel has its benefits.

"My face is up here, Myla." There's laughter in his voice because yes, I just got caught ogling him.

"I'm getting there." I slowly drag my gaze upward. *Yum.* His brown hair is all messy and sexy, which only serves to highlight the strong lines of his cheekbones and jaw even more. Our gazes lock. "Good morning."

"Hello, wife."

"Not until tomorrow." I stretch a little and wake up a lot more because that's when I realize I'm buck-ass naked. "Hey, what happened to my school uniform? I feel asleep in that."

"You did?"

"I know for a fact that I did."

Lincoln leans in and brushes his nose along mine. I'm suddenly very aware of the fact that only a thin sheet separates the bottom halves of our bodies. "You asked me to take it off you."

"Did not." I smile. "But I would have if I'd thought of it."

He gives me the gentlest of kisses. "That's why I'm here. To think of the things you want, but haven't yet given voice to. I even got the Rixa patrol to bring back your fighting suit and my battle armor."

"I like that about you." I total forgot we left that back at the Wheeler Institute.

Lincoln starts kissing my neck. "I thought you might."

"We should stop this. After all, we're in the pink queen suite. You're not supposed to be here at all, let alone naked."

More kisses. "True."

I shift my weight underneath him and feel Lincoln's hardness against me. There's no way I'm letting my guy go anywhere when he's that aroused. It's like a lust demon code of ethics. "So you'll go in a few minutes. Maybe."

His full mouth winds into a lickable grin. "Yes. Maybe."

A low hum sounds from across the room. Jolts of awareness move through my body. I'd know that sound anywhere.

A ghoul portal is opening.

In this bedroom.

The pink unicorn suite.

And there's only one person who'd do this.

Walker.

Dammit.

Lincoln and I scramble to cover up. Meanwhile, a large black door-shaped hole forms in the space beside our bed. Sure enough, Walker soon steps through. My honorary ghoul brother looks undead and super-tall in his long black robes. I wish I had something to hit him with. Who portals into people's bedrooms?

"Good morn—" Walker simply stands there and stares, his body frozen with shock. The situation quickly gets awkward with a capital A.

"Walker." I make sure the sheet is tucked carefully under my arms. "There's a door. Why don't you go outside and *use it?*"

Walker's undead face turns gray, which is his version of a blush. "Yes, Myla. Sorry, Lincoln." He opens another portal and disappears.

I slam my head against the pillow and groan. "Well, that ruined the mood."

A knock sounds on the door. "Myla Lewis, oh Great Scala, are you in there by chance?"

I roll my eyes. "Yes, Walker. I am. And I'm not alone. How sensitive of you to knock."

Lincoln rolls out of bed. His princely getup and my Scala robes sit neatly on a nearby chair. *My guy really does think of everything.* Lincoln slips on his leather pants. Did I mention that they're black and body fitting? Well, they are. He gets it halfway on before leaning over and pulling out Lucifer's coin from my backpack. "See? I told you I have it."

"You've a mind like a steel trap."

Lincoln smiles and tosses me the coin, which I catch in midair. *So glad we got this.*

Walker's voice echoes through the closed door. "Your mothers would like you to join them at the Chapel. I'm to take you there."

I slip out of bed and throw on my Scala robes. There's no point trying to get ready in this place. All my shampoo and stuff is back in my real chambers, which are connected to Lincoln's. I huff out a breath against my palm. Man, I desperately need to brush my teeth. Good thing my toothbrush is back there, too.

"Myla? There's something else you should know." Walker has that "I'm about to give you a lecture" tone to his voice.

Ugh.

I mostly finish slipping on my robes, but not before grabbing Lucifer's coin and setting it against my breastbone. One of these days, I have to get pockets for this thing. Even so, there's no way I'm leaving this magical trinket behind. Lucifer's coin is going the same place as Lucifer's Orb. My father will lock it up. That's another one of Dad's supernatural skills—knowing how to secure dangerous magic like Lucifer's coin.

You may be here now, oh dangerous coin. Not for much longer, though.

Walker's still stammering as I whip open the door and launch into my speech. "Not so fast, buddy. Let's talk about portal etiquette first. You do not go zapping around into people's bedrooms when they're naked and—" The words die in my throat. Mostly because the hallway is crammed with people.

Unholy Hell.

My eyes almost bug out of my head. Thrax, angels, and quasis all line the outer corridor, which is decorated in more pink stuff. My stomach turns queasy. I know these people. They're all top dignitaries from Antrum and Purgatory. Suddenly, I'm super-aware of my scrunched-up robes and hair that seems styled by the Salon of I Just Got Le Fucked.

Shoot me now.

Lincoln moves stand beside me, his demeanor one of total calm. For the record, I have never loved my guy more than I do in this particular moment.

"Greetings, Walker."

"My Prince."

"I see that some of our guests are here. I wonder who let them in." The look on Lincoln's face says he knows exactly who was behind it. "Could it have been the King?"

Walker exhales one of his long-suffering sighs. "Your father is very excited for today, My Prince. He's allowing certain unusual leniencies."

Typical.

Lincoln scans the hallway and nods regally. "How kind of you to greet us."

My tail waves frantically over my shoulder in a way that says, *Attention? Yes, please.* My face burns about twelve shades of red. "Walker says we have to go," I stammer. "So we should leave. I guess." Lincoln's speech to the crowd was smooth. Mine? Not so much.

Lincoln sets his hand at the base of my spine. His touch is reassuring and awesome in general. "Quite right." My guy addresses the crowd again. "We look forward to seeing you tomorrow at the wedding."

Of all people, Mrs. Pomplemousse steps out from the shadows to wrap me in a big hug. She looks just as she did in Purgatory: a plump grandmotherly type who's all smiles. She still wears her tight grey suit with a matching pillbox hat and veil. The scent of potpourri slams into my face as she keeps on hugging. "Thank you so much for inviting me to the wedding!"

I shoot Lincoln a confused look. *We invited her?*

He shrugs. In other words, he has no idea how she got here.

Oh, well. What we both don't know about our wedding is a lot. I'm guessing this kind of thing will happen often over the next few days.

"You're totally welcome." I scooch away from her because that potpourri stink is worse than my breath. "We have to go now."

"But you're coming to the party tonight, yes? I'm counting on seeing you at the ball."

All the air leaves my body. "There's a ball tonight?" I'm not a fan of social events in general, but balls are my personal nemesis. My back teeth lock in frustration. A surprise ball? This whole thing screams of Octavia. She holds a formal ball when the butler buys a new goldfish. I turn to Lincoln. "I thought we discussed there would be no parties other than the reception?"

"We did." Lincoln stares at Mrs. Pomplemousse in a way that says "*I'm the prince and you better back off.*" "If you'll excuse us, my future wife and I have many duties to attend to."

Mrs. Pomplemousse holds her ground. "But what about the ball?"

"Excuse us." Lincoln frowns, and you can almost see the thought bubble over Mrs. Pomplemousse's head, complete with the words "*yipe, yipe, yipe*" written inside.

In other words, she backs off and how.

With Mrs. Pomplemousse out of the way, Lincoln and I march past what feels like a never-ending hallway of people staring at my le-fucked hair and mostly straight Scala robes. There's only one way to deal with situations like this one.

Work it like a pro.

I stroll by, waving and smiling. Beside me, Lincoln still looks regal and calm. For his part, Walker follows us quietly.

At last, we pass the never-ending gauntlet of onlookers and enter the warren of hidden passageways that connect different parts of Arx Hall. Unlike the huge public hallways, these spaces are cramped stone passages. Normally, I get claustrophobic in here. But right now? I'm loving the fact that there's no one else around. I really can't handle any more smiling and waving for a while.

The moment we're out of earshot, Walker stops us all in our tracks. "I must apologize. I portalled into the room to warn Myla about the crowd. However, then you were…And I got…"

I shrug. "It's cool, Walker."

"But it's not." Walker rubs his hands over his pale face. "That was terrible. You're like my little sister and—"

"I've got an idea." I raise my pointer finger. "Let's change the subject."

"Agreed." Lincoln gestures to the far end of the passage. "We're expected in the Chapel, right?"

Poor Walker still looks a little shell-shocked. "Yes, your mothers await you there."

"I know the quickest paths to that spot," offers Lincoln.

"But I'm supposed to lead you."

Lincoln sets his hand on Walker's shoulder. "Will you do something else for me instead?"

"Anything."

"Why don't you check on the Pulpitum at Transfer Central? There have been strange reports of demon alarms going off. It could be nothing more than our unusual wedding guests, but I'd rather not take the chance."

Walker sighs. The relief is plain on his face. "Yes, My Prince. I'll report back whatever I discover."

"Thank you."

Walker's gone so quickly you'd think the man was a sprinter instead of a ghoul. I feel a little guilty. I'm sure his life is crazed today, and it's all about helping us.

"Don't worry about Walker," says Lincoln.

"Who said I was?"

Lincoln gives me a sly look that says, *I know you, Myla.*

And he does.

Lincoln weaves his fingers with mine. "Let's show you the Chapel."

"Right." I shake my head, trying to get my thoughts back into wedding stuff. "We're getting married there tomorrow, and I haven't even seen it." In my mind, I picture a cute little chapel with carved wooden benches and stained glass windows. "Do you have ceremonies there a lot?"

"Not often."

With that, we head off into the tunnels. Lincoln starts explaining thrax traditions that relate to the Chapel. It's super-sweet. Lincoln's gets all excited when he talks about thrax history. It's charming. Even so, he goes so fast, it's hard to take in everything. That said, who cares? And as long as no one ever asks me to repeat every little thing he just said, I'm solid.

Eventually, we leave the secret stone passageways and return to the main corridors. Out here, it's all golden walls, House pennants, and suits of armor as decoration. Finally, we reach a small golden door and pause.

"Is this it?" I ask. "It's kind of dinky."

"It's a side entrance." He rubs his palms together. "Well, are you ready to see the Chapel?"

"Sure." That's what I say, but to be honest, Lincoln's palm-rubbing puts me off a little. My guy only does that when it's a super-big deal. I frown. What could be so huge about some chapel? I'm starting to wonder if I should have paid closer attention to the walk over when Lincoln opens the door.

I step inside and gasp. *Damn, this place is huge.* Like, truly unbelievably massive. And I know large places. After all, I fought in Purgatory's Arena. Yet this Chapel could eat four of Purgatory's Arenas and still have room for dessert.

"This isn't a chapel. It's an indoor stadium."

The place is all grey marble threaded through with veins of white stone. The space is oval, like Purgatory's Arena, and has tiered stone seats that stretch off into forever. The floor is flat and covered with more folding wooden chairs than I ever knew existed. Candelabras and pennant poles dot the floor.

Wow.

All the veins of white rock wind into a single spot on the opposite floor of the Chapel, where a raised stage has been set against the first tier of seats.

"This wasn't what I expected. At all." My voice echoes through the huge space, so my last words are *"at all, at all, at all."* I decide to whisper-talk from now on. That echo stuff is a little creepy.

Lincoln purses his lips. "You didn't catch half of what I said on the way over, did you?"

"Who me?" My tail taps my chest for extra innocence.

"You."

"No, not really. You talk super-fast sometimes."

Lincoln winks. "I'll work on that."

From across the massive floor, a small group of people wave and cheer in our direction. It's both of our parents as well as Cissy and her boyfriend, Zeke. The place is so massive it takes forever for us to meet up at the center of the main aisle.

Octavia looks radiant in her black gown. "Isn't this exciting? Tomorrow, the Chapel will be filled to capacity."

I try not to wince. "What's capacity here?"

"Sixty thousand."

A pang of worry moves up my rib cage. "That's a lot of people."

Lincoln steps in to chat with Octavia, while Connor hangs back and talks with Mom. That's fine with me. Lincoln's father is on my Jerk List.

Meanwhile, Dad rushes to wrap me up in a big hug. "My lovely Myla-la." He steps back and eyes me from head to toe. "You seem a little out of it. Are you feeling well?"

Oh, crap, I forgot about the fact that I didn't get read-ready. Plus, my hair is a post-sexed-up mess, which is doubly embarrassing.

"There's a long and totally believable story about how I ended up this way. I'll tell you once I think of it."

Dad chuckles. "Nothing to worry about. I'm just so happy I can be here to share all this with you."

Warmth and happiness spread through me. "I'm so glad, too."

Dad leans in conspiratorially. "By the by, that was some excellent work at the Wheeler Institute."

"You've been following it?"

"My daughter and her warrior excursion on Earth? I was thrilled when the call came in for Lincoln's private demon patrol to clean things up."

"So what happened after we left?"

"The thrax cleaned up everything. Officially, Prescott had a heart attack."

"And the Acca warriors?"

"The live ones are in custody."

"In Antrum?" My upper lip curls. I can only imagine how quickly Connor will authorize their release.

"Hells, no. I had them shipped off to a secret facility of mine on Earth. I'll disclose the location once Acca gets dismantled."

Interesting. Dad's been alive since the dawn of time, so he has all these little pockets of cool stuff lying around. It's not a superpower exactly, but I'm still putting that in my journal. A secret prison on Earth. Who'd have thunk it?

Talking about keeping things secure makes me remember Lucifer's coin. "Hey, I need to ask you something."

Dad's face gets all serious. "What is it?"

241

I pull my father aside while everyone else talks in small groups about the excitement of the day. With so much chattering going on, I can speak confidentially with Dad, so long as I keep a quiet voice. "Remember when we were talking about finding Lucifer's coin at the Wheeler Institute?"

"Of course."

"Well, Lincoln and I found it." I bob my head from side to side, thinking. "Actually, the human Prescott found it, and we took it from him. In any case, I'm wondering if you can stow it somewhere safe? Maybe up in the Heavenly vault where you put Lucifer's Orb? The coin is simply too dangerous to leave around."

"Of course. Where is it?"

I reach into my robes to pull the coin out. It isn't there. I frown. I could have sworn I put it there, but then again, Lincoln also had it in the backpack. Plus, my brain is a little muddled, what with finding out that I'm getting married in front of sixty thousand people tomorrow. I'm sensitive like that. "Lincoln has it." *I think.*

"Don't worry about a thing. I'll get it from him right away."

It feels like boulders of worry roll off my back. Dad took care of Lucifer's Orb. He'll do the same with the coin, easy peasy. Just as my father heads off in Lincoln's direction, Cissy and

Zeke approach me. My BFF is still wearing her purple senatorial robes, which are super-flattering on her willowy figure. Damn. If I wore something like that, I'd look like a heifer. Cis air-kisses both my cheeks. "I'm so excited for tomorrow."

Zeke lurks behind her, posing in his purple armor. That outfit has way too much padding for my taste. That said, I'm not the one running Purgatory's national guard—Zeke is. Captain Lustboy rakes his hand through his blond hair and winks. "Hey, Myla."

"Zeke." I glare at him. He hasn't said anything insulting yet. However, when it comes to Cissy's guy, it's simply a matter of time. Zeke is part lust demon and can't imagine anyone not adoring his lame ass.

"So, it seems you've moved on from your infatuation with me." The look on Zeke's face can only be described as smug.

"Zeke!" Cissy steps back to elbow him in the ribs. "Don't say things like that."

Now, I can't miss how Cissy isn't calling him a lying liar. Unfortunately, they're both back under the delusion that I once had a crush on Zeke. Whatever. It isn't worth explaining for the hundredth time.

"What?" Zeke shrugs. "I'm only happy she moved on, that's all."

Cissy offers me a sympathetic glance as Mom approaches our group, pulling me into one of her über-clingy hugs. I know this particular kind of embrace, and it's a warning sign. At this moment, my mother may be all decked out like the President of Purgatory, but inside? She's all weepy Mom.

And weepy Mom soon becomes embarrassing Mom.

"My baby is growing up," she says with a sigh. "I can't believe you're getting married tomorrow. And then, once you have sex for the first time, I know you'll become pregnant right away with my grandchild."

And there she is. Embarrassing Mom. I step back from her hug.

Zeke does a totally-on-purpose shitty job of hiding a chuckle behind his hand while Cissy looks even more sympathetic. I stifle the desire to run.

Mom pats under her eyes, clearing away a few tears. "Tell me you're going to the ball tonight. I can't wait to introduce you to everyone and tell them I'm about to be a grandmother."

"That's not a good idea. At this point, I'm adjusting to getting married in front of, you know, sixty thousand people."

Mom shakes her head. "Sex is nothing to be ashamed of, baby. I've been working with Purgatory's inner city youth. They talk about such matters all the time." Her tail straightens the lapels on her sleek purple suit. "For example, it's no big deal to say that your father and I got pregnant right after we banged uglies for the first time."

Oh, no. Mom's trying to act "inner city" in front of my friends. Is there anything worse that a parent can do? If there is, I can't think of it right now. I put on my most authoritative voice. It's the one I use before moving souls. "Mom."

"What? I told you. He wrapped up his junk and everything. I still got knocked up."

Cissy sighs. Zeke all-out laughs.

I raise my voice. "Mom!"

"It's the igni that do it. I think they nibble little holes in the condoms, personally. Not that it makes a difference in getting me a grandchild."

"MOM!"

Cissy steps in to break up the awfulness, which is one of the main reasons why I love her. "Oh my goodness, President Lewis. I just remembered something about the ball."

"What?"

"I'm so sorry, but I already have Myla committed for tonight."

"You do?"

"Oh, yes." I slap on my most my super-sincere face. "Cissy and I made these plans, oh…"

Why can't I think of more stuff to say?

"Six weeks ago," finishes Cissy. "You see, all these gifts have come in from across the after-realms. With so many attendees, that's a lot of stuff. Myla needs to go through the most important things and tell me where to put them." Cissy's eyes gleam. "Some people have even sent live animals."

Nice one, Cis. Mom is a sucker for stuff like that.

My mother straightens her shoulders. She's going back into Presidential mode, and that's not good for me. "But what about all my donors and supporters? I'd love for you to meet them."

When it really counts, I can lie my ass off, especially with my Mom. "And I want to meet them, truly. But dang it all, I already made this commitment to Cissy to help with the gifts."

This isn't bullshit, by the way. We have tons of gifts we're supposed to sort through.

Cissy steps up. She looks even more sincere. "Myla has to come right away. Like I said, people have been giving animals as gifts.

Trouble is, there are all these small, furry, sweet little animals that need Myla's help."

Now, there has been the odd animal gift that's come through, but so far, they're all roasted and ready for eating. Still, Cissy's a freaking genius.

"There are even kittens," I say sadly. "Tons of kittens. And a few baby pandas." I take care to sniffle. "Which is why we have to go now."

"What about your dress fitting?" asks Mom. "We were going to do that today."

No way am I doing a fitting. Mom will wear me down until I agree to the ball. "There are simply too many kittens and pandas, Mom. Besides, Striga can cast a spell to make sure my dress fits. It's all good."

Lincoln strides up to stand beside me. "Did you hear?" he asks solemnly. "The kittens are mewling. Poor little things. We can't keep them waiting."

For the record, my guy has awesome hearing. Plus, he's an even better liar than Cissy.

I loop my arm around his waist. "That's right. Off we go. We'll check on the gifts and kittens with Cissy, exactly like we planned."

Although I'm not putting on the best show, Mom still buys it. "All right, I won't stand in the way of animal health." Mom kisses me goodbye and walks away. On second thought, I'm not sure she totally bought that story one hundred percent, but as long as I'm not going to the ball, I'm good.

Once Mom's gone, Lincoln arches his brow. "Gifts? Do you have a list of who sent them?"

"Sure," says Cissy.

"Does it include Acca?" I ask.

"Does it ever. They've invoked some fake thrax tradition where you have to give them a gift back of equal or greater value. It's rude, in my opinion."

"But it's a list of every noble in the House," says Lincoln.

"Sure."

Ah-HA! I can see where Lincoln is going with this and it's an awesome place. Thanks to this gift stuff, we could have us a full list of all the Acca who could be exiled; it's the exact information that Connor won't provide.

"It's super long though," says Cissy. "Sorry."

"Not a problem at all," says Lincoln. "I have the perfect gift for many of them."

We quickly say our goodbyes and walk away. Cissy stays close. "I hope this isn't a bummer way to spend the night before your wedding. There really are a lot of gifts that need your attention. As well as that long list of the House members. It won't be enjoyable."

I smile. "Honestly? I can't think of a better way to spend tonight."

Because I'm not going to fuss about the gifts at all. What I am going to do is plot with Lincoln on how to systematically break up Acca, while my dad takes care of Lucifer's coin. And that's what I call fun.

CHAPTER TWENTY-SEVEN

A

Twenty-four hours later, I'm standing in a stone passageway that leads to the Chapel floor. The place is packed. All the tiered seats are filled with dignitaries, and an even larger crowd is crammed onto row after row of wooden chairs on the Chapel floor. The hum of voices echoes through the stone hallway.

This is really happening. In a few minutes, I'm about to get married.

I fidget in my white gown. What's wrong with me? I should be overwhelmed with joy. Instead, I can't shake this odd feeling of foreboding that weighs down my shoulders.

Cissy stands beside me, straightening out my skirt and veil. "You look gorgeous, Myla."

"Thanks." The word comes out with a sigh.

Cissy pauses. "What's going on?"

"Nothing."

"Is it your father? He said he might be late."

I frown. "He did? When?"

"Well, I didn't want to worry you, but he couldn't find some coin or something."

My tail does its up-periscope move over my shoulder. "What? Why didn't you tell me?"

Dad picks this moment to march into the passageway. He looks stunning in his gleaming armor. His great golden wings arch over his shoulders. "Myla-la." He shakes his head. "How lovely you look."

It's my wedding day, and my father says I look lovely, so I should be all blushy and stuff. That's not happening. My warrior sense won't let the news from Cissy drop. "What happened with Lucifer's coin?"

Dad gives me his thousand-watt smile. "Coin?"

"Don't schmooze me. Cissy told me you couldn't find it."

"I couldn't, but that's nothing to worry about. I've been personally overseeing the Pulpitums all morning. Nothing magical is getting in or out. That coin is somewhere close by and I will find it...*After* the wedding."

I stare between Cissy and Dad. "You didn't tell Lincoln, either, did you?"

My father steps closer and lowers his voice. "You only have one wedding day. We thought we'd take some of the burdens from you both."

My eyes narrow as my mind spins through this news. "You've been in the Pulpitums all morning." A shiver runs down my limbs. "But the coin went missing yesterday. It was supposed to be in either my robes or the backpack." I stare out over the crowd of supposed friends. Could one of them have taken it from me? It seems too horrible to be true.

Dad's eyes glow angel-bright. "Everything's going to be fine, Myla. Whatever you're worried about, it can wait forty minutes for you to get married. You need to trust us."

Cissy steps up as well. "We care about you and have taken tons of steps to ensure your day is perfect."

I nod slowly. When she puts her mind to it, Cissy is a marvel at organization. For the first time, I notice how my friend looks in her black velvet gown. As my only bridesmaid, Cissy's wearing the colors of the house of Rixa. "You look beautiful, by the way."

"Does that mean you trust us?" she asks.

I straighten my spine and tamp down my worries. "You're both right. Whatever happened to the coin, it's nothing that can't wait an hour."

Somewhere across the Chapel floor, an orchestra starts playing Vivaldi. It's human music, but sometimes mortals really know their stuff. This piece from the Four Seasons is one of my favorites.

I step closer to the edge of the archway and stare out over the crowd. Everyone's gone silent while the orchestra plays. There are so many faces it's hard to pick out any single one. Ghouls, angels, quasis, and thrax...Every seat seems filled with a dignitary. The only big difference is that if you're thrax, you're likely to be glaring at a nearby quasi and vice versa. How sucktastic.

The hate fest between Lincoln's thrax and my quasis continues. Blech.

My gaze locks on one quasi in particular. Mrs. Pomplemousse. She got a choice aisle seat right not a dozen yards in front of me. Something inside my soul goes on alert. I motion Cissy closer. "This is assigned seating, right?"

"Oh, sure." Cissy eyes her bouquet of white roses. "It took forever to arrange."

"And only major dignitaries got aisle seats, right?"

"Everyone was fighting over them, so we had to come up with a system." She gives me a conspiratorial grin. "I guess everyone wants a closer look at the demon who would be Queen of the Thrax."

I nod toward Mrs. Pomplemousse. "So how did a low-level quasi get that seat?"

"Who?" Cissy squints at the old quasi. "Oh, her. Maybe someone switched spots. She looks pretty old and helpless."

I stare at the back of Mrs. Pomplemousse's head. She's still wearing that outrageous pillbox hat and veil. Something about her feels wrong...Like a *"demon cloaked in a fake skin"* kind of wrong. And Mrs. Pomplemousse hugged me in the hallway yesterday. That old bat could have used that opportunity to steal Lucifer's coin. My mind whirs through other suspicious things about the old dame. Desmond was right outside her house, waiting to steal the codex. Why didn't I see it before? She could have tipped him off where we'd be, and with the codex, no less.

Desmond and Mrs. Pomplemousse could have been in cahoots.

My eyes widen. Prescott said that the Lady takes many forms. What if the Lady and Mrs. Pomplemousse are the same person? He also said the Lady can freeze a man on sight. That could just be lust powers, but it could also be the freezing abilities of a dyad demon. If she can freeze as well as shape shift, then the Lady has all the key powers of a pair of dyad demons.

A super-charged dyad demon.

And she's sitting not ten yards away.

But how could a single dyad demon have the powers of a mated pair? Most female dyads wouldn't survive without their tether. When we fought Mourn and Dusk back at the ruined hospital, they certainly didn't. However, those two were lesser demons. Greater demons often have untold powers, and I know for a fact that there was once a greater demon dyad pair: Drusus and Daria. My father fought them at the Battle of the Gates. Supposedly, that's where Drusus and Daria died. An odd chill settles into my heart.

Maybe Daria somehow survived. And kept Drusus's freezing powers to boot.

If that's true, then Daria would fit the perfect profile of a combination lust monster, shape shifter, and freezy demon. Could that even be possible?

One person knows whether Daria might have made it. My father.

I grab Dad's hand as the orchestra music swells. "Tell me about the Battle of the Gates."

"Now?" My father shoots a worried look at Cissy, who shrugs in a way that says *"whatever, let's humor her."* Dad slaps on a patient smile. "Fine. What do you want to know?"

"The only dyad demons who were also greater demons were at that battle, right?"

"Yes. Drusus and Daria."

"How did they die, exactly? Did you kill them?"

"Me? No. One of my foot soldiers stabbed Drusus through with a sword. Good fighter. He cut their tether as well. Do you know what that is?"

"Sure. A tether is a line of dark energy that connects dyads." I stare at him with a *"go on already"* sort of glare.

"That was it," says Dad. "A number of warriors saw their tether cut. We never found the bodies, though. Not that we were going to expend a lot of trouble trying to answer that mystery. Dyad demons can't live without a tether."

More bits of information fall into place. "Is there any chance Daria lived?"

"What is this about, really?" asks Cissy. "Are you getting cold feet?"

Dad sets his hand in my shoulder in a protective move. "If you want to call this off, we'll do it. Whatever you want."

"What I want is information about Daria. Could she have survived?"

"I've never seen a dyad survive having their tether cut." My father bobs his head, considering. "That said, Drusus and Daria were also greater demons. Those kind often have unusual powers. You know, like archangels." He purses his lips. "Although, dyads specialize in shape shifting, lust, and freezing people. Even if those powers were extreme, I don't know how that would help them when their tether was cut."

"But it could happen."

"If Daria somehow managed to keep them both alive, maybe."

So, Drusus and Daria could still be alive, and they might have enough power to stay that way. Damn.

My heart rate picks up speed. "What do you think happened to the bodies?"

"Charybdis would be my guess. Many from that battle got pulled in there."

"That's a magical vortex on Earth," explains Cissy. "Basically, it's a hole in the desert that pulls in supernatural beings. Every so often, it spits one out again."

I nod slowly. *Charybdis. I remember Lincoln saying something about that. It's a popular spot for demon hunting on Earth.*

My father scratches his cheek. "I suppose if Drusus and Daria survived having their tether cut, then they could have gotten dragged into Charybdis. It could have spat them out at any time. That's a lot of 'ifs,' though."

I bob a bit on the balls of my feet. My warrior sense tells me I'm getting closer. "Let's just say that somehow, Daria lived. Would she ever want to help Armageddon?"

"Certainly. Demons can be very loyal, in their own ways. She fought on Armageddon's side in the Battle of the gates. We're in Antrum, though. There's no way Drusus or Daria will get you here, even if they did survive."

"What about the demon alarms? Could Daria have gotten in, especially if she masqueraded as a quasi-demon?"

"Perhaps. That said, even if someone did get through, you have the greatest warriors in the after-realms before you." Dad's eyes fill with worry. "Please, Myla. Enjoy your day."

At this point, Dad and Cissy are done humoring me. In fact, they both look not-a-little freaked out. And the music is about to switch to my processional. I steel my shoulders. This is ridiculous. Whatever this thing is with Mrs. Pomplemousse, Dad is right. It can wait.

"Yeah. Sure." I return my focus to the Chapel floor, but I can't stop watching Mrs. Pomplemousse. She raises her right hand. A small cloud of black dust swirls around her torso.

My breath catches. I saw this happen once before—back when we were fighting the dyad demons in the ruined hospital with Desmond. Mourn pulled in some black dust right before he tried to freeze Lincoln and me.

Hells bells. I was right. Mrs. Pomplemousse is Daria.

My eyes widen as Mrs. Pomplemousse raises her other hand. Something golden gleams in her palm. Oh-the-Hell-no.

That's Lucifer's coin.

I rush forward, screaming. "Dyad demons are here! Run!"

Everyone stares at me in shock. From across the Chapel floor, Lincoln takes off for me at a sprint.

Suddenly, a great burst of darkness erupts from around Mrs. Pomplemousse.

This is just like what happened with Mourn and Dusk. The male dyad, Mourn, released a cloud of black particles that froze Desmond in place. There's no forgetting the unique look of that darkness.

And now, somehow, Mrs. Pomplemousse is releasing the very same power at my wedding.

I can do nothing but stare in shock as the black motes of evil energy wrap themselves around me. My muscles turn heavy as my body stops moving. My last thoughts are to my igni. After all, they were what saved me last time.

Find me, my little ones. Please.

CHAPTER TWENTY-EIGHT

A

I stare across the Chapel floor, my gaze locked with Lincoln's. And this isn't in a cute *"I'm looking at my future husband"* kind of way, either.

It's more of a *"yipes I'm trapped under an evil spell"* thing, which really blows.

For Lincoln's part, he became frozen while he was still running toward me. Now, he's stopped midstride in the center aisle. My heart sinks. My guy's only twenty yards away. However, the way things are right now? He might as well be in another realm.

With all my (not insignificant) will, I focus on moving my body. *Zip*. I can't even flinch, let alone reach him. *Not good.* From my peripheral vision, I scan the Chapel. Everyone else is stuck in one spot, too.

Well, almost everyone.

Mrs. Pomplemousse currently waits at the far end of the Chapel floor, alongside Aldred. They're standing on the very same stage where Lincoln and I are supposed to take our vows. Gross. And after seeing the effects of her black spell? There's no question in my mind.

Mrs. Pomplemousse is the Lady Daria.

She and Aldred have their backs turned to me, but I've no doubt what they're up to: figuring out how to use Lucifer's coin to release Hell on Earth. Well, I have one thing to say about that.

No. Freaking. Way.

Inside my soul, my wrath demon roars to life. These clowns have gone way too far. No one releases Armageddon on my wedding day. End of story.

Closing my eyes, I call out to my igni again.

Find me, my little ones.

Sweet, childish voices echo through my mind. These are the sounds of the light igni, the power that sends souls to Heaven. They're followed by a harsh cacophony of rough tones. That would be the dark igni's song. Like always, the igni are speaking to me, yet their words sound like gibberish. Even so, they're here and that's good news. They can help me start moving again, exactly like they did in the battle with Mourn and Dusk.

The igni's song grows louder until a few small lightning bolts of power swim around my right palm. My little ones have arrived, which is great. Still, I need them to be cautious. Once again, I speak to my igni in my thoughts.

You must surround me just enough to release the dyad's magic. After that, I need you to connect me to Lincoln, the same as you did last time. Form a tether of energy between us. Can you do that?

The voices keep babbling—after all, that's what igni mostly do—but the tone becomes loud and angry. *Huh.* Actually, I'm not one hundred percent certain what they're saying here, but I'll assume they mean *"yes, we'll do that"* anyway. It's not like I have much of a choice.

Wait for my signal. Start in three, two, one.

A few dozen igni appear and swirl around my arms, reminding me of fireflies. The Lady Daria and Aldred face the far wall. However, the moment the igni appear? Those two baddies turn around and stare straight at me.

Fuuuuuuuuuck.

Mrs. Pomplemousse-slash-Lady Daria rounds on Aldred. "Give me the incantation, now." The Chapel is so quiet, I can hear her every word. "Those little lightning bolts are igni. That one's the great scala, and she's using her powers to override my magic. We must activate the coin before the Scala breaks free." She raises her hand, and yes, she's still holding Lucifer's coin. Eek.

Let the record show that Mrs. Pomplemousse definitely stole Lucifer's coin from me when we hugged outside my thrax suite-o-pink stuff. Not cool.

Aldred sets his fists on his hips. "If I give you the incantation, you can open the portal. I cannot allow that to happen. It would violate the terms of the deal I made with Armageddon."

What is it with this guy and his magical agreements? Aldred made a deal once before with Armageddon, one that ended up with his daughter Adair being dead. I still can't believe he went back to the bargaining table for round two.

"Don't be a fool, Aldred. I can't hold this many people frozen forever. Hand over the incantation."

"I must be the one to release the King of Hell. That was our deal; I set free Armageddon. Only then will he kill everyone who's stopping me from becoming King of Antrum. But once that bloodshed is over? Armageddon has to return to Hell. If the terms of our deal aren't met to the letter, then Armageddon could end up staying around after he kills off my enemies."

Yup, that definitely sounds like a deal Aldred would make, all right. And there's no question who he's defined as his enemies, either: Lincoln, me, and our families. The only good thing in this situation? All this blah-blah-blahing about his master plan buys us some time.

While those two bicker, the igni's power begins to free my muscles. At last, I can twitch my hands and feet. However, Lincoln still stands frozen on the main aisle. That's not helpful.

I make shoo fingers at the igni, trying to get them to go release Lincoln already. They get the hint and start to multiply while whirling themselves into a cord, exactly like they did back when we fought Mourn and Dusk. My heart beats faster as that rope of light winds its way up the main aisle, wrapping itself about Lincoln. Soon, dozens of igni twist and dive around his body as well.

Finally, Lincoln blinks. He's starting to coming out of it, the same as I am. Even so, I can't move my legs yet. I call on my igni once more.

No need to hold back. They know you're here. Give us more power. Set us free.

Hundreds of igni spin and dive in a thin coating around Lincoln, me, and the tether that connects us. At last, I can lift my right leg a little. That's better, but it's nowhere near battle ready.

And make no mistake, a fight is coming.

Mrs. Pomplemousse-slash-Lady Daria raises her arm. Little spots of red light twinkle near her skin as her entire body transforms. In the blink of an eye, she's no longer a plump grandmotherly type. Instead, she's a tall vixen with long black hair, bright red lips, and pale skin. She paces before Aldred, making her long crimson cloak and veil trail behind her. Her eyes flare demon-red with power.

Damn.

All signs of Mrs. Pomplemousse are gone. This is definitely the demon in her Lady Daria form. Instead of potpourri, the scent of rose perfume becomes so strong it hits me in the face from clear across the freaking Chapel. The gears of my mind whirl through this particular bit of strangeness.

What's with all the stinky perfume and veil action? When she was sporting them both as Mrs. Pomplemousse, I didn't think too much of it. However, she's doing it again as Lady Daria. Demons change shape as camouflage. Keeping consistent looks between forms simply isn't done. It defeats the whole purpose.

Unless, the demon in question *has to* because they're hiding something. But what could she be hiding?

The Lady Daria runs her red-tipped finger across Aldred's chest. I can feel the waves of her lust demon mojo waft across the Chapel. "The Scala is waking up, as is Lincoln. Let's take them down." Her voice is all things whiskey, rough and sexy.

Aldred huffs out a frustrated breath. "It's Armageddon's job to fight them. I'm not getting anywhere near that pair."

But we're going near you, buddy.

"What about *our* bargain?" asks Lady Daria.

Another deal confirmed. My, oh my…Aldred's definitely been a busy boy. That makes two magical agreements with two greater demons. Jackass.

Aldred folds his stubby arms over his barrel chest. "I'm far more worried about my deal with Armageddon than the magical contract I have with you."

"Even so, our deal was very specific as well," says Lady Daria. "I get you the coin, and you get me the incantation. You've already made things unreasonably hard for me. After all, I took on all that extra work to help you regain your silly codex."

My brows jet up. Sure, I knew the Lady sent Mourn and Dusk after us. Yet the fact that she did so only as extra credit for Aldred? D-U-M-B. Who does favors for that guy? The knowledge adds a whole new level of yuck to an already yucky situation.

"And I've kept my side of the bargain," says Aldred. "I have your incantation. However, that doesn't mean I'll hand it over. I'll be the one to read it, that's all."

This whole conversation is nasty, but at least, they're still fighting over who gets to read the incantation. More time-buying. And once they're done fighting? They have to actually speak the words of the spell. Major incantations can take hours. I mean, I'm no wiz with magic, and even I know that.

Lady Daria slowly licks her lips. She's working her lust mojo and how. "Drusus and I were taken down by a lowly common angel. Imagine! Our tether was cut and Drusus got run through with a sword. We both fell into the vortex of Charybdis. It was terrible. We have diminished in the eyes of Armageddon." She sighs dramatically. More waves of lust roll across the Chapel.

Note: although Aldred seems immune to all this lust demon action, Lady Daria has a plan and she's sticking to it. Points for consistency.

"But you survived," says Aldred. "That certainly impresses the King of Hell."

"You don't know demons. Survival is nothing. I must be seen as powerful again. Allow me to speak the incantation and open the portal. That will show Armageddon that I am a demon to be feared."

"Enough, Daria." Aldred points at Lincoln and me. "We don't have time for this. They're starting to move."

Lady Daria stares straight at us. Her dark eyes fill with worry. Crap. Looks like Aldred is done fighting over nothing. "How dangerous are they?"

"They're the first two I've asked Armageddon to kill. What does that tell you?" Aldred's voice lowers an octave. "Don't ruin this. Allow me to set Armageddon loose, and I promise, I'll extoll your strength to the King of Hell. He will respect you."

Lady Daria shoots another worried glance at Lincoln and me. After that, she hands over Lucifer's coin to Aldred.

Fuck-fuck-fuckity-FUCK-fuck.

Aldred rolls out a super-long scroll and scans the contents. "I've studied this for years. So much fuss, and in the end, this has only three words." He rolls his piggish eyes.

All the oxygen seems to get sucked out of the Chapel. *Three words?* Incantations usually take hours. And that freaking parchment is like a mile long.

I want to face-palm myself. Of course, I get the only incantation in the history of the after-realms that's three words written on a huge sheet of parchment. What else did I expect?

With all my focus, I will my muscles to contract. At last, my entire body breaks free from the freezing magic. Lincoln starts to move as well. That's the good news. The bad news? We're stuck on one side of the Chapel while Lady Daria and Aldred stand onstage at the opposite wall. I still can't get over it: they will release Armageddon on the exact spot where Lincoln and I planned to exchange our vows.

Don't think about that. Fight now. Irony later.

My mind clears as I focus on Lady Daria and Aldred. They are so going down.

Lincoln and I don't need to chat out our battle strategy. Now that we can move, there's no question what we'll do next. Moving in unison, we race down the main aisle. I'm barely aware of all the frozen bodies behind us. Our parents, friends, and subjects... Everyone is still frozen in the last pose as Lady Daria released her spell. Some small part of me wonders how she did that without Drusus, but there's a battle to win here. I can't afford to get mired in that little mystery at this point.

As we race forward, Aldred tosses the coin to the ground. "Infernum."

This is Latin, which normally I can translate pretty easily. However, at this point, I'm more concerned with the number of words than what they mean.

That was the first word of the spell. Only two more to go before all Hell breaks loose.

The entire Chapel vibrates as a massive amount of power ripples through the air. I'm sure they felt that across the after-realms. I almost lose my footing while running on the shifting stones. At the same time, a bubbling pit of red goo forms around the coin. The rock stage looks like some kind of bloody swimming hole. Although the pit is only a yard wide, clawed hands are already reaching up through the crimson muck. Rage corkscrews up my neck.

Hell getting into Antrum? Not on my watch.

Aldred speaks again. "In."

The crimson pool in the stage floor grows larger. More hands, claws, and wings press up through the bubbling red sludge. I recognize a long face with a blade-like nose.

Oh, crap. That's Armageddon. I roll my eyes. *Of course, he comes for me right away.*

And there's only one word left to go.

Finally, Lincoln and I reach the stage. Lincoln ignites his baculum into a long sword while I leap into the air. I make a firm landing on Lady Daria's chest while choking her with my tail. I'm tempted to give myself a high five because that's a tricky move in any situation, let alone while wearing your wedding dress and high heels.

Lincoln stalks forward with his baculum sword blazing white fire. "Take back the incantation and we won't kill you." He holds the sword over Aldred's head. "You know the word to do it: retracto."

Aldred grits his teeth. "Terra."

Hells bells. That wasn't *"retracto."* That was the final word of the incantation. We are so screwed.

Suddenly, Armageddon leaps out of from the pit. My limbs turn rubbery. The King of Hell stands tall and lanky; a tuxedo hugs his wiry frame. His onyx skin looks smooth as polished stone, while his eyes flare red with demonic power.

Since the last time I saw Armageddon, only his stance has changed. One month ago, my father battled Armageddon (who had possessed Adair at the time). In the fight, Dad injured Armageddon's hip. As a result, the King of Hell now stands at an angle, as if he's lost mobility in one leg. So, that's good.

Armageddon snaps his fingers. A wave of power slams into me, throwing me off the stage. My back slams onto the small strip of empty floor space before the raised platform. At the same time, a metal cage appears around me. While the top and bottom are solid steel, the walls of the prison are made of bars. The thing is barely large enough for me to crouch inside, and then only if my neck cranes at an odd angle. I look over to Lincoln. He's been imprisoned the same way. It breaks my heart.

Even worse? I know for a fact that Armageddon used to lock up my father like this, too.

I rattle the bars of my cage. *Solid.* At least, the igni still form a protective shield around Lincoln and me. Everyone else in the Chapel isn't as lucky, though. Just like before, they stay frozen in place, unable to fight. This must be horrible for everyone, but especially for my father. I know he'd do anything rather than see me caged by Armageddon.

Panic and shock wheel through me, emptying my mind of all thought. Some small part of me says I need to focus in order to escape. Not happening. At this point, it's a huge effort merely to crouch in my cage and not cry my eyes out.

While keeping his gaze locked on me, Armageddon's mouth winds into an over-large smile. Battle demons climb out of the pool behind him. I spot some manus, flying succubae, and all sorts of other Class A nightmares. Normally, that would make me a happy girl. Right now? Not so much.

I rattle my bars again and look over to Lincoln. "Are you okay?"

"Relative term, but yes." His baculum rods lay just outside his cage. He strains through the bars, trying to reach them. Lincoln's face flushes with the effort. It's no use, though. Crud. I bet Armageddon did that on purpose, too.

Aldred scurries to Armageddon's side. "There they are. Lincoln and the demon whore. Go kill them as we agreed. What are you waiting for? I already released you."

"You did release me," says Armageddon slowly. His cruel voice makes me shiver.

Aldred waves his tubby arms around. "Go kill them and their families, then. After that, you must return to Hell." Aldred stares at the massive demons that keep climbing from the pit. "And take your demonic army with you."

"I'm not going anywhere." Armageddon waves his three-knuckled hand dismissively. "And neither are they."

Aldred puffs out his bottom lip. "That was not the terms of our agreement."

Ignoring Aldred, Armageddon turns to Lady Daria. "My dear. I must admit, I was disappointed when you and Drusus were so easily defeated at the Battle of the Gates. That said, I've been watching you from Hell for some time. It was you who tricked Prescott into finding Lucifer's coin. I'm most pleased."

Aldred steps between Armageddon and Lady Daria. "My soldiers did all the work. Lady Daria was useless."

I roll my eyes. Way to throw your only ally under the bus, Aldred. Especially when you promised to put in a good word.

Armageddon keeps right on ignoring Aldred. "Of course, the true accomplishment was pinpointing the need for Lucifer's

coin in the first place. It was *I* who did that. It wasn't easy finding a way to free myself after what *that one* had done." He points
right at me. Both my tail and I give him a lewd hand gesture in
reply.

Lady Daria bows her head. The movement makes her long red
veil shift behind her. "We are all in awe of you, oh King."

"Of course, you are. And you haven't even heard the full tale
yet. After I discovered a way to escape Hell, I then used my agents
on Earth to release you from Charybdis. I even made sure that
Prescott had access to the right books and motivation."

"Your glory is beyond words," sighs Lady Daria.

"What a sniveling sycophant you are," says Armageddon.
"Don't stop, though. I'll find a suitable role for you in Hell."

I cup my hand by my mouth. "Hey, I have an idea for a role.
Maybe you two can fight alongside each other again." I snap my
fingers. "Oh, that's right. Teaming up didn't work out so well at
the Battle of the Gates. Dad kicked both your butts." I scan the
room dramatically. "Where is Drusus anyway?"

Lady Daria hisses at me. It's a full snake-y move where she
bares her teeth and everything. "Quiet, you!"

Like that will happen. I point to Aldred instead. "What about
you, buddy boy?" Some small part of me says wonders if I should
shut up, but I put that part in a time-out chair. "How's the master
dealmaker doing now? Doesn't seem like Armageddon is killing
anyone or leaving." I shoot him some mock thumbs-up. "Nice
work, you!"

Aldred stomps his foot. "Kill her!"

"Of course, I'll kill them." Armageddon finally turns to face
Aldred. "In fact, I plan to kill everyone. Except you, of course."

"Quite right." Aldred puffs up his chest. "You'll kill everyone
on that list."

"Oh, you did give me a list." Armageddon raises his right
hand. A rolled sheet of parchment appears on his stone-smooth
palm. "But our contract has very specific—or should I say non-
specific—language in it." He unrolls the document and points to
a line. "Right here, section one, line seven. I shall kill all your

enemies. The way I see it, every thrax, human, quasi, and ghoul in the after-realms are your enemies."

Aldred takes a half-step backward. "But…We…"

"Don't try to outsmart the devil on deals. You'll always lose."

I lean forward until my forehead thunks against the bars of my cage. Aldred is such a dumbass. This makes twice that he's gotten the crap-end on a deal with Armageddon.

Aldred steps forward and pokes Armageddon in the center of his bony chest. "How can you?"

"Quiet!" Armageddon snaps his fingers once more. A wave of power slams into Aldred, forcing him to slide away from Armageddon. To fight the pull, Aldred grabs onto Lady Daria. The pair tumbles to the floor. A moment later, a steel box appears around them both. Now Aldred and Lady Daria are caged, the same as Lincoln and me.

Lady Daria rattles her bars. "This is an outrage. Release me!"

"In a moment." Armageddon gestures to the growing ranks of demons behind him. "I have more than enough assistance for the work at hand. You stay put." The King of Hell slowly turns to Lincoln and me. "Now, it's time to kill you two. At last."

With these words, my mind finally snaps out of its funk. All of a sudden, it's pretty obvious what I need to do.

I simply need a ton of igni to do it.

Raising my arms, I call out in a loud voice: "Come to me, my little ones. I need you all!"

Instantly, the room fills with millions of tiny igni. They sparkle in the air, creating a thick cloud of shifting light. There's more that I need them to do, however.

"Create more tethers. Encase, link, and release all our allies." The music of the light and dark igni echo though my mind as they whip about to fulfill my orders. Small bodies of brightness encircle almost everyone. The igni can see into someone's soul. They know who is trustworthy. After they fulfill my orders, only a handful of demonic delegates remain in a frozen state.

Armageddon lets out a roar of rage. "You little angelic bitch!"

"Really? I thought I was a demonic whore. You and Aldred need to get on the same page."

Lincoln shoots me a thumbs-up. "Well said." My guy always has my back.

Armageddon's voice blasts through the Chapel. "Kill her!" He starts to limp off the stage, his demonic army following behind him. Whoa. Looks Dad really did a number on Armageddon when they were fighting last time. It's taking the King of Hell forever to limp over and kill me. The sight is hypnotic, and not in a good way.

This is where I die.

Lincoln's voice breaks into my thoughts. "Myla, get back."

"What?" I shake my head, trying to focus again.

"There's no room to fight. You must go defensive. Make yourself a smaller target." Lincoln motions for me to slide to the far side of my cage.

"Got it." Much as I hate to cower, I also have all of Hell's worst coming for me and no way to protect myself. I scooch my body until I'm as far away as possible, curl into a ball, and wrap my arms around my head. My tail makes a protective loop around my neck.

There, that's about as protected as I'll get.

The thud of footsteps sounds as Armageddon limps closer. War cries echo in from the demonic horde, but no one screams louder than the King of Hell. Fear prickles across my skin. Everything around me seems more extreme, from the yelling warriors to the chilly metal beneath my body. My mind races as I think through options in what's quite possibly my very last moments alive.

No matter how I look at this situation, there's only one way I make it out of here, and that's if my igni free everyone before Armageddon kills me. Trouble is, last time it took them a while to free Lincoln and me. Is it too much to hope they've gotten better at it by now and can release everyone more quickly? Knowing my luck, it probably is.

Tapping sounds on my cage. I peep through my fingers to see Armageddon's face peering at me through the metal bars. He's only a few feet away. "Nice to see you again." He holds up his arm; a long spear of red fire appears in his hand. "Looks like you want to play hide and seek. Let's see if my weapon can find you."

Everything in me wants to go into a battle stance, but I can't even get myself up to a full sitting position. Instead, I curl into a smaller ball; it's really the best I can do at this point. Armageddon arches his arm back and the thought occurs to me that I'm about to be skewered by Kill of Hell on my wedding day. In my wedding gown. Not the way I wanted to die.

All of a sudden, a blur in golden armor slams into the King of Hell. Huzzah! Armageddon is thrown back, along with his demon horde. My body lightens with a jolt of happy.

Dad's awake. Nice.

After that, everyone starts moving and fighting. A flurry of angels dive in from the sky to attack the demons. Thrax race across the floor, their swords and baculum ready for battle. Quasis get into the fight, too. Some of them wield folding chairs from the Chapel floor. Others grab the standing candelabras and pennant poles. My people look like a frightened mob of villagers about to take down Frankenstein's castle. They're pretty awesome, actually.

The scrape of metal sounds above my head. *Someone's breaking into my cage. This is it.* Turns out, I can't stomach the thought of staying curled in a corner for one more second. If this is the end, I'll meet it head on. I twist my body so I'm in a semi crouch, my tail arched over my shoulder.

There, that's better.

The top of my prison gets peeled back as if it were nothing more than a sheet of paper. I blink my eyes rapidly, not believing what I'm seeing. Lincoln stands beside the Earl of Striga. *Yes.* One of Lucas's magic hula hoops holds of top my cage in the air. I exhale a relieved breath. "It's you."

"Myla!" Lincoln reaches forward and pulls me into his arms. "I thought Armageddon had gotten you with his spear."

"He didn't."

Lincoln presses a pair of baculum into my hands. "You'll need more than your tail for this fight." A gleam shines in his eyes.

We're going to battle demons again. Together.

I scan the Chapel. Dad and his angel buddies are taking it to Armageddon and his horde. Walker's a marvel of speed as he slices the wings off a devil bat. Octavia and Connor have ignited their baculum to take down a pair of crini demons. Mom's using her tail to cut through a knot of demonic serpents. Even Cissy's using a candelabra to fight alongside Zeke as they turn an enchanted corpse into mush.

All in all, it's a really touching scene. My entire extended family is here, killing demons and protecting the after-realms. Even better, the quasis and thrax are fighting side by side. I sniffle. This is one helluva battle. Too bad I have to miss it.

"Much as I'd love to fight with you, I need to work with my igni."

"You can summon more of them?"

"Not more, necessarily. I'm pretty sure all the igni in the after-realms are already here. I need them to take a new shape, though. Lucifer's coin set Armageddon free, but now that the King of Hell is here in Antrum? He and his buddies are fair game again for my powers."

A slow smile rounds Lincoln's mouth. "You'll send them back to Hell. Perfect."

"Yup. I need the igni to create a ton of soul columns." That's the form my little ones take when moving souls around. "I'll send Armageddon and his buddies right back where they came from."

"What about Lady Daria?"

"Good question." I scan the scene, looking for the Lady Daria. She's easy to spot, considering she's still in a prison box with Aldred on the stage. Trouble is, their cage is surrounded by a huge group of manus demons. Not good. Manus are gorilla-like creatures with long fangs and a taste for blood. There can only be one reason why they're on guard duty. Armageddon has decided to keep his word for once. He's got the manus to make sure that the Earl of Acca stays safe. And Lady Daria is along for the ride.

I could try to move her anyway, but Lady Daria's a greater demon. That would take a lot of supernatural juice. There's no way I can send Armageddon back as well as his demon horde along with a second Greater Demon. Unlike Aldred, I know my limits.

I focus on Lincoln. "Lady Daria is protected from the fighting. I don't see anyone battling their way to her any time soon. And I won't have enough power to send her to Hell at the same time as Armageddon and his cronies." A shiver moves up my spine. "Even if I do dismiss the King of Hell and his army, Lady Daria us staying right here. It will take time for all my igni to move so many bodies around. There won't be any left to protect our wedding guests."

"Meaning?"

"Once I start reforming the igni into soul columns, she'll just freeze everyone again."

Lincoln frowns. "How about asking the igni to protect only you, me, and a few top warriors? Maybe your father and Lucas."

"I'll try." Unfortunately, the words come out as more of a question. "Even in the best of situations, my igni are tough to control. In fact, I'm amazed they've done this much. They really like making soul columns and not much else."

Lincoln fixes me with a serious look. All the love and trust in the after-realms shines in his mismatched eyes. "You focus on moving your igni. I'll guard you. Everything else will be fine."

"But Lady Daria—"

"I'm not concerned about her. Your safety is far more important at the moment. Once you start summoning and commanding igni, you lose touch with your surroundings." He ignites his baculum as a long sword. "I'll be here through everything. And afterward, we'll figure something out. We always do."

I nibble on my thumbnail. "I don't know."

"Just focus on those igni." Lincoln gets into battle stance. The light from his baculum sword casts flickering shadows on his handsome face. "I know you can do this." The strong tones of his voice reverberate through me.

I straighten my shoulders. "You're right."

Lincoln winks. "That's my Myla."

The roar of battle surrounds me. I can't let it derail my focus, though. Closing my eyes, I call out to my igni once more, making sure to speak in a full voice so Lincoln knows my plans. "Little ones, I need you to send Armageddon and his demons to Hell. You must form soul columns around the demons. Here's the tricky part. At the same time, I need you to keep the protection and tethers in place between Lincoln, me, my father and Lucas."

The igni instantly shift to form swirling pillars of light around Armageddon and every one of his demons. Pillars of brightness dot the massive Chapel floor. The fighting ends, which is good. All the wedding guests freeze in place. That part isn't as good. At least, the igni did heed my bidding about the tether stuff. A thin shield of igni remains around Lincoln, me, my father and Lucas.

So far, so good.

I lift my arms. "Move them!"

The soul columns grow brighter as they drag the demons back toward the gurgling pit. The igni's song rockets through my mind at an ear-splitting volume. One by one, the bright soul columns reach the pit. Flares of pure white brightness erupt as each demon disappears. The soul columns won't let them go until they're back in Hell.

While the other demons are moving along nicely, things with Armageddon's soul column aren't going so well. As the massive pillar of igni surrounds him, the King of Hell snaps his fingers, summoning his own hell fire to slow the igni down. Crimson light mixes with the pure white brightness of the igni. Their small bodies, once swimming quickly in the column shape, become sluggish and dim. While the other demons still get moved to the pit with ease, Armageddon doesn't budge.

As each demon moves, more power rushes through my nervous system. My mind fogs over with energy. My bones feel like they're twisting inside me. I grit my teeth and stay the course. There simply is no other choice.

Dad marches up to Armageddon. My father can change into his armor with merely a thought. Right now, he's wearing his formal golden stuff, and it gleams in the igni's brightness. He pauses before Armageddon's soul column. "My daughter said it's time to leave." My father raises his arm, palm forward, and begins one of his own spells. The white flames of angelfire pour from his hand and into the soul column that surrounds Armageddon. The red hell fire begins to fade. Armageddon's soul column slowly moves across the floor. It's not fast enough, though.

My limbs tremble with the power rushing through them. Even when I move billions of souls at once, I don't process this much energy. My soul columns send the last of the demons back into the pit. However, that leaves the worst one still around.

Armageddon.

Through my mental fog, I hear Lincoln calling to Lucas. "Get over here! Help Xavier!"

The Earl of Striga rushes out from the crowd, his long purple robes billowing behind him. Not sure what he was doing before, but if I know Lucas, he was most likely healing those hurt in battle.

Now Lucas stops to stand beside my father. The senior wizard then summons shifting hoops of power that loop around the King of Hell. The soul column around Armageddon grows a little stronger. He moves a little faster. It's not enough, though. At this rate, it will still take hours to get Armageddon into that pit, and I don't have that kind of time. As more energy flows through me, my mind becomes little more than a haze of igni voices. Power tears through every cell in my body. My legs turn watery beneath me.

This isn't working. I can't move Armageddon.

"Myla," Lincoln's calm voice breaks through my cluttered thoughts. "Put every igni you have left to Armageddon's soul column."

I try to focus on him. Unfortunately, the igni seem to coat my vision as well as my body. He's a hazy form and a loving voice, nothing more.

"I can't risk it. Lady Daria—"

"You can't hold out much longer and you know it. Ask your igni to protect you and only you. The rest of us will be fine. You need every bit of power to get rid of Armageddon."

I nod, sadly. I hate to admit this, but Lincoln's right. Pulling in a ragged breath, I command to my igni. "Listen, my little ones. You must send Armageddon back to Hell. If that means you stop protecting Lincoln, Lucas, my father, or even me, that's what you have to do. Do you understand?"

In reply, lightning bolts pour down from the ceiling of the Chapel, encasing Armageddon in a fiery ring. Fresh power zooms through me. Even when I first took Scala energy into my soul, I never felt such a rush. With all my will, I send every ounce of that power at Armageddon and the pit to Hell. Long lightning bolts wind across my arms. My teeth vibrate in my skull as I call to my igni one more time: "Get that bastard out of here!"

A blinding flash of light fills the Chapel. At last, the soul column around Armageddon breaks free from its sluggish pace and whirls toward the opened pit. With one final burst of red brightness, Armageddon descends into the bubbling muck. Although he's surrounded by igni, I can still see him howling with rage.

Good.

"That's it." My voice comes out as a harsh croak. "We're done."

The next thing I know, I'm enveloped in Lincoln's arms. A thin coating of igni swirls around us both. I'm exhausted, but I can still breathe, move, and look around. And from what I can see? Everything else is in bad shape.

The Chapel is quiet once more. The battle is over. Armageddon and all his demons are gone. Unfortunately, Lady Daria remains and she hasn't wasted any time. All my wedding guests are frozen in place again, except for Lincoln and me. Even my father and Lucas—who were protected before—are now frozen solid by Lady Daria's spell. And honestly? If Lincoln hadn't pulled me against him so quickly, I think the igni would have skipped him too.

As I watch in horror, Lady Daria becomes encased in red light once more. *She's changing shape.* This time, she transforms into a gooey and red version of herself. The sight reminds me of a Lady Daria-shaped gummy bear. It's enough to make me sick to my stomach, but I can't deny that it's clever. With her new gooey body, Lady Daria simply oozes her way out of the cage, leaving Aldred behind.

Lady Daria's taken the shape of a trafero demon. These are in the same demonic class as the limus, who are big gooey monsters, too. Only trafero are far more dangerous. While a limus needs to consume you whole in order to kill you, a trafero has a lot more options when it comes to fighting, mostly because their gooey skin is covered in acid. And while the igni can protect us from Lady Daria's freezing spell, I'm not sure what they can do when it comes to acidic stuff.

I worry my lower lip with my teeth. Actually, I'm pretty sure we're in deep trouble.

Lincoln and I still stand just by the foot of the stage, in the same cleared out area where we'd only recently been caged by Armageddon. I give another order to my igni. "Keep us protected and tethered, little ones."

Their voices giggle and growl in reply. Still, they maintain the shield that sits right above our skin. A short tether appears on the floor beside us. That's a good start. Unfortunately, there aren't a lot of igni to go around yet, so the shield and tether look pretty thin. Even so, that should change with time. It depends how long it takes my little ones to move all the demons to Hell. As more igni become available, they'll heed my last message and come back to help.

Lincoln and I move apart and get into a battle stance. My guy ignites his baculum into a long sword while my tail arches over my shoulder.

We're ready for anything.

While still in her gummy form, the Lady Daria glares at Lincoln and me. "That was my chance to impress Armageddon. My opportunity to regain his favor. And you ruined it."

I roll my eyes. "I didn't see you changing into gooey-girl during the battle. You easily could've slipped out and gotten some brownie points in. I'd say you ruined your own chances."

Lady Daria whips out her arms. And when I say whips out, I mean that her gooey and semi-transparent limbs actually stretch off the stage. One hand reaches for Lincoln; the other goes toward me. The slimy appendage reaches right for my face.

"Move, boy!" My tail heeds the call, arching before me in a pinwheel motion. With a slurping noise, it takes off Lady Daria's gooey hand at the wrist. Beside me, Lincoln makes the same movement with his long sword, cutting off Lady Daria's other hand.

Lady Daria howls in pain. "How dare you?"

"How dare we what?" I ask. "Defend ourselves?" Meanwhile, her hands start oozing their way back to Lady Daria. She'll be whole again in a matter of seconds. What a crybaby.

Another flare of red light encompasses Lady Daria as she changes shape once more. This time, she becomes a giant wasp demon, what's called an ictus. Only in this case, her wasp shape has a hunch of exoskeleton on one side. It's totally weird. The extra weight on her shoulders will make it harder for Lady Daria to fly. You'd think she'd choose a more sleek form. Not that I'm complaining.

Wasp-Daria flutters her massive wings and lifts off the stage. She holds her bulbous head high as her long body droops beneath her, ending in a massive stinger that drips with green poison. I grin.

Bring it on.

Wasp-Daria swoops at Lincoln first. My guy turns his baculum into a javelin made of white flame, which he chucks at Wasp-Daria's belly. It slams into her exoskeleton and leaves a burn mark but nothing more serious than that.

Fine. All the more for me to kill.

After that, Wasp-Daria rounds on me. Her insect head holds bulbous eyes and a slit for a mouth, the latter of which winds into an evil smile. She's so pumped about her bad self. Whatever.

Once Wasp-Daria is close, I jump up, wrap my tail around her skinny neck and hoist myself onto her back. After I have a good seat, I get to work. In this case, that work means trying to tear her wings off.

Wasp-Daria goes berserk. She takes me on a high-speed flight around my own wedding chapel. Wind whips through my hair and my veil gets torn off. A few angels were still in the air when Lady Daria magically re-froze everyone, so they're still magically hovering around now. In an act of supreme nastiness, Wasp-Daria makes a point to slam into them whenever possible. They aren't hurt necessarily, but still. That's just mean, so I pull on her wings even harder. Damned things don't so much as crack.

There's a bright spot to my little ride of terror. No matter where Lady Daria flies, my igni do a bang-up job of keeping the tether going between Lincoln and me. The dim line of power between us stretches thin as the strand of a spider web. It doesn't break, however. Go igni.

Meanwhile, Lincoln's turned his baculum into a fiery bow. He shoots off flaming arrows at Wasp-Daria. Sadly, every hit bounces off her exoskeleton. And all my work at tearing off her wings is coming to nothing.

This chick is tough.

Wasp-Daria tries a new tactic and flies right toward the ceiling. As plans go, this one doesn't suck. She has an exoskeleton after all. At the same time, I'm pretty squishy, except for my tail. Call me crazy, but I do not want to end up crushed to death on the ceiling of my own wedding chapel.

That's not even the worst part. From a distance, the stone ceiling of the Chapel looks pretty smooth and white. Yet as I get closer, I notice that it's actually lined with blade-sharp stalactites, which means I'll not only get crushed there, I'll also get skewered. Not okay.

As I hurtle toward the ceiling at an ever faster rate, my tail tightens its grip on Wasp-Daria's insect throat. At the last possible second, I leap off her back and swing upside down, hoping my momentum will steer her away from the rock above us.

It works. Sadly, it works too well.

Instead of making a high-speed crash into the ceiling, we're now diving Kamikaze-style toward the floor and my frozen guests. Wasp-Daria buzzes from side to side, trying to shake me. It works. My grip on Wasp-Daria slips until I'm only hanging on by her stinger. Sure, my tail is doing the hanging-on part, and since it's covered in dragonscales it can't get stung, but still. This has disaster written all over it.

Below me, Lincoln holds out arms. "Jump, Myla! I'll catch you." *Damn, do I ever love that man.*

Wasp-Daria speeds toward the floor. I point to a spot about three yards ahead of Lincoln. "There, okay?"

"Perfect."

For the record, it's not easy to think when you're hanging upside down from a demon bug in your wedding gown, yet somehow I'm able to calculate when I should free myself from Wasp-Daria. Ideally, I need a little runway so I have a fighting chance for Lincoln to catch me.

There's also the matter of the stinger. Sure, I could just let go. However, the thing has felt loose for a while now and if I can cause Lady Daria a little extra damage, that's what I'll do. I begin my silent countdown.

Three, two, one.

At the end of the countdown, my tail tightens its hold on Wasp-Daria's stinger and yanks, hard. There's a loud crunch as it pulls the stinger right out of her backside. *Perfect.* For a few seconds, I free-fall through the Chapel. Then, strong arms enclose around me. Lincoln.

"I got you."

"You're awesome, have I told you that?"

He kisses the tip of my nose. "Once or twice."

I chuckle. "Good."

Wasp-Daria lands back on the stage. Red light envelops her body again. *Yipes.* Another form is coming. I realize that I'm still holding her wasp stinger with my tail, so I chuck it aside.

Lincoln sets me on my feet. "She's a tricky one."

"I know. Right? It's like she doesn't have any vulnerability. I mean, beyond the fact that I was able to pull out her stinger and all. But that didn't slow her down."

"My warrior sense tells me she's hiding something. Keep an eye out."

"I've the same suspicion, my love."

The red light around Wasp-Daria grows brighter as her body balloons in shape. Within seconds, she's taken the form of a massive stone golem. These are elementals and super-rare. Unfortunately, they aren't demons, so I don't know too much about them. The form Lady Daria has taken is nine feet tall, bald, and has what looks like elephant hide for skin. The thing also sports the single largest forehead I have ever seen, along with a filthy loincloth and a massive club. For the first time, I'm wishing my wedding gown had some hidden pockets for weapons. That sure would come in handy right now.

I jump up into a somersault, planning to land behind her onstage after spearing her at the top of her spine with my tail. It's a classic soft spot for most creatures. Once I'm airborne, I notice something that throws off my game completely.

There's another face on her neck.

I land behind Golem-Daria, my tail still arched.

Golem-Daria lurches down from the stage while taking a swipe at Lincoln with her club. Lincoln changes his baculum into a trident, spears the club, and wrests it from her grip with ease. His long sword strikes her upper thigh, getting in our first good hit of the battle. Golem-Daria roars. I smile from ear to ear.

That's my guy, ladies and gentlemen.

Lincoln circles her, looking for another opportunity to strike. "You saw something when you leaped over her, didn't you?"

"Yeah, there's a face on her neck. What *is* that, anyway?"

Golem-Daria makes a few more lunges at Lincoln, trying to grab his neck with her thick hands. Lincoln dodges her attacks, but takes the chance to check out her neck. A long moment passes before he speaks again. "Drusus."

My brain seems to go on pause. Suddenly, it's obvious how Lady Daria survived. "Oh, man. She shape shifted to take Drusus inside her. That's why she needed the veil. That's pretty clever." It makes her harder to fight, though. If we kill her; Drusus might be able to keep them both alive.

Lincoln's thinking the same thing. "Let's use Assault Plan Omicron." I know what that one entails. We'll stab the hearts of both demons at the same time.

"Got it."

Lincoln and I rush into action. I make another frontal assault by jumping into the air. This time, Golem-Daria sees it coming. Even though she's big as a barn and busy fighting Lincoln, she's able to move out of the way. I land on my ass, which pisses me off.

Red light surrounds Golem-Daria as she transforms back into her temptress form. Lincoln still stands before her; I'm at her back. Even so, I don't need to see her face to know that she's working her lust demon wiles on my guy.

Too bad he's an expert in that area.

Wave after wave of lust demon power rolls around us. Lincoln stares at Lady Daria, and for a second, there's that blank puppy-dog look I used to see in Prescott's face. Can she really cast one over on my guy?

Lincoln all-out laughs. "Nice try. But I already have a lust demon."

My tail does a happy dance as Lincoln reignites his baculum into a long sword and stalks toward Lady Daria. Her leg is bleeding through her gown and she stands at an odd angle. Lincoln got a good hit in, so she's not able to move any more. You'd think she would get a weapon, yet all Lady Daria does it clutch her veil more tightly against her shoulders.

Something inside me clicks. I know where Drusus is hidden. All those damned veils. He's under them for sure.

With that, I know exactly how to end this.

Running forward, I grip Lady Daria's long veil and cloak, tearing them away from her back. And there he is.

Drusus.

The dude is half dead and mostly rotting. A stench worse than anything I've ever known hits me straight in the face. All in all, Drusus is nothing more than a half torso merged into her back. I'm not one to feel sorry for demons—not for the evil ones, anyway—but my heart does go out to Drusus a little bit. He's all mangy and green, more skeleton than man. In fact, I'm pretty sure this dude was the model for the Crypt Keeper.

I arch my tail over my shoulder. "Let's do this." And by '*this*,' I mean skewer two hearts at the same time.

Lincoln raises his long sword. "Now!"

While Lincoln stabs Lady Daria from the front, I get Drusus from behind. There's a gross squishing noise from my side and some greenish glop spurts on me. I guess that's to be expected since Drusus was already pretty much dead. Still a little gross, though.

Lady Daria and Drusus fall over, dead. I'm about to ask if we should check them when they burst into flames. Within seconds, the two are fried down to nothing but a few bits of charcoal. I let out a long breath.

We did it.

I rush over to inspect the spot where the gurgling portal had opened up. There isn't even any coin left over to deal with. Total battle bonus.

A second later, the Chapel comes back to life again. Everyone is freaking out, and so I take a page from Lincoln's book and whistle super-loud. It's one of those moves where I put my pinky and pointer finger on either side of my mouth and let go. The place falls silent. No one fucks with the battle bride when she makes that kind of noise.

"Here's the deal," I say. I step over to Aldred's cage and lean against the steel bars. "Aldred is a dick. And Lincoln and I…" I pause, unsure what to say next. Beyond whistling and starting to order everyone around, I hadn't really thought things through.

"We're going to the courtroom, right now." Lincoln reignites his baculum and points it at Aldred. "Guess who's coming with us?"

Alfred whimpers. "But this is all a misunderstanding."

"Tell it to be Arbiter, buddy." With the help of Lucas, we magic Aldred out of his cage and onto his feet. Good sport that I am, I help Aldred walk away. Okay, that might be a bit of an exaggeration as technically my tail drags him away after I wrap it around his throat, but the same result is achieved.

The moment we hit the Chapel floor, our parents and friends are upon us. Dad is thrilled to have kicked Armageddon's butt, family style. Mom's relieved and a little grossed out about the snake demon blood on her tail. Octavia looks serene. Cissy asks me if I can train her in personal defense techniques. After years of trying to get her into fighting, it seems she may have family gotten the bug. Zeke says something dicky and I ignore him. Walker gives us both a quick hug before going off to help the House of Striga find anyone who's hurt and ensure they are healed up with magic. Walker really is the best.

All through this, we don't see Connor. Not that I care. In fact, very little could bug me at this point. Why? My tail remains wrapped around Aldred's throat.

With all the greetings and regrouping behind us, Lincoln and I head off to court. We're sorting this Acca thing out right now, one way or another.

CHAPTER TWENTY-NINE

A

A few minutes later, Lincoln, Aldred, and I march into the court-room. The cavern seems unchanged from our last visit—it's still a massive cave with a ceiling that's furrowed by stalactites. Wooden benches line the long stone floor. I let go of Aldred's neck a while back. It was grossing out my tail. Now, Aldred keeps pace right before us, mostly because Lincoln's baculum sword is pointed at the dude's spine. Nothing like an angelfire blade to help you keep your focus.

Across the room, the Arbiter sits ramrod straight on her raised stone throne. Her gaze stays locked in profile. *Huh. Maybe this is how she sleeps?* Before we entered, there was no one else in the courtroom. The folds of the Arbiter's long white robes don't move an inch. Once again, it gives the illusion that she really is a statue.

All of a sudden, the Arbiter turns in our direction. A wisp of a smile curls her mouth.

Oh, she's alive and awake, all right.

"I've been awaiting you," says the Arbiter. Her deep voice echoes through the chamber.

Lincoln, Aldred, and I pause before the raised platform. I give the Arbiter a little wave. "We brought you something."

The Arbiter's features turn unreadable. "And what is this?"

"More testimony." Lincoln extinguishes his baculum. Immediately, Aldred turns to haul ass to the exit door.

That's so not going to happen.

I turn around to grab Aldred by his tunic and notice that half our wedding guests seem to have followed us here from the Chapel. A crowd is gathering inside the courtroom, silently filling up the many benches. Mostly, it's thrax.

And man, do they ever look pissed.

I worry my lower lip with my teeth. Angry thrax could be good for us…Or very, very bad for us. I guess there's only one way to find out. "Hang on." I tighten my grasp on Aldred's tunic and drag him back. "You've some 'splaining to do, Al."

I shove Aldred until he stands before the Arbiter once more. He clasps his hands together at his neckline. "Oh, great Arbiter. Have pity on a poor father. I've been so upset at losing my sweet daughter, Adair. I made poor choices. That's not who I am. Not really." He points to Lincoln. "This one has tricked me into looking guilty." Next he wags his chubby finger in my direction. "And she's even worse, using her lust demon wiles to clutter my mind."

I snort. "As if."

Aldred falls to his knees. "This is all a misunderstanding. Take pity." He lowers his voice to half-whisper. "They're both mad, I tell you. All these two think about is how to gain more power. You must protect us all from them."

The Arbiter's face stays totally devoid of emotion, which sucks. Because if she sides with Aldred, then we're really screwed. Again.

The Arbiter focuses on Lincoln first. "And what do you have to say?"

"Aldred is the one who's mad with power. He sacrificed his own daughter to his ambitions and never shed a tear when she died. He even made a pact with Armageddon to release the King of Hell into the realms of Earth and Antrum, all so he could rule."

Lincoln's parents break through the crowd. Connor is the first to speak. "Are you all right, son?"

"It depends." Lincoln's in total prince mode, which means he isn't taking any crap from Connor. *Good.* "Why are you here? Because if it's to help Aldred, then the answer is that I'm furious."

At this point, I really, really, really want to cheer, but I think that might be bad form. I let my tail do a happy-dance instead.

"I'll do whatever is best for you, son. I'm simply glad you're not injured."

"Hello?" I raise my hand. "Future daughter-in-law, right over here. I'm fine, in case you were wondering."

Lincoln shoots me a sly look. We've had multiple conversations about how son-centric Connor is. At first, I thought it was just a lot of paternal love. Now, I'm not so sure. The guy's a demon-phobe or something.

Aldred hops to his feet. "Connor, you must help me." The crowd breaks out into grumbles. I frown. It's still not clear who they're rooting for here. Which is a little sad, considering these folks were all invited to our wedding.

Note to self: make better friends.

At least, my parents are here along with Octavia, and Xavier and Camilla, and they look appropriately concerned. That means a lot.

The Arbiter raises her hand, palm forward. The room falls silent. "And if this man is found guilty, what is the punishment you seek?"

"I had asked before that he be exiled from Antrum." Lincoln shakes his head. "Now, I wish for something else."

Lincoln and I had discussed this a while ago, so I know exactly where he's going with this. He'll ask for a life sentence in a dark dungeon.

"As the high prince, I request a duel of execution. A battle to the death."

Or not.

I grip Lincoln's arm. "Battle to the death?" Some small voice reminds me that this is the exact same conversation I used to have with my mother, only she was the clutchy one who whined about everything being *"to the death"* and I was one who wanted to fight. I listen to that little voice for a moment, then go right on with my grabby hands and over-the-top worrying.

"To the death?" A small smile rounds Lincoln's mouth. "You used to do that all the time at the Arena. And at the tender age of twelve, I might add."

I lower my voice as much as possible, not that I really need to. The whole crowd is chattering away so loudly, I can hardly hear myself think. "I don't like this idea."

"You must admit; it has its merits." Lincoln glares at Aldred in a way that says *"I've been wanting to kill that guy for a long time."*

"Isn't there anything else? What about the whole dungeon idea? We could make sure he was locked up with rats and old incontinent dudes."

"Appealing as that sounds, our family won't be safe as long as Aldred is alive. A duel is the only option that keeps our family secure while still following thrax tradition." He takes my hands in his. "Even so, if you give the word, we can choose another path."

My stomach does few flip-flops. *Another path.* I know what route Lincoln's talking about here: walking away from the throne and leaving the thrax to Aldred. He'd do it, too. I scan the courtroom. Nervous thrax faces peer at me from the packed benches. Sure, many of them have been anti-demonic assholes, but others have been kind and welcoming, too. It would suck to watch them suffer.

I carefully inspect every line of Lincoln's face. My guy knows he can take down Aldred. And yet, he'd walk away from everything just for me. Sure, we could live in Purgatory and Lincoln would never complain about leaving his crown behind. Even so, I know one thing for certain.

It would bug the crap out of me.

Every time I'd get news about something awful that Aldred did, I'd want to suit up as King and Queen and make it right. Only, I wouldn't be able to. In the long run, neither of us could live with that. Plus, Lincoln really is a kick-ass warrior. He'll flatten Aldred in no time. *Hopefully.* I have no idea how these duel thingies work, though.

That said, I can't let this opportunity pass us by, for Lincoln or for me.

"I have one thing to say here." I lock gazes with my guy, trying to convey all my adoration and trust with a single look. "Go rip his throat out, honey."

A slow smile rounds Lincoln's mouth. "I love you."

I give him a kissy face. "Right back at ya."

"Besides, you know me. I have a plan." Lincoln turns to the Arbiter. "It is decided. I formally request a duel of execution. Nothing else will do."

The courtroom falls silent as the Arbiter raises her hand, palm forward. "I have reviewed the evidence you provided. The high prince's request is granted."

"What?" All the blood drains from Aldred's face. "The prince is a far better warrior. I won't agree to it and you must have my consent."

"Then I allow you to set terms for the battle," says Lincoln. "I won't bring any weapons, if you like."

It's an effort to keep up my calm-face because inside I'm screaming. *No weapons? What is he, nuts?* I mean, technically I go into a battle all the time without a traditional weapon. That said, I always have my tail.

Aldred leans back on his heels, a sly look crossing his face. "In that case, I consent to the duel. No weapons."

Now, I know Aldred enough to realize he has something sneaky up his sleeve. I'm really starting to regret not having taken the offer to grab my guy and go back to Purgatory.

The Arbiter lowers her head and begins a low chant. I can't tell what language it's in, but the unmistakable zing of magic fills the air. So many things start happening at once, it's hard to keep track. The stage on which the Arbiter sits flattens out until it's level with the main floor. The Arbiter's throne whips up into the air until she's seated with her back against the top corner of the wall. Something about this position reminds me of a Roman

Emperor watching a gladiator battle from a balcony high above the arena floor.

"I hereby announce a duel of execution between the High Prince Lincoln Vidar Osric Aquilus of the House of Rixa and the Earl Aldred of the House of Acca. The rules of this duel are simple. No man-made weapons may be held or used by either warrior. You both must fight until the death. I will conjure a force field to keep you in place until one of you breathes your last. Are these terms understood?"

"Completely," says Lincoln. He takes his baculum from his belt and tosses them aside. I really hate to see that happen.

Aldred shrugs, and something in the movement sets my teeth on edge. "I have no weapons to disarm."

The Arbiter lifts her arms. "May the battle begin!"

Suddenly, a box of what looks like glass forms around Lincoln and Aldred, only it's not glass. It's really a magical force field that's keeping them in place.

A force field. I know the Arbiter mentioned it before, but I don't like seeing this in action. There's no way for me to step in if things get ugly.

Lincoln and Aldred pace in a circle as they size each other up. I cross my fingers.

Please let Aldred do something stupid.

And sure enough, that's what he does.

Aldred rushes straight for Lincoln. The Earl of Acca hunches forward, his arms folded across his chest. Clearly, he wants to jam his shoulder into Lincoln's stomach. It's a classic move, if you're a human linebacker. For a thrax warrior, it's not so good.

Lincoln sees the move coming a mile away. He allows Aldred to barely touch him before dodging the bulk of the attack. Aldred's momentum keeps him running forward until he slams into the invisible force field. Unfortunately, he picks the stretch of wall right by me. That's when I see it.

Aldred is holding a weapon in his hand. Only it's not man made.

The wasp's stinger.

Somehow, Aldred picked up the stinger that I ripped out of Lady Daria. That thing is freaking poisoned.

"Watch out!" I pound on the clear barrier with my fists. "He got the stinger!"

Aldred catches my eye and grins again, the bastard. When he speaks, his voice is a low grumble. "Once I kill him, I'm going after you."

I keep pounding away because—screw it—I am out of my head right now. "I'll fillet you! You're going down!"

"Oh, my poor boy." It's Octavia. She stands on the other side of the force field, staring in shock at her son.

Lincoln's still hunched over and he's gripping his belly.

Damn. Aldred must have gotten a good swipe in there. I pound away some more. "No!" I round on the Arbiter. "Stop this. Aldred cheated. He brought in a weapon."

The Arbiter shakes her head. "The wasp's stinger is not man made and is therefore allowable. There is nothing I can do. Continue with the battle." I'd take some comfort in the fact that she seems really bummed out, but damn. My fiancé is trapped beyond an impenetrable wall with a stinger-wielding psychopath.

Aldred struts toward Lincoln. "All this time, I've had to put up with you and your damned family." He tosses the stinger from hand to hand. "Now, I have you just where I want you."

Lincoln crouches lower. A moan escapes his lips. I scream my head off. Lincoln never moans. He could have his arm chopped off and the guy wouldn't even whine. What did that stinger do to him? I can't even imagine the ugly-ass poison that Lady Daria conjured.

Aldred pauses above Lincoln's curled-up form. He raises the stinger high above his head. "Now, I take my revenge!"

Fast as a heartbeat, Lincoln leaps up. His movements are so fast, I can see nothing except a blur. Within seconds, Lincoln has gotten Aldred to drop the stinger. Next, Lincoln moves behind Aldred and wraps his arm around the Earl's throat. "Think I didn't see you pick up that little stinger?" Lincoln's voice is low, but I can hear it clearly.

Aldred's face turns red as he claws at Lincoln's arm. My guy isn't giving him any air. I pound on the invisible wall again, only this time with relief. "Yes!"

"As you die, think on this," continues Lincoln. "I have a list of every noble and thane in the House of Acca, and I've already marked which ones go into exile. Your legacy of corruption and greed dies with you."

Aldred's movements turn weaker. His eyes roll into his head. Lincoln lifts his free arm and sets his hand against the Earl's chin. With one smooth movement, Lincoln's flips Aldred's head from side to side, snapping his neck.

Aldred's dead.

Lincoln drops the body to the ground with a thud. The entire courtroom turns deadly quiet. Lincoln straightens his stance and turns to address the Arbiter.

"I am the High Prince Lincoln Vidar Osric Aquilus, and I have won this battle."

I smile my face off. *Lincoln won.*

"So seen and acknowledged," calls the Arbiter.

With that, the courtroom's configuration transforms back into how it was before the duel. The stage rises up once more. The Arbiter's throne lowers until she's seated back in her original place. The invisible force field around Lincoln disappears. I rush into his arms and kiss his face all over, just because I can.

"You knew he stole that damned stinger."

"I told you I had a plan."

"That was an awesome one, too." I lean my forehead against his. "Only, you know, never ever do anything like that ever again."

More happy wedding guests come forward to congratulate Lincoln and me. I count my parents, Octavia, Cissy, and Walker. Almost everyone we know troops by, but it's mostly a blur.

Except for Connor.

Throughout this whole scene, Connor has been kneeling by Aldred's side. "What have I done?"

Lincoln takes my hand in his. Together, we approach his father. "What have you done?" asks Lincoln. "Nothing."

I want to add in the *"as usual,"* but I think it's overkill. Lincoln's tone really says it all this time.

Lincoln turns to the crowd. "The excitement is over. You all need to return to your homes."

The Arbiter stands. "Not quite."

A chill runs up my spine. Now, this is a total shocker. I didn't know the Arbiter's butt ever actually left her chair. I scan the faces in the crowd. Everyone else seems similarly impressed.

"I have another judgment to make."

Connor rises. "No, the case is over."

I grit my teeth. *Nice. Back-talking the Arbiter. Like that's going to help.*

My parents step forward. Mom has her shit-kicking face on, and Dad looks ready to blow the place up with angelfire. *I'm a lucky girl.*

My father addresses the crowd. "I've seen Antrum from the day the Almighty carved it from the Earth. The Arbiter can rule on whatever she deems worthy." Dad's eyes glow angel blue with power. He can be such a badass sometimes. "What is your ruling?"

"Based on all the evidence I have seen, Prince Lincoln and the Great Scala Myla Lewis are the true royal couple of Antrum. For all our safety, I decree they must be crowned so tonight."

The words reverberate around the room. I wait for everyone to freak out. They don't. Octavia looks resigned. Connor shivers from head to toe. But the thrax? They seem relieved.

Wow. I thought they hated my guts.

In a surprise move, Connor steps forward to counter my father. "We have the angel Verus here for the wedding ceremony. Who'll do their coronation? Because I certainly won't." He looks pleadingly toward Lincoln. "With all due respect, son. You're simply not ready."

The Arbiter steps away from her chair. "In that case, I shall be the one to complete the coronation."

Another stunned silence fills the room as the Arbiter walks to the end of the stage. I speak to Lincoln from the corner of my mouth. "Does she ever leave that chair?"

"Not that I've heard of."

"Huh."

Once the Arbiter reaches the stage's edge, she raises her arms. "Let us cheer our new King and Queen to be, Lincoln and Myla."

After that, there's a pause that goes on for like a millennium, minimum. I'm not sure if the crowd is excited or ready to rush off and find some pitchforks, torches, and a noose or two. I'm not going to lie here. I definitely have some deer-in-the-headlights action going on. This is where Lincoln's years of statecraft experience comes in handy. He sets his hand on the small of my back, guiding us both to face the crowd. Gripping my hand, he raises our joined fists high in the air.

"To the coronation!" he cries. Like me, Lincoln may be wondering if we're going to end up skewered on pitchforks. Unlike me, he doesn't show it at all. That's another thing on my list-o-stuff to learn. Statecraft, which seems to be directly related to my whole *need to learn more about lying* thing.

A rousing cheer echoes throughout the room. I'm pretty sure I hear some people shout *"Huzzah."* The crowd rushes around us. A kaleidoscope of thrax faces moves past Lincoln and me, all of them saying similar things.

"Aldred was blackmailing us."

"We had no choice."

"Thank the Almighty you'll be King and Queen."

All this love gives me an idea. I wave to the Arbiter. "Hey, there."

The Arbiter focuses on Lincoln and I. The room falls silent again. "What is it you require?"

"We have a list of those loyal to Acca. They're all to be exiled. Only, you know, they can take their wedding gifts with them if they want." *Hey, I can be gracious.*

Lincoln pulls Cissy's list from the folds of his tunic and hands it over to the Arbiter.

For a long minute, the Arbiter scans the sheet. Her face returns to looking unreadable again. I start to wonder if I've pushed my luck too hard.

At last she lowers the sheet to address the room once more. "I agree as well."

I raise my fist. "Yes!"

The Arbiter all-out smiles. It's a good look on her. "Let's get you wed and crowned. This is one party I shall not miss."

Wedding and coronation? Yes, please. Not that I'm real Queen material, but I want whatever gets us out of this crazy cycle between Aldred and Connor. The Arbiter's plan sounds like a winner.

Lincoln and I waste no time proceeding out of the courtroom. Behind us, there follows the Arbiter and our families. Everyone looks jubilant except for Connor, who is predictably mopey.

Meh. He'll get over it.

Besides, there's too much of a genuine happy vibe in the air to let Connor get me down. Now this is what I was missing before the wedding started the first time. At this point, my heart feels so light, it's like I could fly up to Heaven.

I turn to Lincoln and grin. "Let's do this."

CHAPTER THIRTY

$\mathcal{A}$

Once again, I stand in the stone corridor that leads to the Chapel. I still want to call it an arena, but whatever. It's not like I'll be hanging out in this place for long. It feels like a flock of demonic butterflies have taken up residence in my stomach, and not in a bad way. I am part demon myself, after all.

Dad looks me over and grins. "You look stunning."

I glance over my gown. There are now a few green goo stains from skewering Drusus. I like them. They say *"warrior bride"* to me.

Dad's mouth winds into that million-watt grin. "I have a surprise for you. There wasn't time to tell you about it before."

My eyes widen. "What?"

"I brought in the Heavenly choir. They were going to sing along with Pachelbel's Canon as a surprise. However, in light of things, I thought you might want a change of tune."

"They'll sing whatever I choose?"

"Certainly."

At this point, only one song will do. "No question. 'You Can't Always Get What You Want' by the Rolling Stones...Or would be the angels be insulted with that?"

"Are you kidding? Do you know how many human rock stars made it to Heaven?"

"Not really."

"More than you'd expect. Normally, they have no one to perform for. This request will make their eternity." Dad's eyes light up angel blue. "Excuse me. One minute and I'll get them set up."

As Dad steps off into the darkness of the corridor, Cissy approaches me. Her bouquet of white flowers is now a squished-up mess. She lifts what's left of the blooms. "Sorry about this. It got stomped on a bit in the commotion."

"Meh. I like it better that way. It's more me, really."

"I should have known." Cissy leans back, eyeing me from head to toe. "You're going down the aisle with some demonic goo on your dress."

I grin from ear to ear. "Awesome, right?"

"Only you, Myla."

"Fucking A."

Cis wraps me in a huge hug. "I'm so glad to be here. No one deserves a happily ever after more than you and Lincoln."

"Not sure a happily ever after is in the cards for us."

Cissy's mouth pops open. "You don't mean that."

"Sure, I do. '*Happily ever* after' is a whole lot of boring, if you ask me. Whatever happens next for my guy and me, one thing's for sure. It'll be exciting."

All of a sudden, the voices of the heavenly choir start to echo into the corridor. I peep into the Chapel. All the angels stand along the walls, their white robes gleaming bright.

> *"I saw her today at the reception*
> *A glass of wine in her hand*
> *I knew she would meet her connection*
> *At her feet was her footloose man*
> *No, you can't always get what you want*

You can't always get what you want
You can't always get what you want
But if you try sometimes you find
You get what you need"

Cissy listens intently. Her mouth is all screwed up, which is her *"I can't believe what I'm hearing"* face. "You didn't ask them to sing that."

"Hells yes, I did." Cissy is so easy to shock it's awesome. I bob my eyebrows up and down. "Kick ass, am I right?"

Cissy bursts out laughing. The mood in the hallway turns downright sunny and awesome. "Absolutely."

Dad reenters the corridor. "That's our cue." He offers me his elbow.

I wrap my hand around his upper arm. "Let's go."

Dad pauses and gives me a meaningful look. That's his mischievous face, right there. I can tell because he's arched his right brow. "In case you're wondering, I have some pretty neat dance moves."

My mouth falls open. "You do not." *He's not going to dance down the aisle at my wedding, is he?*

In reply, Dad starts working his hips. Despite the fact that he's my father, I have to admit that he's pretty smooth dancer. And that's no small feat either, considering the man is still wearing golden armor. It's beyond cool.

"I take it back." I start swishing from side to side as well. "Let's sashay this thing."

"I was hoping you'd say that."

The music breaks out into a rock-and-roll solo with the band. How they got their instruments here so quickly is anybody's guess. Mostly, I suspect it has something to do with my father and his archangel powers. Another item to add later to my Dad journal: *Zaps in rock band equipment at a moment's notice.*

Dad and I start to stroll-dance our way down the aisle as the refrain rises and the band goes nuts. I'm pretty sure it's Hendrix who's working a mean guitar solo as we close in on the stage.

Lincoln stands at the opposite side of the aisle. Damn, does he ever look yummy. His velvet tunic is torn a bit at the shoulder, and he's sporting some evil demonic goop, too.

He looks like a warrior.

He looks like mine.

As we shimmy closer, Lincoln starts swaying from side to side as well. That's when the crowd gets into the scene. Of course, they're a lot of thrax, so it's not like they're jumping up and down. Still, there's some basic twist moves and lots of smiles. The quasis rock down pretty well. It feels silly, spontaneous, and all-around awesome.

As I get close in on the stage, Lincoln's gaze locks with mine. His hips keep swaying in time to the music because really, how can you not? He eyes me from head to toe and gives me one of his double-dimple smiles. Those just slay me. My knees go a little wobbly as Dad guides me to the end of the aisle.

Lincoln grips my hand. Pure joy softens the chiseled lines of his face. He's even working a bit of scruff now. I like it.

"You look beautiful."

I run my fingers along the tear in his shoulder. "So do you, Mister The King."

"Future King. First, I need my Queen." He wraps my hand around his arm, and together, we walk to the stage where Verus and the Arbiter look down upon us. Both are in white robes, only the Arbiter is white everything, including her eyes, hair, and skin. Beside her, Verus has long black hair, almond-shaped eyes and her full wings on display. She even wears her crown of office, which is huge, gold, and looks fabulous on her.

The crowd quiets, and my heart starts beating with such force, I think it might break free from my rib rage. Lincoln rubs soothing circles on my wrist with his thumb. It helps.

Verus is the first to speak. "Dearly beloved, we are gathered here today…" She sighs. "I had a formal speech planned out for this occasion."

Lincoln and I share a sly look. Verus is a bit of an unknown commodity. She was the one who engineered the two of us getting together in the first place. She's an Oracle angel—by all accounts, the last one left—and she never gives the reasons why she makes certain things come to pass.

In this case, I'm glad she stuck her nose into my love life. That said, there's no rush for her to start spouting off fresh prophecies and plans.

"Some of you may not know this," continues Verus. "But I had a vision of the future that required Lincoln and Myla to wed, and if you don't mind my saying so, have children as soon as possible."

I raise my hand. "I mind."

Mom pipes in from the front row. "I don't!"

I try to groan, but it comes out more as a chuckle. They can scheme all they want. It won't change what Lincoln and I have already decided to do.

And yes, I want to start a family with my guy as soon as possible.

"Be that as it may," says Verus. "This isn't my first time encouraging a couple to unite. It is my best effort to date, however. I have never seen anyone rival Lincoln and Myla for respect, love, and teamwork...All in the face of some fairly unbelievable obstacles. Couples like these are why marriage exists. A true uniting of equals." Her elegant features soften with a smile. "I couldn't be happier to perform this ceremony." Verus's wings arch behind her. "Have you, Myla Lewis, accepted the betrothal jewels of the House of Rixa?"

"I have."

"It is time to don those jewels and add your wedding band."

Cissy steps forward and opens a small leather case. I put on the diamond earrings and necklace that mark me as betrothed to thrax royalty.

Once I'm done, Verus ruffles her wings as she speaks again. "Have you rings of commitment?"

"We do."

After reaching into his pocket, Walker pulls out a small jewel case that holds a simple platinum band and hands it to Lincoln. Cissy does the same. Our rings are pretty basic. I felt like my betrothal jewels were already super flashy, so I liked going simple on the wedding stuff. I guess I'll be adding a crown to my ensemble now too, so that makes me extra-glad I went the simple route. "Repeat after me," intones Verus. "I, Lincoln Vidar Osric Aquilus, do take you, Myla Lewis, as my lawfully wedded wife." "I, Lincoln Vidar Osric Aquilus, do take you, Myla Lewis, as my lawfully wedded wife."

He slips the band onto my finger. My upper lip wobbles. This is a lot harder than killing things, that's for sure.

Verus turns to me. "I, Myla Lewis, do take you, Lincoln Vidar Osric Aquilus, as my lawfully wedded husband."

"I, Myla Lewis, do take you, Lincoln Vidar…"

Crap, I can't remember his whole name. Who has a huge name like this anyway? In a flash, the rest of the words appear to me.

"Osric Aquilus, as my lawfully wedded husband." I set the ring on his finger. He winks, the creep.

Now, the Arbiter steps forward. At this point, I'm seeing little white blobs in my vision and feeling a bit woozy. It's been one hell of a day. How happy am I that thrax ceremonies are way short? Very happy indeed. Not sure how much more of this I could take. I have two speeds: fight like hell and nap.

Much as I hate to admit this, I am quickly heading into nap territory.

The Arbiter gazes out over the crowd for so long, I start to wonder if she's fallen asleep with her eyes open. After all, who knows what kind of magic she's under? At last, she breaks the silence. "My role as Arbiter is to watch over Antrum and the legal side of my

people, the thrax. Once, I lived among you, and I try to keep that knowledge in my heart as I sit in judgment over you all. For nearly two thousand years, I have a sat on my throne of judgment in the courtroom. Never once have I stepped away from my dais. Never have I wanted to. Today though? I saw a people in jeopardy and only one couple with the heart and power to bring us into a brighter future. For too long, our people have fought among ourselves for the crown of Antrum. It has cost us much blood. Today, I see a real chance for Antrum to unite under a single rule that is both fair and kind. I know many of you have waited for this day, the same as I have. How blessed for us all to be here, and how lucky I am to make it happen."

I can't help but peep over my shoulder. Do the thrax really see this as a huge blessing? I mean, some of them approached me after Aldred died. That's not necessarily a statistically valid sample of the after-realms, however. I scan the huge Chapel. All the faces are drawn in lines of relief and joy. Even better, there's an excitement in the air. It seems like they all agree with the Arbiter about this being a new and better phase for the after-realms. It's a huge responsibility that's both terrifying and exciting, all at once. I get another one of my ideas.

I raise my hand. "Hey, Arbiter?"

She tilts her head. "Yes?"

"I'd like to say a few words, if that's okay."

"Of course."

I look to Lincoln. "You want in on this?"

"No." He gives me a genuine smile. "I look forward to hearing what you have to say."

I turn to face everyone and clear my throat. "Hello, thrax. I'm about to be your Queen." I wave to another section of the audience. "And my fellow quasi-demons. Lincoln here is about to become the official consort to the great scala, which let's face it, is pretty much a king to you. Now, I know things haven't always been smooth between us all." I frown. "Okay, I can't lie. It's been hard. Really hard. This alliance between our peoples is new and uncomfortable. However, we all just fought off Armageddon together. You could have run the minute the igni set you free and you didn't. That means something big. For those of you who aren't warriors, there's something special that happens when you battle side by side with someone. A bond that forms. I feel a new connection with you all." I scan the crowd, feeling their energy zing through me. "I want you all to know how honored I am to be your new leader. I can't wait to see what the future holds for us."

There's a long pause where I think I may have screwed up. Suddenly, applause breaks out across the room, followed by raucous cheers. Lincoln leans in to kiss me gently on the cheek. "What a Queen you'll make, Myla. I couldn't be more proud." And that makes me blush my face off.

Eventually the Arbiter raises her arms and everything gets quiet again. "It is therefore my great honor and privilege to crown the Great Scala Myla Lewis and Prince Lincoln Vidar Osric Aquilus as the Queen and King of Antrum." As she raises her arms and a pair of cherubs flit over from the walls. Sure, I've seen pictures of cherubs in paintings, but they really undersell the experience. You can't imagine how freaking cute the little baby angels are until a couple of them flit toward you, all chubby cheeks and infant giggles. In this case, each holds a glittering diamond crown, which is the headgear of choice for formal thrax ceremonies. I must say, they look really sparkly.

The Arbiter raises her voice. "I hereby declare you the King and Queen of Antrum." The cherubs giggle as their little wings flit up a storm. With gentle movements, they set on our gleaming crowns.

Whoa. I'm officially the Queen of Antrum. Six months ago, I was on the ghoul's Watch List for Unreasonable Tardiness at Purgatory High. Go me.

Verus steps forward. "And I hereby pronounce you husband and wife."

"As well as King and Queen," adds the Arbiter.

Lincoln grins. "Guess what?"

I think I know where he's going with this. "Hmm?"

"I'm officially calling my kiss."

"You got it, Mister."

Lincoln and I embrace and share a gentle brush of the lips. I know I'm part lust demon and all, but it's been a big day, and this is one huge audience. The choir takes up again, and we process our way out of the Chapel. As we walk down the main aisle, the angels now take flight as they sing while the rock band kicks musical ass once again.

"You can't always get what you want
You can't always get what you want

You can't always get what you want
But if you try sometimes you find
You get what you need"

As we head toward our four different receptions—there was no single ballroom big enough to hold everyone—I take this as another moment to soak into my soul and save up for later. Because what's happening now? It's nothing less than supernatural, unexpected, and downright bizarre.

In other words, perfect.

CHAPTER THIRTY-ONE

A

The rest of the night turns into a blur of ballrooms and orchestras. The angelic choir parties like the rock stars they are. I dance with everyone: Lincoln, Mom, Dad, Cissy, Walker, Octavia, and even Connor. Just because Lincoln's father is a useless pile of dung doesn't mean I can't be gracious on my wedding day.

I'm gabbing it up with some of Cissy's senator buddies at who-knows-what o'clock in the morning when I feel a familiar warmth at my back.

Lincoln.

His voice is all low and yummy in my ear. "Time to leave, my Queen."

My mouth winds into a sneaky grin. "Lead on, my King." Lincoln is an expert at bagging out on long formal events. And even though this is one hell of a party, it's not as fun as being alone with my guy. The thought of it sends heat coiling through me. Now that we've made the decision to start a family, I can't wait for everything to start.

Mostly the sex part.

Lincoln takes my hand, and we weave through the crowd to what looks like a floor-length mirror. Lincoln taps on the frame in an odd rhythm. Instantly, it swings open to reveal a dark corridor hidden inside the wall. My eyebrows lift. "How many of these secret passages are squirreled away in this place?"

"Tons. There are some unused Pulpitum, too. I've found…" He bobs his head from side to side. "Maybe half of them."

"You're such a sneaky guy."

"And proud of it. You'll find my skills come in handy."

"No doubt." I squeeze in through the door and enter the stone hallway beyond. Lincoln navigates the labyrinth of corridors like a pro. After all the excitement today, it's awesome to be someplace quiet. In no time, Lincoln pushes on a section of rock wall, which swings open to reveal the interior of the walk-in closet of his private chambers. I step inside and smile.

"This is super-handy. Who knew you had a door here?"

"I did, actually."

"Ha-ha." I scan all Lincoln's clothes. There's something intimate about being around his mix of casual modern stuff, medieval tunics, and leather pants. Especially the leather pants, if I'm being totally honest.

Before I know it, closet inspection time is over, and Lincoln's mouth is on mine. This isn't a chaste brush of the lips like we shared in front of the crowd. This kiss is possessive and charged. We've spent months getting to know each other's bodies, so we both know exactly what to do next.

I gently bite his lower lip. He loves that.

Lincoln slides his hands around the swell of my breasts and grips my backside hard. Now this is one of my favorites.

Our kiss turns fierce and one thing is clear. There is way too much clothing going on. I break our kiss and tug at his tunic. "Can we, uh?"

Lincoln grins, and this is his sneaky smile, the one he saves when it's just him and me. He knows I want him to tear everything off, but he also knows that if he goes slowly, it will drive me crazy.

One guess what he does.

He goes so slowly that I'm about to lose my freaking mind.

One by one, Lincoln undoes the buttons down my back. His warm fingers brush against my bare skin, making me shiver. My wedding gown pools at my feet. I stand naked before Lincoln, except for my wedding jewels and heels. He steps back and admires the view. There's something heated and even worshipful in his gaze. I love it.

I love other things just as much, though. Like the fact that it's Lincoln's turn to get naked.

"Now you." I guide him in pulling off his tunic, chain mail, and undershirt. In the process, I make sure to include a lot of touching. In particular, Lincoln's bare chest is a work of art. He has super-broad shoulders and well-defined abs. There are even a few scars along his rib cage. As a warrior, I think they're my favorite.

Lincoln's naked from the waist up. I brush my fingertips along his bare waistline. Now, it's his turn to shiver. I help press his leather pants to the floor beside my white gown. Lincoln kicks off his boots and with that, we're both naked. My inner lust demon roars to live, pumping heat through every inch of me.

Lincoln's gaze locks with mine. "Are you certain about this?"

"Oh, yes." *And I mean it.*

We kiss. It's a powerful sensation at any time, but with our naked bodies in contact? Mind-altering. Lincoln backward-walks me to his bed. We stay kissing the entire time, even as I scoot back on the mattress while he crawls forward. My core tightens, I want him so badly.

Soon, I lay on my back with Lincoln settled between my legs. He braces his heavy arms on either side of my head. I feel confined, safe, and ready. An unsure look crosses his face.

"Are you certain?"

I reach up to brush the bristle along his chin. "You don't have to ask again."

"I want to. We have all the time in the world, Myla. You need to be sure."

"With all my heart."

"Should I get protection?"

"I don't think it will matter either way. Besides…" Using my two fingers, I mime a pair of legs running up his arm. It's a move that Lincoln did with me six months and a million years ago, back when he first told me he wanted us to have children. "I'm ready for a family, too."

Lincoln smiles. "In that case, we've one final ritual to complete."

It's been a long day, and being naked with Lincoln is pretty distracting, so for the life of me, I can't think what ritual he's talking about. That is, until a white light glistens over his shoulders.

Lincoln's wings appear once more.

I inhale a shaky breath. My new husband is showing me his deepest beauty, and it's breathtaking. I touch the soft arch of his feathers. "They're beautiful."

"As are you." Lincoln kisses me once, gently. "Ready?"

I nod.

Lincoln enters me gently. There's hurt that lasts a few seconds, and then, Lincoln and I are moving together. Making love. The universe collapses until there's only our bodies in motion and waves of delight. A coil of energy tightens inside me, and I feel the same mounting excitement in every shift of Lincoln's body as well. Our gazes lock as stars seem to explode behind my eyes.

Suddenly, a real white light appears, engulfing us both. The music of light and dark igni fills my ears. The brilliance fades slowly, along with their voices. I suppose I should be freaked out, however I'm too post-orgasmic to care.

Lincoln leans forward, rubbing his nose along the length of mine. "That was a first."

"You saw the light?"

"And heard their music, too."

"Whoa. That *is* a first." My igni have never been audible to anyone except me before. I hope this isn't something they plan to make a habit out of. It's a little off-putting during intimacy.

Lincoln rolls onto his back and tucks me into his side. He kisses the top of my head. "You're amazing."

I'm about to tell him that he's not so bad himself when a wave of nausea careens through me. I pop my hand over my mouth. "I think I'm going to be sick."

Lincoln's brows jet upwards. "That wasn't the reaction I was hoping for."

The igni reappear, only this time, they're not a blast of white light. Instead, hundreds of them swirl above our bed like a school of fish.

Lincoln frowns. "I hope they don't plan to do this through the whole honeymoon."

I can't help but smile. "I was just thinking the same thing." The voices start singing again. "Do you hear them now?"

Lincoln tilts his head to one side "No. Can you?"

"Yes." Closing my eyes, I concentrate on what the igni are saying. It's not easy, yet I do catch a few words in the mix of gibberish:

"Pregnant."

"Boy."

"Scala Heir."

"Name him Maxon."

Wow. Mom was right. They really didn't waste any time, did they? Guess they want a Scala Heir already. I reopen my eyes to watch the igni multiply until their whirlpool-like swirl of brilliance almost fills the room. At this point, the words *pregnant, Scala Heir,* and *Maxon* are a constant refrain, and honestly? It's over the top and getting on my nerves. Suddenly, it's all less pleasant since I feel like I got socked with a serious case of the stomach flu. One guess what that is. Morning sickness. And after all of three seconds, too. These igni aren't screwing around.

I wave my hand. "All right, all right. I got it. Now take off." The igni vanish.

Lincoln sets his knuckle under my chin, guiding my gaze to meet his. My guy looks so happy, you'd think he was six years old and just got a box of puppies. "What did they have to say?"

"The igni?"

"Yes, Myla." He's smiling so hard I'm surprised his cheeks don't crack. I debate about playing with him for a bit—pretending I don't know what he's really asking—but then I decide that even *I'm* not that mean.

"They said I'm pregnant with the Scala Heir."

Within the span of a heartbeat, I'm flipped onto my back with Lincoln over me again. Based on the hardness pressed against my thigh, he's very excited about this news. "Anything else?"

"It's a boy. They want us to name him Maxon."

"That was the name of the last thrax who was Scala." Lincoln smiles even wider, if that's possible.

"It makes sense. The igni followed the dude around for a thousand years or so. It's a nice way to honor him."

Lincoln starts speed-kissing my face. "I'm going..." *Kiss, kiss.* "To be a father. We're going..." *Kiss, kiss.* "To be parents. I couldn't be happier."

I shift my body under his. "I don't know. I have a feeling you could be a *little* happier." What can I say? I'm ready to go again. It's all part of the lust demon package.

Lincoln pauses mid-kiss. "Are you sure? You said you felt nauseous before."

"Well, I'm fine now. There's only one thing."

"Which is?"

My stomach rumbles. "We should take a break soon and get some food."

"What kind of food?" Lincoln's features turn unreadable. "Demon bars?"

"No, not that." The thought of those chocolaty things makes me ill. The image of my perfect meal appears in my mind. "Kale. I really want me some kale. And what are those little question-mark-looking thingies? Quinoa. That too." I'm sure the igni are working their supernatural mojo on my cravings to make them healthy, but whatever. As long as I eat, I'm good.

Lincoln places a soft kiss on the tip of my nose. "Whatever you want, my Queen."

"Speaking of that..." I shimmy beneath him.

All the talking stops and indeed, we do end up making each other feel a whole lot happier. And the good news? My igni don't make a second appearance. Total plus on a supernatural honeymoon.

As I drift off to sleep in Lincoln's arms I try to recap everything good that happened today: Lincoln, a baby, and a crown. Six months ago, I would have said that was everything I didn't want. Turns out, it was exactly what I needed. *Thanks, Verus.*

And with Maxon in the mix, who knows what the future will bring? One thing's for certain, though. Whatever happens next, it won't be boring.

The story continues with THRAX, Book 4
in the Angelbound Origins Series

The day after their honeymoon ends, Myla's husband Lincoln
disappears. Available now at retailers

Also from Christina Bauer is CURSED, book 1
in the Beholder Series

A story of witchcraft, adventure, and love.
Available now at retailers

ACKNOWLEDGEMENTS

To begin with, I would like to send a massive thank you out to my readers. High fives to everyone who encouraged me to write the story of Myla and Lincoln's wedding. Writing this thing was a blast and I hope it shows.

Next, I must bow down to the amazing folks at INscribe Digital, who move mountains and make it look easy. This includes the wonderful Kelly Peterson, Stephanie Gomes, Allison Davis, and Larry Norton. You all are totes awesome. Also, a big welcome the new team at IPG; I look forward to getting to know you all!

Behind the scenes are a team of crazies who keep me writing and happy. Top of the list is my kick-ass editor, Genevieve Iseult Eldredge. It's been a joy to work with you and I can't wait to see what the future holds.

Best for last. Huge and heartfelt thanks to my husband and son. None of this would be possible without you. First and last, you're the best.

Christina Bauer thinks that fantasy books are like bacon: they just make life better. All of which is why she writes romance novels that feature demons, dragons, wizards, witches, elves, elementals, and a bunch of random stuff that she brainstorms while riding the Boston T. Oh, and she includes lots of humor and kick-ass chicks, too. Christina lives in Newton, MA with her husband, son, and semi-insane golden retriever, Ruby.

For more information and updates about Christina and her books, go to: http://monsterhousebooks.com/authors/cbauer

More Books By Christina Bauer

ANGELBOUND ORIGINS
About a part-demon girl who kicks ass, takes names, and falls in love
1. Angelbound
2. Scala
3. Acca
4. Thrax
5. Armageddon

ANGELBOUND OFFSPRING
The next generation of her story
1. Maxon
2. Portia
3. Mistress Dragon

BEHOLDER
An epic fantasy filled with romance and witchcraft
1. Cursed
2. Concealed
3. Cherished
4. Crowned

DIMENSION DRIFT
About a science genius who attends a Learning Squirrel High School...
Her life goes downhill from there
1. Prequel 1
2. Prequel 2
3. Prequel 3
4. Dimension Drift
5. ECHO Academy
6. Corrosion Line
7. Drift Warrior